AGÕTÍME

Judith Gleason

ΛGÕTĨME

her legend

with drawings by Carybé

The Viking Press   New York

Viking Compass Edition
Issued in 1971 by The Viking Press, Inc.
625 Madison Avenue, New York, N.Y. 10022

Distributed in Canada by
The Macmillan Company of Canada, Ltd.

SBN 670-00333-6

Printed in U.S.A.

This edition published by arrangement with Grossman Publishers

Foreword

There have been poets who have sung of the transportation of gods to nether shores and incipient kingdoms, but many the gods who, eluding poetic notice, have survived the vicissitudes of their voyages to haunt hearth, heath and headstone, to come to terms with the local deities and to deign to descend—most often to dance, but sometimes to destroy. These potent voyagers will persist beyond all human memory of their itineraries so long as they continue to be praised, so long as breath bellows them. The gods of Africa came to their new world under more trying conditions than most, but many have admirably survived wherever their worshippers were permitted to beat skins into drumheads. Some, out of neglect, still slumber; others are awakening.

There once was an imperialist Lybian queen who "loved not the shuttling ways of the loom," Kyrene, she of the white arms. This is not her story. There once was a black queen, Agõtĩme, exiled by fate from a real Africa. The gods she brought to a new world have known a modest survival. This is her story, an exploration of her unsung destiny.

To all of the scholars who helped me imagine the times, visions and places through which Agõtĩme moved, my gratitude. Their names, together with a glossary of names from Acarajé to Zagaia, may be found at the end of this book. But the foremost of these interpreters, Fatumbi—of Oshogbo, Porto Novo and

Bahia—deserves special mention here. To all who extended their hospitality to us in Brazil, to Carybé, Nancy, Ramiro and Solange Bernabo, to Antonio and Zora Olinto, to Doctora Flor-de-liz de Nina, to Luiz Braga, who jumped over the St. John's fire for and with me, to Toni the prince of Amazonas and to many more, *abraços*. To the Farfield Foundation for making the pursuit of Agõtíme financially possible, my thanks. To Gertrude Simpson, whose presence, years ago, inspired my unconscious search for an Agõtíme, my continued affection. To Page Edwards, whose editorial intuitions are phenomenological, my admiration. And finally, to my husband, without whose support and enthusiastic confidence I never could have done it at all, my dearest apologies for the disorders left in the wake of my bulldozing typewriter.

But it is to the children, our children, that I dedicate Agõtíme's story, to Maud, Billy, Esther, Richard and Helen Montgomery, with the hope that they, too, live to become what they dream themselves to be.

J. G.

Principal Characters

Agŏtĭme—A former queen of Dahomey, wife of King Agŏglo (1789–97).

Gãkpe—Agŏtĭme's son, later King Gezo (1818–58).

Adãdozã—Son of Agŏglo's first wife, Nahoue; King of Dahomey (1797–1818).

The Bokonŏ—Diviner-priest.

The Panther—Totemic ancestor of the Dahomean dynasty.

Aligbonŏ—A medieval princess from Tado, mother of Agasu, founder of the Dahomean dynasty.

The Hunter—Enemy of the Panther and befriender of Gãkpe.

Fa—Destiny, the oracle, principle of cosmic order.

Legba (Elegba, sometimes Eshu or Exu)—God of chance, sex, disorder, interpreter and messenger between man and the *vodũ*.

Zomadonu—King of the Toxosu, or water spirits, closely affiliated with the Royal Dead.

Sakpata (also Shopona, Omolu)—God of smallpox.

Thunder—Appears as three *vodũ* in this story: Xevioso, Shango (Xango) and Bade.

Gu-Ogun—God of iron, of crafts; Warrior, Opener of the Way.

St. Antony—Patron of ships and of lost things.

Curupira—A fantastic being, with many guises, in this story King of the Brazilian jungle.

The Jaguar—Brazilian-Indian deity, in this story new world surrogate for The Panther.

O Boi—A sacrificial animal.

Gbaguideguide, the Calabash-smasher—A slave from Mahiland.

Oro—A Nago boy.

Saliabsõ—A slave, mother of Alixossi-Afefe.

Suuna—The Fulani girl, a slave.

Batoques—A cooper, later second mate of the *Incompreensível*.

Vivaldo—A Bahian creole, drummer and revolutionary.

The Mãe-de-Santo—Head of the most prominent Nago cult in Bahia.

The Imam—Muslim teacher, priest; in this story leader of a revolt.

Mateus—A cowboy of northeastern Brazil.

Rosinha—A slave on the Fazenda Paraiso, befriender of Agõtĭme, wife of Pãe Juca, a bargeman.

Luiz Braga—Adopted son of Agõtĭme, later a famous abolitionist poet.

Atindebaku—Prime Minister of the Right Hand (Migã) during the reigns of Agõglo, Adãdozã and Gezo; an ambassador in search of Agõtĭme.

Dosuyovo—The second ambassador.

Notes on pronunciation:

The tilde (~) indicates nasalization (n).

The African vowels should be pronounced: a(ah); e(ay); i(ee); o(oh); u(oo); and final vowels should be pronounced as separate syllables. Agõtĭme's name is therefore something like Ah-go(n)-tee(n)-may.

The X in the Dahomean words is close to an aspirated *h*, but the X in the Brazilian words is more like *sh* or *ch*.

Contents

AGÕTĨME

The Wake of the Past

In a quiet provincial city in northeastern Brazil there stands a white stucco house where an aggressive water spirit and certain deified kings of a remarkable West African dynasty continue to dance in company with less particularized forces of nature and the human mind. These gods are worshipped not in affluence but in the proud gentility of straitened circumstances. Should you chance to visit this modest convent, the aristocratic dignity of the proceedings would stimulate wonder at the cult's origin. Should you question anyone there, you would receive a vague reply—*Gôme* [Dahomey?]. Should you persist in your questioning you would elicit a response so elusive as to suggest inevitable forgetfulness superimposed upon a destiny once purposely concealed, a mystery—but not entirely concealed, no, not entirely.

At 199 Rua São Pantalão, or 857 Rua Senador Costa Rodrigues (for all houses in São Luis have a double set of numbers and names), the old house once known as Casa Querebatan still stands. *Querebatan?* not a Portuguese word. *Xelegbata* with a Portuguese spelling? That odd name must have slipped from communal memory some time ago when Mãe Andresa died. Now everyone in the neighborhood, everyone who trudges up the steep cobblestone streets from the market calls it simply Casa das Minas. By which they mean the Dahomean cult house.

For years nobody has talked about Legba in that place. He's the devil to them, not safe to mention. Nobody sends him away at the beginnings of *tambors*. Still, anyone who assumes he's not there is mistaken, for Legba is everywhere. Just up the street there's one of his phallic clay mounds in front of the wrought-iron gate of a respectable old town house turned police station. Better not hitch your horse to that post. But there aren't many horses in São Luis these days, only cars, bicycles, trolleys, and mostly pedestrians, carrying things in plaited palm-fiber baskets. Other mediators have been substituted for Legba, a proliferation of childish pranksters.

Nor, oddly enough, has the name of the founder of the Dahomean cult house been retained, although memories of Agõtíme are everywhere in evidence. Those sandals hanging on a peg in the little room next to the one where the drums are kept, the room where the final interview with the ambassadors took place, they might have belonged to her, for she had remarkably tiny feet for one so tall. And over there in the corner of the sanctuary, that ancient yellow-wood-hafted spear. Ought she not to have taken it with her?

Enter the sanctuary, if you are fortunate enough to be granted special permission; look, the words she inscribed on the lintel are still legible, although few, surely, have entered as she entered, drunk as she drank and departed as she departed. Within the sacred triangular space covered jars, containing the virtual presences of Zomadonu and the water princes as well as the mysteries of Earth, sit half-buried in the ground. Still other energies repose in small deceptively placid stones, now carefully arranged on the smooth dirt, polished by the receding tides of history into perfect ovals like those occasionally to be found along the beach at Ponto Area.

On special occasions the forces slumbering within these stones are renewed by lustral infusions of leaves culled from beneath the cajàzeiro tree that continues to grow, clumsily, in the garden they still call *Gôme*. One of these stones, symbol of a powerful queen who once lived in the world, is never bathed in the sanctuary with the others. Once a year this special stone is taken out to be washed in an unknown, distant and presumably deserted place. Where? Why? Who—was she? One must never tell more than half of what one knows, so say Dahomean elders on both sides of the Atlantic.

It's true, words will never fill a basket. Therefore, leave your questions behind and return instinctively to that particular street, so like all the others. It was not a dream. The house remains, its modest one-story façade merging with those on either side to form a stout wall abutting on a narrow and hazardously eroded sidewalk. All looks boarded up; but no, clap your hands three times and call "*O de casa!*" A novice will open the door for you. Go in, not into the sanctuary this time, but out onto the back porch under the arcade looking out at the stumpy arms of the cajàzeiro sprouting into leaf. Wait, as once Agõtĭme anticipated the arrival of the ambassadors and your flesh will tell you that you have taken refuge in one of the coolest places on this tortured planet. You have located yourself upon the equator, and yet the wind from São Marcos Bay, and beyond, penetrates everywhere —passing between the wooden jalousies, across the transoms of the doors, through the interstices of the curved tiles as they lie loosely interlocked along their hardwood beams. Breaths, presences. The thick walls are cool and slightly damp to the cheek that rests against them in that constant shade. But in the courtyard the sun gnaws at the blue shadows of the herb garden under the tree, strikes the white walls with all the intensity of light and, stealing obliquely into the hidden cubicle where the three drums sleep, turns formless obliteration into carefully graduated contours of mute sound.

The *huntos* have arrived in gleaming shirt sleeves to tune the drums. Back and forth along the L-shaped veranda novices and *vodunsi* move almost noiselessly in sandaled feet. Like luna moths they move for a day, for an eternity, along the cool, dim corridor —all dressed in white, for it is São João's midwinter festival.

one # DAHOMEY

History will never be more than an evocation, verbal and fragmentary, of a reality which has disappeared, submerged in the evanescent wake of the past. Alone survive a few memories, afloat on yellowing pages. This fugitive vision may always be embellished and completed, if not modified.

—*Père Dieudonné-Rinchon*

1 ▶▶ The Panther

One hour before sundown the bats swarm overhead. Flying southward from Savi and the forty-one hills of the Dassa region, they thicken the sky above the capital on their way to feed in the fruit trees that line the royal road from Abomey to Kana.

Agōtĭme turned from the window. "Here's a riddle for you, Fina: What grows grey? As the shadows fall before the door, what grows grey?" From the other end of the room the answer came, "The bat, it is the bat grows grey." "Good for you, Fina." Agōtĭme laughed. "He builds his house right against the fence, in my backyard; a wizard's house, for try as I may, my pole can't strike him. Now, Fina, time flies on ever-moving wings, without stopping for food, for shelter, for love, or dreams. But I am thirsty, so before we go out, be kind enough to bring me some water to drink, water cool and fresh . . ." "As the leaves of Destiny, Na Agōtĭme?" "As the leaves of Destiny, Fina. If you keep on growing your wits at this rate, you'll be a wealthy woman before your years are used up." "I hope so, Na Agōtĭme."

The girl rose at once from her pallet bed which had been wedged into a row of baskets storing satin, velvet and silk brocade. Water and foodstuffs were kept in an adjoining alcove.

Ladling out a full cup from the crock, Fina walked steadily across the main room to the window. Taking the precautionary first sip, she extended the cup and then, as Agŏtĭme drank, shyly suggested that perhaps the queen would like her vermilion shawl tonight. It was late January, the beginning of Harmattan season, and the dry north wind blew cold at the extremities of the day. Agŏtĭme acknowledged Fina's courtesy with a dreamy look that had a hint of pity in it, for she had been recalling all afternoon her own girlhood, spent far from the court, on the granite escarpments of Mahiland where fresh winds blow down from the Atakora Mountains year in, year out. Untamed by slavery, unlike Fina, she'd taken no heed of herself or others then, unless they were old. But she was young, still too young for such solicitude, and, in her white satin headtie, beyond all sorrow beautiful.

She was at the crossroads now. Frightening though her prospects, she willingly committed herself to chance, for nothing could be worse than the dismal path the last five years had taken. When her husband King Agŏglo died, she, unlike those childless wives required to immolate themselves upon the bier, had passed with some fourscore others into the keeping of Adădoză, his son and successor. However, unknown to the commonality, this customary transfer had in her case implied immediate imprisonment.

There were some within the walls who whispered that she had been fortunate in being kept alive, that she might well have been put to death right away, or later with the leaders of the opposing faction. Why not? Because Adădoză thought her less, or thought her more, dangerous than the rest? A certain woman had used her spiritual immunity to establish an evil precedent. Was not Adădoză afraid it would happen again? That was why he planned to exile her soon, they said.

Whatever the cause, Agŏtĭme had been spared and for five years now she, whom palm groves were supposed to delight, had been confined to the panther-wives' compound—an outrageous irony considering that had supernatural advice prevailed she ought, upon Agõglo's demise, to have been named *kpojito*, Queen Mother, the most powerful woman in the land.

There were those who had continued, covertly, to support her cause. Before her son Gãkpe quit the court, she had had the bitter satisfaction of being able to play the role of ill-used aspirant, the invulnerable heroine, marked for preeminence by the unseen. Now, the human imagination being just as fickle as afraid, she was considered no queen at all. What then? Tomorrow she'd begin afresh, and finally, one day . . . Where pots are baked the hearth builds up until a mound is seen.

Let Adãdozã cast her future as he willed, he was impious in so doing and Fa would retaliate. No thunderbush barricades can obscure origin. One is what one accomplishes, let not immediate adversity be mistaken for a sign that the unborn soul maliciously chose a bad fate. Sow patience, and good fortune will cooperate with the harvesters. Let Legba show her the roundabout way, Agõtĩme prayed. Meanwhile, the long-silenced *gonggong* resounded amidst the rubble of the mountain village, Gbohuele, where she was born. Thus memory animates, finds words to summon sleeping forces. Queen or no queen, her face unscarred even by time, she was a Maxi priest's proud daughter still—whatever else she might have been, or would become.

"No thank you, Fina," she said, squaring her shoulders so the coral beads would fall just right, "we'll let the sun wear the royal stole to bed this evening without any competition." Then bowing westward with irrepressible mockery at the splendor windowed from her plain adobe wall, Agõtĩme walked down the corridor and out onto the veranda.

Beneath the lowering brow of thatch and between the carved posts supporting the beam, segments of the familiar courtyard seemed totally absorbed in the last light. Serving maids and

mistresses were almost indistinguishable at this hour. Having put
by the robes of public audience for simple cloths, the wives-of-
the-panther stooped easily and, so it seemed to Agötíme, gratefully into old attitudes of domesticity as they prepared to feed
themselves and their young. *Pocla-pocla.* Ironwood pestles
drummed maize in the mortars a few frantic seconds more. Then
a hush of fine meal fell upon boiling waters and the heavier tools
were put by.

No stones are to be found on the plains of Dahomey, nothing
bigger than a guineafowl's egg. So in those days slaves were as-
signed to carry heavy stones down from Mahiland to the markets
of Abomey for use as mortars and trivets by many whose hearts
were as heavy with exile. All panther-wives, they too had to be
brought in from elsewhere. No royal blood could flow in their
veins. It was the law. Since outlanders, generally, were preferable
to commoners, many, like Agötíme herself, were formerly captives torn from the rugged fastnesses of the north, as it was believed that the Maxi made healthy mothers and spirited concu-
bines.

As denizens of the royal household, these captive women
had to renounce all former religious ties, suppress whatever af-
finities they felt with various *vodũ* of the established pantheons,
and devote themselves exclusively to the cult of the royal dead
and their bumptious affiliates, the Toxosu, or water spirits. To
this rule Agõglo had permitted Agötíme to be somewhat of an
exception. She was not allowed to become an active votary of
her father's earth-born smallpox cult, but she was at least not required to do violence to her paternal heritage by being forced
to exalt the memories of those whom she could never regard as
other than mere usurpers of the land, no more at home than their
cairns of imported queens.

Only the youngest of the royal children were permitted to
remain in the wives' court with their mothers. Their childhood

was short and Agōtǐme never failed to be moved to see them taking full advantage of their time of life chasing each other wildly about the yard, jumping off and onto the porches of the apartments that surrounded it, calling like so many lark-heeled coucal birds perched in the pollarded fig trees. In the center of the court, beneath the feathery leaves of the tamarind, a double line of little girls in gay calico wrappers jerked and bobbed to the rhythm of the jump-clap game while here and there on the porous red ground, where shallow holes had been scooped for Ajido, the future elders with deep-dyed cloths thrown over their shoulders hunched intently over the bouncing seeds.

Agōtǐme thought of her own serious son Gākpe, not so much older than they. Dismayed by the prospect of existence on the periphery of his tyrannical brother's regime, he had exiled himself to hunt along the reed banks of the Weme. She did not doubt he had racks heavy with strips of meat drying above his campfire now. Gākpe was quick to learn the rules of any game. But not having been born to the profession, would he know, intuitively, in the twilight, before the twigs snapped, when the panther was at last prepared to spring? A cold wind seized her by the arm, and that strange feeling so close to faintness came over her again, but she would not give in to it now.

It was the eve of her banishment. The Migā, an old friend of Agōglo's, had let this much filter through to her ear. No one else out there in the courtyard knew how soon. Adādozā was not in the habit of confiding in his wives—Nahoue took care of that. Nahoue, usurping queen mother and Agōtǐme's bitterest enemy, had to keep vigil tonight at Agōglo's tomb on the other side of the palace. So, custom be praised, that woman would not be there to inhibit her leave-taking. Anxious lest her behavior tonight seem any way extraordinary, Agōtǐme steadied herself with a hand on Fina's shoulder and stepped majestically over the rain-ridge and down the five narrow steps to the floor of the court.

As she moved across the yard, avoiding the unrolled mats and clusters of utensils, not one woman so much as shifted an eyelid to acknowledge her advance. She could have spoken first. Given her adversity, it was really up to her. And since whoever makes bold to approach a hostile camp must not be refused civility, most of them would probably have answered her. Once there had been exchange of talk—from some mockery masquerading as elaborate politeness, from some slit-eyed neutrality, from others a muted concern for her well-being. Although compassion now tended to restrain those women who had always been hostile, fear had finally numbed the hearts of those few who had been her friends; and since food offered with a frown is more honorably refused, she no longer solicited their hollow courtesy, nor did they go out of their way to extend it.

"*Ago, ago,* make way for the queens! Avert your eyes, common things of Dahomey." When the panther-wives walked abroad, to market or to the spring, this cry preceded them. Publicly declared unwell, Agŏtǐme never went beyond the walls, but nowadays whenever she strolled about the courtyard, she went accompanied by an invisible bell-ringer, shrouded in deferential secrecy—signs that all must at length come round to see that Agŏtǐme was more powerful, more dangerous, than she was at pains to seem to be. "The pebble feels not the chill of the stream"—one of King Kpĕgla's favorite sayings. She would have liked to have been able to praise herself that way. But for such coldness there was compensation in exemption. If her heart was a bird, well then let it take wing. There was no evil in her transformations, yet, apprehensive of evil, no one dared tamper with the chains she forged to bind herself to the children.

Here they were! Between herself and them, linked as they were, the words flowed in revivifying currents. They had seen her come out and were rushing forward to give her greeting:

"Welcome!"

"Salutations at the closing of the portals of the day!"

"We greet you for watching us at our play!"

And to each she gave an appropriate response:

"I thank you for welcoming me."

"May you not stumble in the dark."

"And your elder brother, have you had news of him? How is he?"

"And your father, the king of pearls, does he continue to exist?"

"Have you had any more trouble with that skinned knee?"

Now they ventured beyond the well-worn formulas.

"Na Agŏtĭme, you are late."

"Na Agŏtĭme, are you not well, why have you come out so late?"

"But you have not lit a fire tonight. Why? Aren't you going to cook yourself any food to eat?"

Having escorted her to her accustomed place beneath the tamarind, despite her protests, they ran off to their mothers for gifts of food. These they laid out on the mat before her knees. She would, she promised, taste a little of each later on; but not quite yet, for Fina already, out of nowhere, had produced a packet of steaming cornmeal wrapped in marantachloa leaves.

"Na Agŏtĭme, I know you said you didn't feel like food tonight, but I prepared this earlier, when you were asleep. Please take it."

"Thank you, Fina, this *akãsã* is like life itself for which I hope never to lose my appetite. I would that all passions might thus be clothed in cooling leaves." Gratefully warming her hands, nodding at the children's talk, Agŏtĭme ate.

Zã-ku, day's death, it was time for nocturnal fantasies to begin. Huddled together in a semicircle about Agŏtĭme, the children vied with each other in riddling while, by the glow of their several fires, the women finished cleaning up. Above, in the tamarind, the tree that no axe could ever break, invisible spirits clustered expectantly. "What will it be tonight?" someone whispered, "what will it be?"

Agōtíme's eyes gleamed. She knew. When a man dies his people raze his sleeping hut to the ground, so she knew there was but one story appropriate for tonight.

Her repertoire for one so young, the women said, was remarkably extensive. But it had been her fortune once to spend long hours with the palace diviner. And if she could not fail to remember countless fables expressive of the sixteen-times-sixteen-eyed wisdom of the oracle, she at least did Fa the grace of adapting them to her own purposes so that all were, and at the same time were not, the wiser when she told them night after night to her attentive following.

But there was one tale of which she really did have forbidden knowledge. No amount of elaboration could possibly disguise its lair. None of Fa's wisdom this, but an ancestral tale passed down from each king to that prince chosen to succeed him. Knowing that Fate was determined to have her son inherit the throne eventually, she, without compunction, had coaxed the story out of Agōglo one night as he lay sick with premonitions of the disease her presence was supposed to keep from him. She had promised the anxious king that she would never disclose this secret of origin to anyone but Gākpe, and to Gākpe only when the time came for him to replace his elder brother. She would keep it in reserve, lest the state become so corrupt under Adādozā's dispensation that priests and diviners no longer dared speak. Her son's horoscope was safely stored in the calabash of memories dutifully carried to and from the diviner's house, why not the shadowy half of his fate, the darker title to his patrimony?

She had her will. The doomed king complied, but the custodianship had not been easy. How could she have known, she who retained horoscopes in fabled form so easily, that old Earth-songs have a strong life of their own? They refuse to be dried or folded. Once told, Agōglo's pedigree had coiled itself like a snake about the base of her brain. For five years it had repeated itself to her—sometimes in new guises, both in dreams and in abstract moments of her waking life. She had fought it off at first, fearing it would consume her, rot her head, but slowly she began to realize that this forbidden mystery was a strength, the secret source of all narrative energy in her. Of all suppressed life too, for in her isolation she came to fulfillment only in and through the stories told to that double audience—the spirits abroad in the night and the lively community of children.

Now, this final night in the royal city, her son as impossibly far from the throne as from her side, she no longer cared about violating the taboo. Let the dynasty fend for itself, she was no longer involved.

She was in no immediate danger. The sacrilege would not be immediately grasped by these dull-witted women who never paused to wonder what *kposi* [panther-wife] really meant. As for the children, since this tale—for all that it really belonged only to her son and his progenitors—expressed her weird turn of wit, her wildest longings as no other ever could, what more appropriate gesture of farewell? Let the spirits in the tamarind understand and forgive her motives. She would, she must, tell that tale tonight.

"*Kpo ñã, kpo ñã*," she began, "the panther goes forth, the panther goes forth."

"*Avū be, avū be*," the children completed the sentence, "and the dog hides, and the dog hides."

"No power can oppose *kpo*," Agōtīme went on. "Now listen. It is the tale of the Princess Aligbonō, daughter of Tado's king, who went down to the banks of the Mono River. She was thin, thin as a willow-rod, but she was well made and her hands were remarkably calloused and strong. She went down to the river, accompanied by her servants, to cull rough leaves for scouring calabashes in the courtyard of her father's home."

Agŏtíme's voice dropped, becoming more intimate as she drew closer. "It was early morning, between cock-crow and earth's-opening-of-the-door. The line of trees along the river-bank looked to be a furl of black brushfire smoke against the grey horizon. As Aligbonō approached, a covey of startled guineafowl flushed from the underwood. A warm wind rasped upon the brittle stalks of the swamp grasses. A white heron skirred along the mudflats and plunged into the stream. Then, a yawn in the canebrake, followed by a dry cough, as if something or someone were clearing his throat to speak. . . ."

Raising her voice, she continued: "It was at such a time and in such a place that the Princess Aligbonō met a spirit in the form of a panther. The servant girls screamed. Dropping their plaited baskets, they fled, leaving their mistress alone with him.

"It was dawn for him also, and having consumed the vital organs and fed for a while on the powerful thorax, the panther had covered his kill and retired to the reeds beside his watering place to rest. He had heard the whirr of quail wings flailing free of the bush, the screech of the waterbird on the marge of the stream. Catching his first glimpse of the Princess Aligbonō, he saw her golden wristlets gleam in the first light, saw the sheen of the white satin scarf about her waist, the smooth folds of her headtie. Her limbs were as sleek as a young antelope's, but she walked on two feet and there were flecks of sea-green life in her eyes. Startled, the panther dropped his jaw and sucked in an awesome breath . . ." A small boy in front of her did the same.

"The Princess Aligbonō smelled that unmistakable sour odor and would have fainted had not a short, angry snarl alerted her. And then that dry cough. Swiftly, silently, the panther slid forward, low to the ground, his cloak as black as storm clouds at midnight. A mere bamboo length away he paused to dig in his hind claws. Then, amidst a crash of dry twigs, he sprang. The princess screamed."

And so, Agŏtǐme feared, had she. She opened her eyes. A calabash of stars emptied into them. The night wind was chill. Nothing could be heard but the soft cry of the tambourine doves, the gentle sough of the tamarind. She looked into the astonished eyes of the little boy directly in front of her, and as if talking to her own son reassured him, "But deep inside herself the princess was not really afraid.

"Returning the next morning with armed men—the cowardly servants found Aligbonŏ quite well. The black leopard had disappeared. Nine months later the princess gave birth to a boy, rust-colored and velvet-skinned. In time, this child grew into a strong young man with whorls of hair on his shoulders, long nails and strange sea-green eyes. The king of Tado, displeased with his daughter, named his unusual grandson Agasu [bastard], but the youth survived to father many kings.

"That, however, is another story. I heard this one from a bird, and no sooner had it told the tale than it changed into a stone. Already it has rolled away and whoever would catch it must run all the way down the royal road to Whydah Beach. So be off with you and get you to bed. It will soon be Zǎ-nǎnǎ [bad night], the hour when serpents crawl forth from the bush to cross the paths of the unwary and all things change hands. So go in peace while it is still possible to salute you with a 'goodnight' and a 'goodbye for now.' " "And forever," she added silently.

She watched the children trundle off in the darkness to doorways now illuminated by flickering oil lamps within. When these were extinguished she would go. At the time of night for which there was no greeting, she would wrap herself in a cloak dark as a panther's fell and slip out of the courtyard to do her final errands within the royal city. It had not been difficult to bribe the guards. Why had she not thought of doing so before? Those ugly warrior-women had proved to be as vain as any other fourteen-ribbed creature, delighted with a short string of inferior coral beads or a tawdry Ceylonese scarf.

"Come, Fina," she said, "you too must go to bed. Already the moon has left her lover's arms and goes to play with her innumerable children in the white foaming sea-of-the-sky. The spirits of the dead are restless. Come, we must not offend them." And Agōtīme led the little slave girl across the courtyard and tucked her into her pallet bed wedged between storage bins in that narrow corridor that had been home to her. I wonder, Agōtīme said to herself, what will become of Fina now? I wish, wherever I am going, I could take her with me. But even if it were possible, it would not be just, for who can ask another to share one's destiny?

She heard the doves moaning under the eaves and thought again of the Princess Aligbonō. There remained a short skein of the tale untold, and as she waited beside sleeping Fina, Agōtīme rolled it up in her mind:

Everyone thought Aligbonō never saw the panther again. But she did. A hunter hurt him badly once and for days he lay hidden in the bush until the princess discovered him and secretly tended his wounds. In exchange for her help, he gave her to know his forbidden name—a name of which Agōtīme herself was ignorant—along with three magic doves to warn her of danger so that she might flee before it.

2 ▶ The Bokonõ

The full moon groped the sky above the Great Wall, extending fingers of light to probe about the crumbling parapets of Kpẽgla's palace. Glancing along the frieze of skulls, still intact on their iron palings, the moonlight restrung them into a grotesque collar for the still-living shadow of that king-of-pearls.

They were Egbado skulls primarily, six thousand mute witnesses to the time Kpẽgla's expeditionary forces broke Badagri, a slave depot located midway between Porto Novo and Lagos. Though six European ships stood in the offing, like vultures awaiting the outcome of the struggle, and although slave prices were high that year, the Dahomean general had orders from Kpẽgla to slaughter all captives. Their heads were requisite to the completion of the new royal residence. The soldiers loaded their litters and force-marched seventy miles upcountry with the cargo of heads. But when these had been spindled at regular intervals along the top of the wall, Hupatĩ the architect was chagrined to find that he had miscalculated. He was one hundred and twenty-seven short. "What matter," Kpẽgla said, "mountain crocks may serve as well as brackish water gourds. No matter how empty our prisons are, there always are the dregs. There must be some Maxis too infirm or repulsive to be sold who would jump at the chance of useful employment. Let the correct number be led forth to complete the decoration."

The Grand Palace, auspiciously begun long, long ago upon the carcass of an unyielding aborigine, was the accumulated work of six reigns and, as Agōtīme was wont bitterly to insist, one regency. No sooner had each successive crown prince fallen heir to the priceless pearls, the embroidered sandals, the three-tiered throne, than custom required him to begin at once to build a lesser palace in which to live, to be entombed and thence worshipped as a force whose bearing on the welfare of the state tended but slowly to diminish after he was dead. And for the second source of his earthly being, his mother, all these arrangements were to be made in diminished duplicate. It also fell upon each king to cut his own gateway and to provide an equivalent exit for the *kpojito*.

The general plan of all royal residences was the same—a series of interlocking courtyards, covered arcades, halls of state and relatively secluded chambers, cubicles and passageways, one of which was required to lead directly from the king's most private apartment to the mausoleum of his immediate predecessor. Upon this a king might superimpose a house of two or even three stories. For the realization of his structural needs, as for the embellishment of honest clay walls and thatched roofing, the king relied upon the ingenuity of the royal architect and craftsmen. He could be assured that, once built, his tomb would remain both well-guarded (by old women) and in good repair (repainted and rethatched once a year at least), but he had to face the fact that the carvings on his noble gateway, the sculpted pilasters bearing the stress of low-browed porticos, and the polychrome bas-reliefs along his section of the Great Wall would not long survive him. Yet there remained the comforting thought that despite the intense defacement by termites, winds and rains the motifs upon which they were based would become a part of history and persist.

The Great Wall had by Agɔ̄tīme's time attained a perimeter of six hundred and seventy-one bamboos (almost two miles) and a rhombus shape. Its northern peak had been formed by the first palace built, Huegbaja's eponymous *Dã-xome* [house-upon-Dã's-stomach], its nadir by the structures bordering Sīboji Square —site of most festivals and where, even on ordinary days, modest crowds could be seen gathering before dawn to acclaim the rising of the king. Only after the Earth opened its door and the king his, could those men—be they artisans or dignitaries—with business in the palace presume to enter it. For the palace was a veritable city of women. Within those hundred acres were housed six thousand people, and those who were not women were eunuchs and princelings too young to be a real threat either to the life of the king or to the virtue of his wives.

Having safely attained the outer wall, Agɔ̄tīme, pausing to catch her breath, smiled at the moon's lustrous dexterity. The sixth king-of-skulls—how apt a praise-name that would have been! They say that great King Kpēgla used to steal forth upon Sīboji Square at night to strew the ground with skulls so that whoever, on some illicit business bent, chanced to stub his toe in the dark might be thus reminded of that supreme power upon whose grace his very life depended. As for those there upon the parapet, had Kpēgla himself lived long enough to fulfill his dearest wish, they might have numbered the severed heads of Agɔ̄tīme's own kin among them. But no, having tried seven times to take Gbohuele, the sixth king was forced at last to bequeath this task to earnest Agɔ̄glo. Her husband! How strange that having spent eight years striving to please and at the same time to settle accounts with him, she should so seldom think of him dead.

And when she did it was her youth she mourned for rather than his unfulfilled career.

Having successfully resisted the raids of prior kings, Agŏtĭme's village, protected by the highest peak in the Dassa region of Maxi, was thought to be invulnerable. The cony is a helpless little rodent, but he builds well into the rock. In Dahomey they say: "The cony has turned his back to the mountain of Gbohuele," meaning, "He has placed himself under the protection of a powerful superior." But King Kpĕgla stubbornly fought this proverbial invulnerability until Gbohuele's chief, Ajinŏ [theft is good], equally determined not to give up, yet having begun to doubt that geographical vantage alone would continue to protect his people, had recourse to surer supernatural means. Going beyond the mountain, Ajinŏ turned his back, as they say, to a powerful medicine—a jar of stones—which, hurled down upon Dahomey's capital city, caused a great tremor to shake both king and dignitaries from their ceremonial seats and toppled sections of the vast wall itself. Never before in Dahomean memory had such a convulsion seized the earth. What did it mean? The terrified Kpĕgla sent emissaries down to Whydah Beach to ask the Europeans resident there if ever they, in their farflung countries, had experienced or heard tell of such a prodigy. To which the wily Europeans replied that the earthquake, a phenomenon by no means unknown to them, was but a visitation by their High God upon the Dahomean king on account of his most horrible sins. What sins? Highly offended, Kpĕgla turned to the interpretation of his own Bokonŏ, a reading well borne out by subsequent events; but meanwhile, in the wake of the dry north wind, there was worse to come. One year after the quake, Kpĕgla, immured from curious eyes within his most private apartment, lay dying of the smallpox.

Before night finally fell on him, Kpĕgla made his crown

prince Agōglo promise to search out an even more powerful medicine with which to humble Gbohuele. But this was not Agōglo's way. He had spent many years patiently waiting to rule, and in the shadow of that proud palace of skulls had come to see life as it is. Although the son dutifully swore to postpone his father's funeral rites until the bier should be washed by the blood of Gbohuele's best sons, he remained convinced that, were the proper pious precautions taken, man power would be enough. And Agōglo consulted the Bokonō.

His first invasion would seem to have proved him wrong. Gbohuele remained impregnable and Ajinō's sister Ninugūgōnō, she of the twisted mouth who talked too much, was emboldened to send back the taunt that, for all Huegbaja's descendants had been at pains to enlarge their domain, Dahomey remained so reduced a plot that but one small furrow could be dug out of it.

As the defeated army, demobilized, prepared to disperse to natal villages and farms, Agōglo, disguised in a commoner's cloak, strode forth to mingle with the throng. A personal sounding of his men's morale might help, he thought, to determine the cause of their continued failure. The king walked along the road to Bohicō with one garrulous warrior who said, "The time has passed for ardent pursuit of victory at all costs. Nowadays, who cares? The officers, well-fed, care but for their own comfort while we, having consumed our meager supplies, there being no women to prepare our food for us and carry it as far as the foothills of that cursed Gbohuele, think but of returning home."

"And the king," Agōglo asked, "the king?"

The soldier thrust out his lower lip. "The king? Why should we fight his battles for him? Reclining his sacred head upon the bosoms of his fourscore wives, what should he know of our sufferings? Why should he know that we have no one to administer to our needs?" When they came to the crossroads of Goxo they parted. The soldier went on to his hut and the king, by another route, to his palace.

The next day Agōglo gave orders for immediate remobiliza-
tion. "This is too much, he must be mad to try the loyalty of our
troops this way," the generals said. "The common bird shies
away from the raffia palm seed," Agōglo said, "but the toucan
doesn't find it too hard for his beak. Having cracked the riddle,
the rock should be easy. Of all perfumes musk is most penetrat-
ing," he added, in a playful vein uncommon with him, "being
privy to the secrets of the deer." So saying, he had twenty
corpulent wives led forth from his deceased father's harem, and
these he distributed to the more seasoned veterans of his father's
wars, charging them to replenish the royal stores with fresh
mountain maidens. The soldiers laughed.

Eight days later, unable to withstand the most impassioned
assault in its history, Gbohuele fell. Trapped with her youngest
children in a thatched cottage fired by burning arrows, Agōtíme's
mother perished; but Agōtíme herself, together with two elder
brothers, twins, her father and the surviving members of her
father's cult, was led in captivity down to Abomey.

By the time the last prisoners straggled into Sīboji Square,
second funeral rites for Kpēgla were well under way. Her handsome brothers were among those chosen as messengers to the
dead king to tell him of his posthumous victory over that most
stubborn of all Maxi villages. For her father, a renowned priest
of the smallpox cult, the seventh king had other plans which, in
accordance with some oracular advice the Bokonō had latterly
communicated to him, involved Agōtíme as well. But she could
hardly have been aware of this possibility then. Too stunned for
tears, that scrawny twelve-year-old, the palm fringe of submission
loosely hung about her neck, stood beside her father hours on
end, beneath the leaden atmosphere of early Harmattan until at
last the sun, master of all victims, had the mercy to incline its
head and the king to recess the interminable ceremony.

So night fell at last upon Gbohuele, upon all those for whom
it was fated to fall, save one. For Agōglo, humane though he may

have been, or tried to become, being no less literal-minded than the rest, was unable to resist the royal Dahomean impulse to make his enemies eat their words served up as gruesome practical jokes. When all the proper sacrifices for Kpēgla were done, Agōglo stepped forward with a hoe. Eight soldiers joined him to complete the job. Then Ninugŭgōnō, the chief's sister who talked too much, was bound and stretched out in the trench. The eight soldiers filled her crooked mouth with clay, then buried her completely. "Chief Ajinō," Agōglo said, "you may have wondered why, in defiance of all precedent, you two were spared. Now my intention may be made clear. Your sister has just been bedded down in a modest furrow. Add this to Dahomey, that other furlong of which your sister spoke, and you've got a plot wide enough for a king. This lesson now you've learned by experience, but such quick knowledge is scarce enough to make a proper farmer out of you. Therefore I've decided to put you in charge of one of my herds. As a solitary cattleman you'll have plenty of time for reflection."

Edging along the shadowy contours of the wall, Agōtĭme heard the hyenas barking in the thornbush outside. Who knew what corpses would be thrown to glut those hideous scavengers in the moat? Foolish Agōglo suspected no one; Adādozā they said, despite his reputed sorcerer's powers, feared, or perhaps because of them foresaw, the harm in everyone. He was a violent man. One day in a fit of rage when he was very young, he struck his eldest sister with his saber's edge. Another time, for a joke, he tied the two prime ministers together right hand to left as befitting their titles and spat brandy in their faces. Yet far from thus making him an enemy of the Migā, this prank but seemed to consolidate the loyalty that ministers felt for Adādozā. As king, understandably after all the turmoil following his father's death and all the acrimony, as well as the threats that preceded it, Adādozā preferred ambitious commoners to men of royal blood.

In religious matters he claimed to be a traditionalist. Indeed, when the Portuguese priests came back for the third time, he told them that Agŏglo was dead, that he himself already had a god, Elegba, and that what he wanted were red-eared men who knew how to manufacture guns and gunpowder, that he wanted a European foundry built, not a Christian shrine. This forthright retort was the talk of the palace. Why then had Adădozā expelled Agŏtĭme's father's cult; and lately, they said, he'd gone so far as to neglect the Toxosu and the royal dead? The hyenas howled again. Agŏtĭme shivered and hastened on.

She passed by Tegbesu's palace, then Agaja's, and left the wall by the ordinary wives' gate that opened out upon the road to Bohicō. A short path to the right led her to the Bokonō's compound. Night stood straight up, but she knew he was expecting her. She hurried across the courtyard, giving the hideous mound-of-all-sicknesses a wide berth. Under the low thatched joists of the veranda the diviner's family and his disciples were stretched out asleep, each wrapped against the chill. Under the eaves of interlaced bamboo, swallows slept and the dusty sill beneath was covered with droppings. Agŏtĭme smiled. Nothing here, at any rate, had changed in five years.

Within the consulting room an oil lamp guttered, projecting a sporadic silhouette of Legba's clay bust onto the south wall. In the shadowy middle region of the room, the Bokonō slumped toward the east in meditation before the mysterious covered jar. He did not turn around, but no sooner had she stepped over the threshold than the narrow black-and-white stripes of his ample gown shifted slightly as he eased up to adjust the sacred tools of his trade.

"I have returned. Greetings at midnight, father."

"Greetings at midnight, daughter, I greet you after a long time."

"I greet you for not seeing, for not even inquiring about me," she dared to say.

"My hands have been tied," he replied. "It was up to you to find a way to see me."

She sat down while he completed the preliminaries. Although she could not see what he was doing, she knew the procedure intimately. As preferred wife, it had been up to her to bring the royal kernels for casting and, in secret, to report the Bokonō's findings back to Agōglo. But she felt ill at ease tonight, not only because of her long, long absence from the consulting room because of the tragedy that remained unspoken between them, but because she had never before come on her own behalf. No panther-wife ever did, her fate being, by definition, the king's.

When it was time to begin, he placed the board between them and turned to look at her for the first time. Five years. Could he see them—as minute traces beneath her eyes perhaps? Impossible to tell. He knew it was she, that alone was certain. His face, like that of most corpulent men, had not aged at all. His gaze was as steady and kind as it had always been, but deep within she thought she detected a new wariness; or was it she who had grown wary? He said nothing. It was for her to make the first move. The sixteen eyes of the oracle never close and when Agōtíme said, "I have a question to ask of Fa," a small sweat broke out on her forehead.

From the jumble of bones, kernels, gourds, mysterious knobs and integuments that he spilled forth from his sack onto the immaculate cloth before him, the Bokonō picked out the tiny *ajikwi* seed and handed it across to her. Reaching into the folds of the satin scarf about her waist, Agōtíme produced a small piece of European money, five francs—a veritable fortune in cowries. The Bokonō smiled at her extravagance.

Coupling seed to coin, Agōtíme raised both to her lips, mutely phrasing her question. Then she gave both to the Bokonō. Pocketing the coin, he placed the seed in the covered calabash of divining nuts. When he was satisfied that the disclosure had taken place, he took the seed out of the calabash again and placed it on the carved rim of the divining board. Agōtīme relaxed a little. The rest was up to him.

The Bokonō took up the eighteen nuts. With the tips of his fingers upright he gently chafed the kernels between closed palms while pronouncing the invocation:

> Inspire me, my teacher,
> Inspire me, my ancestors,
> And you, Alaba, who reside in mysterious Ife,
> Inspire me.
> All those more knowledgeable than I,
> Come to my aid.
> Gods of life and death,
> *Vodū* of the earth,
> *Vodū* of the waters,
> Help me.
> Legba, intercessor,
> Permit me to speak.

Having summoned the defunct members of his fraternity, the Bokonō put down the nuts. Taking a pinch of powder from the surface of the board, he put the stuff on the tip of his tongue and spat in turn to each of the four points. Then, seizing the nuts in his left hand and withdrawing them just as suddenly into his right, returning them to the left again with the same quick gesture, the Bokonō began to spell out the sign. Without breaking the clicking tempo of nuts passing from hand to hand, he drew rapid strokes upon the powder: two marks if one nut remained in place as the moving palm took them up, one mark if two, and no mark at all if more than that. Eight clues and the sign stood completed:

But was it legitimate? The Bokonō continued to throw the nuts until Agōtīme's answer should lie framed by parallel columns of marks that declared either no or yes.

From the detached height to which the strain of the last hours had mercifully lifted her, Agōtīme looked down upon the simple pattern of evens and odds. Strange tracks. The odd shape of the board suddenly suggested the skin of an animal, pegged at the corners. Surely that was how it was first done in simpler times, before there were any woodcarvers. And the *ye* powder must have been sand, blown from distant desert by the dry north winds. And before that, before there were tanners of hides, there was only sand—an immensity of sand, pegged by the four points, upon which a prowling animal nightly left his spoor.

But the Bokonō was speaking; he had begun to develop the configuration known as *Weli Meji!* "Hyena, catching his paw in a trap, yowled for help. 'I'm coming,' cried Brushfire, veering his way!"

"So I depart the kingdom under a dangerous sign," Agōtīme laughed nervously. "I'm not surprised. But," she continued, with ill-concealed annoyance, "why do you begin on such a threatening note? Why intimidate me? I know that road. I know it well. It's dangerous, but not necessarily catastrophic. Some might even call it beautiful, like the road upcountry to Gbohuele. You seem to forget how many hours I have spent in silence here listening to you tell the ways of Fa. I thought you knew, but perhaps you never realized how, walking home to the palace afterwards, I found that each new pattern your hand disclosed had altered the entire world for me. Five years of separation have, if anything, made these forms but the more real to me for being the only eyes through which to see the world. I have even fashioned praises for the greater ones. Weli Meji! How well I know him. Listen:

> The world of Weli Meji is stippled, riddled with sunlight,
> the fish in the shallows of the mountain stream;

It is the world of antelopes, dappled in the shade; of pied
guineafowl, of nubby toads and spotted snakes; of butterflies, of bamboo, of cloths of tied and deep-dyed
indigo;

It is the world of porous laterite, clotted red; of flat-crowned
euphorbia trees with dwarfed, contorted arms; of cactus,
pebbles, granite boulders and deep-rooted peaks;

It is splashes of evening color on the calabash of the sky
when the sun inclines its head to the axe of the executioner; splotched leaves in the dry season; daubs of
clay on the dancers' faces; the chameleon's camouflage;

It is the world of fingers cracked with grime; the splayed toes
of weary feet; the dust of the journey; the fire-scarred
pot; the face of the oldest grandmother;

It is grain broadcast upon the furrowed earth with which
Earth's children are fed; the blisters, rashes, wens, warts
and pustules with which Earth punishes them; of cowries or knuckle-bones knotted into nets, filleted gourds
to shake, shake them away, the vertebrae of serpents."

"Stop!" the Bokonō said, "you convince me, Agōtīme. One
man's collar does not fit well upon another's neck; nor, if it did
fit, would it become him. I cannot believe you would praise
all the major signs so heatedly. This would be indeed remarkable.
There are some," he continued, "who, fearing to view the world
through such an eye, see only ugliness there. Since you do not,
the sign must fit you in some more permanent way, inherited I
dare say from your paternal kin. But it's a deceptive road, my
little guineahen, and you must learn to read it well. Don't forget,"
he laughed, "it is Weli Meji who's responsible for stomachache,
as well as for those fierce disorders of the skin you so rapturously
enumerate—without having experienced any of them. Many are
the ramifications of Weli Meji; perhaps the tale of Guineafowl
and Leopard might seem more relevant to your present situation."

"You insist on patronizing me, on treating me like a child,"

Agōtīme said, "or like one of your duller-witted clients—some warrior-woman come to consult on the outcome of her regiment's next campaign. O, I don't mean to be so quarrelsome, and I intend no disrespect, it's just that I've been so walled up. I've thought of you often. I'd hoped that if I finally managed to bribe my way through the gate . . ."

"So it was not Fa you wanted to consult, but me? What sacrilege," the Bokonō said, looking at her more narrowly. It was impossible to tell whether or not he was still joking—if indeed he had really ever been joking. Then, with a self-deprecatory gesture, "I have nothing original to say. I but develop the signs. Everything that happens here has happened in the sky before; hence the miracle that we are able to know anything. You strip the *fa-du* of their meaning. Setting the succulent poetry aside for yourself, you then proceed to devour the old tales greedily, reduce these to a fine pulp and then spew them forth as pap for babies. You think you feed when in reality you but flatter them."

"Who told you that?" she snapped. "Was it Nahoue? Or that Nago wife of Adādozā's whose name always escapes me—my replacement, so to speak?"

"No matter," the Bokonō said. "If you don't consider it too patronizing, may I suggest that you will never find your way until you begin to reflect upon the original stories. You do remember the one about Guineafowl and Leopard, I take it—part of your repertoire, I imagine. Would you care to tell me what you think it means?"

Why did he nettle her so? She used to hang on his every word but now he seemed less wise and more tedious, narrow rather than inscrutable. And why this strange hostility between them? Who had planted it there? "No, you're wrong, or you've been badly informed," she said. "I do know what the *fa-du* stories mean, or at least I think I do, but only while I'm telling them, when it suddenly seems as though it all had happened not in the sky but to me, Agõtĩme. However, once told, the feeling passes, and with it whatever insight there may have been. But did I not convey the gist in the telling? For me there's only one tale persists, stays real, and even here I cannot honestly say I possess the entire meaning."

"And that one?" He was interested. "Would you tell it to me?"

"No, and I can't say why."

He sat back again.

"It's none of Fa's wisdom anyway," she went on. "Forgive me for bringing it up. Better return to Guineafowl and Leopard. But that's no use. That sort of tale means nothing to me tonight. It's like the fruit whose flesh is much too soft and whose inner husk can't be cracked by the teeth—either far too simple or impossibly arcane. It would bore both of us in the telling."

"The more's the pity," the Bokonō said. "I understand that you are weary. It is very late. You will have to go your own way without listening. But be cautious, Agõtĩme, such is the moral of that little tale you refuse to discuss with me; adapt to circumstance; be discreet, adept at disguise, change of place and you will survive to accomplish that which Fa has decreed."

"For whom? For Gãkpe? I don't see how my absence can accomplish anything for him and, since my only reason for living has been to see him become king, I fail to see how Weli Meji can lead me to anything but old age in a strange place, mere survival."

"Who can say? Fa is cool, absolutely ordered; but don't forget that through Fa's messenger, Legba [fate], works in devious, sometimes tortuous ways. You ask too much of me. I cannot predict, much less create, events or opportunities. All I, with Fa's help, can do is try to sweep the evil a little to one side. For example, since you have not the proper ingredients at your command, I shall make the necessary sacrifice to Weli Meji for you later tonight. And I suggest that before you go to Sĩboji Square tomorrow to receive Adãdoza's sentence, a sacrifice to the messenger on your own account would do no harm. I wish I could be there, but human blood will be shed and I cannot violate the prohibitions of my priesthood."

So that's how he used us, my father and me, as brooms to sweep the evil from Agōglo's path. When my son turned out to be the favored of Fa, he must have been genuinely pleased. It's not every generation that a prince turns out to have the same stars as the Dahomean earth itself. This seemed to justify his advice, cancelled his debt to me. Then it turned out that he hadn't read the leaves correctly, that none of us—not he, nor my father, nor I—could succeed in averting catastrophe. "I have often wondered," she said aloud, "if I had not been led by fate down from Gbohuele into the wives' court what I should have been? One of Sakpata's dancers? This was always Agōglo's idea, but I'm not so sure. Suppose it had been permitted me to go into the sacred wood myself. What would I have learned? What would have come of it? I have heard tell of one or two women who, having done such a thing, became diviners themselves. I have a good memory and perhaps the interpretive wisdom you say I lack is just Fa's way of punishing me for ignoring his call. But above all I sense that I do have a destiny, apart from that of the king, be that king Agōglo or—I won't deign to mention him in this regard—or, even, Gākpe."

"Fa forbid, Agōtǐme, you have a surfeit of powers as it is. Do not, please, if you care for your sanity, do not number divination among them. Besides, it is your destiny that interests you, not that of other people, Gākpe excepted, of course, Gākpe excepted. I am ignorant of the sign that brought you into the world and rather than speculate on that I suggest we return to Weli Meji. You are going on a journey, this much we know. And the sign tells us you must stick to the Earth, not in your father's way precisely—you're right about that—but wherever you go you must come to terms with the local djinns, with the spirits who have infiltrated the trees, infested the streams and learn how to let the greater *vodū* sustain without destroying you. Do you know," he asked, as if to change the subject, "how we Bokonō make the sacred *ye* upon which the signs are traced?"

"No," Agōtíme said, sullenly fussing with the contents of her little drawstring purse, "not really, but it's odd that you should mention that. I saw what you might call a mirage a short time ago, while you were casting. O well, there's no point in going into that. You ask what *ye* is now. Some sort of wooddust I suppose, to judge by the color. How do you get it so fine? Mortar and pestle, probably, but I really don't see what . . ."

"No, Agōtíme," the Bokonō said, staring at her fixedly now, as if to suggest the imposition of a second meaning behind the flow of words he was well aware she found almost too tedious to bear, "we are not impatient housewives. There's no pounding. It's a leisurely process. First we must find a thunder tree in the sacred forest. Then the tree must be cut, but only at the new moon, then passed through fire and left to dry. At the end of three moons we return to have a look. Tilting up the trunk, we knock it against the ground. Having encouraged the termites to do our work for us, we should be able, if they've been busy, to skim handfuls of *ye* off the forest floor, *ye* as fine as you see it on the board. And we know this powder to be the only visible, tangible replica of that greater *ye* that permeates all things. This is why we value it, why we guard the secret of its preparation."

"So that's it," Agōtíme said, fighting to keep the tremor out of her voice. "How absurd of me to imagine my destiny to be mine, to be other than it is, has been, will and must be. I knew in principle before, according to the law of things, but now I feel my fate irrevocably linked with that of the king—be he Agōglo or Gãkpe or, who knows? Not Adãdozã."

"Don't be too sure," the Bokonō interposed.

"No, I repeat," she went on stubbornly, "not Adãdozã, if any proof were wanting of his future downfall, here it is—I, Agōtíme. I may be but a tool," again she choked at the thought, "yet my axe cuts across his grain, small wonder he has to get rid of me! What then am I to do? You haven't answered that. In what way shall I be used? Where will it end? Will there ever come a time when I am free? No," she said rebelliously, "it's all wrong. I have the power to do anything—everything, be a queen in my own right, communicate with the unseen, become a priestess. You're only trying to intimidate me because you feel guilty for having, in the course of making your greatest mistake, tampered with my destiny, and more than that, because you're jealous of me. There, I've said it."

The Bokonō, clearly, had no intention of commenting. He was busily putting his tools away. But Agōtĭme would not stop for the tears choking her throat, stifling her head. As if the very stars were receding in the pale light of her desperation, she kept on questioning. "Or am I by any chance the Princess Aligbonō? Is that what it all reduces to? Is that the secret meaning?"

The Bokonō rose. "Agōtĭme, I have said enough, but I shall say one more thing. No, you are not the Princess Aligbonō, but you are very like the Queen Huãjele [she gasped], or so it has always seemed to me. And now I must perform certain rites which can no longer be delayed. Be patient and the path will eventually be made plain. Goodnight, take care not to stumble in the dark. *Mawu ni co mi.*"

"Goodnight," Agōtĭme said, coldly. "May your work be completed successfully and then, may you live while you sleep. Thank you for the consultation and, in advance, for performing the sacrifice for me. Goodbye until—forever."

Safely within the palace grounds again, Agōtĭme did not return directly to the panther-wives' court. She had further business of her own to perform. She continued to skirt the Great Wall, past the quiet compound where the old women guardians of the kings' tombs lived, until she came to the northeastern extremity of the Great Wall. Here she paused for a look at the first palace built. Was Dã really a stubborn farmer who refused to yield up his lands to the invading panther-king? Or was he Dã-aidohuedo the rainbow-serpent, *vodù* of good fortune and happenstance, brought down from her own Mahiland? At any rate, not much remained of Huegbaja's watchtower now—a mere mound of mud, no more than two bamboos high, scarce distinguishable, at a distance, from the well-repaired wall surrounding it.

Now, turning west, Agōtíme straightened her shoulders, arched her back and, meeting the declining moon full in the face, began her defiant tour of the northern wall, her viewing of the Queens' Gates. There was the gate of Na Adono, mother of three rulers: Akaba, Akaba's twin sister (the only reigning queen), and Agaja—he who first linked Dahomey with the sea. Beneath Na Adono's shrine, checkered with whitewash and soot, a guard dozed—one of the warriors, sitting bolt upright in her sleep, her huge legs stuck out like felled trees from beneath her short, striped tunic.

Agōtíme tiptoed past, on to Na Huãjele's gate. How could she, Agōtíme, be compared to Na Huãjele, Tegbesu's mother, priestess of the sky gods Mawu and Lisa, whose living substitute had stolen into Agōglo's room and shot him? How cruel of the diviner, how outrageous. What did he mean? Am I then a murderess? Nonsense, ridiculous to think. A door opens both ways. The Bokonō erred once, she thought. Not all elders grow wiser with the years, despite what they tell us about being closer to the Earth. Besides, he has become stray witted from guilt. He dared not refer to . . . Did the panther-wives in charge of watering still pass through Na Huãjele's gate, sprinkling a handful of water in her honor on their homeward way? She doubted it. Not now, but when all memory of the secret deed has dried up, when public truth prevails, they will again.

How, if Gãkpe ever becomes king, will they honor me? Agōtíme wondered. Cursing herself for that untimely vanity, she hurried on. Past Gaxoxi gate, through which all cadavers passed, all headless victims of the Migã's sacrificial axe on their way across Ajaxi Market to the burial grounds or the thornbush, or the hyenas of the moat that protected the palace. Past the gate of Cai, Kpẽgla's mother, through which the living came out into the clutter of the market. Past the gate of Senume, the mother-in-law she had never known.

Then, Agõtĩme came upon an opening that was new to her. It was flanked by mud-sculpted elephants between which an elaborate series of steps led into the plantations of the Ajahito quarter that used to be reached through Senume's gate. This must be Nahoue, her rival's gate. How like her! "Well, may her gate's issue be by posterity forgot," she cursed aloud, and then moved on.

At last she came to a line of palm-fiber mats strung between sprouting posts of terebinth. Here heavy rains had dissolved the clay, but here, nonetheless, at the northwesterly apex of the wall, Agõtĩme was convinced that they would someday build her gate. Stooping where she had often imagined the center of the future threshold to be, Agõtĩme started to dig. The laterite yielded unwilling. As she broke nail after nail upon that reluctant element she thought, Not only I but all of us are poor creatures of appearances. To consult Fa, to divine fate is but to scratch the surface, like a guineahen. For what I'm after—whatever it is—I need cruder tools. Even claws make but superficial wounds. What then? and how in the name of Gu to get them?

When the hole was about two handspans deep, Agõtĩme untied her little leather pouch and brought out an amulet. She put it in, covering it well so no one would ever know that anything was buried there. "Di n'gbo fi, di n'ka le," she whispered to the ground, "just now I passed by here, just now I passed by here again." Now I may return, she said to herself. I wonder what Gãkpe, what posterity, will call my gate?

An immense fatigue invaded her. Cutting across the smoking

debris of the potters' yard, picking her way through the ruins of former wives' courts and servants' quarters, she walked a long diagonal back to her room. She walked as if asleep, but she did not stumble.

Meanwhile on the clay of the Bokonō's courtyard, a large rectangle had been hurriedly sketched in broken chalk-lines. In the center the stout Bokonō stood, clothed in nothing but moonlight. "*Se to . . . Ia! ia!*" he cried, invoking his soul. A dull silence pervaded everything. He was alone, his family and disciples slept on, discreetly, in front of the consulting chamber. Then, as he waited, irresistibly a band of grey fog began to unfurl in the east while, simultaneously, in the northwestern sky, a certain star became suddenly illuminated. Piercing the thickening atmosphere, a slim beam from this star struck along the lines of the figure he'd traced, within which he waited. Joyously, the Bokonō turned to address this star in Arabic.

3 ◥◤ Adãdozã

Heels gibbeted upon a beam, tail shafts and barbs splayed out in agony, like a swirling grimace of dishevelled feather-fronds the white cock ripped the dark night into shreds of grey. From the clean slit in his throat the blood dripped onto the freshly white-washed rain-ridge. Agõtǐme smeared her hands with it and moved out into the open to anoint Legba's rough clay head. The thick-set idol glared dispassionately at the coming dawn through slits in those bulging cowrie lids of his, mocking death with the gleaming immobility of his grin. Rubbing her hands clean on the grit of the courtyard, Agõtǐme filled the god's bowl with an offering of kola. Then, prostrating herself before the clay mound into which his shoulders foundered, she praised him:

> Legba is erect in the doorway;
> He swings in the sockets of the hinge;
> He's as near as the edge of the footpath,
> As far as the cup's rim.
> Legba stands by the broken pot on the highroad,
> Munching the shards;

Traveler, you say you stubbed your toe?
Did you get out of the wrong side of bed?
Legba kicks the stone in his anger,
And the stone bleeds.
Traveler, is your easy burden crushing you?
Who piled all those rocks on your head?
Legba slung the shot a week ago
And will stun the bird today;
He strikes the pot with his club
And the world laughs.
Messenger of crossroads,
Vagabond of the future and the past,
With your pointed head that bears no weight,
Make way for me,
Straighten the path.

As she sang, Agõtĩme could feel the skin of the morning tighten across the fine bones of the sky. Somewhere along the great wall all cocks but one were crowing for the second time. *Gong-gong, gong-gong;* the palace crier had completed the praise-songs. On the king's threshold today's dawn-messengers, bound, awaited the Migã's knife. Now through the gate of the panther-wives' court came the water carriers, single file, their heavy jars balanced on gay print head-scarves. There was a stir in the various apartments. Leaving their children to sleep on until bird-chasing time, the women came out to collect their water, then hurried to the common bathhouse, then back again to dress in something appropriately simple for the singing of the Hãye for the king's awakening. When they had all left by the inner passage that linked the wives' court with Adãdozã's, Agõtĩme ventured forth to the washing-shed.

When she returned she noticed that beneath the heavy over-hang the bloody feathers, although slackened, were not yet still.

With a shudder she sloshed the remaining water over the threshold and went in to dress. Behind her, in the courtyard, Legba
continued to smirk.

The wives-of-the-panther were especially quarrelsome on
ceremonial days. They returned from the Hāye and had to begin dressing themselves in their most luxurious costumes at once,
without pausing for breakfast. No cooking was permitted in the
courtyard on such mornings lest untended coals fire the thatch,
nor would there have been time to bring a pot to a boil. Hardly
had the sun left the crocodile's jaws before the officious Gūdeme,
resplendent in yards of bustling yellow satin topped by a black-
felt hat, began tapping her stick the length of every veranda.
But there were elaborate coiffures to plait, and the wives abused
their servants for being clumsy and slow. Emerging at last from
their separate doorways, the queens found their natural vanities
frustrated, their antagonisms intensified by relentless rules of
decorum and rank.

Now the Gūdeme, female counterpart of the Prime Minister of the Right Hand, was using that staff of hers to goad the
wives into their proper places in the line. Outside the compound
the old women's band began to thump out a processional on their
mortuary jugs. Somewhere a split gong clanged and as Agōtīme
waited indecisively with Fina beneath the tamarind, she could
imagine the *kpojito*, venerable representatives of queen mothers
past, starting out from their quarters. In crimson velvet and
ivory satin the living queen mother Nahoue would be lumber-
ing along at the head of that file where she herself belonged.
A few minutes more and the gong sounded again, directly outside the wives' wall this time. "*Ago, Ago,*" the bell-eunuch
shouted, "make way for the queens." The gate opened. As they
left the court, some were handed enormous parasols for the
king's shading.

After all had gone through, the Gūdeme finally pointed her

stick at Agõtíme: "Now you," she said, "the monkey gamboling in the trees is certain to reach his objective," her voice heavy with irony. "There are those who teach us to be tall," Agõtíme said, "and others who cut us down. But the palm tree thrives on pruning."

"Greetings for the journey," said the Gũdeme impassively.

"Thank you," Agõtíme said, "I greet you for remaining behind. And you, Fina," she said, "you must dry your eyes for I can't greet you for sobbing. So long as yam mash is prepared on leaves and broth boiled in a groundnut husk, those destined for full stomachs will not starve nor shall I forget you. Good-bye for a long, long time, but not necessarily forever."

The outer corridor down which the procession passed led into the king's palace just outside his audience chamber. Here Adãdozã waited in a morocco-lined cabriolet, the gift of his English "brother" George III. The wheels had been taken off so that it could be borne on poles like an ordinary litter. Beside him stood his four favorite wives, porters of the royal pipe-and-tobacco, drinking goblet, spittoon and whisk. The Gũdeme stepped up to receive the royal message staff. Transferring this to Nahoue at the head of the line, she then gave the signal for the parade to depart the palace. The musicians tempered their beat to simulate the slow rolling gait of kings.

Once outside the gate the rest of the procession fell in behind: the second-class wives; the various military contingents; high-ranking officials, each with his female counterpart and an appropriate number of attendants; the royal genealogist with the king's "birds"—all clothed in white and bearing the cowtail switches of their bardic office; auxiliary bands of musicians; and, finally, a file of servants displaying the king's riches, a part of which, together with an abundance of flesh and wine, would be thrown to the public from the tower of sacrifices.

How, Agõtíme wondered, could she ever have been part of this pageantry? Once she'd been proud to walk beside the king's litter as cupbearer, her tall slim figure softened into elegance by skillful draping of her priceless cloths. A reassuring smile from Agōglo, but where and what was Agōglo now? An invisible force that left her alone, never spoke to her? A wrought-iron altar waiting inside the mausoleum to drink the resultant blood of this day's festival? His emblem? That at any rate was everywhere in evidence—embossed upon the palace wall, refurbished for the occasion, and appliquéd upon the many-faceted parasols shading his successor, Nahoue's son.

His emblem: the pineapple alone, to save space, or if there were room enough, the pineapple beneath the palm. There were various ways to interpret that. His own, of course, was the accepted one: "Lightning strikes the palm but spares the pineapple," his sentence pronounced on acceding to the throne and thenceforth in abbreviated form his name, *Agō-glo*. He claimed it actually happened to him once when he walked out alone, along the road to Bohicō, and got caught in a storm; and because the tree beneath which he stood cracked and burned while he remained unscathed, he was wont to refer to himself as "the king who laughs at thunder."

Poor Agōglo, strong words were not enough to strengthen his head; peppered yams won't substitute for sauce when there is none. Agōglo, like the pineapple, needed shading, sought shelter. He was always overly anxious to protect himself and as often happens he failed to recognize the true shape of disaster. Her father was to have been the palm planted in Abomey to ground a force so feared that no previous king had dared take the proper steps to placate. Yet, this done, never did Agōglo cease to imagine that dread beast already in the process of devouring him. Nor was his flirtation with the black-robed Malams a mere political expedient. He truly thought that by planting the European sky god in their midst, prosperity would return and with this his own popularity—signs that state and king, being one flesh, had indeed grown strong enough to laugh at thunder.

The procession was already passing by the queens' pavilion, a conical tent raised up on poles two bamboos high and secured a hundred times to the ground. Here all but the favorites would return, when the procession stopped, to take up temporary residence. And to this end servants were now busy unrolling bright bolts of cloth for them to sit on and setting out calabashes for them to string into official currency as they viewed the events of the day. This tent, on festive occasions, was the showpiece of Sĩboji Square, not for its size alone, but for the magnificence of its decoration. Its every gore, like a length of time unfurled, was crammed with significant bits of Dahomean history—with emblems of kings, gods and gruesome practical jokes attendant upon unforgettable victories—the whole, together with the great umbrellas, a testimonial of the Dahomean art of appliqué, the pride of the royal craftsmen. Once Agõtĩme had delighted in the ingenuity with which the stocky, energetic figures were made to fit the snatches of space allotted them, the wit that turned strength to symbol, entire battles into single encounters, dignified kings into wild-eyed animals. But seeing all these again for the first time in five years, the brutalities depicted—the lopped limbs shaped like ubiquitous firearms, the hurtling heads, the ricocheting droplets of blood—horrified her. The patterns seemed awkward rather than inventive, too literal-minded. She felt as if it were her life constrained to fit those segments of canopy, those flaps of drapery. No, that painstaking work now seemed far too frank an expression of arrogant power of a line of kings to which, paradoxically, she would, if she were to believe the Bokonõ, become as time went on but the more firmly linked.

And what of Agõglo's public prophecy that Gãkpe would, in the long run, accede to his predestined place? Ah, that depended on Adãdozã, on whether those special powers were real, or but pretended. If they were real, why did she still live? Supposing his reluctance to trouble with black medicine, there were plenty of established means of getting rid of her. She might have been secretly strangled in some dark passage by burly female warriors. Why should adulterous panther-wives fare worse than an ex-queen suspected of conspiracy? What checked him? Perhaps, in defiance of custom, he planned a public execution to thicken the people's fear of him. The Migā's messenger said banishment. But the messenger could have lied or the Migā been mistaken. Or, it was always possible for Adādozā to change his mind at the last minute. Would the Migā refuse to carry out orders repugnant to him? He never had, never would, and why was she so convinced he was her friend in this? She doubted that in public he would go so far as to acknowledge her existence. No, the Migā liked Gākpe, and out of loyalty to the boy he'd sent her the message to prepare herself to quit the kingdom. But now that Gākpe was out of the way, nothing could stop Adādozā from doing anything he fancied. Nothing, except . . . Was it possible that he, in his turn, was afraid of her? Would she be granted a formal interview with him? Did he dare confront her? Or would her punishment be meted out offhandedly, with no fuss about it. She'd know soon enough.

Ahead of her, the queens' umbrellas seemed to throb in the morning sun like overtones of the funereal jar-drums. The royal progress seemed interminable. Did any in the crowd of onlookers notice her, single her out? Or had five years made them forget what she looked like, who she was? Were there any who covertly pitied her? Among the princes and princesses of the royal blood, Gākpe and she had many silent partisans still, but they would have to stare at her indifferently as she went by, as though she were but a shadow passing across their consciences. So many faces, so many voices crying "Dōō Dada [salute to the king]." Well, if nothing else the crowd was still capable of distracting her; they, at least, were life—as variegated as Weli Meji's surfaces.

It was the exotics who always interested her the most, the Malê element, for example, representatives of the Muslim enclaves of Abomey and Kana. There they sat clustered together on their separate rugs. One never saw their women. No parasols for them, although as foreigners she supposed they were entitled to them. Insulated by cloud turbans topped by *tarbooshes*, these Malês were haughty travelers under the sun who stayed wherever and as long as they saw fit. Were all Malês confirmed itinerants, like the Hausa traders and those leather craftsmen from who-knows-where to the north beyond the Atakora Mountains? Some were Malams, holy men who were willing to prepare amulets or cast lots for those they contemptuously called "unbelievers," for those who in turn reviled them as "charlatans," holy men equally skilled in the secondary arts of writing and espionage, who hung around Sīboji Square hoping not only to attract credulous clients but to be hired in either of these latter capacities by the king or, if they were powerful enough, by the king's enemies. As oncoming events cast shadows across the consciousness, Agõtīme thought that somehow or other her path would someday cross that of the Malês. . . .

At the extreme south of Sīboji Square stood the victims' shed. With this part of the annual ceremony Adãdozã clearly did not intend to dispense. For here, to the sixteen posts supporting the pent roof, sixteen state criminals—chosen by lot from the prison's stores—had been bound as they sat in relative comfort upon wicker basket stools. The scene was exactly as she remembered it: before each condemned man a servant stood feeding him pounded yam and fanning flies away from his face and food while a small two-drum band kept them doggedly beating time with their feet and actuated their raucous voices into refrains suggesting a relish rather than a repugnance for their common fate. The sixteen, to judge from the empty demijohns littered about, must already have consumed the required amount of European brandy. When taken to the tower of sacrifices later on, they'd be half-dead anyway.

Just beyond the victims' shed the Great South Gate opened wide upon the Royal Road to Kana and beyond—all the way down to Whydah Beach. Had the cannons finally deteriorated? No, there they were, one on each side of the gate, still mouldering slowly, rusty as sea wrack stranded more than twenty leagues from shore. Early in Kpēgla's reign, when Agōglo was a small boy, a Dutch sea captain had offered these cannon for the defense of the Dahomean people at the absurd price of one hundred slaves apiece. Kpēgla was tempted, being fond of toys and gadgetry, but for once he let his sober son's advice prevail and refused to buy. The captain then sold them to the ambitious king of Badagri who had them mounted in war canoes for defense against an inevitable Dahomean attack. But when fired, the aging cannons capsized the canoes and in the end Kpēgla got them for nothing more than his soldiers' pains taken to drag them up-country along with six thousand skulls and the other loot. How odd it was that the name of the man who cast them, long ago, and so far away it was hard to imagine the place, had been preserved. At the heavy end of each muzzle, on a brass plate a cryptic legend read: *Conraert Wagenwart me fecit Hagae 1640.* The intrusive priests who were able to translate the inscription told Agōglo and Agōtīme that the cannon must have been made about the time Dako-donu, progenitor of the present dynasty, established himself in the palm-rich land just south of Abomey. No Dahomean smith would dream of afixing his name to one of his artifacts. In Conraert Wagenwart's country, then, were armorers as notable as kings? No, certainly, but then again yes, the black-robed Malam had said, for all men were equal before the Great Creator, the Supreme Being. Agōtīme had smiled. The priest had not understood why the cannons fascinated her. She would have liked, before she died, to leave upon something somewhere a little brass plate that said *Agōtīme made me.*

On the other side of the Great Gate stood the visitors' shed where *caboceers* and slave traders from the coast lolled about drinking British brandy and Brazilian arguadente. Here the resident Portuguese riffraff betook themselves on occasions such as this to beg favors and news of the outside world from their more fortunate countrymen. Victims of a languished trade, some of these ex-sailors and adventurers, accidentally captured in the course of Dahomean raids along the littoral, had remained unransomed prisoners as long as twenty-five years in Abomey, where they were permitted to fight boredom by serving as unpaid grooms and scribes to the king.

It was from one of these, an opportunist named Innocencio, that Agõtĩme had, at Agõglo's bidding, learned to speak some Portuguese. He had wanted her, when the priests came back, to be able to take religious instruction from them in their own language. Then she could communicate the deeper secrets of the cult to him. Furthermore, suppose the Portuguese Empress and her emissaries the priests were deceiving Dahomey; suppose trade would not resume; suppose all this was a trick to place them under an alien sky god's power to force Dahomey to pay tribute. After all Tegbesu had led the kingdom under the Nago yoke, a yoke from which they were still at pains to free themselves. It would be well to have a pair of educated ears in the audience chamber.

The lessons were held in the king's private apartment. Agõglo's death, as it was meant, put an end to everything of this sort. But in her isolation Agõtĩme, painful as the association was, often cast back over these simple conversations with Innocencio, for perhaps someday she might have cause to act as king's ears for her son. The priests would never come again, or if they did they would not be welcomed. But rich traders would come to buy palm oil from the royal plantations, and slaves from Mahiland, she supposed.

She was curious to have a look at Innocencio now. Ah, there he was, grown glossier than the self-important snail of which he always reminded her. He saw her too, and started forth with an expansive smile as if to kiss her hand in the courtly fashion of his own country, then apparently thought the better of it and withdrew to his companions. Not to be trusted, not that one.

Rumor had it he'd so ingratiated himself with Adădozā that he was even now preparing to depart the kingdom as *nuncio* to the Portuguese king in Lisbon.

The procession, now in its final phase, had begun to pass by the temporary cult houses, mere cloth partitions, set up at the west end of the square. The Sakpatasi, members of her father's cult, were, of course, not present, nor would they have been even had they not forcibly quit the kingdom into which they had, during Agŏglo's reign, been just as rudely imported. No, the sons of Malady could not presume to share one piece of soil with the king, their *vodū*'s claim being more ancient than his and therefore the direst threat to his hegemony; but some defiant enthusiast had installed a cactus plant and a perforated jar to represent Him, and Adădozā apparently dared not remove it.

Her father. She hardly dared think of him. Had he survived the journey, the rigors of the way? The indignity of it was congenial; he welcomed suffering as the potter the feel of clay. It was the god in him itching to take shape. They said when Adădozā's soldiers came to evict him, he threw the straw veil over his head and dancing led his followers out upon the road to Adame, dancing all the way, the medicine gourds strung about his body bobbing like seedpods in a dry wind. How far would his withered leg-stalks carry him? If he survived the crossing of the Weme, the prescribed distance, the pale, would he then have tried to return to Gbohuele? She had heard no word of him, or did she expect she ever would again.

But the priests of nature's other forces were there: Xevioso's votaries displaying the overriding energy of their thunder god in squared shoulders and arched backs (none were more acrobatic dancers than they) and stiff skirts cut well above the sinews of the knee; the sullen heavy-lidded votaries of Gu in their pointed straw bonnets, trim togas and iron wristlets; the priests of Dã from Mahiland, festooned with strings of cowrie shells, who squatted tensely, arms akimbo, heads cocked, listening. Because Adãdozã had cancelled the annual procession to the sacred spring, the public watering of the tombs, the high priests of the Toxosu had refused to attend the bloody exercises in honor of the kingly dead, the parade of riches. These denials were the talk of the palace; never since Tegbesu's time, since his famous pact with the prince of the water spirits, had there been enmity. What were Adãdozã's motives? Had he no fear of turbulence? of floods? of grimmer prodigies? Oddly enough, though the priests were absent, the water spirits themselves appeared dressed as fashionable princesses of yesteryear—displaying intricate coiffures into which were plaited corals, pearls and strings of tiny violet snailshells. Against the busy folds of their print skirts, aprons, paniers and sashes, small naked children huddled—those wrenched by fate from the swamps and streams who, uncalled as yet to rejoin their native element, were constrained to manifest their special status in the sluggish protruding features of the imbecile. In former times, such as these were immediately hurled into the ravine, but ever since the pact, the abnormally born had been sacrosanct. Would they still be? Within the farthest cabana, that nearest the king's place, the Nesuxue, ordinary ancestors of the blood royal, stood like segments of wind in their sweeping white cloths which now and again blew open to reveal a solid underskirt of pied brocade.

The procession had come round to the start. Beyond the temporary cult houses, beside the gate of Adãdozã, the king's own canopy extended from the palace façade out to a simple threshold of bamboos laid down to mark off royal space. Copper basins, heaped with skulls, stood guard at the corners. Inside stood Adãdozã's three-tiered stool of office and the sacred *dogba* drum.

It was late afternoon before Agõtĭme's case came up, long after the seven iron-stemmed altars in the mausoleums had drunk the mingled blood of man and beast, long after ancestral feats had been sung, long after the wrestling between retired soldiers of decrepit age whom Adādozā had ordered to fight to the death for worthless European gifts (dwarfish medieval armor, a magic lantern, a music box) from the royal treasury, long after the royal prisons had been emptied and the bedraggled contents marched across the square to the visitors' shed—a meager allotment against which the *caboceers* would have protested were it not for the fact that Adādozā's armies had been notoriously unsuccessful in their raids and the middlemen had no wish to risk the unpredictable temper of an already anxious king, their sole supplier. After that the dances, an aggressive display of martial ardor in which the king himself participated, cock of a squad of kilted female warriors. Who knows how long this would have gone on had not the seasonal gusts come up. Lifting swirls of dust from the parade ground, the dry winds covered the dancing figures with a fine red grit, within minutes transforming them into whirling statuettes. Commanding the drums to cease, the king withdrew at once to his pavilion. The four favorites discreetly held up a screen. When this was lowered to disclose him in golden finery again, Agōtĭme stood waiting by the bamboo threshold, not ten paces from the throne, to which the prime minister himself had guided her. The dry wind subsided.

She had already determined not to prostrate herself but rather to adopt the notorious new manner of greeting used by members of the royal family who disapproved of Adādozā, a mere "*Dōō Dada*" [Salute to the king]. Adādozā did not seem surprised at this, but it was equally clear that having deigned to grant her a hearing, he did not intend to alter the traditional mode of interlocution. Without ceasing to stare out and down upon her with those wild asymmetrical eyes of his, Adādozā spoke *sotto voce* to the Migā who loudly relayed the words to Agōtĭme and returned hers in similar fashion to the king. There was no distortion. The linguist in this case was an honest man.

Yet, the removal of the speaker's intonation from the speech, the odd time lag, so heightened the formality, the irrevocability of what was being said, that their sentences, in the space between the first utterance and the repetition, seemed to have already taken shape as history, as images transfixed upon clay or cloth or sung for some future king's awakening.

"Agōtīme, you are ugly. I wonder that my father married you."

"You know very well why he married me. He was afraid of One-who-prowls-at-midday-when-the-ground-is-hot."

"This being so, he ought to have known better than to pull you into the shade with him—you, the monkey who gorging all day on palmnuts grows but the more starveling-eyed and gaunt."

"So you would interpret my name, *Agōtīme*. But one could with more justice say that it's the fruit of the pineapple which explains why palm groves delight me. However, now that the fruit beneath its tufted crown has been untimely plucked, palm groves delight me not. Nor will they until the hunter returns to claim his heritage."

"Then I shall change your name to Agō-xame [the obstinate], who has borne false witness with regard to me."

"False witness?"

"Yes, you have been telling stories, stories about Guineahen and Hyena, stories about cruel kings—some who keep menageries of wild beasts in their courtyards, some who go so far as to slit open the bellies of their pregnant wives to predetermine the sex of their offspring. One has to be careful, Agō-xame, such tales persist. However, we in Dahomey must tolerate storytellers; a certain amount of vituperative praise, if it be ingeniously masked, is good for the state. But witches, no, them we cannot tolerate."

"Witches?"

"Yes, witches. Do you remember when I sent word to prepare yourself for public appearance on Sīboji Square?"

"So it was you, making your will known through the Migã.

I had thought it was he who warned me. Yes, I do remember exactly when it was. The lustral part of annual customs having gone by uncelebrated, you had gone up to Mahlland in prepara-tion for the second half, you yourself at the head of the expedi-tionary forces—another of your courageous departures from pre-cedent. And as you were preparing to return, empty-handed, from the Fita chain, a messenger informed you that Gãkpe had taken advantage of your absence to effect his own, so you decided as a counterplay to get rid of me. Of which intention I received notice, immediately."

"Gãkpe's departure has nothing whatsoever to do with the facts of the case, but yours does, Agõ-xame."

"My departure? You speak in circles, as a carrion crow to fallen prey."

"You have recalled that time, unwittingly perhaps, revealed the place. Need I review the facts?"

"Do, since I can have no notion of the ingredients you mean, lest you uncover the pot for me."

"Very well. Let me recall them: water, water mainly, thick-ened with fear and garnished with floating corpses. Here's how it was, may the king's birds lay their ears upon the ground and take heed one more time: The Maxi—your stinking countrymen —had set themselves in ambush at the swamp between Diofa Forest and the heights of Lovī. But thanks to last season's ma-neuvers at Agrime, we were able to grapple successfully among the reeds. Pushing them back onto dry ground, we seized the advantage, took numerous captives and confiscated a sizeable village of its supplies, the better to feed them sleek for slaving. Then, as fate would have it, the weather veered. The sky opened to release its rain which began to descend more and more viciously as if Xevioso's hand were pelting us with pebbles. Blinded, no longer able to distinguish friend from foe, we were forced back to the swelling waters of the Zou."

"Ah," interjected Agõtīme, much to the distress of her interpreter, "the pot boils. I can see it now. Isn't this where the white cock comes in? This is not one of my stories. We in the queens' court heard the true history from a bedraggled female warrior who has talked of nothing else since."

"I am not surprised. It drove one mad to see it—that improbable creature, embodiment of our frustration, the projection of an evil whim . . . whose whim? whose emanation? You say you see everything now, distinctly. Need I continue?"

Agōtīme said nothing.

"You are silent, biting the tongue that tricked you. Well let that same tongue now so lick your wounds as to lay your foul heart bare. On pain of death I command you to go on, take up where I left off, continue to describe the scene, Agō-xame. You may say it's but the female warrior's tale retold if you require the device. Go on, I tell you, or your friend the Migā will be obliged to put down the linguist's stick and take up another he's more accustomed to wield."

"I have no choice. Very well, let us say that the Zou was a mass of thick, grey water writhing with uprooted debris. That those unable to swim, and even some who could, perished at the ford and that the rest were cast disarmed upon the nether shore. Gone down the river were the spoils taken from that foothill village. Only one item remained—a white cock, his horny heels viced in one stubborn soldier's hand. But the man went down. Struggling free, the bird flailed the water with unaccustomed wings, tried flight, and in defiance of nature gained the enemy shore. A cheer went up from the left bank. 'Look,' they taunted you above the roaring flood, 'look what happened to your prize.'"

"Agō-xame, you are dangerous. Who's to say that's not an eyewitness account? that anything you have said or might say isn't real? A word, coupled with a leaf, can do anything in the world—the right leaf, the right word, anything you choose."

"I have walked slowly, but I have finally arrived at your thought. Now do you really imagine that I, like the naive guineahen, intend to peck at those seeds of incrimination you have strewn along the path to your lair? You have got our characters confused; it is you shall lick your heart bare and I, the guineahen, though forced to change my abode, shall ultimately elude you. And whatever you may choose to make the humiliated populace believe, call me names, impute translations, force me to give genuine accounts of things I have never but in my mind's eye seen, do what you please to me, you will never live that white cock down. That bird was not I, but it was no ordinary bird, agreed, sent as a sign that you will never defeat the Maxi until the Master of the Earth is reinstalled. Don't you see? Xevioso fulminates, Gu strikes his tools out of fraternal sympathy, both of them. The Bokonõ warned you, but rather than pay him heed you laughed, said all his prophecies were false, and said there was no longer any need for Sakpata. (No, I am not afraid to utter that dread name.) Are you insane? Brushfire burns the fields but spares the green leaves. The Lord of the Open commands those leaves. You must permit the passage."

"There can be no Master of the Earth but me," said Adãdozã.

"So you've all thought. Why then do you suppose that special Malady eats panther-kings?"

"But the installation of your father's cult did not clear the water from Agõglo's path."

"That's the public version. When the Portuguese priests came for the second time, the Migã gave out that he was sealed up inside his room with the sickness. They fled, naturally, for what power has their sky god against Sakpata? And so overcome in every way was he by his opponents, the upholders of tradition, that he was only too glad to take to his bed. He half-believed he was indeed dying of the smallpox. It will do no good for me here to contradict the public version, and I understand the need for it; but I cannot forgive the use you've put to it. There was no need to use my father so, and certainly you'll live to regret his absence. You are not immune. After all, you, as a panther-king are most susceptible. And until those straw skirts, blistered with gourds, whirl in the dry wind here in Abomey, the King of the Bush runs free."

"I repeat, there can be no master of the Dahomean Earth but me. Furthermore, unlike my father, I am not afraid. Do you not recall what my name means? I have 'unrolled my mat' and 'only cowardice can roll it up again.' "

"So you fear nothing, no one? Not even a small boy? He's known but twelve long dry seasons, yet he's growing. Need I review the facts for you? Recall that scene? Do you remember when Agōglo, premonishing his end, stood before the populace here with your elder brother Adukonu (poor fellow) on his left, you on his right, and little Gākpe in his arms? It was a touching scene. 'Soon I shall leave you for the other world,' said he, 'and since Adukonu's damaged foot disqualifies him, I perforce turn to the next in line. This young man on my right is the second eldest of sons produced by the honored women with which my father, the sixth king, presented me upon the attainment of my majority as crown prince. You think it a pity that this little fellow cradled here is too young? His mother, though a latecomer to our couch, I daresay would agree with you. And so would other forces that see what we shall never see. I must speak in riddles, my people, for yours is a double heritage. First I shall plunge your hands "into hot water" pausing to look at you, Adādozā, "then into cold again" holding up Gākpe for the crowd to see.' "

"Agōtīme, you exaggerate. That touching scene was not exactly as you describe it. Gākpe was not a baby. Why do you wish to make posterity think there was such a discrepancy in our ages? Look at me. I'm not anywhere near as old as you are. I only just attained my majority. The unseen world may have designated Gākpe, but the counselors of this world, young as I was, chose me. The people have had enough of poverty, the princes of irresponsible visions of grandeur, and Legba, yes, He, has had enough of rigid procedures that mean nothing. You object to my ignoring the water deities, they too claim to be 'owners of the land' and again I repeat, there can be no master of Dahomey but Dahomey. Gãkpe, he is too much in love with ancient things. I am forward-looking; under me Dahomey shall prosper."

"I say differently. What have you accomplished in five years? Soon," she continued, "bored by your continual defeats, sickened with hunger, made anxious by your impieties, the Dahomean people will say it is time to liquidate their differences in the stream, then, somewhere along the bank, a dry twig will snap, uniting hunter and hunted in a single leap."

"No one tends a field with a leaden hoe, nor fells hardwood with a copper axe. Enough of this Agõ-xame, you talk too much. Already you have more than incriminated yourself. Know now that I have determined—another courageous departure from precedent, as you put it—to send you down to Whydah Beach. Let the whitemen seal you in one of their floating drums. When the waves beat, Agõ-xame, you will dance to a different tune."

"Like the orphan girl in the ogre's drum, I am innocent and my true song will eventually be heard, my true identity made known, my own name preserved. And when, in secret, the people enumerate your crimes, let them recall these my final words to you: Listen, all tales do come true. The third son will one day rule. And when that time comes everything belonging to you will be discarded. Not a whisk, pipe or necklace will be kept as a jog to memory. Your iron standard, your three-tiered throne will never take their places beside the other royal regalia at the tombs, nor will you even be granted the comfort of a mausoleum. Your *asen* altar will never nod on its stalk when water's again poured out to the kingly dead. Your deeds embossed in the palace façade will be blotted out, or attributed to others; your very residence razed to the ground; none of your devices will float high on gaudy parasols; no praises of you sung, nothing remembered. Even this conversation of ours will be forgot—at least your part of it. Here, where history is everything, you, Adãdozã, will come to naught. And if by any chance some whiff of your existence survives, I will have it repeated publicly over and over that you were a bloody tyrant and therefore had, in the name of order to be removed from the throne, cut out of the dynasty."

"You are most persuasive, little mother; I am almost convinced myself. Should I, in another defiance of all precedents, take out my saber and lop your head off here and now? No, I won't do that, I shall spare your life. You, who have so much life, deserve to walk about the earth awhile. But when you are dead, and if I survive, I shall have my say. I shall say that Gãkpe, far from being my brother, was but a distant cousin with no legitimate claim to the throne. And you I will not even mention. So now we are quits. Let us see who, in the end, proves stronger. You tell me to beware of Gãkpe. I ignore your advice. He's no threat to me. But I tell you, beware of my *vodũ*, propitiate him; wherever you go, he'll dog your footsteps; wherever you arrive, he'll be waiting for you. He shall have the last word, that one, for he is and always shall be the interpreter. Farewell, and take your name with you. I give it back. Soon it's all you will have, Agõtĭme. Farewell."

Sweat poured off the Migã's forehead. He stared at the ground, not daring to look at either interlocutor. Dispossessions, fortunately, were not part of his job. At a sign from Adãdozã the second minister of the right stepped forward. Seizing Agõtĭme by the shoulder, he took her a few paces out into the square and made her crawl through a bottomless hempen sack.

And so, divested thus, Agõtĭme reentered life a slave. Her case was unique, she knew. Very well, she had seen several thus disgraced and thousands of prisoners sold. She was a human being still, so were they all, those with the stomach for survival.

Far from being humbled, she felt, if the truth be known, exhilarated. Adãdozã had done his job, done what he had to do; but so had she, the very most, the best of which she, at that moment and in that place, was capable. Her prophecy: how had it come to her? How insipid his imitation. His weak words would never come true. Yet it was unfortunate, in some ways, that she and Adãdozã were adversaries. Their wits allied could weave in and out like patterns of practiced dancers. How clever of him to set that trap of words for her. She was no witch and he knew it, but it was true she talked too much. She must be careful. He was no sorcerer, but he too had force. She wondered if either she or Adãdozã were really capable of all each thought themselves to be.

When Agõtíme insisted on walking escorted down the center of Síboji Square to the Great South Gate, since few Dahomean citizens, and no queens, had ever been thus dispatched before, since the king had retired behind his screen to eat and drink, and since the Migã was ill-equipped at the moment to give any restraining orders, the bewildered soldiery let her go. She walked with a proud head, intent on her goal, oblivious of the crowd. Enough that they were silent and kept the way clear. Beyond the gate she knew the *caboceers* with their rough fetters and filthy jokes awaited her. The scum of the earth, like Innocencio. And beyond the gate? Wisdom? A new world in which to grow? A triumphal return through a queen's gate? A destiny of her own?

The long day was almost over. Already the Earth had begun to close its door, to draw the crimson cloth across His Weariness, when the king mounted the wooden tower of sacrifices to perform his benediction. The conclusion of annual Customs was the distribution of the royal largess—the moment the crowd had waited for all day. They rushed forward. At the king's command strings of cowries, lengths of cloth, baskets of grain, whole fowls, quartered pigs, lambs, goats, beefs rained down upon the "things" of Dahomey that could never, so the first king decreed, be sold into slavery. Calabashes of palm wine, bottles of brandy passed from hand to hand—hands drenched in the blood of freshly slaughtered, greedily dismembered beasts. To the crowd also belonged the headless corpses of the sixteen state victims. These too were hurled from the tower, these too were fought for, torn into pieces. Not everyone was lucky enough to get one.

"Eat life," cried Adādozā from the top of the scaffold, "eat life, my people, consume what you can, consume everything that you have for time flies swiftly, unlike the bird on the wing never pausing, never alighting."

"Eat life," the people answered him, "eat life, long live the king of pearls, long live the king, eat life!"

4 ◗ The Hunter

The coffle left Abomey the next morning.

As soon as it was light enough to distinguish lines on the palm of one's hand, they were turned out of the barracks in the Portuguese visitors' compound, lined up and attached to one continuous lariat, made of interwoven strands of raffia which had been knotted into loose halters an armspan apart. They were then issued headpads and loads—calabashes of palm oil, baskets of parched corn, cooking utensils, bundles of mats and sleeping cloths—the equipment needed for a three days' journey down to Whydah.

There were to be no additional porters, only the thirty slaves under the surveillance of three *caboceers* who, together with two commercial agents from a Brazilian trading company, walked before, carrying authorized umbrellas, and two Dahomean soldiers who brought up the rear, carrying muskets.

These were joined as they stood, after some delay, by an imperious British traveler, red-faced, notebook in hand, accompanied by his English-speaking valet from Sierra Leone, and Innocencio, erstwhile prisoner, wily ingratiator, Portuguese language instructor, now Adãdozã's personal representative to His Portuguese Majesty in Lisbon.

Finally, just as it seemed there could be no possible reason for further putting off the departure, an alarm sounded at the gate and two of the king's eunuchs rushed into the courtyard escorting a lanky, dishevelled man of indeterminate age who had, in the dead of night, been apprehended, so they said, in a ludicrous attempt to scale the palace wall. He should have been beheaded at dawn, and would have, had not Adãdozã capriciously commuted his sentence saying that since the *caboceers* were short of well-seasoned men, they might as well take this one along as a sort of garnish. The *caboceers*, after some deliberation, ordered the soldiers to splice an additional place at the extreme end of the line—just behind Agõtĩme. As they led him past, she could not resist the immodesty of raising her eyes to get a look at him.

To the lead slave, an athletic Mahiman whose fate it was to be strong-named Gbaguideguide [the Calabash-smasher], the *caboceers* had given a double-skinned drum which, slung easily across his left shoulder, promptly began to speak out its ingenious glissandos:

> Now, now, all of you, all of you, come;
> Loosen heart-knotted, heart-knotted fear;
> Bring feet speedily, speedily here;
> Keep airy pace with the, pace with the drum.

The rope tautened, jerked and tugged a few times until everyone managed to fall into step and march in good order out of the courtyard.

Then they were off: down the walled alleyway, catercorner across the open space in front of the Captain of War's estate, through the bustle and din of the blacksmiths' quarter, up over the stile and through the last gate blocking the free sweep of the highroad to Kana.

Agŏtĭme thought of Legba back there in front of her abandoned home in the wives' court, Legba with his cowrie teeth like a death's head grinning, grinning here beside the Kana gate, from the top of his termite mound, everywhere flaunting order, measure. And she grit her teeth and prayed to him to keep her from faltering, stubbing her toe on a rough place, jerking the rope and chafing the neck of the man behind or the boy in front of her, giving cause for complaint to anyone.

That no one had singled her out or even paid her the slightest notice either last night or this morning had come as an unexpected relief. She had been prepared for anything—from cloying solicitude to snide greetings, even jeers. But she had been mercifully allowed just what she wished—protective anonymity. Never before had she felt this curious need to efface herself, to be nobody in particular, a gap, a blur. Always it had been the reverse. But she had been unsure. The Bokonŏ's hints had chastened her. She was for the time being ostensibly free of all ties to Dahomey, free to be anyone she chose—on this journey; and she was particularly anxious to conceal her heavier suppositions from her companions. She craved time on the sidelines, time for the contours of another self—those of an ordinary, viable woman —to emerge from that dream-infested, thought-eroded monolith she had allowed herself to build back there in the wives' courtyard. To tag along at the end of a ragged line of slaves—what a release from the confines of conspicuous personality! From now on there'd be no more sham. She would learn by watching the others how to display a true self in response to a common adversity—the original, the residual Agŏtĭme.

And the others, how did they feel? How did they behave? Of the greater part of them it would have been impossible to say, had there not been the lariat, that they were not ordinary bypassers on the way to some distant village to stay, times being hard, with a reputedly prosperous relative, or to attend a family funeral, or to consult a famous doctor on account of a wife's prolonged infertility or a child's chronic illness. Which is to say they looked resolute, subdued, yet withal relaxed—as cotton once spindled must be spun into thread. There were only four who stood out from the rest and of these only one by design, the others inadvertently.

The little boy in front of her was indeed the irrepressible character he had, obviously, young as he was, schooled himself to be. His name, as he proudly announced to everyone, was Oro-the-voice-of-the-bullroarer. He was a Nago hailing from somewhere up north near Savalu, and his high-pitched nasal voice was the instrument he used, when the fancy struck him, to compete with the drum, the authorized pacesetter. "Wake up, wake up, stragglers," he would say, "money throws people from home like pebbles from a sling. Keep up, keep on going." Or, again, "Wake up, I, who am the offspring of the owner of a clump of sacred trees, declare you out-of-bounds, trespassers on the open road, polluters of the open air. You with your impurities, speed up, you've no business loitering here." When he sensed his shrill singsong was beginning to grate rather than amuse, he ceased his dialogue with the drum and began to imitate now the mincing steps of the Englishman's valet, the self-important stride of the *caboceers*, the lilt of the pregnant woman directly in front of him or, tired of such obvious parodies, the pitter-pat of field mouse feet, the baboon's round-shouldered saunter, the spindle-shanked tred of the duiker. The soldiers laughed. It was impossible to censure him for his bravery, his precocious wit.

Gbaguideguide, on the other hand, sequestered whatever it was that made him extraordinary. He gave nothing out. His drumming was obedient, conventional, its banter seemed to have nothing to do with him. For some reason, the *caboceers* liked to make him the butt of their crude coastal humor, jokes about masculine prowess mainly, but only the knotted veins on his hands, his bloodshot eyes, displayed his anger, showed him full of the tragic force of the Thunderer.

The pregnant woman, salute to her whose stomach is heavy, walked submerged in fear, grief and resentment; but Agōtǐme had the feeling she would, under different circumstances, have proven to be a light-hearted, rather frivolous person. It was not that she was acting a part. She did look unwell, Agōtǐme noted with concern. Her legs were badly swollen at the ankles; the puffy flesh on her neck formed terraces. And fate, although she must with reason have grown up to expect the contrary, had deprived her of everything but the possibility of delivering a healthy child without the proper means, without a proper place to care for it.

Agōtǐme doubted she would ever know the Calabash-smasher's story, but she knew the pregnant woman's well. Not from her lips directly. To all friendly expressions of concern last night along the sleeping shelf in the barracks, she'd responded with a minimal thank you, half-audible at that, and the daylight showed her face as it now was, sullen, the eyes cast down. But the woman (she was really hardly more than a girl) had lived for a while in the ordinary wives' court on the farther side of the royal residence, and although there was no visiting permitted between the two groups, everyone in the panther-wives' court knew all the pertinent facts of her pathetic case—for women's ears range wide and their mouths reach where their eyes may not, which is why there's no shelving of secrets.

She was light-skinned, a mulatto, and her name was Saliabsō [Sally Abson]. She had grown up, so it was said, within the walls of the British fort at Whydah where her father survived an astounding thirty-five years as the only European governor ever trusted by the local populace. When his ineptness was exposed and he fell out of favor, he died of an ordinary fever, was given a proper funeral by his wife's people and buried upcountry under a tamarind—undivulged so that the British could never have him. Shortly thereafter Adādozā, hearing of the daughter's charm and fair-skinned beauty, had his raiders kidnap her. (Sali had been in love, she later told Agõtĭme, with a red-bearded sea captain who had promised on his next trip to take her windward with him to a place where her British citizenship would be respected and where she would find shore life more interesting, more genteel than in disreputable Whydah.)

But Adãdozã was disappointed, for Saliabsõ, dour and inert in her adversity, did not take kindly to life in the common wives' court and so made no effort to please him. ("We were little more than slaves, my girl," she later said, "and no man's a hero to his sweeper, as my old man used to say! If it had been merely a question of sweeping! But we had to spend half our time preparing fancy dishes that more likely than not he'd refuse to eat, and we were even expected to blow his royal nose, wipe his greasy lips, and worse. Imagine it!) One evening when the Gũdeme reprimanded her again for the slovenliness of her dress, for the lack of savor in her cookery, Sali suddenly came alive and dashed a calabash of swill in the Gũdeme's face—as if she had been a pig. "A pig, a pig," she cried, "a regular rooter you are with your mouth like a hoe, with those unsightly warts on your face, with your rolls of flesh, your ponderous gait!" It was in effect her farewell speech to Abomey. Adãdozã ordered her consigned to the *caboceers* immediately—with the proviso that she be sold for a double price on the beach. No captain would dare refuse to speculate on the king's own issue, he said. He would have had the child delivered prematurely, at the mother's expense, had he not secretly relished the idea of calling the noisy Gũdeme a pig.

The latecomer, the man who walked behind her, was extraordinary in still another way. Unusual the circumstances of his enslavement, yes, but oddly enough she gave them no credence. Unusual in his appearance, certainly, but this was not it. One searching look had overwhelmed her with the frightening intelligence that this man was one to be remembered rather than merely seen as if for the first time; that he was one to whom it is said,

"Surely we have met before," and of whom later the speaker perforce dreams and upon awaking says, "Surely I'll meet that one again." All things have happened in the sky before, as the Bokonō says. All lives have been lived and relived. Across the path lies a felled tree, with a tangle of vines beneath.

He was a strange weather-beaten fellow with wild matted hair, almost straight as if mud had been combed into it. His clear tight skin stretched across prominent cheekbones, then spider-webbed at the corners of eyes which seemed more accustomed to distances than to the turmoil of tasks at hand. He wore green and yellow beads and the typical hunter's smock of interwoven raffia and cotton. His knees were well muscled, his shins lean as pasterns, his forearms smooth as the limbs of a fast-growing fig tree; but he had the bony wrists of an adolescent, fragile wrists like those of Gākpe. His unforeseen and yet familiar presence so impinged upon her that she dared not turn around twice to look at him. That the curious bond between them would sometime, perhaps before the day was done, break into speech, she did not doubt. Not for a moment. But when the bird will fly, it's the idle hand pelts stones at him. No need to precipitate the inevitable.

Midmorning! Already they must have walked halfway to Kana. At first the seasonal fog, hanging low in tatters upon the branches of the guava, mango, and sour sop trees that line the first stretch of the royal road, obscured everything. But after two, or possibly two and one-half hours of walking, the sun pushed through with a sudden slap of heat across the shoulders which generalized into a steady, reassuring pressure upon the back, the limbs, the cheek; and the fog dissipated to reveal fields of drying millet interspersed with plots of tasseled maize—the second crop as yet unharvested. And hither and thither the dark heads and thin stick-waving arms of small boys appeared above the stalks, together with quick flights of speckled pigeons, purple starlings and other birds it was their job to chase from the royal plantations. The wind increased, soughing the coolness of leaves across the perspiring bodies of the travelers, parting the standing grasses with a deft sweep, this way and that as far as the eye could see, as the anxious mind remembers.

Who, having been thus circumscribed by towering walls and narrow corridors, who, no matter what the circumstances, could fail to delight in the limitless prospect of that vivid terra cotta road, bordered by dark green intervals of trees, cutting across tended fields to a tawny plain broken only by occasional bursts of silk cotton and far patches of palm grove—the horizon a mere wispish promise of heavier forest growth, of denser mysteries? It had been a mere footpath once, before Kpẽgla came to the throne.

"Should anyone wish to pay me a visit, let him never have occasion to complain thorns or briars have impeded him." Having said this, Kpẽgla sent to the headman of each village along the way orders to broaden his section into a king's highway two bamboos wide. The king's birds praised his accomplishment for it was done: spear grass, bracken and groves were cut back, low places filled, swamps bridged by waterlogged pontoons, seventy miles along that natural corridor to the sea so that travelers could come up to gape at the six thousand skulls along the parapet and then, after a lavish feast and a good look at his wives, to presume upon the king's hospitality to tell him he was sinful, uncivilized. What were their motives?

"When policy requires men to be put to death," Kpẽgla said to them, "neither silk, nor coral, nor brandy, nor cowries are acceptable substitutes for blood." Enslavement was but an adjunct of war. Of the living surplus, those not needed on the farms, or as gifts to the royal princes and princesses, or in his bed could be sold for the civilized riches mentioned above, but most especially for guns. Because guns, Kpẽgla knew (and before him Tegbesu, and before him Agaja, who first established liaison with the Europeans), guns were essential to sustain their new kind of kingdom. In the beginning simple tools had been enough. Flattening their claws into common hoes, the panther-people invaded the fertile wedge between the Kufo and the Weme, and when the plots of ground conceded them were deemed inadequate, they raised those hoes into cudgels and asked the aborigines for more. Generations later, the kings who let their fingernails grow commanded vast armies that pursued the remnants of those resisting tribes up into the hills, enslaved and traded them on the coast for more European guns. (What good, save for ceremonials, is that old-fashioned saber shaped like a crescent moon? Let us sing a praise for Gu, whose priests carry a caveman's cudgel called "his wrath." Foremost of well-traveled wayfarers by land or by sea, wild war god, artificer who never forged palm nuts, O Gu, don't fight against me!)

The sun rose, straight as stone-throw. A toll-log laid across the road, reinforced at both ends with thunderbush barricades, announced the arrival of this, the most recent batch of slaves at Kana—Dahomey's second city which her people shared, in those days, with a depressingly large population of Nagos; holy city, where the chief priests of the royal cults lived and where the king journeyed once upon a lifetime to receive the mysterious incisions on his forehead, and annually to perform his sacred ablutions.

The customs officer dozed in his lean-to, head cradled in the crook of an arm whose fingers continued reflexively to caress the overturned palm wine jug beside him. "Did we not survive our sleeping?" the chief *càboceer* greeted ironically, and then, without bothering to wake the delinquent, scornfully righted the jug and deposited the requisite cowrie toll. Then he had them all step over the log and into a spacious clearing, a roadside shrine, dominated by a giant African teak called Leleloko [Loko of the sonorous voice].

The tree was the largest in the neighborhood (one hundred tons of heartwood—could anyone have weighed it—secretly rooted to over a thousand acres of ground), as old as man's first descent from the sky. Agŏtĭme had visited this place years before in the king's company, and, pressing her ear against one of Leleloko's sedulous thighs had listened, in vain, for the voice of the indwelling *vodŭ*. But now, standing well back from that immense torso, girded round with palm fringe, and craning her neck so she could see where the crown burst into the sky, she could indeed hear something breathing in giant sleep behind that flowing drapery, smooth grey, that cascaded down from lofty armpits. In the interstices between the gnarled feet with their clawlike toes all covered with the same loose-fitting bark, offering bowls of Mahi-millet had been set out by those who suffered from chronic fevers: for Loko assuages rather than gives force; everlasting, honey-tongued, cool-leafed Loko calms. Opposite the tree were ranged a group of dwarf thatched sheds consecrated to Legba. Before one of these stood a priest, like an ancient bird limed to the place, enmeshed in innumerable strings of cowries, snailshells, tiny gourds and vertebrae. Jerking his rachitic limbs, he intimated calamity for the tight-fisted, good luck for the generous. The *caboceers* filled his twisted hands with cowries to which he replied, in a harsh quavering voice, with the following praise stanza:

> Legba, I salute you. Here in the clearing,
> Where Leleloko holds you fast, I salute you, happenstance.
> Bottlegourd warps his own, not the fruit of another plant;
> The traveler is rootless, bound only to chance.
> Legba, I salute you. Let this strange snake pass.

Since Adădozā was not in residence, the *caboceers* were permitted to file their coffle down the main street, past banana and plantain orchards beyond which red clay walls of wealthy compounds cast off their shadows to stand naked beneath the noon heat, past the market where prosperous householders from elevated platforms kept a wary watch on their bartering wives, past long thatched sheds which shaded the several gates of the minor palace from all eyes, including that of the sun. Its turbulent history seemingly forgot, Kana at midday exhaled tempting odors of *akāsā*, fish stew and green soup. Everyone was either at market or indoors, save for two leprous vagrants dozing in the dusty snatch of shade offered by a tattered palmyra. Except for these two the road was deserted; they alone were there to notice, to greet them: "We salute your walk in the sun." "We salute your rest," everybody mumbled politely, everybody but Oro, who said, "Wake up! Once spittle's spat it never leaves the ground." "Why, Oro," Agōtǐme said, "how cruel of you." He turned to look at her, grinning. "My head aches," he said, "I am a child of the road. And it is not I, it is the world that's cruel."

Just south of Kana, where Hlā Brook flows through a deep cut to the sinuous accompaniment of a tall line of silk cottons and swamp mahoganies, the coffle halted to drink. Putting down their loads, they knelt side by side, and, all at the same time, cupped hands, carefully skimming the top off those black eddies that, when puddled, show batik patterns of livid clay.

It was out of the Hlā that the turbulent Toxosu had first sprung, in the form of dwarfs no bigger than newborns, to harass the fields with floods and other chicaneries. Here Tegbesu made his famous pact with them, swearing that never again would the panther-clan ignore their priority: "You will be kings also, but stop tormenting us." Now that Adādozā had broken the pact, would they not retaliate?

Fording the Hlā, the coffle surprised a troop of little boys engaged in sliding down the steep flanks of a great rock stranded midstream, the rock which gives its name to the place: Gede-sits-down. Agōtǐme had traveled this far and no farther with Agōglo. Beyond this rock all was hearsay and wild report, communal memory of places she had never actually seen. Did living forces inhabit these legendary places still? Times changed, relentlessly transforming hunter's bow into farmer's hoe, machete into mattock, angry cudgel into tempered spear, slingshot into gun, and the Toxosu's stream, here by Gede's stone, where once only a king was allowed to bathe, into the joyous profanity of a children's swimming hole.

Suddenly, as if in answer to an unphrased supplication, Agŏtĭme heard a muffled voice speak out of the Gede stone. An illusion? No, the voice, as if from an immense distance, went on sounding the depths of the old story that seemed, for the first time, to tell not only of Gede's destiny and the fate of three thieves, but in some mysterious, frightening way to anticipate her own.

And as the coffle, leaving Hlă behind, proceeded southward in the direction of Ko Swamp, Agŏtĭme's voice rose, hesitantly at first, above the thud of their many feet, above the neutral discourse of the drum. "Listen to the story of the Gede stone," she began. "We are listening, mother, we have laid our ears on the ground," Oro responded. "Good. When Dako-donu, chief of the northbound prowlers from Alada . . ." Her voice soared like the swallow, confidently now. And why not? The one who has lost his luck takes up a bag full of hunger. Who shall disbelieve the storyteller who speaks of wonderful things? Least of all the storyteller herself.

"When Dako-donu arrived in this palm-rich country, the strongest people living here on the plateau were the Gedevi. They owed their strength to their founder, King Gede, who upon his death had taken refuge in a stone for which act of grace his people promoted him from ancestor to *vodŭ*.

"Good. Now while Dako-donu and his followers were engaged in ensconcing themselves on borrowed land with their hoes, the Gedevi took the precaution of moving their guardian's altar to Gbanicŏ. But they reckoned without the vigilance of their neighbors, the people of Zagnado, who, long covetous of the beneficial power of the stone, took advantage of the confusion of the times to attempt to secure King Gede's protection against the incursions of Dako-donu. No sooner had the Gedevi priests arrived at Gbanicõ than three spies from Zagnado, under cover of midnight, made off with the stone. Hoping to confuse their pursuers, the culprits decided on a southerly detour and started off for Zagnado by way of the Kana road. But they in their turn reckoned without the hard and fast loyalty of the *vodũ*.

"Slowly, firmly, as a wise group of elders makes its wishes known, the stone began to bear down upon the head of the first man elected to carry it. So this one passed it on to the second, saying he'd complete his turn as soon as he had a chance to rest. Staggering under his load awhile, the second carrier passed it on to the third who, after a few excruciating steps, decided two men would be better at the task than one. So they improvised a litter. But this mode also proved unsatisfactory. Only a sledge and ropes would do. So branches were cut and vines were bound and they started up again along the road to Kana from Gbanicõ.

"Now there could be no more doubt. No fatigue's illusion had weighed them down. For the stone was not only growing heavier, it was growing larger too. Horrified, the three thieves watched it swell like a grey cloud before a thunderstorm; but they refused to give it up. "Well then," roared the stone; and, summoning more force from every fast-multiplying granule, it rolled forward upon its abductors and crushed them, there at the ford."

"*È è è è è*, mother, you tell a good story," Oro said, "but what became of the *vodũ?* I saw no chaplets there by the stone, no offerings, no attendants—unless you count those boys, no hint of a shrine."

"Good," Agõtĩme said, "it's the wise child waits to scrape the pot. He shall not go hungry. I shall say more. Now, since even the Gedevi couldn't carry the stone back to Gbanicõ, the priests came to the stone, for a time, until the Dahomean king forbad it. Eventually, the Gedevi, robbed of their strength, were sold into slavery like ourselves; and the stone, unworshipped, was vacated. Only an echo, deep inside, remains to tell of Gede's whereabouts. Listen: he followed his people to the new world. His ancient rites have been revived, but he is known as Lord of the Gravestones now, Sentinel of the Burialgrounds. Perhaps," she added, in an undertone, and thought the better of it; "No, the thought escapes me. It's gone off down the road."

"Don't worry, we'll catch up with it," said Oro.

Four hours later they encamped near the village of Agrime on the northern marge of Ko Swamp—first and gravest of that series of depressions and dunes that corrugate down from the plateau to their ancient home beneath the Bight of Benin.

Released from their collars, Agŏtĭme and the other women put their loads down and began at once to prepare the evening meal—the first that day. The *caboceers* and the foreigners uncorked their rum. The Englishman drew forth his notebook and began to sketch the assembled company while his bespectacled body servant struggled with the guys and gussets of his tent. The soldiers and the male slaves neither worked nor drank but, putting aside their antagonistic stances, lay back side by side upon the grass beneath the great rain tree that marked then, as it has always marked, the beginning of the treacherous swamp path. Hands pressed behind their stiff necks they relaxed, idly watching the little crimson-breasted scythe-beaked sunbirds flit nervously about their dangling puff-ball nests as the wind shuttled delicate fernlike leaflets through the last shreds of a violet afternoon.

Beyond the sheltering magic of that tree the grass was charred by seasonal fires which villagers from the environs of Agrime were even now pursuing westward towards the Kufo, quarrying terrified warthogs and duikers as they went, and leaving a heavy odor of smoke behind them to taint the natural freshness of the evening air. Before the regular thuds of pestle on mortar stone began, Agŏtíme could hear an anxious spur owl cry out to his mate from the abandoned fields as he searched for a few parched seeds that the retreating brushfire might have left behind, while high above the still-smoldering ricks a red kite lamely flapped its wings hoping for an evicted rat or two, or perhaps a wounded guineahen.

That night after the food had been put away and the sleeping mats spread out, Agŏtíme, too exhausted to sleep, lay listening to the stub-nosed jackals baying about the camp, fancying she saw, exposed in the hazy moonlight, the bones of Agri the stubborn farmer whose carcass served Dako-donu as foundation for this town. How oddly the patterns of history repeated themselves. Did Dako-donu's palace here serve his son as moral precedent for Daxome? Or was it memory of past deeds that likened them, the storyteller's art, the sleeper's obsessions? What did that cruel emblem mean? Or did it merely happen that way once, twice, and by extension eternally?

As if he guessed at the direction her thoughts had been straying, the hunter now for the first time spoke out into the darkness, saying, "No sane man would ever take a night journey along a path not previously traveled by daylight. Are not all towns, truthfully, built upon the bones of those gone before? Strong men are restless, scratching their way across the face of the earth in search of milder seasons, more abundant harvests, plentiful game and quiet backwaters where fish leap to the net, hornbills to the shaft. The less aggressive must give way, taking flight to less hospitable terrain high in the mountains or deep in the swamps or out onto deserts where, though they may not live well, they may at least preserve their customs. Or," he continued, "adverse to flight, the conquered merge with the conquerors like cloth dipped in the vat. And the homeless conquerors hasten to absorb all the propitious local forces to strengthen their clay, support their thatch. Where I come from they say that when

King Ede founded Ketu town a local hunchback was buried beneath the thick gate where his weaver's stall had been, so that only He who could straighten the hump could destroy the new-founded city."

Little did Agōtīme know how closely she followed his thought's path when she answered him, "Yes, but bones decay, Fa works in mysterious ways. Only the *vodū*'s power is certain. Tomorrow may destroy today. Only the taste of friendship lingers in the mouth forever. Your strong wanderers would have established nothing without the pact. When Dako-donu left this place to push on up the plateau he met my father's forebear, Gbaguidi Aho, son of Idesu the archer, by a white-barked tree not far from Kana. Long before that, the sires of these two had befriended each other along the shores of Lake Aheme, so it was natural for the two young men to 'drink the earth' together. Having done so, it was Aho who interceded with the local headmen on Dako-donu's behalf, Aho who secured for him the right to till Gedevi land. And when Aho, hearing how Dako-donu treated his hosts, had the foresight to flee with his own people to the foothills of the Atakora, Dako-donu sent messengers after him promising perpetual immunity. He was afraid it might seem to Earth as if he'd done violence to the awful binding power of the pact and so, every year at Harmattan, King Dako-donu sent bamboo cuttings, palm branches and garlands of raffia to the base of Gbohuele Mountain as tokens of his spiritual vassalage to Gbaguidi Aho, son of Idesu the archer, clan founder of my father's people, the Maxi."

"And whom did your Aho dislodge, only the eagles? and what was the nature of his treachery? Yet you do well to speak of the pact, my queen, for in so doing you touch upon matters of the greatest concern to me."

"And what might those be?" she asked, calmly, although her blood pounded heavily in her ears as if it were palm wine, not words, she was drinking.

"Encounters, chance discoveries—these, after days of silent

tracking, hazardous waiting, fastidious observation, are the hunter's blessings, the only titles to amazement he shall ever take. But we were talking of sworn brotherhoods, of migrations, of the founding of towns upon the bones of aborigines—none of these, you realize, ever could have been accomplished had not the hunter gone before. Ranging far and wide in pursuit of game, it is the restless hunter who finds the suitable place for others to settle in. Perhaps the croaking of frogs at night tells him water is near, more water than the solitary needs to drink; perhaps the tree to which he returns in the evening suddenly strikes him as proper shade for a future market place. So Allalumon led my people by devious forest paths to Ketu country, so Idesu the archer led his clients here to Agrime. The hunter knows the way because the forest god protects him. It was with the hunter that the pact was first made."

"King Agōglo told me that his father Kpēgla used to stalk about the palace with a quiver slung over his shoulder, bow in hand, as tokens of a time when his ancestors hunted their way up the gap, across the swamp, to the plateau. But surely the panther-kings were never hunters except in dreams. They relied, as you say, upon others for that."

He looked at her strangely across the huddled forms that divided them in the moonlight and she could have sworn he whispered, "Aligbonō, Aligbonō, why do you play thus at forgetting." But now the irritated voices of the others broke in.

"Will the frogs croak all night long?"

"Red-pated rails, I say."

"I say they are sleep-marauders, snub-nosed calabashsmashers like our friend here, spilling words out all over the place. What a disgrace."

"Slit 'em open in the morning, you'll find shards in their intestines nine times out of ten."

"Let us be masters of silence at night, seeing that by day . . ."

"Who does she think she is? No queen I say, but a noisy

junior wife who keeps the compound awake and ought to be . . ."

"What's all that noise over there, quiet down or you'll all feel the lash of my whip, that's what I say."

It was enough. Her eyes smarted with shame. She deserved to be reprimanded. But it was the hunter's fault. He spoke up first. She only followed him. What did he intend to convey in those weighted phrases? Yet they were beautiful. There was no denying it—words washed with moonlight. Who was he? Why so familiar? Could she have heard that last correctly? O that they might converse again before daylight stripped the shadows from common things!

She must have dozed, for she started at the touch of the hunter's hand on her shoulder and saw that the moon had risen high above the canopy of the rain tree. "I greet you for sleeping and waking," said he. "Forgive the importunity, but little time remains and I must ask you to hear what I have to say to your private ear. Come with me."

She followed him out into the stubble field, beyond the first row of smoldering ricks.

"Who are you?" she asked, peering intently at those cool eyes set in that weathered face. "You got me into trouble; I felt like a girl of sixteen; I might almost . . . it was as if you charmed me, drew me along, made me go on and on about things that really are of no concern to me."

"My name is not important," he cut in, "I hunt along the banks of the Kufo now, although once along the Weme, and before that, westward . . ."

"Ah," she said, "now I understand. I thought—O who can say what I thought. I was on the wrong path. You come with some message from my son. Who would have thought it possible? Is he well? Is he taller? Shoulder-high? Can he really shoot well enough to fill out that long belly of his? He's got a big head, but such thin bony wrists; strong legs though, a man's thighs; I should imagine he could outrun anything. How did you meet him? Tell me."

"Gākpe, yes, he's remarkably quick for a boy his age, not boy, youth, with a man's thighs, as you say; and so deft it's hard to believe he grew up in the soft robes of a princeling. I met him by chance one day, took him for an antelope"—the hunter laughed—"but fortunately my arrow went awry. Then and there we concluded the pact. There'll be no such mistake again, and I shall continue to keep my eye on him, do what I can. He tells you not to worry, that the throne and the embroidered sandals will one day be his, and that when that day comes he will send ambassadors to bring you home again—wherever you may be."

Agōtime smiled. "And just how does he plan to roll up the usurper's mat?"

"With the help of friends. As a fellow hunter I have counseled him that only by a network of ties such as that binding him to me can he hope to snare the unnamed. It will take time, years perhaps, but we've begun already. One by one his brothers and sisters, incensed by their elder brother's arrogance, his neglect of hallowed practices, are promising to come in secret to take the oath with him. Adukonu, Tometi, Lipe-hu and To-fa have already agreed. The others will follow them eventually. I prowl about Abomey, talking, or, as you say, charming those prepared to listen to me."

"And they caught you? That's why you're here?"

"No, my queen, I am never surprised. I have many disguises, stealthy feet, amulets to make me disappear. No, we heard it rumored Adādoʑā planned to send you away. So I loitered about Sīboji Square yesterday dressed in a Malam's burnous, turban, everything," he laughed, "until your precise fate had been decreed. Then, later, in the night, after a slight scuffle at the wall, I managed to get taken into this coffle that I might converse with you, as I have done, and bid you farewell-for-many-a-season's-change from him, as I have done, and there remains a third thing . . ."

"Wait a moment," Agōtíme said, "while you were speaking of the pact with the princes of the blood, something occurred to me that I don't want to lose in your conversation. For Gãkpe to ally himself with royal blood is a splendid beginning, but to succeed in his business he must have guns, guns that speak power even when they're silent. Now this is my idea. There is a man, a slave dealer from Brazil, who must have warehouses full of guns and who hates Adãdozã even more than Gãkpe does. He languishes now in Cãboji prison—the occasional victim of one of Adãdozã's more curious punishments. Every now and then, they say, as his humor moves him, Adãdozã takes this man out and dips him in a vat of indigo."

"Why so? If that's an old saw acted out, I never heard of it."

"No, it's a new idea, one of Adãdozã's own pronouncements made to be taken literally. When de Souza, that's the trader's name, went up to Abomey to collect an immense debt for guns, cloths and rum which the king could not possibly pay, Adãdozã flew at him in a rage, saying, "Mulatto, neither white nor black man dares thus confront the king of pearls. Perhaps if darkened to my color you will come to venerate me as you ought. And if this won't work, we'll try bleaching—a more painful process I assure you." Forthwith began the first of the famous baths. I'm surprised you've never heard of them. They've gone on several months now, but de Souza refuses to recant. The debt still stands. Somehow Gãkpe must manage to see the man in prison, conclude the pact with him and then, with your assistance, of course, help him escape. There is nothing de Souza would not do for Gãkpe then."

"I shall do my best to arrange this, my queen. It's a track well worth pursuing. But we must act with extreme caution. Until now Adãdozã has suspected nothing of the real scheme. He thought you the conspirator and with you gone, the wind can easily blow our scent his way. Now, as I suggested before you interrupted me, there is one more thing to be accomplished here before night turns. You yourself are embarking upon a hazardous journey. It is of the utmost importance that you survive. You may not understand this, but I must warn you never to be tempted to take the easy way back to Abomey. Think, should anything happen to you, of the effect on Gãkpe. I am therefore asking you to take the pact with me so that if ever your life be threatened you may take up a handful of earth and call for help. No matter how far away, I shall hear and do what I can to deflect the danger. Otherwise, I shall not interfere at all. You go your way, I mine, and whether our paths cross soon again remains to be seen. Yes, I know what you are thinking. No woman's business, this oath-taking. But you shall not be penalized for that; the forest knows and has agreed to let you be the exception. There may be more, who can predict? Adãdozã, in your case, has set an awful precedent. We have fallen upon evil days and worse, I fear, are to follow. We cannot afford to be too nice in our distinctions, too rigid, too squeamish."

"But I don't see . . ." She started to question his claim, but thought the better of it. Because of that eery sense she had of prior meetings, she would do as he suggested, required really. It was his coldness, coupled with his familiarity, the almost servile politeness with which he addressed her, that perplexed Agõtĩme now. She had thought that when he finally spoke to her alone his words, less remote, less general would release hidden springs of passion in her, dreams of her girlhood, fantasies of Aligbonõ among the reeds. But no, although he seemed to depend for his effect upon some previous image reflected in her eyes, his eyes showed no trace of her. They were opaque, chilling; and there was something diffident and at the same time insistent about him that recalled a distant range of mountains.

Returning to the slaves' camp beneath the rain tree, Agõtĩme lay down upon her mat again with no thought of sleep. He had remained behind in the maize field apparently seized, as she imagined hunters often must be, by an irresistible impulse to take out a flute made from a bushbuck's horn and play an improvisation on the disembodied sounds of the forest creatures. She could barely hear him at first, but then her ear became accustomed to his cadence and when he put down the flute and began, with the same intonation, to sing, she was able to distinguish every word as if it were to her he was addressing his praise, as if it were through her hair that plaintive wind was blowing.

> Long, long is the neck of my antelope,
> Dark, as if ringed with antimony,
> The hesitant glance of her eyes.
> The spear grass quickens to her stride.
> Lovely my bride's brazen feet in the dry season;
> And lovely her mud-daubed fetlocks in the rains,
> As she treds the primordial waters dry.
> Brushfire: the antelope takes flight;
> The lake is swollen with sorrow, regrets,
> But cannot unfold its flanks and depart.
> The mottled thicket tries to conceal her,
> But the singed leaves whisper, fly, fly while you can.
> The Hunter sings, do not despise the arrow, little wife.
> Grief felled the trees, and the vines laughed;
> But they, too, will fall upon evil times.
> Long, long is the neck of my antelope,
> Dark, as if ringed with antimony,
> The hesitant glance of her eyes.

Agŏtīme fell asleep and began to redream the beginnings of that which she had thought, by the telling, to have been finally rid. But now, again, she was the Princess Aligbonŏ in the reeds by the rocks of Kpove. Where were her serving maids? No, it was to be different tonight. The place changed. She was standing in a rain of lianas at the edge of a clearing and an insistent voice was whispering in her ear, "May I perish under fang and claw or by my brother's arrow mistaking me for game, if ever I abandon you in danger."

In the center of the clearing stood a tree with stunted limbs whose species she did not immediately recognize. At the base of it, on a bed of dry leaves, a doe had just given birth to a little spotted fawn. Above, in the fork of the tree, a hunter crouched, bow in hand, white owl and parakeet feathers limed to his hair. Was it her hunter? She could not see his face, but those knees were the same. He sprang up, took easy aim, drew back the string, and then let the bow fall to his side again—out of pity? Fawn and doe vanished and in their place a curious one-legged creature was seen writhing this way and that, that way and this. She moved closer and saw that strands of his long fine hair had been snagged in the bark where the wrinkled roots formed little rifts, or crevices. With horror she observed an army of red ants deployed upon his helpless flesh. They were devouring him, bit by bit! No wonder he screamed. Leaping down from the crotch, the hunter drew his knife and cut the snarled strands free.

The creature jerked himself upright and, leering at the hunter through his single dog's eye, said, "I thank you, Hunter, for delivering me. Twice today you have shown compassion for those of us who go our ways beneath canopied trees in the dim light of the forest floor. Now I am prepared to reveal the secret virtues of our plants to you, provided that you promise never to talk of them to anyone. Furthermore, I intend to convey the power to perceive and make use of the fine strands of the forest spirits' invisible hair. Whenever you chance upon one of these wisps, snarled in vine or snagged on briarthorn, you must chew a bit of pepper and spit it out upon the hair. Then you've but to pluck the strand, close it in your medicine gourd and you yourself may become invisible whenever you choose—safe from thrusting horn and stampeding hoof. But first the pact!"

So saying, the king of the forest, for it was he, the fabled Aziza, slashed his own right hand in the soft web of flesh between index finger and thumb, then slashed that of the hunter as well, so each could drink of the other's blood.

"Between forest and man, linking everything that breathes by trust in the oath and fear of Aziza's ban," whispered that voice in her ear. This time she turned, but it was not the hunter who spoke. He was over there. It was Oro. And, in that nasal falsetto of his, Oro began to sing this praise—as if it were a lullaby, or a warning:

> Handsome the hunter sleeps,
> Hard by the rain tree,
> Will you awaken him?
> His eye's as fine as a needle at dawn,
> His glance is as cold as the dry north wind,
> His mind holds an image of all that lives.
> Will you awaken him?
> For every man that's dissatisfied,
> May another be content;
> Path over river, stream over track,
> Follow the hunter.
> The hunter knows where the grass is high,
> Where the arroyo is always dry,
> Where the silk cotton casts its net to the sky,
> Follow the hunter home.
> Say, whom did you meet when you skirted the lake,
> Was it a panther crouched in the brake?
> Spare that python coiling there,
> Its droppings are the beads you wear.
> That tawny cloth conceals your bride,
> Spare the antelope. Cull the leaves.
> And you may wander, endlessly.

Agõtĩme awoke with a start. The moon was down. The leaves of the rain tree had contracted, just as she had always heard they would, diffusing soft moisture to the ground. She heard the *chur-chur* of the straggle-plumed nightjar, courting. Drawing her cloth up tightly around her, she fell asleep again.

The next time she awoke it was morning and, much to the mystification of all but herself and Oro, the Ketu hunter had disappeared.

5 ▶◀ Zomadonu

On the outskirts of the swamp grew waist-high grasses through which the coffle serpentined like ceremonial dancers clothed in the very element through which they passed. The bottomland displayed its wealth in rampant crowns of crested pineapple, in the mothy blossoms of the wild potato plant; and here and there contorted turrets of fierce termite kingdoms towered black above the subtle morning colors of the vegetation.

Then the grass gave way to an expanse of cracked mud flakes littered with logs and other debris. Here water had been and would in four or five months begin to flow again, gradually increasing until travelers such as they would stagger swaddled to the armpits in that thick stagnant stuff of which life itself is made. But it being midwinter now, the swamp had spread its viscous skin to dry into stiff black scales that abraded rather than engulfed the feet.

The long rope flailed their necks like a whip as they plunged down a fifteen-foot embankment to a ravine pockmarked with pools of black water that seemed to have steeped there since the world began.

On the other side of that ravine the path became truly

tortuous, snarled with the slippery roots of giant ficus and clogged by clusters of the gregarious raffia palm. After an hour or so, they broke through the undergrowth into a clearing which had been paved with dung and furnished with *vodū* sheds and split-log benches. This was Wodonū, the halfway house where, during the rainy season, travelers were wont to put up for the night.

Though set upon a sort of island that never floods, far from inspiring confidence, this Wodonū had an unkempt, temporary look about it that frightened everyone. The shrines were deserted, their blood-stained altar bases stuck with flies. Nor was there any custodian to serve the freemen fresh fruit or palm wine; but the jugs beneath the hostel roof were full enough to provide all with a draught which only a limp fringe of bats along the beams prevented anyone's taking. Serious repose, moreover, was out of the question, for the logs, on closer inspection, proved to be infested with woodborers and the paved ground carpeted with living mats of red ants and tiger beetles. So the slaves were left in harness, fidgeting to be gone, while the dignitaries stomped nervously about, unlit pipes in their mouths, fly whisks ever vigilant. The disappearance of the Ketu hunter had set them all on edge. No soldiers could, in the *caboceers'* judgment, be spared to go after him. Before leaving Agrime they had decided not to spend more than an hour or two at the halfway house and to push on down to Alada for the night. There huts would be available for more effective detention of the slaves and more suitable accommodation of themselves, the commercial agents, Innocencio and the Englishman.

It was Saliabsō, not the foreigners, who required consideration, and yet the *caboceers* seemed oblivious of her very existence. Not so the slaves who, one by one, courteously turned to her with the encouraging "Salute to your capacity for enduring pain, discomfiture, bodily suffering." "Take heart, ma'am, take heart," said Oro, "and your unborn child should take heart too. For surely the worst is passed, and the yam which survives the harvesting is not likely to break apart in the coals." But how irrelevant proverbial wisdom, even Oro's, bizarre as it was, to the struggle actually taking place within that distended belly of Saliabsõ's! Or was it within her own? So alert had Agõtĭme suddenly become to the poor girl's condition, that, strange to say, she could not be sure. Then, as she strained to catch Saliabsõ's mumbled reply, she heard, near at hand, as if from inside one of the sheds, the unmistakable pronouncement of a hidden slit gong: *thonk thong thit thong, thong thong thit, thonk.*

The creature inside Sali's womb responded to the pattern, thumping wildly, hurling itself against that restraining wall of flesh. A series of sympathetic contractions gripped Agõtĭme herself now and she recalled and expelled that ancient pain in a great cry which burst against the tautened fibers of her diaphragm, recoiled rapidly upwards along fluted corridors to her throat, caught chords and sounded forth at last in an articulated form that her tongue had moistened and her lips dispatched before her mind had time to grasp its meaning: *Ale voheeeeeeeee-eeee!* It was the traditional call to the Royal Water Spirits, their birthing cry, and the women of the coffle automatically answered her:

> *Ale die vohee*
> *Ale die vo.*

Again Agõtĭme threw out the shrill loop of her voice, by her own volition this time, shaping the sounds precisely as the spirits wanted them: the first three syllables high-pitched staccato, like quick wing beats before the overriding ecstasy of the vowel:

> *Ale voheeeeeeeeee*
> Open the waaaaaaay
> *Ale vo*
> Open way

The road is free
Your force dominates the world,
Swallows seas, breaks mountains,
Softly, softly, like the chameleon.

Ale die voheeeeeee
Open is the way
Ale die vo
Open the way.

Gbaguideguide began to drum. The water spirits, apparently, were satisfied with the strength of the summons for, having firmly seated themselves upon the heads of the singing women, they began to dance with deliberate majesty, forcing the men attached to them by the lariat to dance along in a slow serpentine movement before the astonished eyes of the *caboceers* and their associates.

Once under way the song held its own rhythm and the gong diminished, retreated rather, high above the canopy of broadleaved trees along the path to the great ravine that drains the northern reaches of the swamp. And Agŏtĭme's call detached itself from the responding chorus to follow after. As if snarled in the coils of her own voice, her second soul rose upon the open sound, spun up and, then in wild orbit, down to the edge of a black pool at the nadir of the ravine.

There, reconstituting herself, the first thing she saw was the fabulous humpbacked gonofo bird busily probing the waters in a series of clumsy dives. It was a rare theophany—unprecedented, so far as she could recall, since Tegbesu's time.

He was too absurd to be frightening. "Salute to the Fisher-king-of-the-world," she greeted him as he surfaced, finally, for breath.

"Thank you," he said, "but I am not fishing. I am searching for a lost stone."

"In that case," she said, "may its whereabouts be revealed to you in a dream: salute to the Dragnet-of-the-unseen."

"Do you really know who I am, or are you just bluffing?"

"I take you for a Toxosu," she said cautiously, "in the guise of a gonofo bird."

"More specifically," said he, "I am Zomadonu, King Akaba's abnormal son." And with that he arched his neck back until his duckbill bit the end of his tail, continuing to contort himself until the hump on his back flexed in and he became entirely contiguous—a bearded sphere with six apertures for eye sprouts. "Don't stare," he panted, emerging thus, "I might have been born to you."

Agŏtĭme cringed.

"Don't you remember," he went on, "the night a Toxosu was born to Nahoue, first wife of my royal cousin Agŏglo, now in the process of poling himself along Selu River on his way to the land of the dead?"

Remember? How close the air had seemed as she sat in her place beside the laboring woman: the lampwicks sputtered as if that bloated breathing were sucking up the very oil. Rising to fill the clay bowls once more, she had stepped outside for a bit of fresh air and heard the screech owl's ominous cry—modulated on a single note. And the unconscious woman had shrieked in reply, that mound of flesh on the plank bed heaving for the hundredth time. And when she fled back indoors, the pockmarked midwife from Dasa-Zoume had hastened to reassure her: "Be patient, my daughter, she will be all right. The medicine is working now." "Yes, mother, praised be the simple recipes of the esteemed midwife." But Agŏtĭme knew that despite all the potions, infusions, massages with herb-scented hot oil, Misfortune gaped. She knew because it was she who, months before, had caught the first glint of this in the Bokonŏ's eye—a premonition that for a time had given her strength born of pity to put up with the first wife's incessant gibing.

"But whatever the outcome," Zomadonu broke in, "the old woman was right. The medicine did work. That birth was my responsibility and I made sure she found the correct shrubs from which to strip the bark. Lots of them cheat, you know— afraid of crocodiles."

Yes, the medicine had worked. Nahoue survived the night and by dawn the midwife was able to extricate the child. Well, not exactly child. It was a monstrosity, of course, with twelve fingers, a full set of teeth, the beginnings of a beard, and a rudimentary third eye. But they performed all the usual rites and, when the time came, named it simply Wemu [stranger-to-the-group].

Unable to persuade herself that Wemu did not feel like a real child inside, unable to cope with her own outraged feelings, Agōtīme kept as much as possible out of its sight. But the other panther-wives, for fear of offending the unseen powers responsible for its existence, forced themselves to be ostentatiously kind—an indulgence Wemu repaid with excessive irritability— especially after dark. Then, to everyone's secret relief, as soon as he learned to walk, Wemu disappeared—presumably into the marshes beyond the northeast gate. A thatched altar shed was erected in his honor beside those of Zomadonu, Adomu and the rest; and when, at the beginning of each ceremonial year, the rites for the royal dead were performed, Wemu was scooped up from the waters of Dido Spring and carried majestically back to his altar in a covered jar. Every year, that is, until this one.

"She was much too old," Agōtīme said, "she ought to have known. And what's more, malformations are congenital in her line. She ought to have told Agōglo when he married her. Official history has it that Adukonu smashed his foot in a hunting accident, but that's just another of her lies."

"Hardly sufficient to wish her dead in childbirth though," Zomadonu observed, rotating on his axis so as to be able to look askance at her successively with all six eyes.

"Gu only knows what she wished on me," Agõtĭme replied.

That night, before her own Gãkpe was born, she had heard them laughing together in the courtyard. "Agõtĭme, she's so odd, there's no telling what form her child will take," said Nahoue. Then the others began to clap out the old satiric rhyme:

> Woman, your head is misshapen,
> Modeled in haste
> Before the creator
> Had properly kneaded
> His clay. Woman,
> Your face is as ugly
> As cassava porridge.

Nahoue was jealous. She had no right to send the others out of the room. Gu be praised, the old woman from Dasa-Zoume had sense enough to station herself just outside the door or there's no telling what Nahoue might have got away with.

It was Agõtĭme's turn now, young as she was, and she had refused to lie on the bed after the degenerate fashion of the court. Her child would be a stalwart Maxi born on the ground and his horoscope, so the Bokonõ intimated, would be that of the Dahomean soil and he would live to have men call him Buffalo, Blagbe grass, Invincible. That back-rending pressure of the first born. She could stand no more. No, she would not scream; she'd show Nahoue the stuff of which Maxi women were fashioned; but she would retch, retch until she spewed the lining of her stomach out. Bear down. It splits me like an axe. Bear down. Who screamed? Not I. "A stone, a stone, I told you so, the Maxi has given birth to a stone!" She could almost believe it—hard, cold, clothed in slime, cauled in mud. "Cut, now, mother, I am going to cut him into life." Terror shook her perspiring flesh and she reached blindly about on the ground for a blanket. The midwife persisted in questioning her. Yes, by all means, cut; strike the stone for sounds. "Go," she heard Nahoue say above the hoarse, high-pitched little scream, "go tell the king it is as we feared." "No, please don't leave me, old woman of Dasa Zoume," Agõtĩme heard her own voice saying, "please don't go." "Where are the others?" she asked Nahoue, angrily. "Where are they? You know very well custom requires there be three."

"Where are you going with the newborn?" she heard the old woman say at the door. Why couldn't she open her eyes? What made them smart like a serpent's oath? Now the midwife's reassuring voice again, matter-of-fact, as if nothing were wrong, "I have sent a servant to fetch the king. We must tidy up a bit before he comes. You had better give the prince to me, Na Nahoue." A stone? No, she held him now, slithering like a tadpole on the massive billow of her breast. The midwife struck her belly to expel . . .

"But like a scorpion in a dark cranny of the wives' court that rumor persisted for a long while, did it not, Agõtĩme?" Zomadonu said.

"It may still persist," Agõtĩme replied, "but such rumors cannot be relied upon except in the long run and Nahoue is not one to sit around waiting for termites to make wood dust. When the Bokonõ first cast Gãkpe's horoscope and found it indeed to be that of the Dahomean Earth, undaunted by her first defeat and in defiance of all prophetic legacies, Nahoue intimidated me again. 'Official history is flexible,' she said, and who should know that better than she? 'A crosscurrent of rumors keeps truth eddying,' she said, 'even now it's not too late for you to ford the Zou and return to Mahiland. I have talked to Agõglo [a lie] and he is willing to let both you and your father depart the court. We shall say it was I gave birth to Gãkpe; that you, on account of my ill-health and your unfortunate loss, were for a while his wet nurse. Such situations are no rarity. And if you do not agree,' here she stung, 'I shall do my utmost to prevent Gãkpe's ever being king.' I should have left then. All that conniving exhausted me. I was never made for such a life. I'd have gladly exiled myself, except that I did not trust her. I feared for Gãkpe's safety. I refused to leave. Then she decided to approach Agõglo directly and frighten him into designating Adãdozã crown prince.

" 'If you don't declare my son your inheritor,' she said, 'no son of yours will succeed.' 'You speak in riddles,' Agõglo said, 'and I have passed the age of fireside games. What do you mean?' 'What I mean is this,' said Nahoue, 'the royal family is tired of Tegbesu's line. They have gradually placed Dahomey under the influence of distant kingdoms, first the Nago, and then the European traders on the shore, and now you plan to let Portuguese agents into the very capital. They want a crown prince chosen from Agaja's line, someone who will set the kingdom free of these foreigners who sap our strength, infest us with debts. Now here's my scheme. I have told them Adãdozã is not really your son but the son of Prince Tofa of Agaja's line who voluntarily exiled himself to Mahiland. To keep the scandal from popular ears, to maintain the appearance of unbroken continuity, they have agreed to let you name Adãdozã as if he were indeed your son. But if you do not agree to this plan, they will stop at nothing short of revolution.' And Agõglo conceded. So numerous were the fears that plagued him in his sleep that, waking, he no longer knew what he believed. He thought Adãdozã was his own son, but he was at the same time convinced that he and Nahoue were contriving to murder him by letting water into the palace. Sometimes a tattered garment would appear by his bedside: 'Out with it,' he would shriek, 'it is the shroud of one of your father's incurable patients.' Nothing anyone could say would convince him otherwise. And yet, though he finally agreed to name Adã-dozã his successor, Gãkpe was always his favorite. There was no wild look in Gãkpe's eyes, no, they were always deep and calm as polished teak. Adãdozã may have been formidable as a child, but from the beginning Gãkpe was beautiful: ten perfect fingers, ten perfect toes, silky skin, and his solemn eyes—only two of them."

"Agōtīme, how stupid to think such insults capable of offending me. Words, words. Bringing language into the world, the Eighth Great One said, 'Wind preceded me with a rope to bind together all man accomplishes, but water can never be bound by rope or winnowed by wind.' Which brings me to that most pressing question of your destiny. As I said before, Agōtīme, you might have given birth to someone like me, Wemu, for example, but instead . . ." „

"O I'm sorry if I offended you. I didn't think . . . but let's forget the past. What do you know of my destiny?"

"Know?" the Toxosu laughed. "I am your destiny."

"You? I have, or rather had reason to believe my thread wound to the spindle of Dahomey—which is to say Gãkpe, the royal family. But this hint may be unreliable. All I really know, and Fa's voice must be believed, is that I left Abomey under the sign of Earth, Weli Meji."

"You belong to Water now. Consigned to my element, shall we say. For how long? Who knows? And after that? Who knows, again. Let's just say that for the time being we Toxosu, outraged by Adãdozã's neglect, have preempted you, as a kind of hostage to our collective destiny."

"Why me? Because I owe a debt of solicitude to Wemu—may he forgive my lack of humanity."

"Lack of maturity, rather, or realism. Yes, it was you who behaved abominably, not he. But setting that aside, hoping eventually to bring you around to our way of looking at things, you have, shall we say, a certain flair for the unseen. You are susceptible, your dreams are real—as real, let's say, as I am powerful. And not only that, you have a reliable memory. You are loyal as lice on a man's head, persistent as a tick under his toenail. Perceiving this, whatever else he may have failed to perceive, Agōglo chose

you to replace Nahoue as his go-between with the Bokonõ. A
good choice, as it turned out, but scarcely calculated to ingratiate
you with that schemer. How she would have loved to get her
hands on Gãkpe's horoscope! Well, you can hardly blame Nahoue
for putting up a fight with the only means available to her—her
primacy with Agõglo as his eldest, his least loyal perhaps, but
nonetheless his most passionate, in short, his favorite wife. Ah,
that offends you, doesn't it? Hurts your feelings, your pride.
Now we are quits. For a long time you deluded yourself, hoped
against hope it was otherwise with Agõglo, that your youth, your
fanciful intelligence, your own kind of magic would triumph in
the end. But don't worry, if you lost that fight with Nahoue you'll
win the other one. For you are not just a little *gbo* [medicine]
gourd belonging to your father, a bit of homeopathic medicine, a
sprig of euphorbia planted in the midst of the yard—all the things
Nahoue was fond of calling you. No, you are more than that, as
you yourself have suspected all along. But no one, except perhaps the Bokonõ, ever took the trouble to wonder just who you
really might be. Nahoue reckoned without you and now history
will reckon without her, without Adãdozã. It is, in sum, on account of your entire situation—present as well as past—that we
have preempted you. Your exile, which is after all a part of you,
shall provide us with force greater by far than that which
Adãdozã denies us now. And this future empowering of me, of
us, is, for the present, the substance of your destiny."

"I don't understand. And before you tell me any secrets I'd
better tell you here and now that I'm not as trustworthy as you
think. Not too long ago I let a secret out that I fear must stalk
me the rest of my days."

"Forget Agasu. He's no concern of mine. Our paths never
cross. And what is more I bear no love for him, nor for the one
who wounded him, though we were born out of the same sign, I
and that one. No, the only Dahomean kings who count for anything with me are the descendants of him who had the wisdom to

conclude the pact, or those who fathered Toxosu before and after the pact was made. Until the Agasuvi ventured into our territory, they were no threat and therefore no incipient kin. No, Dako-donu was the first as far as we're concerned. You must begin with him."

"What do you mean 'begin with him?' I should have thought to begin with you. But how, exactly, am I to 'empower' them, you? And what does my exile have to do with your getting back at Adãdozã?"

"Come now, my little queen, you've had hints enough to be able to tell me straight-out, if you wanted to. But I shall speak clearly now, so there'll be no mistaking my intention: You must find a way, in the new world, and I shall help you, to celebrate the Toxosu and our brothers, cousins—kings of the royal Dahomean clan."

"All the kings? All the Toxosu? And what of your common kinsmen, the innumerable Nesuxue that roam upon the rivers of the dead unquaffed by human memory? Those too?"

"Only those who can be called *vodũ*. The dead are always near at hand, but they are not your responsibility; you cannot control their comings and goings; I warn you, don't try to do it. The ordinary Toxosu are local spirits—rooted to the mud-bottoms of these streams, these pools, here on the plateau and on up into Mahiland. But you will find equivalents of these common Toxosu in the new world, with whom you will tend to confuse my people. You may do so. I give you my permission. Of the royal ones, I alone will be there to welcome you, to speak when I wish and be silent when I choose, for I am your *vodũ*. The others will follow when you've found jars for them. Some may manifest themselves unbid as soon as you have room. We and our kingly cousins and brothers will live together as one family there—no distinctions made among *vodũ*. We have sworn to share hegemony with them, wherever we rule, and we will abide by our agreement—whatever they do. Now, don't let numbers and fine distinctions trouble you. They've got nothing to do with words as we use them."

"Now at last I do understand—I think. Not content with a mere supportive role as far as Tegbesu's clan is concerned, Zomadonu, a king in his own right, seeks to dominate. Gãkpe's purposes are subordinate to his; Gãkpe's prize—the price Zomadonu doesn't mind paying, bait thrown to his own self-esteem and at the same time a nice means of revenge on Adãdozã and his group. Well, *vodũ* have played their part in politics before and I, now I understand why the Bokonõ compared me with Na Huãjele. I must say it comes as a great relief to me to think it is because we both are founders of cults to secure kingships for our sons. After all, I'm not a living substitute for anyone. I am an original. Whatever my living substitutes may do in the future is no concern of mine. Let them murder for your sake, Zomadonu, but you'll be possessing them, not I. The original Na Huãjele must have been a shrill, unpleasant person—a mammy trader they say who insinuated herself into her future mother-in-law's favor, a die-hard Nago—but she did a good thing for her son. More power to the sky gods for making Tegbesu triumph over all contenders, and more power to the Toxosu for asserting themselves against the intruders. Am I right? Is my understanding good?"

But Zomadonu was speaking again: "Listen, Agõtĩme (you don't have to look at me). Forget Agasu, all that wild nonsense —a tall tale told by a hunter, an illicit lover's lie, a disloyal wife's daydream come true, the hysterical fears of an adolescent girl. It is I who have prior claim on you. Listen, and later, tell—tell all and anyone, with no sense of betrayal. Listen, there have been four worlds: first Ocha and Nana-buku, the crone (a Maxi woman); then the world of Dã the serpent; then twins; then the world of the Toxosu—first conceived by beautiful Amina, sired by the wind. When this fourth world was securely fixed, when it had begun to evolve, first-man Ocha decided it was time for him to go inhabit the east. But he promised Nana-buku to visit her from time to time and as tokens of their parting gave her two gifts: a string of eight cowries and the moon. You think me obvious and crude, but I too have strains of gallantry—well hidden as they are within this self-inflicted shape of mine, and I should like to be able to duplicate the original gifts. The moon, I'm afraid, is out of the question. I was dredging for its semblance when you first arrived; but being a simple swamp dweller, I have to catch as catch can. No use trying again. But here, Na Agōtīme, is the second best, a necklace from the reefs of the Maladives, once the envy of all wives whose husbands plied the upper Nile. Which is to say it is ancient, Agōtīme, almost out of time altogether. I might have been content to give you a chain of tortoise scales from the deep, or discs from fish backbones, had I not fallen in love with you."

So saying, he translated himself back into the form of a gonofo bird and pecked about the reeds in search of his hidden treasure. He found it and she took it from his beak with a modest smile, shyly shielding her face with her left hand. They were the most beautiful cowries she had ever seen: gleaming white along the dental seams, yolking slightly yellow on the lumpy side which was slightly striated and conveyed a grey hint of vanished animal life beneath. The shells cheeped in the cup of her hand as she jostled them—like small birds conversing.

Now Zomadonu ticked them out of her hand, catching up the center of the strand so that both sides swung free—back and forth for a moment only, and with a deft flick flung them out onto the black mud. They landed in a perfect U, open-ended towards Agōtīme. The two rows were the same, denoting a major sign. The tips lay concave—labials; the other six showed humpbacks. It was Akla-Meji.

"Akla-Meji," the Toxosu said, "let the forked-stick catch the rain, the wind blows it away. Who can braid a rope of earth? Can water ever be bound? This time round you leave the swamp purified in your intent. Your tongue will find words to cover your nakedness; but like the raffia, you must learn how to strengthen your head or you will talk needlessly. Farewell, Agŏtĭme, I shall seek you out over there."

How odd of him, Agŏtĭme thought, why all this incoherent rush? He was, clearly, impatient for her to be gone, for he had begun to flex himself back and forth from bird to sphere, from sphere to bird as if hoping by chance to hit upon some third shape. And he had forgot to give the cowries back to her. She stooped to pick them up, started to polish off the mud with the edge of her skirt, then thought the better of it and, twisting the ends together with a bit of grass, slipped the strand over her head at once.

Ah, he'd found it, that other shape, but she could see only a vague outline of it before Zomadonu disappeared completely. In his stead the gong began to sound, over and over until her head throbbed. She felt nauseated. There was nothing to grab on to. Where was she now? She bent forward so as not to faint. "Zomadonu!" she shouted, above the clamor invading her consciousness, "please, there are one or two more things I must ask you. What about Saliabsŏ? Will she, is she giving birth to a Toxosu?"

"O no," his voice laughed, "don't worry about her. That was just a ruse to permit me to have your head awhile. There was no other way I could think of. No, none of Adădoză's wives will ever have the honor of giving birth to one of us. You don't think of it as a privilege do you? Ha, ha, ha, ha, ha, you'll get over that hump soon enough, I warrant you."

Impossible creature. "Please, Zomadonu, one more bit of wisdom before you go. In Mahiland they say that whenever man and woman unite a Toxosu is born. You cram our streams like fish spawn and yet, being unconceived, you remain invisible. Why is it that you materialize on the plateau in the guise of the misborn?"

"How else," laughed Zomadonu bitterly, "could disorder possibly manifest itself to the literal Dahomean mind? How else assuage their guilt? Assert freedom? Creativity? And how else, were some of us not born to kings, could we be sure of our immortal sovereignty?"

6 ▶▶ Whydah Beach

The Englishman was interested. He drew out his notebook and began, hurriedly, to sketch them in the ecstasy of their dance. The commercial agents were bored and irritated by the evident lack of discipline which permitted such a display at such a time and in such a place. The *caboceers*, although their gestures counseled calm, as if this were but a passing affair, a bit of spontaneous recreation, were extremely distressed. Whoever heard of slaves possessed in caravan, either singly or as now—far worse—collectively? It was impossible to stop them, impossible even to interrupt them without giving offense to the *vodū*.

But they were in luck, for when the slow processional was done, one of the soldiers automatically raised his gun and fired straight up—as if to blast a hole in the broad-leafed canopy covering Wodonū. This report would, normally, have been a signal for Adomu, Tegbesu's abnormal son, to begin, in the person of his priest, praises of the five royal Toxosu. That no Adomusi was present would perhaps, in the present circumstances, have made no difference. Adomu might, for his purpose, have picked any one of the heads just ridden with such elegant bravado. But Zomadonu, his elder brother, first-born of the fluid dynasty, had no intention of making this a full-fledged ritual. His own purpose accomplished, he allowed Agŏtĭme, at the sound of the gun, to come to herself again and ordered his four brothers and their kinsmen to return at once to that stagnant hole at the nadir of the swamp to which dry times in the court of Adãdozã had driven them.

As for Saliabsŏ, when her convulsions left her as suddenly as begun, she had fallen into a sweaty sleep as she stood. She did not waken when they cut off her neck rope and hoisted her into the canvas litter, and she continued to sleep soundly all the way across the swamp. When she finally did awake, she had no memory of what had occurred at Wodonŭ, nor could she imagine why she was being borne along like a potentate, but she did not complain.

The sodden trail leading south from Wodonŭ was suspiciously marked with spoor. The soldiers, poles slung across both shoulders, could not be trusted effectively to manage their guns, nor did the *caboceers* wish, at this point, to have Gbaguideguide begin playing the drum; so they urged everyone to shout, sporadically, as lustily as they could; and that noise, apparently, was enough to keep the lurking beasts away, for they saw none. One hour more of anemic fig boles braced by strangulating clusia vines, of dark overhang and undergrowth, and then sunlight, high grasses, and the gradual dispersal of those formidable ranks of trees into isolated clumps, informed them that there was no more need for shouting. Ko Swamp was at an end. They had crossed it in a mere three or four hours—with considerable time out at Wodonŭ. In the rainy season, it would have taken them a full two days.

As they hurried along the downs of that beautiful open country, Agŏtĭme's anxious thoughts saw their patterns reversed by swarms of butterflies which now and again started up from the path—puddle-dipped and dyed blue as the sky into which they now seemed bent on merging.

The Gede stone and the hunter in sounding new (or were they merely disused?) tones of feeling had unsettled her. But the encounter with the Toxosu, quirky as he was, had changed her into a new order of being. Yet all had been implicit. Her pride, no pretense after all, foreshadowed more power than she had ever hoped for. Simply to be Agōtīme, a self of which legends are made, would in the ensuing years become onerous. She did not refuse that implication. So why not now take fugitive joy in the new awareness attendant upon such personal expansion?

Leaving Kana she had felt the need to pick up elusive impulses from the past. Now having crossed the swamp, she was suddenly able to hear that which her new-found vocation authorized her to hear, made mandatory. Communal memories of local happenings, clashes of energy, shows of force, manipulations of chance came unsolicited to her ear, as wind to cheek. Why did such random events, most of them violent, all outside her own experience, move her to tears like haunting partials plucked from zither strings? How could she know that the Toxosu had in effect commissioned her to transmit her historical feelings—if such they could be called—to susceptible compatriots stranded on some distant shore? She had yet to learn how to transform their yearnings into religious facts, learn how to provoke the manifestations of those whose strong names were drawn from deeds still implicit in this expanse of land through which she now passed for the first time. Now she heard the deeds, but how, from some new world vantage point, to extirpate these forces from their ancient habitat? How but with the well-honed tools of memory? There must be other ways—the use of which she could learn—over there. And for now she'd do her best to carry what strengths she could in the form of *huenu xo* [time-words], which, gleaned from these mellow fields as she hurried past, garnered during the long voyage to come, would put forth roots in some distant soil to be a perennial crop of praises for the insatiable Toxosu and, at the same time (she hoped), a far-flung source of energy for her insurgent son.

Just north of Alada, on the left side of the road, a battery of twenty-eight cannon, some mounted on ship's swivels, some propped upon logs, corroded peacefully in the setting sun. Here legendary time-words paused to wrestle with the relics of recorded history. The fields of memory darkened. Agõtĩme came to herself again. A gently inclined stretch of sandy ground, stalked upon by shadowy oil palms with clusters of red bats clinging to the drupes, the sound of peasant voices speaking a Fõgbe as pure as the nearby waters of sacred Sodji Spring told them they had at last reached the ancient capital to which the kings of Dahomey and Porto Novo still journeyed for their investiture.

That night, seated on the threshold of one of the huts the town provided as hostelry for all travelers, slave or free, Agõtĩme told Oro and a few stray dogs the story of the founding of Alada. She began, inevitably, with the story of Aligbonõ. Why not? Alada was inconceivable without Aligbonõ. But she had her qualms. Not the old ones. The Toxosu had made light of those. And what better test of her new power than to confront old phantasms with a clear gaze, a singsong voice? However, he had plainly said she should forget Agasu and begin with Dako-donu. Surely a local prejudice of his. For Zomadonu, the panther tribe did not exist until their feet muddied the waters of Hlã Brook. Would he, over there, with all the assurance of a well-traveled universal *vodũ*, continue to feel the same about Agasu, Ajahũto and all who came before Dako-donu? If he did, she would do as he wished, but now she needed a strong frame across which to stretch the loose strands of hearsay she'd been picking up along the way. And what better frame than old, old history which policy over the years had shaped into the simple, stable contours of an artifact. Therefore she began her education of Oro with the story of Aligbonō.

"But Na Agōtīme," Oro said, "it's a man's yam that pushes his hand into the palm oil, why should Agasu have been blamed for being what he was—the result of his mother's escapade in the reeds by the River Mono? Do you know what I think? To find a buffalo, one must hike to the grasslands; to find an elephant, these days, one must go a good way into the forest; but it would take a long, long time to come across a pure black leopard."

"It is so." Agōtīme mused. She was silent a moment, staring at the ground, then her face lit up like a mischievous young girl's. "I have it," she said, "just now a bird threw the news to me and I caught it. Listen, but don't tell anyone else until I give you my permission. All things have happened in the sky before, no? Well, suppose there was once a hunter had two wives. To flatter you, let's say he was an eastern man, a Nago. Now the first wife was a princess of the royal family of, well, it doesn't matter about her city; but a princess she was and the second wife was only a commoner, or worse. Let's say her father was a musician and her mother a . . . a . . ."

". . . beggar woman turned troubador, a professional praiser of Ogun," Oro interrupted.

"Good," Agōtīme said, "how quick you are to follow. Now the first wife was like a bad seed yam that refuses to sprout and yield, and when the second wife, she of common origin, began to grow a big belly, the princess, furious with jealousy, convinced the hunter to abandon the poor girl in the bush he knew so well, she not at all. And so, having wandered several moons in her solitude, the musician's daughter stumbled across the ford and into the court of Tado. There she was delivered of her child and the king took pity and adopted both into his household, calling her Ali-gbo-nõ [mother who passes along the road] and her son Agasu [father unknown].

"Now, let us take up the tale where we put it down. The legitimate sons of the king of Tado were envious of Agasu, and unwisely taunted him about his origins, inventing the story of the panther to account for his superior strength, his green eyes, his shaggy appearance. But Agasu was content to bide his time, for he knew his horoscope, knew he would live to father kings of four kingdoms: Tado, Alada, Porto Novo and Dahomey—greatest of them all.

"This is how it came about: the Agasuvi prospered. Succeeding generations, proud to call themselves sons-of-the-panther, grew into a clan formidable enough to wrest the throne from the male descendants of the king who had originally befriended Aligbonõ. But it was not until one Agasuvi wrongfully installed himself upon the throne of his own elder brother that their true pulse began to sound, the *lici-co-cia* of their marauding feet. You heard Gbaguideguide take it up at Wodonũ, you yourself were dancing it, remember? *lici-co-cia, lici-co-cia.*

"Well, once that beat began there was no stopping it. The outraged brother killed the usurper but because of his impiety was forced to flee with a group of loyal kinsmen, south to the shores of Lake Aheme. There Ajahũto [fratricide] and his people learned to build their houses on slender poles like wobbly-kneed waterbirds; but Ajahũto's descendants, pursued by vindictive kinsmen from Tado, were finally forced to abandon their homes and once more take to the road. Ascending the gap between the Kufo and the Weme, they eventually settled here at Alada—named after them [place of the accursed]. The invaders pacified the local inhabitants, little people who made their homes in termite mounds, by letting their diminutive ancestor be guardian of the market place. Here Ajahũto, ancestor of the migration, became *vodũ* and under his protection this branch of the

Agasuvi prospered and, inevitably, split again. Three brothers, this time, disputed the throne; but rather than kill each other, two took to the road. The eldest remained there in Alada; the second, Dako-donu's father, turned north—whence we have come; while the third went south to the sea and founded Porto Novo. And that," said Agŏtīme, "is enough for now. Goodnight, Oro, take care not to stumble in the dark."

"Thank you, mother," said Oro, "and let us hope these dogs, should they see a panther's face, will now have sense enough to keep silent."

The double-tiered clay palace with its five shuttered windows spanning the royal gateway stood intact; but as the coffle marched out of town the next morning, no trace could be seen of the famous nine miles of wall; and where handsome compounds must once have lined the street, maize stubble and ragged banana trees stood begging for fire and rain. It was Agaja, fourth king of pearls, who had turned that well-founded town into a thoroughfare, he who first involved Dahomey in the trade. His emblem is a man-made thing—a ship, although he himself never put to sea. But those who did, saw him, the first Dahomean king to be described in European writing—"short of stature," "pockmarked face." And certain deeds of his, stripped of their numina, have taken their place in the crowded annals of European history.

When Agaja came to the throne usurped from his nephew, he found fat King Xufŏ comfortably ensconced in the thriving Xueda kingdom of Savi, whose capital lies south of Alada on the north bank of a brackish estuary—a leisurely distance from the sea. Through the eyes of his spies, Agaja watched Xufŏ welcome foreign merchants to the Xueda strand, permit them in the course of time to build forts in the seacoast town of Glexue (which they called Whydah—a deformation of Xueda), and eventually to penetrate inland as far as Savi itself.

Oblivious of local place names, European traders had the habit of calling the various shores off which they anchored after the raw materials they were able to obtain. Grain Coast, Ivory Coast, Gold Coast—rugged shores concealing impenetrable interiors. But when they came to the easy lagoon-laced stretch between the River Volta and Cape Lopez, they found no rare or precious matter—except men. Over this plenteous commodity, hospitable King Xufō held sway. And as time went on, he controlled a massive influx of trade goods as well: iron bars, tobacco, fine cloths, intoxicants and guns. Sullenly, Agaja dug his hind claws in and waited. ("Don't throw a green branch on the fire" was the phrase from which he drew his name.)

Another fraternal struggle for the throne of Alada gave Agaja an excuse to move south. The legitimate heir asked his powerful kinsman to intervene, thus enabling Agaja to establish a strategic hold on the parent kingdom now grown too weak to bar Dahomean access to Xueda country. Agaja's army occupied Alada, but rather than restore Agaja exiled its rightful king. Some months later, using Alada as base, the army of Dahomey marched down to the Xueda capital of Savi, paused long enough to burn everything, and then, the very same day, their battle-painted faces further decorated with soot, marched on down to Glexue. "*Helu mi!* [malediction]," they cried out to the terrified Xueda, "do you recognize us?"

Hardpressed by invading horsemen from Nago country, Agaja could not then spare enough troops to hold the seaport; but he returned the year after to complete what he had so successfully begun. In the twenty-second year of his reign Agaja established order in Glexue, an order that, in persisting to the end of the nineteenth century, would outlast the fluctuating trade it was designed to dominate. A detachment of Dahomean troops was perpetually stationed in Glexue to ward off further attacks by the exiled Xueda, an elaborate system of customs and exchange set up, and an equally elaborate bureaucracy, headed by a minister of external affairs, the Yovogã [whites' chief]. The Europeans, having witnessed the ruin of their establishments at Savi, wisely decided to confine themselves to the bastions that they continued to call Whydah. Temporary factories were set up along the beach and ships began to anchor off the Slave Coast once again.

Passing by the place where the Xueda people had hidden their tutelary snake—vainly hoping by this means to forestall Agaja's advance, Agõtĩme sensed a slight swaying amidst the sodden fern banks at the ford, a trembling of stippled croton leaves—their stiff-tongued homage to inconstancy. "Down here when you meet a python," she told Oro, "you must kiss the ground and say 'my father.'"

"But I don't know him, Na Agõtĩme," Oro protested, "he is not one of our *vodũ*."

"What does that matter? Are all Nagos so parochial? Hardship taught us both to speak the same language, did it not? He's not my *vodũ* either, but he lives here. Besides, he may know you very well. Rain forms clouds for the deaf and rumbles for the sake of the blind. Who knows from one place to the next what form a force may take? You Nagos think you invented iron, but Gu came down from the Atakora Mountains long before you had anvil-altars to welcome him. Now in Mahiland we also have a snake who, after rains, stretches his beautiful striped cloth across the calabash of the sky. Who can say the Royal Xueda python is not his brother? You must keep your eyes on me, little hunter, or next year you'll bag only a buffalo, and the year after next—a mouse."

In Savi itself no shrines or cult houses could be seen, flanking the road, and of the former European installations, only moats could be traced, like old scars on the face of a fertile land, winding numbly through recently harvested fields of maize, cassava and calavance in search of the healing waters of the estuary. From that inlet Agõtǐme caught her first hint of the sea which, being the most mobile surface of all, is the Greater Serpent's favorite resting place. She heard the rasp of the seabreeze upon the brittle palmyra leaves, smelled the heaviness hidden in the air—saline and yet sweet.

Whydah lies in a slight depression and, as the coffle ascended the final rise of the alluvial plain, those who looked carefully could see—beyond the sharply crested sand ridge on the far side of the town, between the thin line of palms etched against a bluish-white horizon—the spectral masts of European ships. And Agõtǐme felt a shiver run along her spine, confirming her pious suspicion that the Xueda pythons were not only local spirits, but that their force, being elemental, was everywhere, and informing her that whatever encircles the earth three thousand, five hundred times also coils itself about the base of the brain to ripple the skin from neck to finger tips. For mobile, elusive Dã sustains and animates everything. All that verges, vibrates, wavers is Dã, the snake; yet without him there would be no perpetuity for Dã is fortune's vehicle, excreting riches.

Life passes, she thought, like Dã himself, cleaving the stagnant waters with a sudden flash of light. How brief! What multiplicity! No matter how powerful an ancestor, if he lived long enough ago he'd be forgot by now, were it not for Dã. Even gods drop out of mind when there is no one left to worship them. Behind all the known *vodũ* stand their progenitors, denizens of other worlds, forgotten now, and these nameless *vodũ* would be neglected now, were it not for Dã. He alone, who inhabits space in the guise of Aidohuedo [rainbow], stands surrogate for all of these and, too, for slaves led far away in fortune's chains (emblems of him), so that everyone who has ever lived can be invoked, placated and, in some vague sense, retained.

> Take our songs
>> but not our singers' voices;

Take your speech
but not our drummers' hands.

So the living cautiously dismiss the invisible swarms each
year at the conclusion of Nesuxue rites for the dead. So Agōtīme, on that sandy hogback overlooking the sea, took prudent
leave of the times, places and deeds animating her world whose
confines now stretched south of the Atakora Mountains as far
as the Bight of Benin. Bereft of locality could those, whose surrogate in the new world she had been chosen to be, find their
way to the drum-heads? Hands and voices there would be. And
perhaps the greater *vodū*, those well-traveled ones whose elemental avatars were everywhere, would show the others the
way. The cowries Zomadonu had given her gleamed cool as
moon-bits on her firm black breasts; and above the slim column
of flesh that encased her spine, her head, with carrying pad
coiled upon it, for all that it needed strengthening, seemed sufficient for the calabash of memories she bore.

Oma! The cry mouthed itself and sped like brushfire
through the town. *Oma! Oma!* Wild-eyed, their faces plastered
with kaolin or mud, their bodies bristling with fibers yanked
from the earth, wrenched from the palm, brandishing sticks or
clubs, kola nuts, snail shells, spindles and bobbins strung around
their necks, coiffed with bottomless calabashes or battered hats
that were sprigged and bracted, dishevelled with leaves or topped
with bamboo birdcages housing brandy bottles or cast-off European boots, the *vodunsi* ramped through the town.

Inside one of the barracks huddled along the adobe ram-
parts of São João Baptista, Agōtīme heard the call and shuddered, wondering what sacrilege had been committed to which
god thus to send his distraught worshippers out into the streets
proclaiming anarchy and calling forth curses on the heads of all
casual passers-by. Whatever the cause, once the sacred order is
outraged, anything is possible; and until the culprit can be

found and atonement made, the offended god's votaries are compelled to embody the threat of universal disorder in hysteric disarray.

"Someone got a cloistered novice of the Sea God quick with child," Saliabsō said, "that's why Oma. Xunō proclaimed it at dawn. But other crimes have been committed in the wake of that one. Before you woke up I heard the guards gossiping about everything that's been going on. This poor town's been aflame with evil doings. I mean literally aflame. Smell the smoke? Even in here you can smell it. They suspect sorcery, of course, and the chief priest has also given orders to kill all vultures, cats and screech owls on sight, supposing the wicked one to be hiding in feathers or furry-pelt. Shortly before dawn, it seems, a fruit vendor, a widow getting along in years, came to the market to open her stall. Discovering that overnight she had been robbed of her stock, the woman took up a torch and ran distractedly about the square crying 'May he who stole from me be extinguished sooner than this brand.' Well, as you can imagine, she attracted quite a crowd of early-risers; and then the dry wind came up (she might have known, this being the time of year for it), and blew the sparks from her torch about, tindering the thatch of more than a dozen stalls before they managed to beat the fire out. By this time there was no question of recovering property or punishing a thief, for the victim, turned criminal for want of self-control, had to lose her head to a stake for firing the market place! Her only daughter, they say, so unnerved the Yovogã (a touchy fellow, always making a great show of his prerogatives and cloth-of-gold) by her shrieks, that she'll be sold along with the rest of us—if anyone will buy the poor mad thing. It's either that or the sharks for her. Well, no sooner had one rage been calmed than the priests of Dã announced another bit of firey business to come. And this amid continuous cries of *Oma! Oma!* Really, I can't imagine how you slept through it all. Anyhow, it seems that late last night (while who knows what else was going on) a drunken caretaker from the British fort on his way home from some nocturnal mischief of his own had the ill-luck to step on a royal python (squashed the life out of him) and now the fellow's got to undergo the prescribed ordeal. His master tried to buy the Dāgbenō off, unsuccessfully of course. Whydah's always been a wild place, Na Agōtíme, but never wilder than right now. How I wish my father were alive to see it! 'Forces, Sali, forces,' he used to say, 'nothing dull about old Africa, my girl.' But he was wrong. It can be dull. He never had to serve out a term in the common wives' court under the ever-watchful buttocks of the female Migā. Maybe it wasn't so bad over on your side of the palace. Not Whydah, though. I hadn't realized how much I missed the place and now, how laughable for me to be a transient slave in my own home town! I should be doing the honors, showing you around. What a privilege—to show a queen around. But we won't be staying here long. I heard the guards say five ships stand in the roads anxious to complete their cargoes and be off. Well, even if I could escape, Adādozā's spies would find me out. My mother's gone back to her village, poor soul; but I couldn't stand bush life, not me. No, there's no place for me here any more. We'll take our chances in the New World, my little unborn bastard prince and I. You'll do as midwife, I can tell. Let's hope the royal lot of us end up in the same boat," she concluded warmly, squeezing Agō-tíme's arm.

Agōtíme couldn't help it, she recoiled from that over-effusiveness. What's got into her? she thought. She must have caught fire too. Not more than two coherent words the entire trip down and now there's no stopping them. The long ride in the litter must have rested her. And then, as she says, she feels at one with things here, even confined as she is behind bars in this foul rookery. (But when the talk died down, Saliabsō looked more helpless, more exposed than ever. Her eyes held a frightened look.) She is hurt at my lack of responsiveness, Agōtíme thought.

"Nor will I be sorry to leave, my daughter," she said out loud. "Old Africa and I have already bade farewell."

Saliabsō was right. They were to be dispatched as soon as possible. Although the *baracoons* on the beach were but half full, the Yovogā feared the impatient captains would, without further ado, load up and be off to complete their ladings in Badagry, Lagos or Bonny. It had been the worst of a run of bad years and everyone involved in the trade was in a bad mood, Yovogā included. A few British and French ships, released from their warring obligations, had begun to arrive again; but there were not enough slaves to go round, for which they blamed him, the Yovogā. Well, the Brazilians who went up to Abomey, under the pretense of attending Grand Customs, would have found out the true cause by now; and how could Adādozā, absurdly unsuccessful in war, be so untoward as to harass the Portuguese king with requests for exclusive rights of supply and other favors? And why should the young king of pearls have picked such an unsavory fellow as Innocencio to represent Dahomey in Lisbon? Was there not one of his own kind whom he could trust, the prime minister for example, or one of the royal princes?

Well, what the Yovogā could not prevent he could at least postpone. He would see to it that Innocencio stayed in São João Baptista for a long visit. Meanwhile, the batch quartered in the fort had to be got down to the beach before it was too late. The Yovogā was curious to see the queen, but he had no intention of forestalling her departure. Let the wrath of Agōglo and the ancient kings fall upon the head of Adādozā, he, the Yovogā, wanted in no way to be responsible for harm done to her. The sooner that one was on the high seas the better. And the dead British chief Abson's daughter, too, he'd known her from her childhood, why in the name of the good serpent was Adādozā selling her? He the Yovogā would take her home with him if

he only could. *Oma!* ugh, those priests were making external re-
lations impossibly difficult. They too would lose him his job if
he didn't watch out. That business of the bumbling foreigner
outside the British fort last night, he'd managed to put that out
of his mind for a while but now he shuddered to think of it.

As a consequence of the above deliberations, it was not yet
midmorning when the mulatto guards of São João Baptista, importantly equipped with a noisy collection of antiquated keys,
unloosed the slaves from their shackles and led them, linked ten
to a file, along the crumbling parapet to a ramp at the south end
of the fort and thence down into the streets. *Oma!* the bizarre
vodunsi jostled through an increasingly agitated crowd, impor-
tuning everyone with obscene references to a crime for which,
until confessed, all men were provisionally accountable:

> When the bearded piper pipes
> The dangling dugs must dance;
> Flames black the bottom
> Of the cooking pot;
> The cook is quick,
> The flame's still hot;
> Who boils a stone,
> Must quaff the broth.

Oma! Nothing exceeds the surf on the lips of an angry sea
god!

"Make way for the fortunate slaves," someone shouted.
"They're chained, therefore they're innocent," shouted another.
"Greetings to those whose hands are tied. Keep back your sticks
and let them pass!" "I buried my youth in Salvador," a blowzy
woman said, "I wish I'd never bought myself back. Should you
all be sent to that rich place, give my greetings to Senhor do
Bomfim." "Who's he?" someone asked, "and just where did he
bury his youth? Surely not in that bag!" The crowd laughed.
Agŏtíme grit her teeth. Such indecency, such impossible vul-

garity, surely they were all mad down here. She noticed that Saliabsō was laughing too.

But the throng's attention was soon diverted from the slaves, even the masqueraders stilled their scurrilous nonsense, for the ordeal of the pythonicide was about to take place. The coffle halted in its traces. The *caboceers* wanted to watch.

A small hut, thatched with dry grass, had been hastily constructed in the center of the square and the guilty man, so Sali informed everyone, his body smeared all over with palm oil, had been sealed up inside. At a sign from the Dāgbenō, a young votary held a torch to the thatch. In seconds the hovel flared up and the criminal broke out. Everyone in the coffle gasped. To their horror they recognized him—the English traveler's servant, the young man from Sierra Leone. They had stripped his European clothes off, his gold-rimmed eyeglasses as well, and in their stead had incredibly encumbered him with a dazed dog (lashed to his chest), a brace of fowls (bunched across his pitifully narrow shoulders) and bandaged his head with a score of amulets. Almost blind with the agony of it all, the young man paused, despairing of the way to take to the nearest watering place. But this doubt didn't last long for the crowd fell back to form a corridor, lined with Dāgbesi who emerged from the anonymity of the bystanders to flail him with sticks as he lurched past— hands held up to protect what was left of his face. Agōtīme and the others never knew whether or not he survived the run because, as the populace closed the gap behind him, the chief *caboceer* gave Gbaguideguide's arm a tug and the coffle moved on.

"So this is what Dā considers a fair chance," Oro snapped. "You ought to have forewarned him, not me. But he would have had to say 'my father' in a foreign language. Still, it's not in bending to kiss the ground one breaks one's eyeballs. Send me a second pair so's I can look both up and down. I've no need for white man's attire. No matter how tattered my garments, I shall follow my *vodū*. In a raffia skirt, or with no clothes on, I'll go along. Hey, hey, let's hurry down to where the breakers roar. Some like it hot, but as for me, I'd rather run the risk of drowning!"

Two miles of sand and swamp separated the town of Whydah from the customs house—one of a cluster of outbuildings on the edge of the lagoon which lay closely parallel to the Bight. The soft track they took was anticipatory of the experience of the sea: those cambered palms with reddish copra strewn about beneath provided a landsman's vision of ribs and beams looming buoyant above a gentle series of rises and declivities that seemed like sand-waves southered by an offshore breeze.

The *caboceers* had intended to market their wares beside the solitary dwarf ficus known far and wide as the Captains' Tree, but here on the strand, apparently, there had been some distressing breaches in the moral continuum during the night. The local customs officers declared the immediate vicinity of the tree unclean which, to judge from the flies, it was indeed, and so the coffle was lined up before one of the warehouses.

Two more coffles, brought by Nago suppliers, had come down the Weme by canoe early this morning, but the allocation of these could not begin until the king's slaves from Abomey were disposed of. Manoel Pinta de Fonseca, as first of the present captains to put into Whydah, had priority of choice which, it turned out, had already, by proxy, been exercised. The two commercial agents who had accompanied the coffle down were representatives of the owner of Fonseca's ship, one Sequeira Lima, the most powerful trader in Bahia. Having gone up to Abomey to ascertain why slaves had been so scarce during the last four or five years, they had taken the liberty, while there, of dashing the *caboceers* to let Fonseca take the lot—providing the ship's surgeon had no objections. And this was why the coffle from Abomey had spent the night in São João Baptista instead of being quartered, like the others, in *baracoons* next to the warehouses on the beach.

"Stretch forth your bellies roundly, my friends," the irrepressible Oro said, "for we have come like new-made pots to market where they must examine us for quality. That pale-fingered connoisseur of fine black crockery would have you jump up and down to test resiliency. See that you don't spring a leak, or let the slightest wind escape. He would examine our orifices? Perhaps he has it in mind to make a necklace of our best teeth. Little does he know what strong medicines are hid beneath our well-worn lids."

Eucaristus the surgeon pronounced them all fit. All were not as young as they might be, but at least none were over thirty, he'd swear to it. One bad case of logorrhea, he laughed, but being the youngest, he'd probably grow out of it. Not a trace of yaws or leprosy among the lot of them. Although the pregnant mulatto might be considered something of a risk, she looked to have inherited reserves of strength from the black side of her ancestry. "This one can serve as midwife," he said, poking Agõtíme in the ribs, "she looks the type to know the proper native incantations."

"Yes," the chief *caboceer* agreed, "she is the owner of many strong words, and her rags are those of experience," he added, well knowing the proverb would be lost on them.

"She is a queen," the Yovogã said in his most ponderous manner, "I should warn you gentlemen to treat her with the utmost respect, for if by any chance her son should succeed to the ancient throne of Dahomey, it is not unlikely he would seek to ransom her."

Fonseca bowed with mock courtesy in the direction of Agõtíme. "Queen she may be to you," he said to the Yovogã, "but drone to me. We've no patience with queens in our black hive. She'll lie below with the rest. Strong words she may have," he said to the chief *caboceer*, "but she looks skinny and rather frail to me; I'll pay only the minimum price for her, no less no more."

And so Agŏtĭme was sold to Fonseca for ten rolls of the much coveted Brazilian tobacco (molasses-smeared to keep the short leaves from drying out and therefore more pungent to the Dahomean taste than the long-leaved first grade sent directly to Lisbon). Had she been bought by a British trader he might have met the minimum price with one hundred gallons of Jamaican rum, or with a hodgepodge consisting of eight fathoms of patten chintz, eight fathoms of blue baft, two muskets, twenty-five powder kegs, six iron bars, six clay pipes and one large brass pan. A Frenchman, had there been one, might have had her for six anchors (thirty-six gallons) of brandy and four hundred heads of cowries (at forty cowries the string, fifty strings the head) or, instead of this wondrous currency from the South Seas, ten fathoms of so-called Siamese cloth—striped cotton woven in Normandy to simulate silks worn by the Siamese ambassador to the court of Louis XIV or by hospitable King Xufŏ in Savi.

While the commercial agents, the *caboceers* and the Yovogã moved into the customs shed for a final settlement, the surgeon led the coffle across the sand to the place where a large bonfire had been kindled on the lagoon's edge. Fonseca and the other captains followed. "Courage, comrades," Oro said, "for we are now become like green twigs gathered for initiation. They've stripped me of my bark, as I the great bull-roarer predicted, but still I follow my *vodŭ;* and surely only the great smith himself could have fashioned those evil-looking instruments."

When the appropriate iron had been selected from the pile, sufficiently heated, plunged in and out of a pot of hot oil (to prevent sticking), Fonseca deftly applied it to Oro's left hip. Unlike most captains, Fonseca assumed the responsibility of branding them himself, and the others commended his courage, his finesse. The slaves glanced wildly at one another, every muscle tensed, feet braced wide apart, fists clenched; but not one cried out when his turn came, not one flinched.

"Bloody bastards," the British captain, Fonseca's competitor said, "their skin's as tough as it is black; lucky for them they don't feel things the way we do."

"Nonsense," Fonseca's first mate said, "they have a code of honor, exactly as we do, which their fetish compels them to obey."

"Wrong, both of you," Fonseca said, "they feel everything, of course, look at their eyes; but that silent suffering is an affront to us which they intend as such. Look at that husky one there [pointing to Gbaguideguide], look at his face. He's the most dangerous. Starve them, their wasting flesh vaporizes into anger; beat them, each scar mouths a threat, oozes invective. They resist, whatever you do to them, they resist."

Now the women; in their case Fonseca preferred the more vulnerable flesh of the left breast. Agŏtīme eyed Saliabsō narrowly. Was she, despite her half-birth, one of them? Could she feel the fierce pride which had passed from one to the other when the first brand struck Oro? Would she keep the unspoken agreement to save face at all costs? Agŏtīme shivered in sympathetic pain, but Sali was the best of all. Sali grinned at the captain, and then vomited.

"Now the queen," Fonseca said. "My forefathers' chivalry not being entirely dead in me, I've left her for last. Too bad the gallant Yovogā is not here to see." The smart tore through her skin then stopped, hovering on the point between numbness and feeling, and then began to ache, to throb, flooding her body with pain. Sweat poured from her face. The captain turned away. No, she would not look down, she would continue to stare out across the lagoon to the sea. Yet the truth was that having been thus mutilated, the left breast no longer belonged to her. Perhaps this was the secret, the way to survive. Only now, having come to this resolve, could she look down at the wound. What did it mean—that gash shaped like a striking snake? Later, when, hopefully, without proper remedies, that stigma had sealed its hurt into a scar, there'd be time enough to inquire what it meant.

Having completed his quota, Fonseca was ready to embark. The other lots were led from their pens to join those at the bonfire and Xueda ferryboats, in the Yovogã's employ, began to punt them, in chains of ten, across the lagoon to the shingle.

Agõtĩme, recalling the old story told of Gbe-Gouda, her son's natal sign, eagerly searched the ferryman's face for signs of avarice or guile. But the face was as old and impassive as the element upon which the man, as if he were on the way to Dead's Land, poled out his time. Could the offshore breeze that puckered the surface of the lake be blamed for the tiny wrinkles about his eyes? Her burn throbbed. Would it, after all, become infected with some poison she lacked the means to extract? How odd that she should thus scrutinize the boatman, how odd that despite everything—pain, fever, the shame of being chained and jammed naked into a crowded boat—she should be preoccupied with traces, insatiable for vestiges. These eyes, with their slight tint of green, set in leathery pouches, recalled the hunter's.

The tattooed Kru-men were something else again. As soon as the scow scraped the reeds, the slaves were taken out and led through dune drifts to the strand. Here, released from their chains, they were at once rudely heaved by Brazilian sailors into seagoing canoes manned by the fiercely scarred Kru-men.

"Handsome, aren't they?" Saliabsõ remarked. "Don't put on those queen-motherly airs of yours. I saw how you looked at them."

"Kru-men, you said? I've never heard of them. They speak a foreign tongue. Who are they?"

"Well, there are many things you possess no knowledge of, aren't there? Fisherfolk they were once, I imagine. They floated down to Cape Coast Castle from who knows where, and stayed to be picked up by slavers cruising along the Bight and hauled aboard, canoes and all. They're paid in gold for their work, with a bottle of brandy a day thrown in; but they have to get back on their own, against the current, mind you. You needn't worry;

these canoes are as strong as their bodies. Cut from a single tree, and look at the size of them. 'Indispensable adjuncts to the trade,' my father used to say, 'indispensable adjuncts'—whatever that means. They're hired because none of your lagoon-soaked Hue-damen, and certainly no Europeans, dare run the breakers. And out on the bars they rise up even grander than these, high as those horrible palace walls in Abomey. Aren't you frightened? Even you, Na Agŏtĭme?"

Indeed, it seemed impossible to surmount them, but the re-markable Kru-men did not flinch. They stood astern with their single club-shaped paddles poised for the dip, four of them only, their eyes—ignoring the terrified faces of the passengers—fixed on the seaward bow. Then, at a signal from their leader, the one with the sternmost oar, they struck their paddles; and as they dug in with furious energy, four of their fellows, who waited ankle-deep in the receding foam, ran the canoe off the back of one wave and before the onset of the next, managed to jump in, grab paddles, and stroke in perfect time with the others. They had made it!

But Saliabsŏ was correct. Thirty yards out, the waves were breaking on a sandbar even more violently than on shore. Agŏtĭme held her breath. The leader sang out and, riding low this time, the canoe broke through the breach and slipped easily over the oncoming swell. An equal distance out lay another bar which the Kru-men apparently considered most treacherous, for they rested on their paddles until, she supposed, their sea god should give them a favorable sign. Was their sea god the one she now, on this the very crest of fear, recalled her grandmother's telling of? The one to whose palace Xume, the hero of the south, used to ride out on a white bull every year to spend seven days feasting? The Maxl savored their distant memories of the sea, why did the panther-people prohibit them? Was that a leopard's tooth each Kru-man had knotted to his wrist? Why not a shark's?

But the Kru coxswain, seeing his chance come at last,

screamed out above the roar. All paddles dug in, and the canoe rushed through a chaos of tumbling surf and on over a lesser succeeding wave. They were drenched but upright, alive. Certainly the slightest miscalculation of that Kru-man would have destroyed us all, Agŏtĭme thought; but how else could elemental power be measured and the *vodũ* satisfied? At the last moment, Xu, pleased with his son, had deflected his ire.

It was the last bar. There rode the ship. So this was the monster they'd been branded to on the beach. It dwarfed the canoe which seemed, after its heroic ordeal, to have shrunk into a stick. The salt smarted her burn—recalled now like death's seal on living flesh. And now for the first time Agŏtĭme's thoughts struggled to escape. She wildly willed the Kru-men to strike out for Cape Coast Castle—wherever it was. Nothing could be uglier or more inevitable than that ship. Zomadonu . . . but there was no more time to think. The sailors up there had been impatient all day for their arrival. And with Fonseca gone they had managed to still their impatience with drink. Now in a rush down came the ladders over the side, followed by additional ropes with knots on them, and hooks. Thus goaded, one had to climb at once to that swaying height.

Impassive, the Kru-men steadied the canoe while the boarding took place.

two THE MIDDLE PASSAGE

Let us hear no more then of Ulysses and
Aeneas and their long journeyings, no more
of Alexander and Trajan and their famous
victories. My theme is the daring and
renown of the Portuguese to whom Neptune
and Mars alike give homage. The heroes and
the poets of old have had their day; another
and a loftier conception of valour has arisen.

—CAMOENS

7 ▶▶ Agõtīme's Account

I have seined the shallows and dredged the deeps; water holds no more terrors for me. Look, I throw a silver net out upon the tranquil surface of the sea. Slowly, as a spiderweb drifting downward through the heat, my net extends itself into the liquid layers beneath. Languid coral fans entice it into the gloom of reefs where jewelled eyes keep vigil. See, I have caught a fish! Rest in your *hamac*, little fish, child-of-the-Sun that you are, sway with the cool shift of mutinous tides. Sleep.

So you will not sleep? Listen then, do you know why the children of far-off Dahomey call fish "children-of-the-Sun"? *Hue-vi*, they call them, *hue-vi*. If you lie quietly, I'll tell you why this is.

Long ago Sun was not the lonely king you know him to be. He had many children, more every day, and the people basking on the earth beneath declared: "That overlord of ours has become a menace to mankind so many hot tongues lapping all our water up, withering plant life, shriveling animals, drying up the dugs of our wives, depriving our children of the right to live." So the next time elders' council met, they consulted the diviner. The diviner threw the kernels and announced a curious piece of advice: they must fill five hundred and twenty sacks with stones and leave them at Water's receding edge. Then they must go away and wait for the silver path to open up. And the elders saw that it was performed as spoken.

Now Moon also suffered from the increasing size of Sun's family. The days were growing longer and longer with accumulated light and she was able to spend less and less time in the sky. When there was scarce time for her to venture out of her house to bathe herself and when it seemed that her gracious bathing pool had shrunk to a mere puddle by the dusty roadside, she too had recourse to Fa the oracle. Fa told her to go down to Water's edge as soon as it was dark and, before it became light again, quickly to collect all the sacks of stones men had prepared for her and take them up to Sun's house, saying, "My children have become a nuisance to me, haven't yours? Too many mouths and too little food these days. I'm tired of working so hard. See, I've bound all mine up in bags. You do the same and we'll both throw all our young into the sea at once."

Moon did as she was told, said what she was told to say, and guileless Sun agreed thinking that, once the deed was done, Moon would have lots more time to play with him.

The sacks were thrown. Stones and Sun's children sank into the sea with an awful splash and a hissing scream. But that night Moon's children reappeared, for the first time in many months— a host of dancing stars.

Furious, Sun flung down a big net saying, "Woe is me, to him who casts ashes, ashes must return, misery to the perpetrator of evil deeds, children are, beyond all blessings, the most dear to me." He managed to pull a few score of his offspring in, but to his horror no sooner did they reach the strand than they gasped for air, flopped their bleached bellies over and died. Then Sun, the compassionate father, put by his net and covered his flaming head with clouds of grief.

So, to this day, *hue-vi*, Sun's children, abound in the sea. And to this day, Sun pursues Moon, no longer because of love, but vengefully. For the most part she eludes him, but occasionally he succeeds in eclipsing her, and the children of Dahomey call this *hue-wli-su*.

I used to tell this story to the children on the slave ship. They weren't many, but they were frightened, and I watched out for them as best I could. "The old tales will keep your minds aloft," I used to say. "You mustn't forget anything—except this voyage." How wrong, how foolish I was. If they still live that passage must insist on coming back to haunt their dreams. "Don't forget, you must not forget," those phantom ships cry upon the night wind. To me, after all these years, that voyage seems as strange, as transparent as a tale told by a flying fish. Could any one forget?

How do you suppose we all got here—Leocadia, Benedito, all our people? Every black face that you see has been in some sense buffeted by memories of that voyage, if not their own, why then memories of memories—rounded features polished by the wind, tidal marks on aged faces. I too, Luiz, not my grandmother or my father's father, fortunately for them, but I myself have known the stench between decks. I have witnessed storms of fantastic intensity, suppressed revolt, disease, mayhem; I have known the aftermath—the boredom of day after day the same; I have been blown along by those the sailors call Trade Winds; I have been baptized and salt water holds no further terrors for me—fresh water, either, if the truth be known, nor the seagoing Portuguese.

Poor blind fools to think it was but a quick catch of black fish they carried across the sea. They thought us empty heads, like those casks Baroques fashioned on the quarterdeck. They had no idea of the hidden cargo, of the secret forces more powerful than their Antony. Poor Antony, it's been a long time since . . .

I will tell you, Luiz, how it was aboard my ship, the *Incom-*

preensível. But it will take us all night long to get as far as Cape Lopez—just below the line and the place from which, if you are wise to it, you will take your last sight of Africa—the whole mass of land sailors call the Dark Continent, not what we mean when we talk about "over there" where our dead live. Yes, it will take us all night to get our bearings, and then, you will have to sleep all day tomorrow to make up for it.

In the beginning there must have been about two hundred and half again a hundred of us. The men, who far outnumbered the women, were kept in the hold. They lay side by side, they said, the bent knees of one fitted to the hollow hamstrings of the next and all about the edge huge sacks of grain slumped in sleepy sentinels' position. Most of the women were housed where the sailors normally slept but some of us were fortunate enough to be stored on special platforms built for the purpose just below the halfdeck. I shared such a shelf with six other "choice females" —among them Saliabsõ, a mulatto woman heavy with child, and a young Fulani nomad who later became a very close friend, companion of my later wanderings.

Sali and Suuna did not get on at all well in the beginning. I laugh to think of it. Sali, who had grown up in a port town, thought Suuna wild as you might think some *caboclo* from the hinterland; and plucky Suuna with her comical hooked nose was at pains to defend herself against Sali's merciless chatter for, in the beginning, you see, the Fulani girl could not speak our language. Though the sea was deadly calm, the first few days out, Suuna was sensitive to the slightest rolling of the ship and was sick and there was nothing to wipe it up with. "Come now, Sali," I said, "don't blame her if she can't get used to the ship. It was the death of the fish brought the fish to market. Being all of the same catch, we must out of necessity be friends." And friends we were, after a time, after Sali's baby was born, inseparable shipmates, *malungos* long afterwards. But I anticipate.

The children were kept apart from the rest in a special compartment built for them next to the gun room, where the firearms and ammunition were locked up and where, after the storm, the body of the first mate, Santos Lima, was discovered. Only the body, not the head—but again, I anticipate.

The first few days we were brought up on deck midmorning to be fed and were allowed to remain there until after we'd been fed again, late in the afternoon, when we were herded below and locked into our places. What a relief it was to be able to stand up straight in the fresh air. The atmosphere in our little cubicle was stifling and the shelf so short that if I did not keep my knees drawn up, my body twisted like manioc root, my head lolled over the edge. The afterdeck, which we women shared with the children, was spacious, if crowded. For there sat also Batoques, the ship's cooper, a black man, chained to his bench for supposedly plotting a mutiny, a crime of which he was entirely innocent—then. From the beginning I knew that one to be no ordinary craftsman, though he knew everything about the rigging of the ship, explained everything to me—how yards were braced, how sails hoisted to the masthead, sheeted home, how they drank the wind and other mysteries. His hands were deft, so skillful that he seemed to think with them. When he was not actually engaged in making barrel staves (bent big-bellied, with metal hoops clasped about them), he whittled little dogs.

The women were not entirely idle. Like the queens of Dahomey on state occasions they were given cowries to string into *cabesses* or beads into necklaces. Black and red for Elegba, white and red for Thunder. This amused Batoques no end. There was little for the children to do except when the cook brought out yams for them to peel with rusty knives which were always carefully counted afterwards. One day Oro, the little Nago boy who came down in the coffle with me, conceived the idea of using these knives to scrape out holes for the counting game they used to play at home in their courtyards. But the first mate, when he saw those gouges in the deck, threatened to give them fifty lashes each if he ever caught them at it again.

The raised portion of the afterdeck was divided in half by a little glass-roofed shed the sailors call the binnacle. Enshrined within was the sensitive mechanism the Portuguese use to find their way around the Bight of Benin to the open sea: the palace of the four points. I sat there and stayed under the shade of the spanker sail, limp as it was those first few days. With my head, with my aching spine propped up against Elegba's house, I told stories to the children in broad daylight, for there was no other time or place to tell them. If the spirits of the dead clustered up there on the yardarms at night were offended with me, I begged their forgiveness for my impiety.

Then, on our fifth day out, the ship's priest, Father Martinho, decided to break the monotony by baptizing all of us. He should have done this ashore on Whydah Beach, after the branding, but he had apparently been ill, or squeamish, for until that fifth day none of us had ever seen him. Whether it was his or the captain's idea, I know not, but the ship's passage having been thwarted by smoky calms from the coast, it was evident that the Christian god, having been for some reason or other offended, now must be placated. Whereupon Father Martinho arose from the companionway in a cloud of black cloth.

This priest was a curious combination of the ecstatic and the ridiculous. I was always suspicious of him, as he of me, I suppose, for he always looked at me as if I were a witch, until—but I anticipate. Now, for all the world like a masquerader, he sprang into our midst, climbed the ladder to the poop and thence up to the captain's place behind the binnacle. Raising the captain's speaking trumpet he bellowed forth his intentions in a language that I alone of all the slaves could understand. He would baptize us, he roared, in order that "those whose lusty bodies had been but lately clothed in baft might not sink to damnation with

shamelessly naked souls." Then he prayed aloud in what I took at once to be the secret language of his cult.

After which he began to name us. Beginning with the women and the children, then moving forward to the men on the bow, he gave us every Christian name he could think of from Agatha to Zephryinus, little dreaming that we cared not a whit how he praised us. An important occasion called for a new name. We were used to that. But I, for one, determined never to respond to this priest's praise. Let my future masters learn to pronounce "palms delight me" in my African tongue. Yes, Luiz, once I too had a Christian name, but I have forgotten what it was.

Not content with merely naming and receiving a satisfactory attempt at the curious sounds of that name from the lips of its new owner, the priest had the effrontery to breathe into our faces. Unpurified by alcohol of any sort that breath as I remember it was in every sense repugnant. And not content with this indignity, he proceeded to mark us with a quick crisscross upon forehead and breast. Then followed something even more suspicious. With his own fingers he pried open our lips and placed a pinch of salt on every tongue. Did this salt contain a few grains of medicine that was strong enough to give the whiteman perpetual power over one? I know better now but then I was so terrified that I broke out into a sweat, tried not to swallow and fought against that unknown force with every resource I commanded. I could tell from their eyes, when their turn came round, that everyone felt as I did. But none of us dared cry out, dared refuse or reject the salt, until Father Martinho came to the strongest of the men on the bow, the slave we all called Gbaguideguide.

How he earned this praise-name I know not, nor what he was called before the slave-drivers began to refer to him thus as we walked the long road down from the capital of my country to the beach where they sold us. But once I sensed the sort of man he was, it was not difficult to read his sullen downcast look and imagine that he had done some unconscionable thing up there in the mountains where they hunted him down. From the way he walked, from his powerful back muscles, from the way he beat the drum, I guessed he was a thunder worshipper. But I did not know for sure until they branded him on the beach. Unlike the rest of us, he felt no pain, no shame. He did not clench his fists or bite his lip till the blood came. I watched him closely then for I thought if anyone would choose that moment to revolt, to strike out at his oppressors it would be he. But no, as the hot brand touched his flesh, Gbaguideguide's face lit up with a fierce joy. His bloodshot eyes gleamed with the incandescence of a supernatural manliness. At that moment he could have walked through the bonfire, heaped coals upon his head, run a steel knife through his swollen tongue. I turned my eyes away, and when I looked again he had come back to himself. No sign betrayed him.

I do not know exactly what happened on the forecastle deck. But suddenly a shout went up. "The Calabash-smasher spat the salt out into the priest's face!" The words were taken up and passed round the ship. The sailors standing by seized him and bound him to the capstan, a huge anvil-shaped protuberance on the upper deck round which the anchor cable was coiled. Surely this will put an end to the baptism, I thought; but the priest went right on as if nothing had happened.

There was no further incident. When all the names and salt had been portioned out, Father Martinho jumped up on the bowsprit. Through the captain's speaking trumpet he performed so all could hear, if not understand, the final exorcism. "I conjure you, every unclean spirit, in the name of the Father, Son and Holy Ghost, depart from these creatures all and most especially from this violent savage whom our lord has called to his holy ark. Begone, I say, depart." Upon which he stepped down, picked up a waterbucket the cook had set out upon the bow for him, and wove back the way he had come, ladling out a scant amount onto the head of each new Christian. Drinking water had to be carefully rationed, but oil was even more scarce, so there was no anointment. When he reached the binnacle, Father Martinho took up the speaking tube again: "Now consider yourselves," he said, "from this moment the children of a powerful, compassionate God, now at last properly embarked for the New World. Think no more on your native land, think only of the eternal life to come. Forswear your savage practices. Shed no blood, unless it be your own in victorious martyrdom. Eat no dogs, rats, or horses."

This last bit of advice interested me a great deal. If there were prohibitions to be observed, how cruel not to make them clear to everyone. But since we'd been offered no meat at all in our five days on the ship, only beans (which we detested), maize grits, sauceless yams or cassava porridge, I judged there would not be much danger of incurring the wrath of the whiteman's forces on this account, so I clung to my resolve not to step forward and interpret him.

When Father Martinho had finished we all stood expectantly. Was that to be the end of the ceremony? Was there to be no *tambor*—no songs, dances, possessions? But the priest just stood there scanning the crowd with a doubtful expression on his pale flaccid face as if attempting to surmise the cause of our own uneasiness. Then Batoques spoke up. "St. Antony?" he said, giving the priest a narrow look before bending his neat head once more to his whittling. Martinho smiled. "Why, of course," he muttered, "why didn't I think of that myself. St. Antony'll cheer 'em up. They're used to representations, to fetishes."

Descending into the great cabin where the authorities slept, the priest momentarily emerged from the companionway struggling with the weight of a sizeable wooden statue. Two sailors ran at once to give assistance and together they bore him shoulder-high to the center of the ship. While Father Martinho held this wonder in place, the sailors bound him to the mainmast.

A cry of rage escaped from Gbaguideguide on the capstan, but the other men ignored it. Antony was the first Portuguese *vodũ* they had seen and naturally they began to clap. The tension broken thus, they then began to dance, drumming upon the deck with their feet. "Silence," cried Father Martinho, turning in consternation from the obstreperous slaves on the forecastle deck to the sullen saint as if uncertain to which he ought to address himself. "Silence. You see before you a powerful provocator of winds, patron saint of this and all Christian ships that venture forth upon the fickle surface of the sea. Stay, Antony, and provide us release from our chains, whip us up a breeze sufficient to the amplitude of our undertaking. Now, my little brothers, you may continue your dance." With this the priest retired to his cabin—all wrung out from the look of him.

Little Oro, the Nago boy, was enchanted. "Please, Na Agõtĭme," he begged, "let us go down to the sacred clearing where the great tree plunges its roots into the ocean, please let us go down to have a look at the sacred carving." All the sailors had gone forward to supervise the men's wild dance on the bow; no one was left on the afterdeck to care what we did. "All right, Oro," I said, "we'll go down; but we mustn't stay more than a few minutes." None of the other women were the least bit curious about St. Antony. The baptism had confused them intc a woeful state of despondency and they sat hunched together in snail-like fashion, all their thoughts turned homeward, humming quietly,

> When I was born, my father said,
> "Gu also consoles, consoles me";
> When I was taken, I said,
> "Ooldiers, soldiers, if a moth run
> Against thorns
> She will tear her clothing."

When the vulture called me
Kañumō, kañumō in the white-man's tongue,
I answered . . .

So, with my heart's prow firmly set in the direction of the new world, I led Oro down beneath the tangle of shrouds and ratlines to the shrine of Antony.

His cool gaze undistracted by our presence, by the noise on the forecastle, or by those countless halyards, stays and clew lines that fell aslant his face, his bare feet treading lightly upon a little pedestal embossed with fish (children of the Sun before whom he once, out of desperation at unheeding men, had turned to preach), his right palm sprouting flame, his left arm cradling a tiny man-child, the saint hovered above the fife rail contemplating the vague juncture of sea and sky. I thought it a remarkably skillful carving—despite the undersized heads of child and man, the peculiar stiffness of the knees beneath the too soft folds of gown, the small feet, the overly solicitous curve of the lips. To show force one should let the head swell forth beneath the adze, enliven the major contours with a knife, diminish the body and ground such strength with robust feet. All the same it was a skillful carving, a quiet face. The iconography, however, was confusing. The regalia was that of a teacher, of a contemplative elder. Only the flame gave promise of elemental passions. Was the child supposed to express fecundity or innocence magnanimously preserved from shipwreck? The latter, most likely.

Knowing nothing then of Our Lord of the Good End, I was perplexed. Not so Oro. No sooner had he beheld the saint than he began to hop excitedly up and down, singing,

> Antoneeee is everywhere in the world;
> Captain of the boat,
> When my Antonee returns from his wars,
> What sort of robes will he be wearing?
> When he returns all covered with blood,
> How shall we . . .

This confused me even more. As Oro continued to sing, I stared up at the saint and as I stared his painted eyes seemed to catch fire from the carved flame in his hand. Somewhere, out of the past, a rusty cannon exploded, and from the smoke another Antony appeared in armor, barbed pike in hand. Now, at last, everything was clear. "Durable father of iron!" I exclaimed, throwing myself upon the deck.

But when I finally dared raise my eyes to him again, the destroyer had vanished and the first Antony, the carver's quiet Antony was saying, as if for the seventh time, "Rise pagan woman," I alone heard him say. "I don't care for this sort of grovelling. I am not that iron-headed Titan of yours whom you saw just now descend into my poor worm-ridden frame, although he does, I must confess, inhabit me whenever he chooses, there being no suitable replica of him, God forbid, on Christian ships. Just one split-second manifestation, though. He couldn't resist, but he's not got time for more than that now. Some kindred force of his races across the skies in furious pursuit of him. A promiscuous river goddess is the source of their quarrel, I believe, but one can never be sure of his motives. By Barbara (my sister on land, at sea my direst enemy), I fear before Martinho unties me this time, we'll be swamped. That other one has completely turned her head. She always takes his part, these days, fights for him like a virago. But I won't be drawn in. Not me. Let *my* crude tenant fight his own battles, I say. I hope he loses her in the end. Good riddance to bad waters, I say."

"Most holy saint, your words, first cousins to your deeds, alike confound me," I said. "The owner of the tools that carved your splendid mask had all but convinced me of your wise restraint. Why then that sudden show of battle dress? Where flies swarm, one says, there must be the courtyard of a wealthy headman. A hat does not sit well on all heads; only the owner's will fit properly. Surely Gu's choice was not fortuitous. If anyone is in control of his fate, it is that one. Were there no alternative repositories? That strange box against which I've been wont to lean, there's a loadstone within that binnacle, Batoques says."

"Someone else, who shall not, I repeat, shall not be named, got to the compass first," St. Antony said. "But you are correct. Even had that one the run of the ship, he would have selected me. For superficial reasons, mind you. And as for me, a Christian comes as he is called, pagan woman. Whenever he's about to descend, he forces me to put that impenetrable costume on—far more expressive of him, he says. Nor, I'm afraid, is he the only one to summon me in that guise. Why, I've even got a lieutenant's commission for my pains. My monthly paycheck keeps my altars rich, my images well painted (once a year at least). I enlisted, so to speak, in Spain; and now, in Brazil, they plan to promote me to a colonel's rank before the decade's out. But I take no pride in all of this. Such honors are decreed in spite of me. My living legend feeds on whatever's offered. I am now only that which men make of me." He paused. "My mortal disposition was far otherwise."

I clutched a bitt to steady myself. These words of Antony's frightened me. Was it possible that I, too, by posterity might be thus misinterpreted? I had to find out what Antony had been like at my stage. "Esteemed elder," I said, "laying my ears on the deck before you in seemly humility, I beseech you to tell me in what way, when you were but a man, your destiny appeared to you."

The saint looked at me curiously, then laughed and said, with some bitterness, "As if that destiny were complete! No, not yet, and I sometimes fear it never will be. I appreciate your interest. Hear then, pagan woman, my true unembellished history. Hear and repeat. Perhaps you and your people will some day be inspired to go forth and ransom me." "I am listening," I said.

"When but a simple friar, I began to cultivate the hope of becoming a holy martyr among the Moors. Hope bloomed into opportunity. A ship was found and I sailed forth from Portugal on my way to Carthagenia. But a tenacious fever forced me to turn back before my unshod feet had fair chance to try the burning sands of Africa. Beset by contrary winds, I ended that fateful voyage in Sicily—far from my homeland which I then vowed never more in mortal life to see.

"Chastened by the failure of my enterprise, I changed my mode of existence—became a scholar and strove to bend my soaring intellect to the Franciscan art of special compassion for the poor. My master, Francis! Even as he spoke words to all men, all beasts, to Sun and Moon, so I by emulation was eventually able to make the very fish leap to my harangue. I did not seek sainthood, no true saint ever does, but to me, by grace, was granted the privilege of holding the Holy Child in my arms. Centuries after His birth, He came to me (as you see Him now) and for this and other miracles, upon my death I was promoted to the highest spiritual rank our creed permits.

"Since then, my personality having been willfully misinterpreted, I have served generations of crusaders in a host of quasi-military capacities. But other functions have been found for me as well. And I most willingly attach myself to ships, hoping that a fair wind, conjured by my agency, may some day chance to waft me to the golden shores of Africa where I may at long last be put upon by the infidel and die if not a first, why then a second glorious death by scimitar.

"Preferring ships, I nevertheless do not object to that most modest (if most time-consuming) of all my patronates—lost things. In which capacity I may be able to be of some use to you one day. You have few possessions now, I realize, but once in the new world you too will doubtless begin, modestly at first, to accumulate things, and . . . Ah, that beautiful necklace you are wearing. However did you manage to salvage it? Should you ever lose that, you may—without further instruction in either faith or morals—pray to me for its recovery."

"Thank you, Father Antony," I said, "I salute you for having taken the pains to rewalk your most difficult path with me. And may the fair wind you seek enable both of us to reach our fated destinations. Now, I fear, I am forgetting my own responsibilities. I must see the children safely back lest, our absence noted, it be thought that we are not entirely abject, not even obedient, that we stay not within fixed limits. Soon they'll be bringing the kettles out. We must be in our places when it is time to eat."

Discreetly then, the saint retired behind his mask, and I drew Oro aside for a brief word. "Whether Antony likes it or not," I said, "we must provide our durable father with dog. He needs all the strength he can get to out-maneuver his antagonist, and besides, we must let him know what side we're on. Otherwise I fear the ship be doomed and all of us with it. Now come along with me. We two must have a little talk with our friend Batoques. Do you know, by any chance, if he's 'received' that knife of his? It would be best if he had, but under the circumstances one cannot afford to be too nice."

Shortly after four the sailors forced the men's dance to a halt. When everyone had consumed his allotted portion of beans and meal, with no sauce, with nothing hot to strengthen the blood, we all were herded down as usual. All gratings fastened down, hatches secured, the crew were issued a dram of rum each. Then, their proper seamen's quarters being occupied by our men, the sailors retired to the afterdeck where, under a tarpaulin thrown over the spanker boom, they dozed away the time until their dinner.

And while they dozed, we went to work—Batoques (chained as he was to his bench), Oro and I. We did not go below with the others. We hid in two of the cooper's casks until it was safe to come out. Fortunately for us there was a dog on board—the captain's mastiff. Had I not heard him barking down there in the great cabin, the thought of such an ambitious sacrifice would never have occurred to me. "It should not be difficult," Batoques said, "for the boy to slip down through the ventilating hatch. Already I have put a jinx upon the captain. Already he hesitates to set foot outside his cabin. One more stitch, one more twist, one more pinch and he'll not stir from his bunk till long after the storm is over."

No sooner said than done. Oro managed to get down, muzzle the dog and lead him hurriedly out along the companionway. That was just the beginning. From that time on, unbeknownst to any but ourselves, Oro had what you might call the run of the ship. But again, I anticipate. Batoques slit the dog's throat. It was my task to tie him to the mast, head down, while Oro stood guard at the fife rail. If St. Antony was displeased at the sight of that dog dangling before his very eyeballs, he did not show it but rather kept withdrawn. Resigned to misuse I suppose, he chose not to manifest himself; or perhaps the God of Iron had, at the first smell of blood, come down to evict him, poor Antony. At any rate, I had just finished winding the statue's head with a charmed circle of batting when Oro tugged at my skirt. "Na Agôtîme," he hissed, "drop down at once. The first mate has just come out on deck. He's walking this way. I think he's seen us." There was no time to be sure of this last. We slipped through the tangle of cordage on the other side of the mast and by the time Santos Lima discovered the sacrifice we had got ourselves safely down the rear hatch that led to the steerage, and thence to our respective shelves. At least that's where I went. I think Oro must have spent the night lurking along the passageway that connected the children's compartments to the gunroom. But he refused to incriminate himself—even to me.

One who excretes upon the path should not be surprised to see flies greet him as he returns home again. When the Thundering Man ran off with the God of Iron's wife, the High God said, "There's but one way to get her back, urinate on his head." "All things that happen here have happened in the sky before," a wise diviner I once knew was fond of saying. Give a god a nut and he'll uproot the tree. And so, and so on without end.

Two hours later the weather struck. From our vantage point three and a half feet below the halfdeck we heard that column of cold air attack the onrushing scud and then with renewed strength recoil to fang the *Incompreensível* from the northeast. The planks lurched beneath us throwing us hard against the beam while we strove to brace ourselves with the flat soles of our feet. Thunder shattered the night sky into outrageous rifts through which bolts of lightning were cast down upon the plunging ship like spears into the back of a stampeding animal. The Portuguese had made no material preparations for their invited wind and therefore the contemptuous *vodū* who commandeered a resting place in St. Antony's statue, in the perversity of his anger, did the work himself. It was horrifying to hear him hacking at the jib stays with his iron club, then at the lifts and braces of the upper yards, hollering forth upon the straining sails, flailing topsail tacks and halyards to the breaking point, and like an infuriated rodent with his great stone teeth chafing away at the unparcelled sheets. "Now let him come," the rabid Craftsman cried, "without the added triumph of resistance!"

And Xevioso heard. One crescent crack of flame spit forth from nimbus lips and the mainsail, already half-rotten in its slings, came crashing down upon the deck, followed by the main topmast.

Huddled below, knees clasped to chest, backs pressed to neighbor's knees, we heard, amid all the stench of fear, the whine of straining heartwood as the two great spars began to splinter deep in their shafts. And this was the moment Saliabsō chose to begin her labor.

What happened above decks after that was of no immediate concern to me. When mosquitoes are buzzing round one's ears one does not stoop to examine toes for ticks. I was entirely preoccupied with midwifery. Batoques told me something of what befell afterwards, and since it was Batoques who was promoted on account of having helped the second mate save the ship when the first mate was found to be missing, why should I assume his version of the storm to be incorrect? It was John Fellowes, the Englishman, who told the captain of Batoques' heroism, and John Fellowes was a sober, good-hearted man incapable of exaggeration.

What happened, apparently, was this. Cleaved free of his bench by a piece of falling iron, Batoques was at the wheel before the thunder struck. While the terrified crew cowered beneath their tarpaulin on the poop, together he and Fellowes took charge of the foundering ship. Leaving the cooper to do his best at the wheel, the second mate rushed to the waist to take care of the mainsail. Unable to clew her in, he let her go. He planned to cut loose the foresail next; but, freed from their fastenings, the gawky chain sheets flailed the main deck with such fury that Fellowes was forced to retreat. Throwing their combined strengths against the helm, the two then managed to bring her up to the wind only to have that malicious element, at the very moment of their success, shift two points to the east and catch the tethered foresail flat aback.

The foremast, miraculously, held; but the impact was too much for the flawed and battered mainmast to take. Just as a man's chief virtue may often prove to be the cause of his greatest distress, so the backstays braced to support her now conspired to bring her thundering down. As she stove, there came a final clap of thunder and a flying celt grazed Batoques' cheek. He flinched, lost grip of the wheel (which spun away from the second mate's hands) and the ship broached to. Rain came to swallow fire and the sea spewed across the deck in search of living victims while the fallen masts attacked the sides of the ship. She would have filled then and there, as she lay helpless on her beam ends, had not Batoques been inspired to rush, at his peril, down through the waist and up onto the forecastle deck. Pausing to stare at the capstan where—manacles dripping from his wrists like iron sea-weed, his wild hair turned white—Gbaguideguide, still alive, glared back at his antagonist. Batoques, taking hold of a stout piece of iron, slashed through the gears and set the foreyard free to swing. After which, clothed in water, sweating blood, he hauled in the forebrace. Not daring to look upon that suffering face again, Batoques gave the capstan a wide berth and hurried aft. Together he and Fellowes were able to heave the helm to larboard and the ship righted instantly.

Meanwhile, below in the steerage, we held fast to Sali's arms and legs, keeping her steady as we could so she'd breathe easily with the rising pains. Hour upon hour we chanted down there, praising Gu:

> Durable father of iron,
> You who can make or mar all things,
> Don't take your anger out on us.
> Captain of the boat,
> As the grass in the riverbed
> Blooms the year long,
> Spare the newborn child;
> As watercress floats above water,
> May you prevail against your enemies.

When the time came, it was I who received the head.

She was beautiful. Gleaming with slime, sleek-stemmed as a water lily I held her up for all to admire. "We will call her Alixossi [born on a voyage]," I cried and Saliabsõ smiled. Setting the baby down on a soft wad of oakum, I cried, "Now, mother, I'm going to cut her into life."

"No, no, do not sever us," Sali protested.

Five times the question was denied and then, the sixth, seventh and eighth times there was no answer so I took up the knife. Not an ordinary knife. No metal can be used at such a time for fear of incurring Gu's wrath. No, it was a perfect little wooden scalpel Batoques had whittled for the purpose. Having cut the cord, I knotted the baby's navel up with a bit of rope. When the placenta was born I wadded this up in a piece of old canvas. There was nothing to do but throw it overboard, but I hoped, in a few days, to be able to find a proper place to bury the dried umbilical.

Now I rubbed Alixossi's little body all over with cocoa-butter that one of the children had managed to steal from the cook's stores, then wrapped her up in a fine silk shirt another child had stolen from the laundry. Meanwhile Suuna, the Fulani girl, took care of the mother, sponged her off with wads of cotton batting soaked in brine, bandaged her and made her as comfortable as she could. After this was done, we all mopped up the floor, unrolled the grass mat that had been taken up for the occasion, and spread out sail patching as coverlet.

By the time the ship's doctor popped in to have a look at us, both mother and child were already fast asleep. He was, obviously, astonished. As soon as the worst of the storm was over, he had come below to see how many slaves had survived. "Well, this is a reassuring spectacle, indeed," he said with an amused and slightly sentimental smile, "is there anything I can do?" That I responded in Portuguese did not seem to surprise him at all. I imagine at that point he thought anything was possible. "No, doctor," I responded crisply, "we wouldn't dream of having a man attend us. If all things were as they ought to be, the baby ought to have mouth and throat moistened by an infusion of *akukomo* leaves. I don't suppose you have any of these in that bag of yours. However, I know there is plenty of corn in the ship's stores, and so for the mother here I prescribe a warm maize gruel."

"The fire is out in the galley," the doctor said, "and who knows when they will manage to get it lit; but I'll see what I can do. Anything else?"

"Like the chameleon, he walks softly, but he arrives. He will get Sali special foods," I said to the others in Fōgbe. Then to the doctor, "Please make sure we get a large bucket of water down here, sweet water, and since they probably won't be letting us above decks for a while, would you be kind enough to throw these rags overboard?"

The doctor daubed his forehead with a scented cloth, took the blood-sodden bundle and holding it gingerly at arm's length backed out of the steerage and kicked the door closed.

It took a long time to clear the top decks of debris, install a temporary mast, repair the rigging and bend spare sails to the task of getting us up to the island of São Tomé where the captain counted on refitting the disabled ship. For nine days we remained below decks; but there was fresh water to drink and maize gruel, as the doctor promised, and the baby thrived on Sali's milk and none of us, to speak the truth, were any worse than poorly. Not so the men in the hold. According to Oro, who occasionally paid us a sly visit, although all but six or seven had survived the terrors of the storm itself, more and more were dying every day from a vicious malady the Portuguese call the "bloody flux."

"From the look of things down there," said Oro, "from the smell, the saturated reek of it, I'd judge our stale-breathed, pox-covered, straw-maned, pestilential gourd-carrying god has climbed aboard with the others. There's water on the path down there, Na Agōtíme, and most of the men are lying in it."

"Oro," I said sharply, "be careful how you speak of Earth's favorite son. He is well known to me. My father is (or was) a chief priest of his cult. The men ought to perform a sacrifice. Now I'll tell you and you tell them what they must do."

Whether their bowels would have sealed themselves up again at the request of Sakpata or whether that long-sufferer planned to exterminate them all just to show everyone how strong he was, whether the sacrifice worked or not, none of these possibilities will ever be known, for on the ninth day the Portuguese doctor took matters into his own hands and ordered all the slaves brought up on deck for a great cleansing while the sailors, armed with swabs and buckets of hot tar, went below to fumigate the hold.

The steerage too, if the doctor had had his will, despite the fact that we had remained high and dry throughout the plague. "No slop buckets overturned in here," I said, "but cleanliness is like moderation, you can never have too much of it; therefore if you provide us with the proper means, we'd be only too glad to scour our own shelf. No men, though, and no tar—the fumes would kill the baby. No, she can't go out yet. Today she can be carried as far as the threshold of the companionway, only to return at once. Her introduction to the world must be gradual, no matter what sort of a world it is she's been born into." The doctor agreed, and when we had done our work, leaving Sali nursing the baby, the rest of us went above decks.

In my hand I clutched Alixossi's dried umbilical. No one can possibly appreciate the importance of his bottom until it grows a boil, nor of his feet until they get taken prisoner by a pair of ill-fitting Sunday shoes. What an old person sees sitting down, a young person standing up perforce ignores. So distraught was I with the thought of there being no proper palm beneath which to bury the baby's cord that I could neither stand nor sit. The mainmast would have to suffice, but what sort of rootedness would that ensure? Born on a voyage, voyage all your life, I thought. Well might that not be said of all of us, I thought. Sixteen voyages, if we are strong. Well, should not all things happen on earth as they happen in the sky? He who sits under a tree too long will grow grey from bird shit. Why *not* a moving tree then? I thought for the third time.

It should be easy, in the general confusion of the cleansing, to slip the cord behind the pikes about the base of the great mast unobserved by all save Antony. But there was Antony to be taken into account. What hope was there of enlisting his benevolence?

And not benevolence alone. If ever there were to be an indwelling tree spirit on shipboard, St. Antony would have to be he. Could I ask him to take on one more patronate, as he called them, play one more part for Sali and Alixossi and for me? Then I remembered what he had said about the conditions of the legendary life. "A Christian comes as he is called, pagan woman," he had said, and "I am now only that which men make of me." Very well then, it was worth trying.

"I greet you, Father Antony," said I, "for having withstood the ill-mannered incursions of our *vodŭ*. For forbearing to retaliate, or even to curb his excesses, I salute you." (I did not mention the sacrifice.) But he did not respond. His face, gnawed and polished by the storm, had lost all precision of expression. The tip of his sharp nose had broken off. His torch was gone. He was dangerously withdrawn and would not look at anything, even the horizon—his favorite spectacle.

"I greet you, Father Antony," I tried again, "for your endurance, the only sacrifice surely acceptable to our common creator. Tell me, how did you manage during the storm?"

"How did I manage indeed, pagan woman," the saint responded angrily. "I was not, as you remember, wholly unaware of the charged virulence of the atmosphere, but I felt bound to intercede on my friend Martinho's behalf for a breeze, a breeze which did verily, in accordance with my secret fear, provide those rival forces with just the impetus they needed. (That and the bloody dog—O devilish crucifixion, perverted paganism.) Now that Barbara should have then proceeded to wrest those gentle winds from my grasp, twist them into a tornado and hurl the results back at me and my ship was a humiliating, but alas not an uncommon experience. However, to have had to stand by helplessly while my self-styled heathen counterpart, the house-guest who moves in and throws the host out onto the street, to have had to stand by while he defied all weathers by getting the jump on them, and then to be forced to watch him all but destroy the ship

even before the storm hit, that was beyond the point of humilia-
tion."

"Forgive, forgive him, Father Antony," I said, "he was insane
with rage. As you yourself implied before, the Thunderer had
run off with his woman. Well, all's quiet now. Either he got her
back or he decided he was better off without her. Who knows?
But in the end he took hold and saved the ship, did he not? Drove
the storm away, did he not? We're still afloat, are we not? We
have triumphed over all our enemies—for the time being, at
least."

"Very well, pagan woman, what do you want of me? When
I lay fallen flat on my face beneath a tangle of ratlines and other
debris smashed to the deck by the falling mast, flat on my face
with that canine corpse polluting whatever air there was for me to
breathe, I swore never again to have anything to do with you. But
you convince me; you have (I won't ask how you got it) the
power to speak to me, to see me as I am. Ask any boon you
choose—on one condition: that you never forget me. Do this,
perpetuate the legend of the true Antony and I shall make you
an honorary patroness of lost things; not of objects, you have
little use for these, but of intangibles—memories, half-forgotten
tales, old prophecies, songs and sayings. Now, pagan woman, ask
what you will of me."

"Thank you, Father Antony," I said, "for being kind enough
to listen to what I now have to say. You lost your torch, snatched
out of your hand in the midst of the fray. But the child remains.
We too have a child. Down there in the steerage she sleeps in her
mother's arms. For the deliverance of this new life I hold you responsible. We have called her Alixossi and we've added a tutelary
namo, Afofo, after the wind. These names should please you. Your
little sister the wind, now you must shelter her. Guard well that
part of her she leaves behind at the base of this stout mast of
yours for it is her luck, her rainbow, her wealth, her part of the
Snake. Inhabit this tree from time to time, strengthen it, infuse it

with your force. Child-of-the-voyage she, see her safely out and home."

With this I slipped the umbilical cord behind the stanchions and, placing my hand upon the mast, consecrated it as best I could—may Loco-the-first-tree-in-the-world forgive the make-shifts of necessity!

> Be this, Alixossi-Afefe, your umbilical palm,
> Your deep rootedness;
> May no one ever discover
> What's hidden here,
> Lest harm come, lest harm come.
> May Antony the sailor's *vodū*
> Keep silent, lest harm come.
> May Antony, your inhabitant,
> Keep evil away.
>
> Tell me, shorn tree,
> What wealth have you
> To give Alixossi?
> Not palm nuts
> Not oil
> Not palm wine, certainly;
> But those bolts of white cloth
> Furled on your yardarms
> Will be blouses and underskirts
> Laced with foam
> Clouds of white linen
> Carried home from the stream
> High on her proud head,
> *Bahiana, Bahiana,*
> Child of the voyage,
> *Bahiana* to be,
> Born on the wind,
> *Bahiana.*

We spent the night that followed the great cleansing stretched out upon the decks. After feeding time, we women and children moved down to the waist while the crew went aft to their accustomed place. Batoques, now second mate, kept watch and spoke to us in our native languages. He had been born, so it turned out, in Whydah town and at an early age had got used to making himself understood in a variety of dialects. More importantly, we found out that once he, too, had been a slave like us.

His father, an important *caboceer*, had exchanged him to a Bahian slaver to cancel a gambling debt when he, Batoques, was only twelve years old. But once in Bahia, Batoques was fortunate enough to be bought by a sympathetic gentleman who apprenticed him to a barrel-maker. Working day and night he was eventually able to buy his freedom and become a master craftsman in his own right. Then his woman deserted him for another and, determined never to run the risk of seeing her again, Batoques shipped as cooper aboard the *Incompreensível*. Six passages were completed without incident, but one day, on the seventh voyage out, the captain suddenly ordered him chained to his bench on suspicion of plotting an insurrection. "What a fool I," Batoques said, "to think that such skill as mine could ever be countenanced in a black without the reassuring thought that I must be up to something. Well, I cursed the captain then and let him know that as soon as he loaded up the ship again I'd put a jinx on him. I told him that I knew far more about sailing a ship than he or any of his crew except the Englishman. I told him there is nothing that cannot be changed with the right word and the right leaf and that he would find it more and more dangerous for him to venture out of his cabin. I swore that when the first storm threatened the ship, I, by a dread hand, would be rived free and he, by that same hand, be made fast to his bunk from which he would not stir forth until I had been promoted to my proper rank. 'There's an unseen captain of this ship,' said I, squinting narrowly up at him, 'and you are not he.' "

Now it gradually became clear that the invisible captain had determined to put an end to our voyage as soon as possible. Batoques was delighted to announce that none of us would ever reach Brazil. Why subject ourselves to the indignities of customs house and market street, to the painful years of drudgery, to a cringing impoverished life when we had it in our own hands—the block of wood from which to carve out a free life? He had thought it all out. This was his plan:

We must bide our time until we were hard upon the island of São Tomé. The winds were favoring now, he said, and would continue to freshen as we completed our loop about the bight and hauled up to the line. Even the *Incompreensível*, rum ship and damaged as could be, could not fail to take advantage of the veering gusts and tides to cruise up easily along the windward side of the island. Why, in two days' time we should be able to see a mist-bound peak riding high on the horizon and know that we were but eighty leagues from liberty.

We would not be allowed on deck that final day, but as the ship coasted up towards her mooring at the protected end of the island, the men, at a signal from him, Batoques, would burst through the hatches (having previously weakened the grills) and overcome the crew while he would seize the helm and drive her onto the reefs. Then, still quite beyond the range of the guns on Point Nunez, the men would liberate the women and children, abandon ship and seek refuge among the wooded glens of the interior where we could live in impregnable *quilombos* [communities formed by generations of run-aways] in peace and dignity. In conclusion he admonished us all, especially the men, to glean what potential implements we could from the decks next day in the course of our seemingly apathetic exercise. Each one of you must see to it, he said, that beneath your freshly laundered rags you carry down concealed bits of iron surreptitiously torn from the forecastle door, odd nails, spikes and pump bolts—anything useful. Then tomorrow night you must appear to be holding a celebration. Sing, drum on the planks, and under cover of all this noise, file, file away at the gratings.

When Batoques had finished talking, one by one the men began to give their opinions of the scheme, to convert the forecastle deck into a village square, coiled ropes into woven mats, cleats into carved stools upon which the older and wiser sat, and the foremast into a protective shade tree, the ironwood of the market place.

I sat midships with the other women hanging my head like a banana leaf by the river, thinking. Everybody seemed to be agreeing, more or less. Indeed it was hard not to get carried away by Batoques talking. As his confident voice swept past islands of salient fact that none of us had ever seen, it accumulated such momentum of belief that no one doubted the sufficiency, let alone the existence of those *quilombos* on São Tomé. No one, it appeared, save me. Was it because I alone had the promise of a grander destiny to seal my ears and keep me sane? What, I wondered, would my Zomadonu say to all of this? It was my responsibility to find a *terreiro* for him in the new world. Over there, he had said, he'd be waiting for me, provided I got there first with a strong head. Would such a Toxosu be willing to settle for São Tomé? Strengthen my head as I might, would he even appear in such a place? Let alone take up residence? To descend like so much seabird dung on a rocky islet—what a comedown for my royal ancestors-in-law and their relatives! What a pity that my destiny should run contrary to that of Batoques and, presumably, of the rest. But what could I do—short of turning traitor? No, I would never betray anyone.

Then, without even pausing to knock, wisdom entered my head. I would go along. I would ride the adventure out and afterwards, perhaps, I could escape from the *quilombo,* get myself recaptured by the Portuguese—there, where the guns were, on Point Nunez, I thought—and take slave's passage on another ship. Of course! That was it. To what devious lengths would I not go to keep my pledge? Thank you, messenger, I mutely said, and I moved up close to the ladder so that I could plainly hear what the men were saying.

The only serious objection came from the famished lips of Gbaguideguide. His remarkable endurance of the storm on the open deck had made him every man's champion. Secretly everyone wished that it were he and not Batoques who would lead them through revolt to refuge on the island of São Tomé. But if this were not to be the case—no man dares kick the doctor until the doctor's healed him—at least the Calabash-smasher would have to be released from his irons in plenty of time to participate in the uprising. Batoques said nothing could be more easily arranged. He had the means, if not, strictly speaking, the authority. "No," said Gbaguideguide, "this will not do." It was the priest who was responsible for his situation and it would be the priest and the priest only who could release him. The Calabash-smasher then proceeded to disclose something which gave Batoques a bad moment, a very bad moment indeed. While Gbaguideguide was speaking I, sensing the hatred between them, watched Batoques carefully. If he takes out his knife and begins to pare his nails, I thought, it will mean he has betrayed the prisoner. And knowing that those who contain an excess of wrath in their heads are unable to bear treachery, are unable to bear even minimal unfairness, knew there would be bloodshed on the forecastle deck; but I anticipate. "I don't think this can be so easily arranged," said Gbaguideguide, "for the priest well knows my feelings, and so far he's done nothing. It seems he would rather have me die of starvation than yield. Well so be it. When the ship strikes the reefs you all shall go free, but I shall wait out my time. And when I am dead, misfortune shall settle upon the priest's back like flies upon a wounded animal. And the next time a storm strikes, whether he be upon the deck or not, he shall not survive. Next time the ship will burn."

"What does he mean, Batoques, about dying of starvation?"

someone asked. "We have been below, we don't know the situation. Have they been so cruel as to keep him bound to the capstan all this time without feeding him?"

Then Batoques had to divulge the truth or the Calabash-smasher would have contradicted him, part of the truth, at least. "They have tried to feed him, but he won't take any food. He told me to interpret him thus to the priest, 'I shall never eat, unless he frees me.' But rather than free him, the captain ordered the doctor to employ every instrument the whitemen have devised to force a man to eat. Ingenious pries, prongs and wedges—all have been inserted into his mouth; but when the soup or gruel was poured down, he invariably choked up everything. Eventually, the doctor stopped trying."

For nine days then, Gbaguideguide had gone without food, and yet for all his gaunt and grizzled look, he seemed strong as ever. His arms, the powerful muscles forming taut ridges on his chest looked as if they could uproot the capstan from the deck if he wanted them to. Try as he might—the strange thought occurred to me—Gbaguideguide would not die.

"I shall speak to the priest again," Batoques said, "perhaps this time he will be able to persuade the captain to relent."

Later on that night Batoques came to me and asked if I would intercede with Father Martinho on Gbaguideguide's behalf. "What would be more natural than for you to speak to him of your starving countryman? Of all of them you have most chance of success," he said. "Before the storm I used to watch him observing you, the way you talked to the children. Clearly, you fascinate him. Tell him you're a priestess, that'll put you on even footing. If I speak to him, he'll suspect something, some bond newly formed between myself and them."

"You mean he'll wonder why you have suddenly changed direction," I said, staring pointedly at him. "You were off your guard just now. I know you never interpreted Gbaguideguide to the priest. I am convinced you said the opposite, that the man was dangerous and ought on no account to be released. You your-self could have set him free the night of the storm instead of keeping him exposed. Your hatred of him runs very deep, doesn't it? And do you know, I think Gbaguideguide knows very well that you've betrayed him. But he won't denounce you. He'll let his fellows decide. He's thrown the whole matter to the winds. Now the pressure's on you. You won't let the revolt fail. And how odd to have the lot fall to me, to me who would rather, for obscure reasons of my own, go on to Brazil. For the sake of Gbaguideguide and the others, I'll speak to Father Martinho, al-though I'm not so confident as you that I'll be able to persuade him. I take it the captain will do as he advises in this matter. I understand from what you told me before that the captain is terrified of you. I suppose if I fail, you could appeal directly to him, force him to force Father Martinho, risky as that would be. Now if by any chance I should succeed, and if we make it to São Tomé, I must ask you to swear to help me when I need your ad-vice."

To all of which Batoques made no reply but continued to stare at me for a long time, as if a war were going on within him, a struggle involving fear, dislike, and astonishment.

The next morning I sought out Father Martinho. "I hope you are in good health, Father," I said, "for I have come to plead for one whose body is not well at all. The man chained to the capstan, the one we call the Calabash-smasher, has repeatedly said he will not eat unless you free him, and unless he begins to take food, you will have his death on your conscience. Even so, I should not presume thus to address you had I not had a long talk with St. Antony beforehand. The good saint says he fears you have for-gotten him. When the new mast was set in, some thoughtful sailor picked his damaged statue off the deck and tied it up where it had been before. But by all rights, St. Antony ought to be allowed to return to the cabin. He did summon forth a wind, but some force greater than his whipped that steady breeze of his into a tornado. Although the storm was not his fault, he says he is willing to be punished for it, to remain tied to the mainmast for the duration of the voyage if you will release my suffering fellow countryman from his torments. In short, St. Antony counsels mercy in the name of your high god and his, the All Compassionate, and that god's son, Lord of the Good End."

"So you've been speaking to St. Antony, my good woman," laughed Father Martinho. "And I, who had no idea you could even speak Portuguese, am supposed to believe that you have been privileged to receive a visitation of this amplitude? You're right, of course, in assuming the statue ought to go back; it's true that in all the confusion of the storm and its aftermath I had forgot to tend to this; but these things a clever woman like you could have figured out for yourself. What else did St. Antony say?"

"We've had more than one conversation, and he's told me many things—about sailing forth to Carthagenia, about holding a high post in the army, about his ability to speak to fish, and about other things as well that touch me more nearly."

"Very interesting," said the priest, "and he says he is willing to substitute himself for that pagan rebel on the capstan?"

"Yes, he is," said I, "for all his complaints, I think it fair to say that St. Antony enjoys suffering. My father, himself a priest, has or had a similar temperament, a similar vocation. Is not this one of your most esteemed virtues, this humility?"

"Christian ideas, all," Martinho laughed, "and how quickly you've caught on to them. You are a curious woman, a priestess in your own land perhaps? I understand you people worship fetishes. Perhaps sometime at your leisure you could explain some things to me—the sacred snakes in Whydah town, for example. Now that you have been baptized, it wouldn't hurt to give a few secrets away. You look doubtful. Well, we'll have lots of time to discuss these things. In the meanwhile, since you say his case is urgent, I'll speak to the captain about releasing the prisoner. You'll vouch for him? That blackman who used to be ship's cooper doesn't trust the man. Well, I for one don't trust Batoques. You say he insists that I release him with my own hands? Some pagan notion of honor, I suppose. And for me a salutary exercise in humility?"

The following day, not long after we'd been brought up on deck for our feeding, Father Martinho emerged from the companionway carrying a silver cup upon a silver plate. Glancing up at the binnacle he motioned me to fall in behind him. The puzzled sailors stepped out of the way to let us pass along the waist to the forecastle deck. Halting before the capstan, the priest asked the first mate, Mr. Fellowes, where Batoques was. "Aloft, sir, with three men of his watch, taking in the foretops'l; shall I call him down, sir?" "By no means," replied the priest, "I shall no longer require him as interpreter to the slaves. This woman speaks excellent Portuguese. I merely wanted to make sure he would not interfere with the proceedings." "How strange," said Mr. Fellowes, directing a questioning look at me.

Then the priest took a deep breath and said, "I understand that you whom your friends call the Calabash-smasher have refused these eleven days to eat—why you did not refuse before the storm hit is anyone's guess. Presumably you made some sort of vow during the fury of the blast that if spared, you would rededicate yourself to your own principles. You consider your punishment unjust. I suppose from your point of view it is. But from my vantage point, look what you did—profaned a holy sacrament, defiled a priest. What would you have done if I'd stepped on one of your blessed snakes?" He paused to let me translate.

"Such pride as yours betokens noble birth," Father Martinho continued; "you are perhaps a banished chief, or king. However, what you once were is no affair of ours. It was not we who de-

graded you, but your own people. You were misfortune's slave
ere you were ours. However, what you are now is our affair.
What sort of example does your obduracy provide? You have
set yourself up as an obstacle, a regular Cape of Storms. We tried
our best to round you, now we must fall off. As a pagan slave
you can have no claim to Christian clemency, yet we shall provide
for the lost sheep even though he be a wild ram. Such is the nature of our creed and we shall be true to it no matter what the
price. There is one condition, however, upon which I insist. And
surely you yourself would wish to end your fast with some
ceremony. I say you must take your first food in Christian fellow-
ship with me here in the sight of all. I have prepared the fare,
but you must have your freedom first. Fellowes, unhitch the
man!"

The first mate unlocked Gbaguideguide's chains and helped
him to his feet. Meanwhile the priest spread out a small white
cloth upon the planks on top of which he placed the cup and
plate. Then he sat down upon his knees and indicated that the
Calabash-smasher was to do the same. With this direction the
tortured man complied. Then Father Martinho bit into the biscuit
and drained half the cup of wine, again indicating that his guest
was to do the same. There fell a silence so thick it clogged the
nostrils. All our people pressed forward, straining to see what
would happen next. I alone stepped back. When he saw that
Gbaguideguide did not respond, Father Martinho became red in
the face and said, under his breath. "If that pagan devil denies me
a second time, I'll have him thrown to the sharks." "Don't translate that," the first mate whispered, drawing back by my side,
"rather ask him if he has any objection, what it is he'd like to
say." Knowing Gbaguideguide to be the most silent of men, I
hesitated; but he surprised me by speaking up without urging.
"Tell that rotten head," he said to me, "tell that broken chamber pot, that this is how the dead eat." And so saying he clapped
his hands three times in the air above his head. Then, seizing the

cup, Gbaguideguide poured the contents out upon the deck, saying, "And that this is how the dead drink."

With this both men leapt to their feet and stood facing each other, their glances locked in an inexpressible rage. Then Gbaguideguide contemptuously turned his back and sprang upon the capstan. There he stood, smoldering inwardly, staring upwards at an unseen tower of wind. Martinho mopped his brow with his sleeve and glanced wildly around the bows as if uncertain what to do next. But if a man hesitate in a crisis, events will rush in to fill up his empty head; and in this case the entire slave population of the *Incompreensível* decided the priest's fate for him. In a mass they swarmed upon him—from every direction, from ladderway and cathead, from starboard and larboard sides of the deck; and those who were closest raised him high above their shoulders and heaved him from hands to upstretched hands across to the bulwarks and over the edge.

"Man overboard," John Fellowes cried. Ropes uncoiled and struck the air. A few sailors raced to the longboat. But the slaves, sensing it was now or never, picked up belaying pins, their feeding pannikins, whatever they could get their hands on and began to wield them, bashing the sailors and, in some cases, their own people on the head. The wisest of the sailors swung like so many monkeys into the main shrouds. I looked up and saw that Batoques was missing from his perch on the yardarm. He must somehow or other have managed to slip aft to grab the wheel. There was nothing to be seen on the horizon; a stubborn fog bank had moved in blotting freedom out. The first mate had also disappeared but minutes later he emerged again on deck toting a case of pistols which one by one he threw up to the sailors, exhorting them to "Fire over their heads. Frighten the living tar out of their seams, but don't kill 'em, by my honor don't kill 'em."

A few shots and our revolt was over. The beginning was not as we had so carefully planned it, that night after the great

cleansing, nor was the end. But once a palm tree begins to burgeon with fruit, it is useless to tell him that it's the wrong season.
In a race for harvest, if the birds win, then we cannot blame the
fruits for not attaching themselves more securely. Most of our
people fell flat on the decks. A few jumped overboard, hoping
thus, if the fabled island be forever barred to them, to have their
dead souls washed up upon the shores of their hospitable homeland.

When the smoke cleared, but three of us remained standing
on deck: Gbaguideguide, immobile as an image on the capstan,
myself and the Englishman. Now it was John Fellowes who was
undecided. Once loosed, the Calabash-smasher ought not to be
tied again, but on the other hand, how long would he stand there
like that? And wouldn't he provide the rest of them . . . ?" But
again fate, this time in the form of Batoques, rushed in to fill the
vat. Rushing up the ladderway, Batoques cried, "Don't fire, don't
do anything; leave that man to me."

Once the fight had started, it was impossible to intervene.
Gbaguideguide, sensing his great rival come to do battle with
him at last, swung around, jumped down and measured Batoques
squarely as if, once again, the deck were village soil beneath his
feet. Fire and iron, they fought as gods fight only when a river
goddess is at stake; and standing by the cathead with Mr. Fellowes, I saw Batoques kilted in the feathers of seven birds and
Gbaguideguide with a double axe sprouting from his head. They
fought for more than an hour before eleven days of starvation
at last began to tell on the body of the Calabash-smasher. Pressing his advantage now, the wiry Batoques executed a series of
maneuvers with feet that had learned to dance *capoeira* to a con-
traband Angolan beat in Salvador. The Calabash-smasher tripped
backwards, hit his head on a crankshaft, and was still.

Batoques then rushed up to me and said, "Turn the cooking
pots and water jars upside down when they are empty. Press
them close to the parched ground in the name of Gbaguideguide.

You, daughter of disorder, go in peace where your path leads. I leave alone to realize my plan. For whatever the bravery of a man, the time finally comes when he must find a place." Then to Fellowes he added in Portuguese, "Soon all rampant forces shall have quit this ship or, rather, shall remain, but in a quiescent state, not to be provoked again. Let there be tedium, my honest English friend, and a modicum of discipline; for when you hit the southeast trades, the ship will all but sail herself. Mine is the last to quit. And when I leave, tell the captain he may come up on deck with impunity to take command in deed." Then, again trusting the first mate not to fire, Batoques jumped up upon the bows, dove off and began to swim.

There was a startled cry from the stern. I knew at once what had happened. Oro, the Nago boy, had dived off in pursuit of Batoques. And for the first and only time during the voyage, I put my hands to my face and wept.

An hour later the fog began to lift. There was the mountain. We were in full sight of São Tomé. The heads of the swimmers had disappeared. And so had the body of Gbaguideguide.

The island of São Tomé exists, little Luiz. To the extreme south of the Gulf of Guinea, it lies but seven minutes north of the line that divides this great calabash upon which we live into two hemispheres. Yes, the island of São Tomé exists, one hundred and fifty miles distant from Cape Lopo Goncalves and São João on the African shore and about two thousand, five hundred miles from Brazil. When you are well you must take out your map, the one the white fathers gave to you, and look for it. The slave ship *Incompreensível* came to anchor in the gusty roads beyond the shallow bay called Anna de Chavez which lies on the north side of the island between the paws of the fortified headlands São Sebastião and Diego Munez. Here we put in for repairs.

While the sailors, under the direction of John Fellowes, worked on the ship with new tools and fittings purchased from the governor's chandlery, we all were removed to the mainland. What a relief. We were housed on the ground floor of a spacious villa belonging to a widow named Senhora Ke-ke, herself a former slave who had the good fortune to marry a retired Portuguese naval officer from whom she inherited a good deal of property. She, slave though she'd been, owned several of our people who fed us well and guarded us well too, for none of the men, despite their hopes, were able to escape to a *quilombo*. When the work on the ship was done, we were ferried back in longboats, together with a new supply of yams.

We left São Tomé in the middle of March and two days later Fellowes pointed out the dim ridge of Cape Lopez to us. "Mr. Fellowes," said I, "I appreciate your thoughtfulness, but we have already taken leave of our native lands and not only that, we already carry with us calabashes full of all of Africa that we shall ever need to sustain us in our adversity." He looked perplexed, then smiled that embarrassed smile of his, his well-meaning smile, gate-keeper of his ignorance.

"Look," cried one of the children suddenly, "there's a fish that flies—one of Sun's children, Na Agótĭme, trying to get home again. See, its belly is whiter than foam, but on its back it carries streaks of sky-blue memories."

"Watch, here comes another one!" Suuna the Fulani girl said, "and another!"

"*Hue-vi*," chanted the children, delightedly, "the fish are quitting the sea. "*Hue-vi*, the fish are quitting the sea. Na Agótĭme, you told us false. They are returning!"

Within minutes a score of these remarkable creatures had managed to attain the ship's deck where, horror of horrors, the waiting sailors began to grab them, hack off their lovely translucent wings and gut them as they squirmed. "Who are these flying fish, Mr. Fellowes?" I asked him.

"I know no other name for them," he replied, "but a more wretched creature never lived. Striving to fly, which if it be fortunate enough to avoid sea hawks it may do so long as moisture remains in its wings, it plunges back into the sea only to fall victim to its watery enemy the dorado fish; or, if it manages to fall upon the deck of a ship, a comparable end awaits on account of its succulent meat. The flying fish is a creature of the middle passage, betwixt and between. This is its fate.

"Banished by nature from all elements," he went on, warming to his subject, talking freely for the first and only time during the voyage, "its brief span of flesh finding no refuge upon earth, sea, or air, this creature speaks wondrous mysteries to me. In him I see myself, a sailor, cut off from his native land by some restless urge that will not permit him to return and settle down, calling all ports home, all chance acquaintance friends, beset continually by lee shores, adverse winds, rough seas and those rougher passions within that molest, coerce and will not let him be.

"I had no wish to serve aboard a slave ship," he concluded, "but because like all sailors I occasionally forget my loneliness in drink, I was defenseless, *panyarred* one night in the back room of a Bahian place, of ill-repute I guess, by that blackguard—may he rest in peace—Santos Lima and a gang of henchmen. Kidnapped because of my "nautical competence"—supposedly common to all British tars. Well, I swear now that if I ever do get back to England, I'll fan that inner light that burns in me and join the abolitionists."

"Mr. Fellowes," I said, looking him straight in the eye, "I believe and you know very well that there is just about as much chance of your getting back to England as me to Africa. We all have many voyages to make before we're done. Sixteen, by our reckoning. And who knows which we're on? But hush, listen children, lay down your tender ears upon this blood-bespattered deck . . ."

And do you know what it was I heard?—St. Antony preaching to the flying fish.

Thus Agõtĭme concluded the story of her middle passage, recounted to Luiz Braga one night as he lay sick in his *hamac* with a touch of malaria in the year 1817 or thereabouts. She told him that when he grew up he must write a great poem in Portuguese about everything that happened on the *Incompreensível*. She had but given him the ingredients, she said, and it was up to him, who would be a lettered man, to provide a proper form.

Several times in later life he attempted it, but never finished. Among his papers in the archives of the university he once attended, there exists the fragment of an epic *O Tumbeiro* [the slave ship], which begins:

"Ceuta's gates are barred. Across the strait, Lusitanian armor rusts behind oaken doors; grandiloquence warps into peevish wit; and on the headland of Sagres, overgrown with brambled tamarisk, the ghost of the Navigator strains for a sight of his returning ships. But in vain, for the castled caravels have diminished into floating coffins and Fonseca, Guimaraes, and Oliveira—heritors of de Gama, Albuquerque and Diaz—have gone to ferry lost souls across a briny Styx to the blessed canefields on the other side. . . ."

three   BRAZIL

When the *vodū* descend
Some like certain cosmic forces
    of destruction and terror,
Others like somberness,
    silence and peace.
When the *vodū* descend
They do so heedless of the will
    of novices or mother.
          —*Nunes Pereira*

8 ▶▶ The Big House

Sheltered between the flanks of Itaparica and a peninsula of the main, nourished by the sweet waters of six Indian rivers, the Bay of All Saints languidly stretches its feelers to the sea. Coming up from the south, one sees the land, low and muted green, against a monotonous horizon nicked only by occasional clumps of coco-palm. Then, all of a sudden, the harbor widens. The ruddy sails of a hundred rough-hewn sailing vessels, polacre-rigged, come into view and St. Antony's promontory rises abruptly, as if from bended knee, to display the domes and towers of the discovered city: Salvador, city of all saints and sins, a covenant with three continents made of two ribands of white stucco with a layer of green foliage crammed between.

A shot fired from the promontory was repeated at the Forta do Mar, an ancient bastion squatting offshore from the quays; and a crimson pennant exploded above the turret-top to welcome the *Incompreensível*, a brigantine. She dropped anchor and in a matter of minutes half a dozen launches arrived to conduct in-quiries. No foreigners were permitted to trade in Salvador–Bahia and the presence of an English captain without proper papers was cause for grave suspicion; but Sequeira Lima, promptly notified, came down to identify the ship and secure proper berthing privileges, to listen to several eyewitness accounts of the calamitous events off São Tomé, and, with cynical forbearance, to believe. It was a risky business. He hoped the sale of the cargo would offset the enormous cost of the repairs.

Once matters were finally settled (it took two days), the hatches were opened and the slaves got out upon the decks to await transportation to shore by Sequeira Lima's hired boatmen. These proved to be as black as their passengers, but far from wearing rags they were splendidly dressed: top hats pushed back to the hairline, striped jerseys worn like tunics over canvas britches rolled to the knee. They wore gold earrings, and on the sternboard of each canoe rode a goldfinch or a parakeet in a wicker cage.

The docks were jammed with broad-beamed small craft, *saveiros*. Itinerant greengrocers from the inlets of Itaparica and the farthest reaches of the bay were busily unloading their produce, stepping cautiously from deck to deck, the huge familiar baskets on their heads heaped lavishly with bananas, melons, mangoes, cocos, tomatoes and genipaps. The tall bowed masts of their ships froze the confusion of loads and carriers on the cobblestone quays to the linear array of warehouses, shops and arcades behind, and by forcing the eye upward to the stucco houses that faced the green path-scarred steep, gave an apparent unity to an otherwise incoherent scene.

The canoe sidled up to the slimy steps of the landing place. The first gang of slaves was hauled out onto the quay. A crush of curious, half-sympathetic onlookers broke across Agõtíme's consciousness like a wave, leaving her naked and ashamed.

The slaves were herded onto an open portico in front of the customs house to be examined for infectious diseases. This done, still chained in small groups, they were led indoors to be inventoried—sex, approximate age and origin noted.

Five slaveships, newly arrived in the harbor, had been gradually unloading since dawn, and the floor of the customs house was, as a consequence, a frightful confusion of scrawny-limbed, red-eyed fear. Above them all a corpulent dealer from the interior paced up and down—arms folded across his leather poncho, broad felt hat dipping to greet the moustache on his swarthy face, a bullwhip, whisk of his office, gripped in his jewelled right hand. Various pale-complexioned gentlemen occasionally arose from a long table which extended the length of the rear wall. Hanging over the table, in identical gilt frames, were portraits of Iphegenia and Benedito, the black saints. Picking their way through the black flesh on the floor, these gentlemen finally emerged in the open air market where they conversed and enjoyed their cigars. Beside the door at a high desk in a corner a one-armed scribe wrote uninterruptedly, despite the squawks of a caged bird suspended directly overhead.

In the corner opposite the clerk's perch stood a curious statue apparently intended to portray the victim rather than the master of the hunt. A score of real arrows, brilliant blue and green, impaled his bare wooden chest to the wall. His upcast eyes stared vacantly at the distant ceiling. He who shakes a great tree, shakes himself, thought Agōtíme; his imprecations brought him shafted rain.

Here and there about the hall, charcoal braziers had been placed to burn incense against that devil of a stench that pervaded everything. Agōtíme observed a small boy about Oro's age take a sooty stick from one of these and begin, with a sure hand, to record his experience. He had almost completed an intricate cross-section of a slaveship, drawn in such a way as to make the tiny men seem like seeds strung in concentric necklaces, when a guard noticed and with a quick cuff sent him whimpering back to his place.

The municipal market was adjacent to the customs house, but Sequeira Lima's wealth and position entitled him to display his wares in front of his own residence in the upper town. Therefore, his unloading done, the trader eased into one of the ornately carved and curtained chairs parked amid a host of liveried porters in front of the Alfandaga. Two stalwarts easily lifted this ark aloft and his several chained lots followed behind, like tattered penitents, past the dismal arcade where those of less desirable consignment lay hour after hour in their own filth, swatting flies and chewing ragged sugar cane.

Wading through a mash of vegetable debris left to rot on the cobbles from one day to the next, the procession cut across the square until forced to halt while a gang of carriers, called *ganhadores*, ran a succession of immense casks, slung between shouldered poles, down to the landing. They were dressed in brilliant toques and voluminous pantaloons. Two small boys with tambourines ran along beside and as the carriers ran they exhaled in measured tones that were deep enough to be scarcely audible, yet unmistakably African. More *ganhadores*, single runners, bearing bales or cases on their backs, tortoise fashion, followed after these. When all had gone by, Sequeira Lima's porters picked up their relatively modest burden and moved on across the square, then up one of the numerous alleyways that lead into the Rua da Praia, the only street to run the length of the lower city.

The uphill side of the Rua da Praia was banked by a solid row of warehouses where *ganhadores* sat plaiting straw or simply sleeping before the cavernous entrances. Along one warehouse wall a row of immaculate Bahianas sat on low stools selling trays of *acarajé* or *abará* cakes. Their lace blouses gleamed white against the dingy grey cement; their turbans flared; and shawls of blue-and-white-striped African cloth were folded across their shoulders, falling severely as if to temper the extravagance of their multicolored skirts. Such opulent dignity (those golden chains, those numerous strings of shells and beads)—were they still slaves?

On the other side of the street, under tile-roofed arcades,

Bahia's artisans—metalworkers, weavers, jewelers, potters and Muslim sandal-makers—plied trades and displayed wares. And wedged between all these stalls, wherever there was space, vendors of fried fish, cured meats, palm oil and sugar cakes sang out their wares behind woven trays balanced on crates. Even the animal kingdom, Agõtĩme was amused to see, flourished uncurtailed along this fabulous commercial street. Down the center an evil-smelling sewer ran and here pig wallowed, dog foraged, goat browsed and rooster strutted—all apparently unperturbed by the dismal omnipresence of vulture.

The coffle turned off the Rua da Praia and began to climb the hill to the upper city. The *ladeira* was steep and slippery from last night's rain, the slaves scanter of breath and strength than they had realized. Edging along the outer bank, toes feeling for protuberances in the clay, fingers groping for firm grass clods or reliable creepers, they were astonished at the facility of the porter's ascent with Sequeira Lima's chair, and at the grace of the local inhabitants who climbed quickly past while balancing baskets of foodstuffs from the quayside market.

As the *ladeira* narrowed to zigzag across a treacherous ravine, descending pedestrians had to halt at each bend to let the caravan pass; and at one of these corners Agõtĩme beheld a frightening mask of perforated metal, cone-shaped, like a dog's muzzle or the snout of some monstrous wild pig, a mask which completely obscured the features of its owner who, to judge from the rest of her, was a wretched young girl of fifteen or sixteen. "*Nila, nila*," Agõtĩme muttered, and then, unable to resist asking their guard in Portuguese, "Is it the white sickness [leprosy]? Do they have that calamitous malady over here?"

"No, woman from the coast," he answered, "that unfortunate wears the whiteman's cure for the earth-eating disease. Some out of desperation try to return home that way. See that you be not one of them. There are better methods."

"Yes . . . ?" But the guard had turned his back and walked on ahead. As the coffle rounded the bend, Agōtīme saw the sun gleam for a moment on his metal arm band.

In front of the slave dealer's townhouse, they were fed black beans garnished with parched manioc powder from cauldrons set down in the middle of the street. After their meal they were told to bathe in the neighborhood fountain directly opposite, where a steady trickle of spring water from the grimacing lips of a stone chimera mixed with frequent rains to fill a basin so large you could wade in it. Wax drippings all along the rim bore witness to the fact that candles were occasionally lit here. For what purpose? Who cared? Agōtīme took scant notice of them. What went on at night was not yet her affair. Nor could it be; for having been issued clean cloths, they were all locked into the storerooms and stables on the ground floor of the townhouse to sleep.

The following day being the Feast of Corpus Christi, no human flesh could be bought or sold. The Africans understood it to be a day devoted to the worship of one of the European saints and saw nothing odd in the postponement. They too observed closed market days. And what, after such a voyage, was one day more or less? It was a relief simply to be able to stretch out on good firm ground again.

In the sky, bright pieces of paper danced on strings. Agōtīme shielded her eyes to watch them nervously search out air currents. Occasionally their flat masklike faces nodded, dipping down upon slackened strings to approach an elusive partner or, at other times, like experienced if bodiless wrestlers, they would suddenly swerve sidewise in an attempt to cut rivals off their tetherings. She later learned that the kite-strings were maliciously serrated with a mixture of ground glass and resin, but this first day she knew only what she saw: that the calabash of the sky brimmed with the gaudy red and green ephemera of a Bra-

zilian holiday, while the ever-circling vultures discreetly kept their distance.

Bell-laughter broke the stillness, and moments later a procession issued forth from the blue-painted face of the church at the end of the street.

> *Pange, lingua, gloriosi*
> *Corporis mysterium. . . .*

The slaves jumped up and stood well back along Sequeira Lima's wall to let them pass.

Borne aloft on a flower-strewn platform St. George enjoyed the full impact of the sun upon his shining armor. This was his annual outing and he made the most of the occasion. On his head was a plumed helmet of real steel; his frilled tippet was fine cambric; his red tunic and black leggings rivaled those of a king; but his corslet and anklets were, if the truth be known, only painted pasteboard. The horse beneath him seemed to sweat blood from its painted flanks and the dozen gentlemen bearing the litter shared his vindictive splendor as they sang:

> *Et antiquum documentum*
> *Novo cedat ritui . . .*

Among the ranks of the black men who followed after, Agõtíme recognized Sequeira Lima's overseer whose iron bracelet now shone with a different luster: a token piece of the warrior's armor, it seemed. Surely Gu would prefer this splendid cavalier to that worm-ridden dreamer. She would like to find out if, in Bahia, there were any shrines for Antony.

Senhorinha Prequiçosa sat side-saddle in her *hamac* fretting over the difficult minor chords of the latest *modinha*. As her index finger pressed two strings stubbornly to the bar, beads of perspiration broke out upon her nose and forehead. She persisted, stretching her little finger down for the final positioning.

She was thirteen, and to her parents' knowledge had never spoken to a man. Had she not been adept at deciphering handwritten verses whose vocabularies consisted of words like *suspiro, morrer* and *coração*, she might have been called illiterate—were this not entirely too harsh to say of one whose soft pale cheeks, luminous dark eyes and auburn hair entitled her to read *beldade* from the glass which took all her attention when she was not occupied with her music. Esperança, Felicidade, Suuna, and even Agōtīme took turns embroidering shifts for her, helping her to dress, and keeping her fine hair free of lice and snarls. Her father, whom she adored, made all decisions for her; and her mother, Dona Maria das Dores, whom she disliked, indulged all her whims. Her brother, Raimundo, injected a certain life into her by teasing:

"After such binges of voluptuous modulation, little sister, you ought to sober up with a stiff dose of liturgical chant. But I fear you are not to be trusted out of the house, even to go to Mass. Who knows? Some waxen-faced young seminarian might catch your eye, write a languishing *modinha* in celebration of your forbidden charms and the whole dreadful business would be reenacted right here in our midst. If such be reality, we are better off as we are. But the boredom, the boredom, the boredom—a French disease whose symptoms work worse havoc on the mind than [his mother gasped] . . . Oh well, tell us a story, Agōtīme!"

"In Africa, young master," she said archly, "we tell stories only at night."

Dona Maria of the Pangs refrained from chiding that impossible creature for her impertinence only because she wished to avoid the inevitable argument with her son.

"You say it's out of deference to the spirits, but I say it's because in Africa everyone works in the daytime," laughed Raimundo. "Here we turn day into night, Agōtīme, at least as far as our women are concerned we do. What unhealthy lives we mushrooms lead! It's a wonder you three don't become as puffy and pale as we are. If I had my way I'd rip all this latticework from the windows and pull reason in by the tail."

Dona Maria clutched at the heavy gold cross she wore at all times about her neck even when, as now, she was clad in nothing but chemise and petticoat. "It was a mistake, my son, to send you off to be educated in France."

"What nonsense, Mamãe, it was just a trip; I wasn't educated at all. Look, here I am right where I began, my head in your lap. Like a good boy I keep still and let you groom my hair. What nonsense," he went on, unable as usual to stop talking, "that's the trouble with us provincials—every one of us not only moribund but infantile, stuffed with sweets and swung in our *hamacs* until we are, technically speaking, men. Now don't be offended, Mamãe, I'm really no different from anyone else. What profit my so-called enlightenment? You daub scent on my philosophical brow and I love it. Ah, is not home after all the best? All right then, if you won't tell us a story, Agõtíme, we might as well listen to Prequiçosa sing. And do not sing that one again. It raises the hair on my head like grass over a grave-site. Those fashionable bourgeois *cadenzas;* all that tasteless ornamentation. Simplicity, that's what I crave. Sing me . . . no, no, not the one composed by that obsequious confessor of yours, Mamãe; forgive me, but that's not the sort of simplicity I mean. Sing me the one that begins mi, mi, do."

Agõtíme knew the song he meant. Although most of the feelings expressed by those mournful praises of nothing could not have been more alien to her, there was one song that had a kind of magic capable of evoking real memories of unreal places —memories that she supposed were but longings intensified into *tovodũ, aivodũ, atĩmevodũ* [spirits of the waters, of the soil, of the trees], custodians of the homesick imagination. All the rest were, as Raimundo said, vulgar and, she would add, inanimate. Or was it only that this special song had succeeded in insinuating itself into her private world she'd thought closed to all like intrusions and that others would follow and infect her blood, so attenuate her strength that eventually, though black-skinned and handsome as ever, inside she would be scarcely distinguishable from a colonial Portuguese?

> What nights I spend here
> Cloaked in meditation
> On this cliff by the sea.
> What nights seize me here!
>
> Rainfall. Rivulets
> Run down humid hovels
> On the beach, where widows
> Are moaning. Listen.
>
> Clouds shift. On summits
> The moon silvers again.
> How fate has shifted since
> I began to sing.
>
> *Saudade* for earth,
> For childhood's backcountry,
> *Saudade* for those loved
> And now lost to me.
>
> *Saudade* forest,
> Flush of hidden voices,
> *Saudade* paths, sources,
> *Saudade flores.*
>
> What nights I spend here
> Upon these palisades
> Of weary endurance,
> What dark thoughts seize me!

"Why look at Agōtĭme's face," said Raimundo, "you have at last succeeded, little sister, in moving someone to the point of tears. Ah *saudade*, to have given voice to a universal human emotion, our poets . . ."

"But my son, I must correct you," said Dona Maria das Dores, "you seem to have forgotten that the custodians of our language have given us a special word for the morbid yearnings of the black people. Why not, when the occasion warrants, be more precise? It is not *saudade* Agõtĩme feels, but *banzo*. Now I beg you, my daughter, to put by your instrument for a while. You can't imagine how trying that continuous noise can be."

It was the hour when Dona Maria's migraine bloomed and so, with a final piteous gaze at her son, she retired to take a nap. Suuna obediently followed. (The Fulani girl had been purchased, on account of her youth and unusually aquiline features, to be the Senhora's personal maid. Saliabsõ and the baby had, regrettably, gone to another household.)

There was the sound of angry voices, the banging of an ambry and then the smack of a practiced hand, followed by a series of moans—indications to the present company that Suuna had scorched, or misplaced, or perhaps even broken something again. No one in the front room said anything. Raimundo pulled on his boots, his jacket, and went outside. Prequiçosa, in defiance of her mother's wishes, again took up her guitar. Esperança and Felicidade bent their turbaned heads over their embroidery hoops. Agõtĩme stood up. Taking a large handful of parched corn from the woven tray by her side, she threw them into the tall cylindrical mortar, raised the ironwood pestle, and began to pulverize.

Time flies on, unlike a bird, without ever resting. Things had not turned out as she had expected. Zomadonu had not appeared. There had been no sign. Cargo from Whydah continued to come to the quayside, but the new arrivals brought no word of her son. He was still, apparently, in hiding. Could not the hunter have managed to get through to her? Again, no word, no sign. Occasionally, on holidays, instead of going down to the lower city, she walked out to St. Antony's church on the promontory.

She was afraid of losing her mind. That was something he wouldn't be able to recover. She had begun to attend a certain *candomblé* on Saturday nights. Like most of them, it was dominated by Nagos. Should she ask to become initiated? But as whose daughter? Zomadonu's? No one had ever heard of that *orisha*. But if he should descend to possess her, surely that would be all right. What unpropitiated force, what Malevolence prevented it? As she pounded, her own head began to ache with the "dark thoughts" of Prequiçosa's song. At least, she reflected bitterly, she now knew what to call them—not *saudade*, but *banzo*, which meant *saudade* without hope, life—annihilating *saudade*.

9 ◤◢ Candomblé

Evening, the twenty-ninth of June, and again the sky above the city of Salvador was graced with fire balloons.

Agõtĭme, woven tray balanced upon turbaned head, deftly mounted the *ladeira* to the upper city. At the top of the hill she paused for a moment to let the sweet breeze fan her and to watch the stately progress of a company of paper luminaries on their way to extinguish themselves among the advancing stars.

She did not turn right along the road to Vitoria, but continued straight on across the Praça where sets were already forming to dance quadrilles in the diffused light of two hundred Chinese lanterns donated by the Municipal Council. A brusque hand on her shoulder startled her. It was Raimundo. "Good evening, Mãe Agõtĭme, where are you off to now?"

"To sing a *ladainha* to Saints Peter and Paul, young master," she replied promptly, "I've been busy since before dawn and have not yet had time."

"Two little birds on the Roman Wall," he broke in,
"One named Peter, the other named Paul;

"Fly away, Peter, fly away, Paul—
"Come back, saints, your heads have fallen."

She smiled quizzically, excused herself and hurried on, wondering what he meant and how much he knew. Was that cryptic song supposed to be a trap, or a warning? The *terreiro* had been raided during the Feast of Corpus Christi just a few weeks before, but no arms could be found anywhere in the *barraçaõ* nor in any of the adjacent shrines, so the police had contented themselves with lashing the drummers for disturbing the peace. That was all. They had not returned. But she knew the Mãe-de-Santo was considering a move which would place her even farther from the center of the city. Agõtīme thought Raimundo was probably insinuating more than he knew, and that this, like all his past efforts to draw her out, was grounded in idle curiosity, but one could not be too careful. Those who know least are apt to reveal the most. Raimundo, obviously, assumed her to be a powerful force in the clandestine black world for which the cults with their ambiguous saints, double-faced, provided protective portals. How surprised he'd be to learn how peripheral her involvement—up till now. She was still not an initiate, only a regular visitor, an empathetic participant. Nor did she aspire to the kind of knowledge he assumed her reticence hid. Not that she was disinterested. What she knew of their politics in a vague way excited her. The possibility of a grand retribution for day after day of drear indignity made her own stifled anger easier to contain. And besides, she knew Vivaldo to be at the hub of all such activity. She would like to know more than she ought to know about him—far more—considering that this very night she was prepared to use him as a means of attaining something that had nothing whatsoever to do with any concern of his—unless she by any chance was one. Her pace quickened.

Dipping down the back slope to the Diqué, she skirted its

right bank and then climbed a winding mud road to the site of an abandoned sugar factory now hedged with *iroko* saplings—an indication of why it had been selected for its present use. As she mounted the cut-out steps to the clearing she could hear voices getting rid of troublesome Exu (Elegba) by sending him on a mission to the intersection of this world and the invisible:

Bara obebe tiriri lona
Exu, O Exu, long time a-traveling . . .

sang the soloist, and the chorus answered her:

Gowned in the dust of the road, O Exu . . .

The interior of the candle-lit *barraçaõ* gleamed with fresh whitewash and the rafters beneath the thatch were crisscrossed with the red-and-white garlands pleasing to Xango, guardian of this *terreiro*, king of the fortnight of entertainments proclaimed in honor of Saints John the Baptist, Peter and Paul. Agõtīme left her tray propped up beside the open door. From the folds of her shawl she drew forth a pair of sandals; in defiance of Dona Maria das Dores, the Municipal Council and the prefecture, she slipped on free footgear and crossed the threshold. Walking directly to the center, she embraced the Mãe-de-Santo and the other officials of the house, then took her place along one of the benches on the women's side.

The drums now burst into the ardent warrior's tempo appropriate to Ogun:

"Ogun Onire O
    Welcome Ogun of Onire
From across the ocean
    Captain, you have heard our summons.
When we behold your bloody robes,
    Durable father of iron,
We shall step back to let you by.

Welcome Ogun of Onire
Open the way through the bush,
   Put by your wrath, warrior,
Ogun, come and dance with us."

The *filhas-de-santo* moved withershins around the central pillar where the Mãe-de-Santo and her council sat enthroned in ornate wicker chairs. Dressed in lace or eyelet embroidered blouses and immaculately starched skirts, the sisters swayed decorously to the pulse hidden beneath the wild overlay of drum beats. Feet flat on the earthen floor, wrists, elbows, shoulders, knees, hips moving to the pull of diverse currents, these ephemerae of the Afro-Bahian night, each drawn inevitably to her own fire, united in imploring the first of the Great Ones to come down and dance for a time in mortal company.

The girl Nasinha faltered, then caught herself, shoulders twitching, her head heavy with the influx of such power, lips pursed, dulled eyes half-closed, turned within. The drummers increased their pace. As Agōtĭme stared, not at the dancer but at Vivaldo—proud head thrown back, knees gripping the cylinder, right leg flung straight out for balance, or for punctuation, or perhaps bravado, she saw a herd of wild horses thundering down the beach and for some reason the vision filled her with unspeakable grief.

With a white-gowned attendant beside her now—a cool hand for her forehead, a strong hand for the small of her straining back, Nasinha the saint's daughter fought through her convulsions and emerged triumphant as Ogun. The onlookers shouted their welcome—*Ogunie!*—and began to clap out the domineering rhythm played now by all three drums in unison. The Mãe-de-Santo rang her silver bell to discharge the atmosphere of the room. Meanwhile the attendant had removed Nasinha's sandals to permit her to dance barefoot, as if on African soil. Then, suddenly, it was over. Nasinha, still in trance, was led away to a back room to don regalia appropriate to Ogun, and the summoning of the *orixas*, in proper sequence, went on.

The Mãc-de-Santo smiled contentedly from her chair. It is a good beginning, her expression seemed to say. The girls are elegant, controlled. They've been well-schooled. With the least effort they respond to the drums, relinquish hold, devolve almost imperceptibly. Surely none of the saints will fail to appear, but not to all; and my dancers know better than to pretend. My vigilant eye can tell in the trembling of a leaf whether the trunk be shaken or the wind respire.

The process was almost intolerably beautiful, and Agõtĩme envied her! She had not imagined it like this, but surely it was something like this that Zomadonu had promised her. Yet how modest, how fragile, when compared with the vast pageantry of Africa. It was as if all had been bleached in the diminishing: the entire out-of-doors reduced to four white walls; priests, princes, warriors, wives, noisy dance teams, masqueraders all elided into the least of women—slim housemaids, husky fruit vendors, chorewomen, and that toothless great-grandmother over there who outdanced them all. And yet again, into the midst of such deprivation the deepest forces of the universe descended to renew all strengths. The *barraçaõ* became the cosmos then, the dancers heroes, passions, elements, and nothing else existed.

> *Oke rekoke ode oke rekoke,*
> Hail to the Hunter from the distant hills
> Fastidious, invulnerable . . .

Down from his place of concealment, Oxossi, in leather hat and flaring skirt, holding bow-and-arrow and long-bristled switch, danced in mimicry of all animals, danced pursuit; and Agõtĩme put up her hands to push back the green force from the forest. She knew him once, she would know him again, but her path did not yet lie in that direction.

Ago lonake xaoro
Son of the swampland, slowly, slowly,
Lord of the sultry air, softly . . .

To that sad *opanije* rhythm, the god of Agõtĭme's exiled father from Mahiland came down to dance as he danced in far off Yoruba country—the disfigured face covered with swirling strands of straw, elbows out-thrust, wrists back-bent to paddle through the pestilential air that is Earth's excoriating element.

Araka ada olorum
Oda de owo Oxumare o. . . .

Glissando voices, skeining hands winding heaven and earth, call the rainbow serpent who enlivens, perpetuates, brings fortune. "*Arrobobô*, I greet you, Dã, my countryman," said Agõtĭme, "in whatever guise you choose to appear. I, who shall grow old and sad and be sold for a pittance, remember me."

Ioba odè de Irecê é kié Iemanja
Apota pe lebe owo io lo ko iwa she ewe . . .
Between the waters, clothed in sea weeds,
It is She, the mermaid goddess Iemanja.

Odoia! Mother of waters, of all the *orixas*, in your golden crown, pearl fringe, translucent beads, grant me what I hardly dare hope for; of all your bounteous beauty is there not some to spare for me?

Oya li o ji gbe ina jo
May Oya arise and dance
with firey sword in hand

Oya arojo ba oko ku
Courageous Oya
Prepared to die with her husband
Koji mido ke Oya

> Let the priests of the departed spirits
> Go up to the mountains of Yansan . . .

Tower of storms, vigorous, mature, possessive, come with impetuous arms outstretched to drive the souls of the dead before you, lest they come too near us. Only you can manage them. Look, in your panniered skirt of simple Guinea cloth, you are hovering, above the feckless winds. Had I been born by the riverbank, I should have worn the horns of a buffalo.

> *Awa oki mi mpe oba wa*
>> We salute our king!
> *Oba wa jo oba taro*
>> King, come dance at your festival!
> *Oba nro ojo waiye o*
>> King, as the rain falls, come down,
> *Igi terere o di odo*
>> As tree felled grinds corn,
> *Oba wa jo oba taro*
>> King, come dance at your festival!

This was the moment the Mãe-de-Santo had been waiting for. Not only was he her horseman, ruling *orixa* of her *terreiro*, but also midwinter master of ceremonies everywhere in Brazil. He would not disappoint them. One, two, three drums took up his rhythmical imperative and, double axe head stemmed in a washerwoman's hand, Xango came to the call. *Kawo Kabiesile!* they greeted him, Royal Thunderer.

The invocations were over. The congregation arose from their benches, yawned, stretched, and began to move out into the air or, if specially invited, into one of the back rooms to feast on Xango's favorite *cararu* with *acarajé* beans and *acaçá*. In another cubicle, Xango's daughters had already begun to be clothed in the scarlet robes of his authority. Those already dressed in the distinctive costumes of their gods, rested in armchairs behind curtained doors. There would be a leisurely intermission. The drummers stayed on to tune their instruments while the skins were still warm.

Agōtíme remained where she was, on the bench. Her eyes, half-closed, resembled the cowrie shells of the necklace the Toxosu had given her long ago by the black pool at the bottom of Ko Swamp, a token of survival she now clutched, calling, silently, over and over, not in Yoruba but in her own tongue, "*Ale die vohe, ale vo.*" [The road is free, open the way.]

At length she got up and walked over to the drums. She knew the man who played the *rum*, largest of the three, the man they called Vivaldo. It was he upon whose arm she'd noticed the iron band as he led them up the *ladeira* for the first time three years ago. She had spoken to him briefly then. She knew that he no longer worked for Sequeira Lima, that he'd been jailed twice on suspicion of killing a man in a street fight, that he now lived more or less in hiding, but that he turned up regularly to drum at the Mãe-de-Santo's *candomblé*. (He must have known in advance about the police raid, for that night he had not appeared.) They never met, by chance, any place else, and even at *candomblé* they never spoke; but she kept coming back and he was conscious of that fact. Even so, she could not be absolutely sure of his granting the favor she was about to ask; she had become so little sure of anything; and her request was extraordinary, to say the least. But she had decided that this was the only way open to her, her only alternative to the precipitous, dark cliff. She had watched the dancers night after night, and she admitted enough about her own feelings to know this for a certainty: if he were willing to play the right rhythm for her, she would become possessed.

"Greetings to the hands of the drummer," she said, advancing, "and to their owner, for he is fortunate in his continued avoidance of mishap."

"Greetings for having safely sat out the dance—with enjoyment," he added.

"Do you know me, son of Ogun?" she asked.

"I would know you anywhere," he laughed, "but I have not spoken to you for three market days, for three years more than that," he laughed again, his eyes mocking her beneath the shadowy tilt of his hat brim. "Nor am I accustomed to exchanging these ancient formulas, so forgive me if I forbear, discourteous *creole* that I am, to ask about the health of your ancient relatives —I doubt you've had much news of them—or about that of the inhabitants of your Big House—I rather imagine you'd just as soon they were dead; but instead I shall say that I remember you from the first day, from your arrival in our city. You struck me as a person of great consequence then, but withal an expectant, open-hearted sort of woman. Since that time, although you've learned how to dress like a Bahiana, you've not expanded, but rather drawn farther in. You haven't made yourself at home here, have you? Haven't wanted to? You took my advice about the earth, much as you, from your looks, have hungered for it. Surely those long walks along the promontory haven't got you back to Africa either, not yet, by St. Antony, not yet. You look surprised. Yes, I've seen you here and there and now and then, but you've always looked so formidable, I haven't dared . . ."

"Please," Agõtíme said, "spare me that for the time being. You say you know me, but you can have no notion of who I really am, nor of my situation. For now, there is but one simple favor I would beg of you. Could your hands be coaxed to recall my *orixa*'s pattern? Breath of my destiny, it is no gust, no gale, no hot wind, but rather a subtle air, redolent of disfigured water spirits much redoubted in the kingdom I come from, yet so far as I know still unestablished here."

His expression softened (He looks at me with compassion, as if he thought me mad; but what do I care? I have begun to walk the royal road again and must scale my speech accordingly. The grasses part this way and that, as memory sorts them, and my mind may not move beyond that plane, must concentrate upon those swaying intervals) but his speech retained its casual, bantering manner. "Dahomey? or Mahiland, perhaps? I have heard many praise songs from those places, and my hands can remember anything if they first touch coin."

She reached into her sash. "I was prepared for that," she said, "and I for one, having nothing, am prepared to hazard everything. We have, of course, no assurance that what we bring to the feast will be well received."

Vivaldo shrugged. "What's that to me? It's always a dangerous business, the awakening of forces. But I've good protection. And so far as the Mãe-de-Santo is concerned, I'm but a conduit, remember? And, by reputation at least, the best there is. Now, how does it go? Would you remember if you started clapping, or would you prefer to begin with the song and let me pick up the accents?"

"It's been a long time," she said, "or so it seems to me; and in my sadness I have forgotten many things; but if I remember correctly, the first syllables sounded something like this:

> *Wi ti gŏ   xi ka*
> *Wi ti gŏ   xi ka*
> *Wi ti gŏ   xi ka.*"

She continued to catch at these sounds and shove them out with a rasp as if her life depended upon the successful overriding of each contraction. "Confound the enormity of you water wits," Agŏtĭme panted angrily, "what a price to pay for good riddance to disaster!" And with that a second rhythm cut across the first:

> *"Tato bo*
> *Tato whi*
> *Tato jaĩ*
>
>   *whi li ga*
>   *whi li ga*
> *Wi ti gŏ*   *xi ka*
> *Wi ti gŏ*   *xi ka*
>   *ri ti ko di ja.*"

There it was at last! She had brought forth the praise from the restrictive caul of her own breath, accomplished, unified it; and the drummer, who had kept pace with her, alternated hand and stick upon head and cylinder, three against two to complete the pattern.

Although she herself had never danced to anything of the sort, Agótíme's knees shifted easily back and forth to the pulse below that frantic virtuosity. Confident now, she reached out beyond herself for an invisible stick which, once found and grasped, she raised at once like a sword measured between exultant hands. Now the ground beneath her feet gave way as if she were dancing upon a hummock of mud. No, not mud; it was a bull. She jumped down, recoiled and thrust thrice at the neck of the chosen animal; and as she did so, in that newfound rasp of hers she thrice intoned the following:

"My hand longs to perform
All our ancestors have done.
We the strong,
We are alive,
We knock at the door,
We alone survive."

Then Vivaldo spontaneously varied the pattern and Agótíme began the arrogant steps permitted exclusively to members of the royal clan. Springing from one foot to the other, she threw out her arms behind her and tossed her head high on her long neck as if to out-leap mortality.

The tempo relented and she began to parade disdainfully about the floor, her spine arched like a bow, head still erect, lips pursed, eyes now heavily lidded:

"The way is open;
My force dominates the world. . . ."

The Mãe-de-Santo, horrified, had rushed into the hall as soon as the drumming became audible above the milling voices of the guests. Although Agõtĭme herself was as unconscious of her as she was of the crowd that followed, Zomadonu was not. He made her seize her invisible stick again and begin to tease the spectators thus: presenting the saber horizontal first, she next pointed it high in the air, then threw it back in preparation for a thrust which unexpectedly transformed itself into a swift planting motion. The ferocious warrior had become a decrepit dignitary, tapping impatiently, now right now left, as if imploring the soil to open up.

The Mãe-de-Santo rang her silver bell and all present put up their hands to ward this horrible power off. Then someone threw a glass of water in Vivaldo's face. The drumming ceased. Agõtĭme called out Zomadonu's name and fell exhausted to the ground. Two white-gowned assistants carried her, still shaking, off to a back room. Vivaldo struck out with his left leg and sent his assailant sprawling. Then he too quit the hall. The Mãe-de-Santo was hunched beside Agõtĭme in an armchair. Nodding with fatigue, she became alert immediately she sensed Agõtĭme awakening.

Agõtĭme saw her and became confused. A cock crowed in the misty yard outside the adobe window that might well have opened out upon the palace grounds. A misty chill pervaded the room. It took all her strength to pull herself into a sitting position and throw her long legs over the bedside. Gripped by unaccountable waves of anxiety, Agõtĭme wondered out loud what she was doing there, and laughed like a child when the Mãe-de-Santo told her.

"And who is Zomadonu, my daughter? We do not know that *orixa.*"

Agõtĭme giggled. "O he's a funny man, Godmother, round as a jug with six protruding candle ends for eyes. He can change into a bird when he wants to, like this," she said, flexing her shoulders. "He calls himself king of the water spirits, but really he's only a deformed son of the royal family. They tossed him away and that outraged him. He terrorized them into making him a regal ancestor, but the latest king refused to worship at his shrine. That outraged him again. Did you know that I, though not of royal blood, was once a queen? They threw me away, too, beautiful as I am." And with that she arose from the side of the bed and began to traipse around the room, prodding the earth with her cane, "old, too, older far than Zomadonu, and I shall be sold many times."

"Agõtĩme," the Mãe-de-Santo said sternly, "you must never come back here. Yours is an unwanted *orixa*. Powerful, who can doubt that, but with limited scope. It is most unlikely he would ever mount to any other head. Furthermore, this is a Nago house, and although we do have some saints from your nation, they are major forces, fixed long ago in Yorubaland before making the voyage here. Besides, this Zomadonu would seem to be more like a spirit of the dead than a true *orixa*, and we do not worship the *eguns* here. We have a separate island home for them." She paused. "You are unconvinced? Well, there is something else you ought to realize. You say Zomadonu's a defunct prince of the Dahomean line? I ask you, how can you expect us, victims of your Dahomean kings, to receive the ancestor of those who have burned our villages, enslaved our people and sold them, homeless, to the Portuguese? No," she added emphatically, "we do not know either of you here.

"Perhaps," she resumed kindly, "you could establish Zoma-donu some other place, among your own people. I realize the Minas-Gege cults here, at the moment, are not very well organized—nothing like what we have here. So many of your people have been sold up north to work in the rice fields of the place they call Maranhão. But new postulants will come and, hopefully, some priests. Those houses will pick up again. No, I don't know how far away this Maranhão might be, but I'm sure you could find someone to tell you where it is. Ask your friend Vivaldo, he probably knows. You'd have to buy your freedom first, unless of course you wanted to run away. The first shouldn't take you very much longer. From what I hear you've got on well as a *quitandeira*. As for running away, I shouldn't advise your trying, unless you number yourself as one of St. Antony's favorite children. But some have been successful. There's a *quilombo* not twenty leagues from here; those people are always more than willing to put up fugitives. Contact any of St. George's men; they'll be able to help if that's what interests you. But the best way would be to wait until . . ."

Agōtǐme embraced the Mãe-de-Santo and left the room. She hurried down the long silent corridor, across the ceremonial hall and out into the early morning. Her tray was still there, but not as she'd left it. Bending down to pick it up, she noticed an iron bracelet half-buried in the dust. Vivaldo's? She slipped it on, pushing it well above her elbow so it wouldn't fall off. What now? She supposed she'd better go back to the Big House. Let Suuna tell them she was sick. She needed time to think things over.

As she passed by the fountain across from Sequeira Lima's establishment she paused, irresistibly drawn to the thin stream of water dripping from the stone lips of the custodian of the pool. To drink from the source she would have to hike up her skirts and wade in, knee-deep, cautiously slipping her toes along the slime until she reached the rocky alcove where the spring leaked through the grotesque masonry. No sooner had she done so, and cupped her hands in anticipation of cool freshness, than she heard an unmistakable laugh.

"Greetings upon the successful completion of your journey, inchoate water bird," she responded, "the going must have been most tedious, seeing that the arriving was so long postponed."

"Think nothing of it," he snapped, "some find traveling

easier than others; but now that I'm finally across, not wind nor rain shall interfere again. All subsequent passages shall be instantaneous. To facilitate that, I must present you with an *asogwe*. You have found the gourd, now all you have to do is grab it by the neck; you have tied the net, now all you have to do is shake it."

"Thank you in advance, bearded stone, for the gift. It will be the second I have received from you," she added, touching her necklace.

"Yours by inheritance," Zomadonu said. "Don't think me the least bit generous. You deserve, and you shall get, nothing superfluous. Long ago, before we had been established by our conquerors, I gave the only man who did not flee our prankish inundations a similar instrument with which to summon us at will. His by chance, you might say, for had he not been disabled by the guineaworm disease, he would not have stayed on bravely to confront our regiments. But, once aware of our legitimate grievances, and having dutifully reported these to King Tegbesu, this man by rights became our first Dahomean priest. Those were luminous years for us. Grand temples were built, cool long sheds topped by rounded roofs, wherein our jars were placed so that we might brood on undisturbed, our stamina renewed each year by solemn processions to the water's edge. You who have been bold enough to roost me upon your head and strut my mutations for the first time here in the new world, you now shall have the power to seine me forth from the sweet waters of any ordinary spring, stream or river—even from half-filled jug or cistern. And when you shall have passed the requisite months of your novitiate, you shall, as previously agreed, become our first priestess here. I shall not fail you."

"Fail me again, you mean," Agõtĭme muttered under her breath. Out loud she said, "This novitiate you speak of. I'm afraid it will be impossible to complete here in Bahia, but I have heard of a place called Maranhão . . ."

"No matter where," the Toxosu said, "I leave all housewifely details to you. It is almost sunrise. Dankness calls me. These be but borrowed waters. She crowds me out. Hold off, imperious fishtail. Agōtíme, don't forget. Don't let other concerns distract you. Strengthen me, make me a prince in this strange land and in the land of life I shall have your son reign over all. Farewell until you shake the confined seeds, or until I choose to manifest myself again."

The Toxosu dove into the fountain and was gone, but on the edge of the basin, amongst the candle ends and wax droppings—remains of fires fed to Mãe d'agua—Agōtíme saw a gourd enmeshed in a miniature fishnet beaded with tiny vertebrae. It was the dance rattle, *asɔgwe*. Sadly she took it up, wrapped it in her shawl, and carried it back to her cubicle in the slaves' quarters.

10 ◗◖ Holy War

It was Vivaldo who first took Agõtĩme to visit the Imam. She did not know precisely where he lived, but had occasionally strolled through the Muslim neighborhood, smiled conspiratorially at the shy veiled women, dared to admire their children, had even seen the holy man himself seated cross-legged on a stump in the square of Monte Belem de Cima, settling disputes, and occasionally, skirting the Diqué on her way home from *candomblé*, had heard the lonely voice of his *muezzin*. She had long thought of asking him for a consultation—infidel and woman though she was; but had hesitated to go alone. There were priests of Ifa attached to the *terreiros*, but none who impressed her as worthy successors of her old friend the Bokonõ. The Imam, perhaps.

Not wishing to be seen about the Big House himself, Vivaldo had sent a small boy to the slaves' quarters to tell Agõtĩme he'd be waiting for her at noon on the southern bank of the Diqué. It was Sunday. Senhor Orlando was still in the country. Dona Maria das Dores was confined to her room with a winter cold; and Senhorinha Prequiçosa was only too pleased to sit unchaperoned behind the trellis-work of the upstairs pergola. Agõtĩme told

Suuna to say, should anyone inquire, that she'd gone off with her tray to the lower city as usual.

Vivaldo was stretched out on the grass with his battered hat over his face and from a distance, so strong was the sun upon him, he seemed to be outlined in indigo. But he was not asleep. He jumped to his feet when he heard her coming and pulled her down beside him, saying as he did so, "My very special friend, I have a message for you."

"For me? From whom?" she asked nervously.

"From the Imam. From whom were you expecting news?"

"Not certainly from the Imam. How strange. I don't know him."

"Nor he you, except by reputation," Vivaldo said, his canny eyes crinkling with amusement.

"Why, then?"

"It's a long story, having to do with the revolt or, rather, revolts; for there are two, or have been up till now."

"One for each eye, I suppose," she laughed.

"No, two in this case is most unlucky. In the beginning there was but one; as long as I can remember there has always been this one. Sometimes it festers, sometimes breaks out, and so far has never been successful. Call it the Durable War of the Iron Bands. That's what the Confraternity of St. George is all about. But some months ago, prompted by obscure happenings in the old country, the Malês, most of them new arrivals from Hausaland (I'm not sure exactly where that is), got the idea of waging one of their holy wars—against everyone, ourselves included. Does that startle you? Well, think if you were in my position. You can't imagine the hours we've spent bargaining with the Imam. Now, at last, just yesterday in fact, we have managed to convince him that without our help they've no chance of success. We know the lay of the land in a way they never will. We don't rule it, we walk the streets which we've broken our backs to pave barefoot;

but it's our city all the same. Furthermore, we can count on arms from the backcountry. They've no such resources, the Malês. But I'll hand it to them, they've got another kind of strength in the Imam himself. Never have I seen a man endowed with so much authority. His head's as vast as the Reconcavo and he grinds considerations like cane stalks in a sugar mill."

"Yes, I've heard," Agõtíme said, purposely swerving back to catch up something of special concern to her, "that there's a *quilombo* not twenty leagues from here. That's the backcountry support you were talking about, I suppose. You're in contact with them. Do you ever go there?"

"Sometimes. If the going gets too difficult, we, the leaders, can hide out in the *quilombo*. I doubt they'll risk coming into the city, but they'll probably send guns and we can count on the field hands from the plantations joining us—with their masters' weapons, their tools, anything they can get ahold of. Our real problem lies in accommodating the Hausas without losing ourselves. Be patient. I shall come to the Imam's summons soon, but it is a complicated situation and I want you to understand what it is you're getting into. . . ."

Summons? Getting into? she thought. How is it possible? I've done nothing; I hardly know anything about all of this and yet here I am, apparently right in the thick of it. Never have I felt so removed. Who's responsible? But Vivaldo had gone on talking, unaware that she had dropped behind. If she forced herself to concentrate, she could keep up; the facts themselves were not beyond her comprehension.

"Up till now the *terreiros* have been indispensable to us as well-organized sources of popular support, headquarters, and fronts. In addition, their drums generate force without which we would have no hope of overwhelming the white soldiery. However, the Imam cannot bear to hear the Mãe-de-Santo spoken of, and calls her and the other Iyalorixas 'pagan matriarchs of the most vulgar sort.' Yet, in part convinced by our arguments, he has agreed to accept us as allies if we disassociate ourselves, our confraternity, our followers, completely from the cults, from all that he calls 'animist idolatry.' And because of some obscure Hausa legend which local events have pressured him to recall, he has, in exchange for our putting by our gods, given us the honor of providing a suitable 'pagan consort' to reign (in appearance only, I should imagine) first over our combined revolt and then over his future Islamic Bahian state.

"We have no intention of forswearing the *orixas*, that would be suicidal, but we have managed to persuade the Mãe-de-Santo and the others that rather than run the risk of betrayal, of failure and mutual extermination, we must pretend to go along with the Imam, let him run things. To stop *candomblé* would, so we told him, incur further suspicion on the part of the police. Therefore our drums will continue to beat, but I for one won't do the beating. The *orixas* will not be neglected. They will be fed. They shall descend. But all who take the Imam's oath will stay away from the *terreiros*.

"If, by chance, the uprising should prove successful, it will be only too easy for us—who so vastly outnumber them—to change his 'Islamic Government' into something far more in accordance with our 'infidel' way of doing things—a loose federation of 'nations,' perhaps, a council of elderly headmen, and, it's even possible, a queen. Back to our *orixas* then, back to them in any case, for we shall not in any important sense have left them.

"Now here is where you come in. You must have guessed. It's you I propose for queen of the Hausa uprising. Your image came straight to mind when the Imam spoke of the old prophecy; and the more I considered, the more apt you seemed. Already you've made a name for yourself as a *quitandeira*; but you've kept your own counsel—that has its advantages. Those ruling passions you dramatically displayed that fatal night to everyone at the *terreiro* . . . when the news gets round to the rest of our people that you've even brought a special *orixa* over with you—a wild one, that nobody's heard of . . ."

"Stop, please stop, Vivaldo, you've said too much already. It's not the Imam that's clever, you are. You've thought of everything. Please don't be angry. With me in the queen's place, the pattern would be complete. How could the revolt fail? But I'm not free to step into this scheme. Already I've outstayed my time in Salvador. Each day is stolen from another plot. No, I'm not to be queen in the new world, in Bahia or in any other place. No, no, not me. Faint as the tracks upon the sand at times have seemed, indistinct to the point of vanishing, they're still there. I've been reassured of that much recently, and I must follow them. It's a strange history, Vivaldo, and even had I courage to explain and you patience to listen, even if I dared violate sacred confidences, test unaccomplished charms, court evil hindrances, I fear you would be at pains to believe me. So I must simply say I cannot accept your offer and give as my reason for doing so that I have decided, as soon as I've earned enough money to pay my debt of honor to my best friends, my *malungos*, to run away to Maranhão where I believe . . ."

"To Maranhão?" The tension broke. He doubled up with laughter. "Why, that's absurd! How long have you lived in this world that you don't know Maranhão's not a place you run to, as if it were a *quilombo*. That's a place where the murderous riffraff, stubborn Maxi fools are sent." Whipping off his hat, he put it between his knees and began, in exaggerated pantomime, to drum:

> Wake up and scorch the earth, São João,
> They're packing me off to Maranhão
> For I tried to kill my master,
> And he sold me for a song.
> First I slapped him in the face,
> And he threatened Minas Gerais,

Then I drew my knife
And for love of his life,
He sold me to Maranhão.

So long, Felicidade,
Put on a widow's gown
For I'd sooner be back
From the land of life
Than from Maranhão, from Maranhão,
From the rice fields of Maranhão.

"Enough," Vivaldo said, "I don't know whether you're laughing or crying, but whichever it is, you're alive once more. Come on," taking her hand, "let's go to the Imam. At least we can see if he finds you satisfactory. You owe your special drummer that much. So you have other plans for the future? How long are we going to live in this world that we have to put on iron clothes? Postpone your dreams awhile longer. You don't have to be so mysterious. See how that gust of wind wrinkles the stolid waters of the pond, scuffles with the top boughs of the mangoes over there; look, the pond is smooth again; the lustrous leaves are stilled. What are you to me or I to you? If we're successful, you can always abdicate. You'd probably be forced to, anyhow. Can you imagine how the Mãe-de-Santo would take to being ruled by you? Suppose we lose, you'll probably get sent to Maranhão, all expenses paid. And I wouldn't dream of going with you."

What could she do? Vivaldo was not a *vodū*, he was a man, and not the sort of man to brook refusal.

The Imam lived alone in a whitewashed cell, unfurnished save for a sheepskin rug, an elaborate coffee tray and a low table covered with writing tablets and tattered manuscripts. The *muezzin*, who apparently doubled as a servant, slept in a little hut behind, where a goat was tethered to a scrawny banana tree and a few chickens reconnoitered their impoverishment. The turban which swathed the Imam's head looped down beneath his chin to fill out a haggard face partially lit by a burning intelligence.

"Peace be with you," Vivaldo greeted him.

"And with you, peace," responded the Imam.

"This is Agõtíme, Master, the pagan woman I was telling you about."

"I see," said the Imam, "but my vision is imperfect. *Fal mujarrib l-fala:* let us consult fate. Please be seated on the floor while I complete my preparations."

The device, which the Imam called Dragon's Tail, was known to Agõtíme as *Guda Meji.* The Bokonõ's voice, thrown against the hollow walls of memory, warned her: "The Moon downs. Knives blunder the stream. Owl hoots, but the hunter does not respond. Cock crows, and he trips a trap for the king. . . ."

"A dangerous sign, is it not?" Agõtíme whispered. The Imam did not reply, but turned to stare in her direction, remotely, as if she were at the very horizon of his thought.

"If the scythe goes to the fields and cuts grass," he finally said, "it will return to the house. If it cuts nothing, it will likewise return to the house." He paused. For some reason these words infuriated her. But there were more to come. "What you have been or will be, infidel woman, is of no concern to me. Your poor knowledge is but an insignificant smudge on the surface of the great eye that sees everything. Allah is the light of heaven and earth. His vision is as a niche in which there is a lamp and the lamp is set in a glass like a glittering star and the oil within would burn though no fire touched it. Be silent and you will be led to this light, released from your bondage, and be the means by which others are illuminated. What do you know of the day of decision? Be silent at break of noon; and in the cast of midnight, obey."

To Vivaldo he said, in a hurried, matter-of-fact manner, "She is too thin for my taste, but she has bearing. She will do. The sign is more favorable than expected. You may arrange some kind of coronation for her when the Christians celebrate their Epiphany. For the time being, I assign her to work with you in Barra. She must become known to the people gradually. Like the snake's, hers is an emergent destiny. You will continue to collect arms and distribute them to our caches. Bring to me all who would indemnify themselves against Allah's wrath. Go in peace, and take her with you."

"But what about my swearing the oath?" Agõtíme asked, as they hurried along the path to the Ladeira do Belem. "Does he know about my *orixa?*"

"Certainly not," Vivaldo laughed, "and there's no reason to suppose he ever should. Don't worry about perjuring yourself. There'll be no pact for you. Don't you see? To him you're but a mirage in the desert, even if you are a queen."

The Imam stood in the doorway, his eyes narrowing to the diminution of their retreating figures, his fingers counting prayers like beads on an abacus. When they were out of sight, when the correct sum had been said, purified, he turned to go in.

And Vivaldo took Agõtíme for a long walk along the beach.

The revolt was set for the night between the twenty-fourth and twenty-fifth of January when the masters and mistresses of Bahia annually quit their homes for a pilgrimage to the church of Nosso Senhor do Bom Fim. The insurgents envisaged a simultaneous set of surprise attacks on various military posts about the city followed by a unified march along the strand as far as the peninsula where they planned to massacre the pilgrims collectively at their vigil.

To expedite these plans, the Imam had his Koranic students prepare five hundred maps margined with summary instructions in Arabic. These were for the true believers, the literate. For the rest, Agõtíme designed another set of maps modeled on those which the Dahomean spies made to show slave-raiders the way to Mahiland. Agõtíme supervised the sewing of a thousand appliquéd schemes of the city in a dilapidated shanty on the beach, Vivaldo's hideout where she came every night as soon as she could get away from the Big House. Each of the five sectors into which the Imam had divided the city—Baixa dos Sapateiros, Vitoria, Conceicão da Praia, Pilar and Bom Fim—was cut out in its approximate shape, correctly positioned, and on top of this floppy pattern various strategic places were marked with *x*'s: the barracks and armories first of all, in white thread, and then, in black, the district headquarters—Francisco the tailor's shop on the Baixo dos Sapateiros, Agostinho the herbalist's tenement, Pae Pacifico's *palafita* [stilt house] at Algados on the way from Pilar to Bom Fim, the Jaquaripe pottery stall at Agua de Meninos market, Vivaldo's place on the beach in Bahia; and to complete the job a crescent moon was appliquéd upon the approximate site of Monte Belem to indicate the whereabouts of the Imam.

These "handkerchiefs" were distributed all over the city, to field hands in the Reconcavo, to criminals or escapees hiding out in the *quilombo*—wherever partisans could be recruited to risk their lives on the night of the twenty-fourth and to acknowledge the provisional grandeur of Allah. The latter stipulation being as difficult to comprehend as to enforce, no one troubled too much about it. And the rumors of a queen come from the Guinea Coast to deliver them tended to confuse the imaginations of those in the outlying districts still more. But with regard to the first, there was a heartening response and pistols, machetes, knives and a few stolen fowling pieces began to pour in to each of the headquarters schematically represented on Agŏtĭme's map—a harvest of "yeas" for Ogun, if not for Allah.

The Imam gave his most important Islamic followers titles—like Wiziri, Galadima and Magafin-Gari—and bade them tend, until such time as more substantial administrative services would be required, to various ceremonial aspects of the uprising. The Wiziri, for example, was put in charge of designing the Islamic revolutionary costume and promoting its universal adoption, by true believers only, of course. The others envied the Malês their white robes, red sashes, blue toques, and would have incorporated some of these distinctive items into their own wardrobes had not Vivaldo insisted that European suspicions must not be aroused. Malês were expected to dress alike, in white robes. The Nagos would have to continue to dress as they always did—in the multi-colored cloths of fortune.

The *gris-gris* were something else again. Both Muslims and devotees of the *orixas* wore these talismans—small leather pouches containing medicine made of the Koranic word. The little packet was characteristically decorated with a patch of animal skin, a bit of wood, a cowrie shell, and an embroidered star. Agŏtĭme thought the non-Muslim revolutionaries ought to add a special emblem of their own—something more universal than the iron arm bands worn by the Confraternity, something neither partial nor offensive to any known *orixa*. The black panther was a natural symbol of black strength. No one, not even Vivaldo, need be aware of its local origin. The image, as she knew it would, did appeal to him, and soon the bestial forefather of the Dahomean kings sprang forth in dark running stitches or scraps of deep-dyed indigo cloth on the covers of the amulets. And when various leaders had to adopt revolutionary aliases, Vivaldo naturally took the name O Pardo Preto and Agŏtĭme, although she never told him why, that of La Rainha Aligbonon. Upon which the Imam fearing that idolatrous pride had gone too far, insisted that Agŏtĭme's coronation be postponed until after the uprising.

Although the insurgents had been compelled, for strategical purposes, to disassociate themselves from cult life, they had no intention of doing so. Far from it. During the weeks of intense anticipation, while a hard core of anxious Mães-de-Santo, Babalorixas and their initiates kept *candomblé* alive in the suburbs, freedmen, *negroes de ganho*, and all slaves who could manage to ignore the curfew met together to dance to the strengthening rhythms of the *bata zota* [war drums] under the pretext of practicing sambas for Epiphany celebrations. And although the Angolans were one of the minority nations not officially a party to the revolution, some of their best athletes were prevailed upon to teach *capoeira* fighting to anyone who wanted to learn.

These weeks, these months, were the happiest Agōtīme had ever known. The seaside shack in Barra, a wanderer's hostel, was like a half-way house, cleared of mysterious undergrowth which she understood must proliferate again as soon as the revolt was over. To ignore that unseen tangle, as now, was to be free of its incipient hold on her. But such a human clearing, thus defoliated and uprooted, gradually beginning to erode, would not be habitable forever. She now understood that to be Agōtīme, to be strong enough to evolve, was to be merely an agent, a medium for forces as malevolent, as protective and as captious, as persistent as fire, water, wind or forest growth. It was a relentless process. But there were letups. Here was one. And that this moment of personal fulfillment should occur in the midst of somebody else's revolution, occasionally gave her pause, but did not deter her. It had never occurred to her that she might love and be loved by a real person, certainly not Agōglo. In the wives' court her only thought had been preeminence—a desperate (although she had not realized this then) quest for personal survival. Why not, if ever, now? And Vivaldo? His remarkable intelligence, his aggressive humor, his physical strength—these qualities had a healing effect upon her. She never questioned him about his past; partly because he never mentioned it, partly because she had no wish to reciprocate. This much of his history she knew and no more: that he had loved her from that first encounter on the *ladeira;* that he had stubbornly waited for her to disclose herself; that night after night they had grown inseparable. Much later she would be surprised to learn of her own reputation as a revolutionary. "Nonsense, Luiz," she would say, "everyone, the Imam first of all, needed a queen; but that was only, as Vivaldo himself said, a mirage, an alias, an illusion." For despite her very real, if modest, part in the uprising, she had the impression that she was, for the first time in her life, transparent, invisible; that she had but marked out a civilized space for Vivaldo. Of the retaliatory forces she was, also, at the time, oblivious.

On the appointed night, thunderclouds hid the moon. The main streets of Bahia were haphazardly lit by whale oil lamps that the slightest breath blew out. No wonder then, that everything was obscure.

The Imam stood at his door when the white thread could no longer be distinguished from the black, stood looking down over the darkening city and beyond the riding lanterns of the ships, to Itaparica, island of the dead, and beyond that to the hidden void of the sea. Before calling the *ixà* he asked his *muezzin* to give him the *goron yaki* [kola nuts of battle]. The singer shuddered in the rising wind as the Imam cast them. "Fire is stronger than iron, the prophet says, but water shall quench fire, and by giving it motion the wind shall overcome the sea."

"And what," ventured the *muezzin,* "shall overcome the wind?"

"Nothing," replied the Imam.

Along Vitoria ridge the colonial women wrapped themselves in their black cloaks, adjusted their mantillas and stepped out into the street on the arms of their frock-coated, beaver-hatted, patriarchal escorts. By the time they reached the Ladeira Conceiçao da Praia, recently paved by *corveias* of slaves, the stoutest were already out of breath. Seeing them reach into their bags for smelling salts, their husbands said it would be midnight before they reached Bom Fim.

At certain specified intersections, the insurgents began to gather and greet: *salam alaikum* from Muslim to Muslim, *e k'ale* from Nago to Nago.

The first contingent moved at once to the armory of St. Bento, and would have been successful in their raid had not a fire broken out by chance in the barracks which caused the Hausas to flee before a wild exodus of imperiled soldiery. Realizing that a direct confrontation under such circumstances would be disastrous, the Imam, hoping that the fire would reach where his men could not, quietly led them away to the Campo Grande to await the Vitoria contingent, as planned. But if the Imam's men were early, Vivaldo's were more than delayed. They were supposed to take the Fort of St. Pedro before uniting with the Imam's group to move on down to the cavalry post that barred the shore route to Bom Fim. However, a certain Nago houseslave, hoping to curry favor with her master, suddenly took it upon herself in his absence to alert the prefect of police who forthwith sent sixty armed men to the relief of the platoon quartered at St. Pedro before hurrying off on horseback to the cavalry post to alert them.

Unaware of these mishaps, Agõtĩme, with a handful of women from Barra, strode north along the promontory to perform the one iconoclastic operation of the war. Within the austere, romanesque walls consecrated to the worship of her own "*malungo* saint," as she called him, stood a statue of St. José to whom the slave dealers came with offerings whenever their ships returned with cargoes more alive than dead. Pausing to beg Antony's pardon, the intruders seized the image of the traders' patron, hauled him out of the great door, across the cobblestone court, through the iron gate and, with a shout of triumph, shoved him off the cliff to break on the rocky selvage where St. Antonio himself had miraculously drifted up a century and a half ago.

Meanwhile, despairing of the delay, the Imam led his Hausas forth from the Campo to the lower city, the appointed place of meeting with the third group. In agreement that more crucial time would be lost if they tarried longer for Vivaldo, the united contingents surged forward in the direction of the cavalry post only to find the Rua da Praia blocked by hastily stacked kegs. Somewhat daunted by the barricades, they turned back up the hill and followed the Ladeira do Taboão, hoping to fall in with the group from Pilar. But at the Largo do Pelourinho they unexpectedly encountered Vivaldo's group who, having lost half their own men in the process of eluding the police, had decided it was both too late and too risky to attempt to keep their appointment at the Campo and were preparing to descend directly to the lower city. It was past midnight when the entire army, thus reunited by chance rather than design, turned from Pilar towards the bay. At the Aqua de Meninos they emerged at last into the open—to face a cavalry charge.

"The word may bind the arms of man, but horse hooves on the beach thunder '*Kaddarace*'! [It was fate!] Fight those who would persecute you and turn you from your religion. Seeking the good and avoiding the reprehended are the crescent arms of perfect virtue, the completion of which is the Holy War, that I, in the name of the prophet, order you unto death to perform! *Kaddarace!*" the Imam shouted again, as, waving his sword above his turban, he ran to the encounter. "Allah is great," cried the Hausas as they surged after him.

When the first shots were fired and failed on account of darkness to hit their mark, the Hausas were ecstatic. "Beans, mere beans, see how the Word turns bullets to provender in the barrels of the Infidel!" they cried. But such jubilation was premature, and in their heart of hearts they knew it. Relentlessly the horsemen began to push them into the pond.

Those who could not swim went under—the Imam first of all, snarled in his flowing cloak, still clutching his amulet which contained washings from the one hundred and eighth *sura* ["He who hates you will perish . . ."]. And those who could manage to keep themselves afloat were submitted to a barrage of gunfire from the frigate *Bahiana* which happened to be anchored offshore.

Vivaldo, who, with the rest of the Nagos, had taken cover behind the natural barricades provided by the Jaguaripe pottery stalls, watched with horrified fascination as the flares from the ship went off like falling stars across the waters of the pond. He did not have to see more than he saw; even without the flares, the sounds were nightmarish enough. Pushing back the brim of his hat, licking away the awful taste of sweat, thinking distractedly of Agõtíme, Vivaldo stood up. "Well, it's our turn now, my brothers, and if we're going to do something, we've got to do it right away. Those who care to slip away are free to do so, free to go back to your hovels, your beds of straw. I've got no charms to bind you. And I'm not going to tell you bullets are beans, *camaradas;* those bullets are real; those horse hooves—they're real too. The Imam has tested both the fire and the water for us. We stayed behind. That kind of caution has kept us healthy, that kind of caution has kept one part whitemen in control of three parts blacks, cowards, and mulattoes.

"The horsemen have passed by us to drive the Hausas into the pond, and those of us who decide to stay will attack those horsemen from behind, not because we enjoy being kicked and trampled upon, but because, in the language of the masters, we are dogs. And we've nothing to protect us, *camaradas,* save 'cold iron.' Our brothers from the cane fields have sent their regrets, but they were kind enough to send gifts. Gifts of iron. Grab hold of these gifts, heat them, temper them in blood. Who wants to spend his life, and his son's life, and his grandson's life working his way back to the beginning. Our ancestors weren't all kings, some were working men like us. The only way we can all get back to Guinea is to use these tools to cut away the strangling vines, and fashion us another Africa, our own, right here in Salvador. The sun gave us our insignia. Who are we to serve like shadows on the ground? Stand up with me, and may Ogun and all the *orixas* protect us. In the name of St. George, *camaradas*, if you are with me, come on!"

They fought for an hour, for a little over an hour. Twice in the name of the Warrior, Vivaldo refused to give up arms. But the third time, he thought better of it and surrendered. The Battle of the Children's Pond was over. But no child would venture there, let alone swim there for a long time to come. The Nago remnant, together with a very few surviving Hausas, was hauled away at once to the Forte do Mar. Down at the south end of the inlet the doors of Bom Fim were thrown open and the pilgrims began to trek home along the corpse-strewn beach.

Agŏtíme sat on the stoop of the Imam's house when the black thread could again be distinguished from the white. The *muezzin* had already mounted the ladder to the tile rooftop and crowed *"Allahu Akbar, Allahu Akbar."* She could have strangled him. He, by the All Compassionate preserved, rather than follow his master into the pond had instinctively returned to Monte Belem to perform this futile summoning. He was, so he proudly told her, as if introducing himself, the Prophet's own *muezzin*, the first in the entire history of the faith, and although a humble man, a black slave, he had a well-trained voice, so piercing it could be heard all the way from Mecca to Monte Belem and back again, and so vast was his breath, so great his control that if put to it he could recite the entire Koran without a pause. He could not remember exactly what happened on the beach, but certain images kept coming back into his dislocated conversation so that after a while she was able to reconstruct the scene: horses, the black water, the clammy white robes of the faithful acting as premature shrouds to pull them under while their proud blue toques bobbed out unseen with the tide as far as Itaparica to be salvaged one day, she imagined, by small boys or itinerant fishermen—sea wrack of the Hausa uprising.

There were times when the two threads were better not distinguished. This had to be the Imam's revolt, it was fate, but there would be another one. Vivaldo? Would he be alive to lead it? It was impossible to think him dead—in prison, perhaps, or on his way to the *quilombo*. There would be no second farewell, no chance for inquiry. They'd agreed that she was to take flight at the first hint of disaster. She was to proceed along the north shore to Cachoeira where she must beg, or if need be, steal a small boat from the fishing colony there. She would take Suuna. Saliabsō was well fixed. She and Alixossi would stay on in Salvador.

"Are you at peace, Agōtīme? Am I late?" asked Suuna. "I've had quite a night I can tell you. The Senhora of the Pains did not go on the pilgrimage. She chose to stay behind on account of her swollen joints. And when she woke up and began once again to question me of your whereabouts I told her, 'Don't worry, Senhora, they've all gone to a dance in the lower city. You and I are alone. It is the day of decision, of the descending terror.' And then she began to chase me around the room saying she'd really give it to me this time, seeing that the two of us were alone. And then, Agōtīme . . . May Allah in his infinite compassion pardon a poor nomad for going so far as to wage a holy war of her own!"

The police estimated the Malês at one thousand strong, but actually there were no more than half that number at the Agua de Meninos. They did not attempt to estimate the number of Nagos and "others" who took part in the affair, but directed their energies to composing a letter to the governor of the province urging a cessation of importations from Whydah. There were too many Nagos, too many Maxis, too many slaves from the

Guinea coast already and a mutually intelligible slave population constituted an ever-present threat to public security.

The slaves who returned to their masters' houses with powder burns on their faces, their clothing smeared, tattered and dank, were taken to the prefecture for questioning, as were all those who, when searched, were found in possession of those mysterious undecipherable maps—of two kinds, what did that mean? Some of the suspects were imprisoned, but most were returned to their masters five hundred lashes the wiser. The Nago housekeeper who betrayed them to the police was given a handsome reward. But none of the survivors repented or revealed anything; for, as Vivaldo was fond of saying, "It is not uncommon for a trail blazer to return covered with scratches." Those fifty-odd stalwarts who would not surrender easily at the pond, who would not give up until Vivaldo said they might as well lay down their arms, were held at the Forte do Mar until they could be formally tried. Although to a man they refused to the end to admit their participation in the uprising, the circumstantial evidence was overwhelming and they were sentenced to be hanged at the docks. When the gallows were taken out of storage they proved rotten and so, in the end, the revolutionaries had to be shot.

Every year in early February a host of tiny butterflies passes over Salvador Bahia. They fly, as time flies, without settling. Upon their pale dusty wings they carry a gentle burden of black markings—dots and curlicues reminiscent of Arabic calligraphy. Their exact point of departure is uncertain—somewhere in the backlands of the northeast; but their destination is sure—south to the Atlantic. As Agõtĭme set out for Maranhão with Suuna, she saw these butterflies pollinating the sky on their way to oblivion. Her journey lay in the opposite direction.

11 ▶ The Dark Portage

Her uneasiness had begun the moment they left the first of many rivers, the Jacuipe, seeking a certain salty stream, tributary to a great one which, according to their informants, flowed north for a while into the open plateau country. Eventually they would have to cross this plateau on foot in order to reach the sea-bound watercourses of Maranhão. But first things first. Exhausted by continuous upstream travel on the Jacuipe, Agõtíme had actually looked forward to a portage across level sandy ground. Had they reached the specified place? At first it appeared so. It was certainly flat, but the right bank, from which they were to take off, seemed depressingly overgrown.

"They told us wrong," said Suuna, "and we were fools to have listened to them. Take it from me. Where I come from it's well known that you can never trust a fisherman—except to deceive you. Whatever made Vivaldo think we could rely on them?"

"You're being narrow-minded," Agõtíme said, "and unfair. Those Cachoeira fishermen know more than you think. The Tapuías come downstream all the time to barter with them and the Tapuías know everything about the wilderness. Besides, why should they have lied to us? What profit to them? They're men of good will. They gave us the *montaría*, didn't they?"

"But only because you suggested that by refusing to do so they'd offend the Mãe d'agua. What else could they have done? Theirs is a chancy business; they can't afford not to be generous. But your ability to be overbearing, to imply you're somebody special, who knows what sort of spirit in disguise, wouldn't keep them from cheating a little, just to be on the safe side. 'Good journey,' they cried, only too glad to be rid of us. Cautious, gullible people always lie."

But the dubious character of the Cachoeira fishermen was not of primary concern to Agõtĩme. She thought there must be some hint of the truth in their directions. What really worried her was the moral climate of the place they had now reached. The air was thick with moisture, but no rain fell. Across the river the forest was an impenetrable wall. Surely all that green tangle was a mask. Concealing, representing, but what? Closely observed, the growth on their side was blighted, thorny, grey tones predominating. Nothing seemed awake, or alive, or if it were, then nothing breathed with a frequency she knew. There were no signs to read. She had counted on Gu-Ogun to open the way, and to that end had stolen a scrawny cock from the Imam's yard (a dog was impossible to get) and sacrificed it as soon as they reached Cachoeira. Just last night they'd had the rare fortune to trap a white-crested currasow in one of Suuna's crude snares, and hungry as they were, they'd sacrificed that too, leaving it dangling over the river; but the thicket, after several false starts, remained impenetrable. They decided to spend the night in the boat and try again next morning.

When they awoke there were footprints on the shoal, little footprints heading downriver. "I don't think they belong to a child," Agõtĩme mused, "the toes are too long, too well-defined . . . no, I think they must belong to a Tapuía."

"How ridiculous," Suuna said, "who could possibly wander

tremendous distances on such dainty feet? It's just some monkey come down to drink while we were sleeping. Perhaps the current pulled him into the river."

"No, I think not," said Agōtǐme. "Look, whoever he is and wherever he went, he came down along that path. How stupid of us not to have noticed before. It appears well-traveled, a hunter's track. Let's follow in reverse and see where it leads. Perhaps there is a camp back in there to which he returns by some other route. If he's there, maybe he can help us; or maybe this track leads on through the bush to the stream we're looking for. It isn't exactly the way they described it, but let's assume the fishermen were right after all. Come on, Suuna. We'll have to leave the boat behind."

"When we get there," Suuna said glumly, "if we ever do, we can build some sort of a raft to go downstream. We don't need a fancy *montaría* for that."

Encouraged by an occasional footprint leisurely collecting seepage from foul-smelling humus, Agōtǐme and Suuna kept up a fast pace. Time and distance became distorted by the monotonous snarl and overhang, and gradually they noticed an increasing somberness which warned them they'd better turn around if they wanted to regain the safety of their boat by nightfall. But why go back? This was leading somewhere. Couldn't they try sleeping in a tree? They stopped, undecided, in the hush of the hanging vegetation that threatened to silence them forever in its fibrous net should they stand too long. Then, before either spoke, a strange noise broke the stillness—a resonant thud as if a piece of metal were being purposefully struck against a tree trunk. Where? Fifty paces back along the trail, perhaps. A few seconds later, the sound was followed by a scream—coming from the midst of the thicket, not a stone's throw away. Another thud, another scream—as if in answer, then a low melodious whistle— like a human voice mimicking a dove's. Agōtǐme shuddered. In Dahomey this was a dire warning signal. Silence again. Then a low husky cough, right behind them. They whirled around. Nothing to be seen. There it was again, on the other side—more yawn than snarl. Agõtĩme's hands froze. Her heart beat until she thought it would shatter. From which direction would it spring? She stood poised, too frightened to move, expecting the inevitable.

Not so Suuna. The foolish girl broke into a wild run for the river. Agõtĩme shouted after her. A swish of branches, cracking twigs, hollow foot beats on the earth, then silence. She was gone. Now what? There had been no assault, nothing. Turning for one more frightened look down the path before following after Suuna, Agõtĩme chanced to see a strange little man concealed in the grey folds of a Samaúma tree. He squinted through the smoke of his pipe with an expression that seemed to say, "Well, you've had enough now, have you?" A cascade of raffia falling from a crown of buff-colored feathers made him seem rooted—like an airplant. His face was streaked with genipap juice. Otherwise, Agõtĩme noted routinely, he was stark naked save for a little penis sheath. His feet were turned backwards, heels to the front —the better to deceive the unwary pathfinder.

He did not speak, so she, addressing him for some reason first in Fõgbe and then in Portuguese, said, "I know you, Forest Father, protector of animal life, guardian of the secret properties of leaves; and on this account I beg passage through, at the same moment promising never to molest one of your creatures unless by your agency, never to set snare, draw bow, or," she added as an afterthought, "throw spear." With this she prostrated herself before him, kissed the earth and reverently covered her head with decayed leaves.

When she got up and looked at him again she knew that even if he hadn't understood a word, he had not misinterpreted her gestures. He extended his hand, palm up, fingers slightly curved and said, "*Pa che tan tan aiouca atou pave*" [I am strong and I have eaten many]. Now it was her turn. She nodded, stretched forth her hand in like manner, then stooped to pick up a small wad of sticky black soil which she presented him. Apparently accepting the pledge, for he let it lie still in his hand, he repeated the word *curupira* three or four times, then frowned. She replied, "Agõtĩme." Next, packing the soil in the bowl of his pipe, he put his hand to his head and extracted a feather which he gave her. It was a beautiful soft brown one, black-streaked, like his face. Thanking him, she bound the feather to her left forearm with a bit of rag torn from the bottom of her skirt. Then she bowed, turned and walked deliberately down the path.

She permitted herself to look back once more. He had not moved. The smoke from his pipe hung low along the roof of the forest corridor like a listless python. His eyes, though askance, continued to watch her. Half malevolent, half amused, they gleamed in their darkened sockets, inscrutable as gypsum.

Whatever strange thoughts flickered beneath his wide, impassive brow, she knew that somehow or other the interview had been a success despite unavoidable blunderings. The forest would hold no further mystery. Henceforth all paths would be clear, all watercourses attainable. They would kill no more birds (she supposed fish were all right) but from now on all edible fruits, roots and leaves would so proclaim themselves to the touch.

That night the voice of The Hunter came to her in a dream, telling her to take up a stick and trace a circle on the ground. Having done so, she should step within and it would be as if she were once again in Dahomey—beneath the rain tree on the edge of the great swamp. She did as she was told and saw him—lined, lean as ever, his far-seeing eyes unclouded with remorse. She reached out her hand, but he signaled her not to approach. "For the time being," he said, "I have only certain words to give. Do not ask about your son. You yourself have set the limits of our discourse. It would hardly do for you to be the one to overstep them now. Listen, your quick wit has been your preservation.

Curupira is and is not Aziza, yet you were right to treat him as you did. Now, so far as he's concerned, you may traverse the backlands free from harm. But even under his tutelage, you will not be entirely safe. There remains one danger even Curupira cannot prevent. Come what may, the red star will devour the moon when it is ready. That is a Tapuía mystery. You must not cease your watchfulness. The Destroyer knows you better than you think. You have offended him and in that barbarous wilderness you've come to, he can hardly be counted upon to miss his chance. I alone have the power to deal with him. Should you encounter each other in the open, pick up a clod of earth and summon me."

When she awoke there was a red feather on the edge of a circle by her feet.

Agôtíme said nothing to Suuna of what had happened in the forest or in her dream. She simply said that she had reason to believe they had inadvertently stumbled upon the right path—thanks to that dwarfish Indian whom they would probably never see, whose footsteps, if seen, would never lead to him. Such sounds as they had heard were commonplace in the interior. They must not let their inexperience get the better of them; and they must not kill any more birds. "Now, down the hunter's track with you," she laughed. "Stay right behind me. I'll lead."

And if Suuna wondered at her comrade's new-found confidence, she didn't show it. She had grown used to her sudden spurts of certainty and knew better than to question them. Her own impulsiveness was of another sort. Slack lines depressed her; but once the warp beam had been wound up tight, she took fate in hand and wove defiantly—according to her own design. So that when the route was sure, it was Suuna who made the journey bearable—her jokes, her stamina, her ingenuity. She could kindle a fire in the rain. It was at her instigation that they took time to knit themselves *hamacs* out of vines. And because Suuna had no idea they were being followed, she slept like a sloth in hers every night.

Not so Agõtĭme. That dry cough of his and the muted crunching of ribcages in the crotch of a nearby tree kept her awake. He kept out of sight in the daytime, too, although each morning she came upon fresh spoor and could tell by the amount of moisture remaining how early he had preceded them along the path. In fact, it would have been imprecise to say that he was following them, rather they him. What was it she had said, prophetically, to Adãdozã? That the hunter and the hunted were one. In what sense were they? "Forgive me, Ajahŭto," she cried out to the attending dark, wondering when it would be. And a nightjar answered her.

Where high forest growth gave way to the parched drab of caatinga country, they located the stream that the Cachoeira fishermen had told them about, and Suuna, without apology for her skepticism, again suggested they improvise a simple raft which could be sent before them over the most treacherous places. If that shattered, they could always make another. Two broke. Three were necessary.

Beyond the confluence, when the parent river began to veer east, they set off in a northerly direction across desolate reaches of mesa, a country tortured by drought, irritated by chaparral, pitted with dead lakes and, finally, crowned with thorn trees. Low clouds moved in nightly to impale themselves upon the tree tops. Agõtĭme called this land the Scourge of Sakpata. It was her father's emotional landscape topographically substantiated. Not hers, but she had inherited sufficient grit to endure it, sufficient compassion to find it beautiful.

Gradually the land rose to form a watershed—if water there had been, besides that in the roots of the white blossoming Imbú tree or in truffles on the roots of wild bromelias, or in an occasional cactus. Scrambling up and picking their way down the stone-clogged passes of the mountain ridge known as Dois Irmãos, they slowly descended the fissure made by the Canindé, finally coming to the main body of the Parnaiba. There, with the amused assistance of an entire Indian village, they were able to build a second *montaría*, more or less like the one abandoned on the Jacuipe.

But it was not until they had almost completed the twenty-mile portage to the Itapecuru that Agōtĭme sensed the time at last had come to have it out with Him.

There was something about the yellow swamp grass, its density, the trill of it in the early morning heat, the random disposition of the stunted casuarina trees, the black pock marks in the dry silt of an abandoned watercourse that reminded her of the place where she feared everything had already happened.

She signaled Suuna to stay back and keep silent. Then, advancing slowly into the open, Agōtĭme stood listening attentively to the rough breathing of the reeds. No, not just the reeds. She stooped to pick up a handful of mud.

From the smooth grey flank of a nearby mimosa, a jaguar leaped effortlessly into the sunlight. Touching the ground from fore paws to hind in a graceful flowing motion, he bunched his claws and raised his haunches slightly for the final spring. The low-throated snarl widened, modulating into a scream.

Agōtĭme's fingers closed about the damp clod, crushing it in the palm of her hand until her wrist ached. There was a streak of black and gold in the grass, a horrifying roar, and the tense quiet voice of the Ketu hunter commanding her to jump out of the way. She lurched backward and felt the gust of the falling animal as he met the oncoming spear.

She rolled free. Putting her hand to her eye, she found it sticky with blood, but she could still see. One paw must have grazed the flesh so lightly that she'd not even been aware of it. Surface scratches always bleed more than their worth, but scratches such as these could be worth everything! Had all five claws left their mark?

The ancient kings had been so scarred, but with five incisions on both temples and a trefoil frown between. Those kings never left the palace. They ruled from within, their lives as secret as their bestial origin. Things were different these days. A substitute took the scars and it was he who remained hidden while the king himself was free to stalk abroad.

And the first king's ancestor—was he the hunted or the hunter? She now understood. It was not the panther, but the hunter who had loved Princess Aligbonō. The hunter had killed the panther. No, the panther had loved her first, had given her a son. Or was it the other way around?

She would never know the answer in this life. The Hunter had gone, and in vanishing, had left her his spear propped up against the mimosa. How strange, he must have borrowed it from a Tapuía. They were always leaving their regalia about, those forces of hers. Memorabilia of their bouts. She already had quite a collection—like the keepsakes an old woman's trembling fingers bring forth from the musty bottom of her storage jar to show to a grandniece or nephew. Too large to fit, that spear would have to be propped up in a corner. But how ridiculous all this was. Some things got lost, the *asogwe* for example. Strange, she hadn't thought of that till now. In her haste she must have left it in the slaves' quarters of the Big House in Salvador. Could St. Antony be prevailed upon to get it back for her? Again, how ridiculous. Now where was Suuna? She couldn't be lost. She'd be around as soon as the hunter's charm wore off. The corpse of The Destroyer lay still on the silt of the stream bed—half again as long as a man and three times as heavy. What would Suuna say to that? She had better go down and wash the blood off her face and hands.

The inlet was alive with birds. She had never seen so many in one place. Scarlet tanagers whisked the tips of the lower bushes along which herons stood gravely considering whether or not they would ever move a wing. A pair of egrets remained aloof on a sandbank, as if pretending not to see the intrepid little jacanas with their spindly legs and big feet, striding towards them across the floating leaves. From high in the crown of a solitary Tucama palm came the sound of macaws cracking nuts.

At length, Agõtíme joined the creatures wading in the shallows. As she bent over, an unseen waterfowl spat angrily at her eyes, then with a quick snap of its beak, broke the string of her cowrie necklace. Horrified, she began to grope for it in the soft mud. "Don't think you can ever get it back, with or without the help of your St. Antony," Zomadonu sneered. "Disloyal. Prostitute. And you call yourself a queen? All portages are past, my dear. Your iron-mongers, your pipe-smokers, your gods of the open air will no longer be of any use to you. You must now travel by water until the end, and travel you must. Until the Toxosu dance upon Brazilian soil, you are, shall we say, 'indentured' to me. Lest you forget."

"But without your cowries, how can I possibly establish Zomadonu?"

"When the time comes, I'll give them back for you to hide in the proper corner of the proper room. But you may never wear them again. What have you done with the *asogwe?*"

"I've lost it. O Zomadonu, I welcome your chastisement. But, you know very well I left it behind. Why didn't you warn me?"

"Extraordinarily careless. You'll have to do without it. Don't worry, I shall descend, but to one of your initiates—not to you, never again."

"But the cowries were beautiful . . ."

"Oo, once upon a time, were you."

This was too much. How could that distorted creature be so cruel? "Please, Zomadonu . . ."

The gonofo bird dove into the still backwaters of the Itapecuru.

12 ▶ Bumba Meu Boi

Everyone belonging to the Fazenda Paraiso gathered at dusk to watch Pãe Joachim light the bonfire. The logs had been stacked, as usual, crisscross and higher than a man. The field hands, under cross-eyed Tia Rosinha's supervision, had strung paper lanterns and streamers between the *carnauba* palms that flanked the yard. A table, laden with green corn cakes wrapped in husks, ceramic pots of sweet cane wine and other delicacies, had been set up just inside the gate. Untended kites nodded and banked at the end of strings tied here and there along the fence, while by the harness shed a group of small boys knelt fidgeting with the hoops and stays of paper dancers. As soon as it was really dark, these would take off, far above the everyday kites, in pursuit of an incandescent ecstasy.

Gregorio and Bastião had got themselves up in feathered headdresses and kilts, but the girls, in their Sunday frocks of flowered calico with dimity ruffles and flounces, were obviously less impressed with this display of ancestral finery than with the immaculate linen shirt, short leather cape, tanned cowhide doublet and chaps that Mateus sported. The other *vaqueiros* wore the usual *pindova*—a sugar-loaf shaped cap of soft untooled skin that fitted snugly to the tips of the ears and nape of the neck; but Mateus had chosen this occasion to try out his new *sombrero,* ornately tooled by the wearer himself and tied on under the chin.

As the sparks caught the twigs at the base of the pyre and set the inner pyramid of thorn bush blazing, Gregorio and Bastião began to beat upon their *pandeiros,* the largest and liveliest tambourines in the northeast. Mateus took up his little handmade guitar. Several ganza gourds joined in. Hands clapped, joints loosened and bare feet began to shift in place as Zabalinha's strong contralto delivered a challenge to The Sleeper:

> *"Acorda* João!
> *Acorda* João!
> João *esta dormindo. . . ."*

"Não, Não," the voices of the crowd protested:

"Don't wake up João
He'll wake anon,
Let him sleep, or
He'll scorch the ground.

O Mother, when
Is my name-day? [Zabalinha sang]

It is over and gone, São João! [shouted the chorus]

You know I wanted to go down . . . [Zabalinha again]

Too late, Saint John, go back to sleep!
Who can dance on a cinder heap?
Too late, the ox is in the byre,
This year the world won't end in fire!"

At this point not São João but Dom Verissmo himself appeared on the veranda. He was dressed according to his own conception of the festive: casual silk shirt opened to disclose a pale bony chest, puce satin britches clinging to beige silk stockings at the knee, a vermilion sash and brocade dancing slippers. Raising his spider-like arms to frame a scraggly bearded face, Dom Verissmo commenced to entice an unseen dancing partner with a nervous pair of castanets. Behind him stood his little ashen-faced daughter, Estrela, flattened to the house as if stuck to one of the unpainted pilasters that braced the door. She was awaiting her great moment in an agony of excitement and fear. Her dress was a yellow tutu and her frail little arms were supported in their outstretched position by a pair of stiff gauze wings.

"*Ai está Senhorinha!*" cried Mateus in his generous, enthusiastic way, and the others set up an obliging cheer. Dom Verissmo, with a gallant bow, introduced his daughter to the company and then stepped back to give her room to perform. Accompanied by Mateus' softly plucked strings, Estrela minced forward to the edge of the veranda and sang in a true, yet barely audible soprano:

> Good evening, ladies and gentlemen,
> I wish you happiness every one.
> I am a little butterfly
> Who comes to you from the sertão.
> Though I'm timid, though I'm homely,
> There's magic in my golden wings. . . .

But it was too much. She could not continue, and with a brief imploring glance at her father, fled to her room in tears.

Gregorio and Bastião promptly took up their *pandeiros* and thumped out the lusty measures of the *lundu*, Dom Verissmo's favorite dance. Leaping off the veranda, the *fazendeiro* executed a nimble series of Angolan leaps, clicking his heels together, each of which met with an obliging cheer. Then Zabalinha, with a knowing wink at Mateus (which the latter ignored), stepped forward to dance with the master. Hand on her hips, head thrown back, feet pointed in the European manner, Zabalinha shrugged off each of his supple advances with a deft twist of her provocative hips. From a second-story window Dona Julia's invalid face, like a sorrowful moon, looked on.

When that was over, Dom Verissmo retreated to the Big House and in the lull that followed you could hear old Procopio, the retired dancing master, tuning up his violin. Pãe Joachim, still foreman on the *fazenda* despite his seventy years, jumped up on the steps and shouted for all the able-bodied to form a double line. Gregorio and Bastião began the quick double ground of the coco—the poorman's vigorous equivalent of the quadrilles danced within by Dom Verissmo and his guests. The bonfire was blazing shoulder high by now, sending clouds of grey smoke to mingle with the thick white haze creeping up from the riverbed. Roberto, Zabalinha's kid brother, sent off the first balloon. "Take care of it for me, São João," he called; "for I'll never see it again."

As the dance wore on, several of the girls began to sense that something was wrong. The heart had gone out of it. Someone was missing and that someone was Mateus. Where was he?

O embolé embolée, o embolé embolá . . .

To compensate for that certain distraction, that lack of abandon they themselves were now conscious of, Gregorio and Bastião whipped up the tempo till the dancers shook like pebbles in a gourd.

O emboléembolée, o emboléembola . . .

"There he is!" Roberto spied him first. Mateus: coming across the bluff from the corral with a long rope over his shoulder, leading, a wonder of wonders, the master's prize steer, O Boi: immaculate and obedient as a bride.

"*O da casa!*" Mateus shouted, as soon as he was close enough to be heard, and he clapped his hands three times.

"*Entre, entre!*" the crowd cried.

"No, don't stop dancing," shouted Mateus, "go on. I've got

a proper partner for once. None of you girls is really strong enough to tussle with. Did you say *embolada?* Take a bow, *meu boi.*" Coyly lowering his lashes, the humpbacked animal bent forward at Mateus' command until the tips of his horns touched the broad wheels of his spurs. Everybody cheered. The *pandeiros* began again. "*Oi a canga do boi, oia; oia a canga do boi!*" shouted Mateus, and the dancers serpentined hilariously about the yard led by Mateus and O Boi.

> I heard the hoofs of the cattle
> I heard the seeds in the gourd
> Say my only true love's Catarina,
> The most beautiful girl in the world:
> *O embole embolee, o embole embola* . . .

"How did he ever manage to train him like that?" whispered Bastião to Gregorio above the din.

"Who knows?"

"But what if the master finds out?"

"They're too drunk inside to notice anything."

"Yes, but what if he did?"

"He'd send for the Capitão do mato, that's what," Gregorio said.

> *Bumba meu pai do campo,*
> *Bumba* old man of the backlands,
> *Bumba meu boi, bumba* . . .

As the line swung around by the gate, Mateus, far more alert to anything that might mean trouble than he gave the impression of being, noticed two ragged stranger women standing just outside. "What have we here?" he shouted. "Vultures descended from the heavens to gawk at our feast?"

Floating down the Itapecuru at dusk, Agõtĩme and Suuna had seen a plume of smoke in the distance. It never occurred to them that it might be a bonfire for São João. Let that blaze be a sign of human habitation, let it only be that! Although the sun did not usually deceive them into staying longer on the river than they knew they should, particularly if they wanted to find a safe place to sleep, this evening they kept on poling, following the smoke until they came to something that looked promising: a series of steps cut out of the clay embankment and, a stone's throw farther on, a group of snub-nosed dugouts nuzzled up to a wallowing barge.

Ever since the interminable portage from the Parnaiba, Agōtíme had been fighting attacks of *srá-xome* [dissolving bowels] and fever which left her drenched in a cold sweat and so light-headed that she remained for long periods all but oblivious to everything except the yellowwood shaft of the spear she poled with and that sluggish mass of brown water, occasionally rippled by snags, upon which their flat-bottomed *montaría* purposefully drifted. Agōtíme knew that Suuna was well aware of her desperate exhaustion, but there was an unspoken agreement between them not to complain, not to commiserate, and never to permit expression of those depressing fears that clogged the long hours of their incredible journey like those clumps of swampgrass which obscure and, detached into floating islands, actually distort the navigable contours of an apparently effortless stream. They had no idea how far they were from the sea. The river had noticeably widened, begun to veer off into a confusing series of temporary alternatives, some of which led into blind backwaters, some of which looped back into the main, or into what deceptively appeared to be the main course. Yet having gone this far, Suuna did not really care about distance or destination. What magnificent grazing country! Look, there in the distance beneath that stand of headstrong carnaubas, that might be a herd of Fulani cattle, resting in the shade. "Are you sure that's not a mirage?" Agōtíme would say. Now and then they floated by a deeply pitted water place littered with cow dung, a seeming substantiation of Suuna's belief. But for miles and miles there had been no other signs of man or beast.

Agótime thought it wiser not to use the landing, so they beached downstream in a small cove formed by the bank's erosion. Shoving the prow across a split log that seemed to have served some sociable group of laundresses as a pummelling board, they grabbed their sticks and poked their way up a narrow footpath to the top of the bluff. Here they found themselves on the verge of what appeared to be a temporarily deserted settlement. Somewhere a dog barked, apparently tethered. Two or three answered him. The footpath broadened and turned to run parallel to the riverbank between a double row of cabins which, on inspection, proved to be wattled and daubed rather than woven of saplings. If not a Tapuía village, what then? A *quilombo?* They did not dare enter. They could now hear the throb of the *pandeiros,* and cautiously moving across the flats, they came upon the grand entrance of the *fazenda.* There they stood, for a short while unobserved, astonished by the sight of the dancing steer.

Still dancing, Mateus broke away from the circle, seized Suuna by the wrist and drew her in. "What's this? I was wrong. No stray Tapuía wench, no, by São João, I've a rare beauty here, a black caatinga creeper, a trumpet flower of a girl, that's what I have. Don't laugh, don't laugh I say or you'll live to regret it. She's more beautiful to me, hook-nosed and in rags as she is, than all the rest of you girls put together. What's your name, my little flycatcher?"

"Suuna," said the Fulani girl in a low voice.

"Suuna? What sort of outlandish name is that?"

"Call me Catarina then, if that suits you. But a common name makes not a common thing of me, so mind your tongue, leather man," and with that she wrenched herself free.

"Well, well," said Mateus, taking her hand this time, "she's a peppery little cashew, she is. Let's see how she tastes roasted.

I beg your pardon, *meu boi*," he said, "the Senhorinha and I have a little dance of our own to do. Hold my lasso, one of you; you, Benedito, here, catch it; and don't let him bolt or we'll have the devil to pay." Whereupon he pulled Suuna over to the bonfire which by this time had sunk to its knees in embers. "Are you afraid of fire, my little Bemetevi bird?"

"I am not afraid of anything, senhor, and certainly not of you," said the Fulani girl, with increasing conviction. "I once murdered a woman I didn't like and I suppose if there were a man who was mean to me, if I had the right weapon, I'd murder him too. Let me go."

"That's the spirit," Mateus said, "that's the sort of thing a girl ought to say. No more simpering compliments, whining, pleading, no more tears. But whatever you say, I won't let go of you—ever," he added in an undertone, holding on even more tightly than before. "Now," throwing back his head as if to address himself to the stars, "may Saints John, Peter, Paul, all the worthies of heaven as well as the assembled company bear witness that crook-nosed Catarina with the funny name is my *compadre*. Jump!" he cried, giving her a push.

The *pandeiros* began again, softly. Pãe Joachim took up his guitar:

> At Fazenda Paraiso
> They've milled no rice for three long years;
> Stalks are trampled in the grasslands
> By the hoofs of runaway steers.
> Stay your wild heart, my *caboclo*,
> The good life's here where dreamers dwell:
> > The little Bemetevi cries,
> > "I saw you well, I saw you well."

"Tell me," Mateus whispered, "tell me, my little migrating one, what must I do to keep you here? What is your heart's desire? Tell me and I'll give it to you—anything!"

"All right, senhor leather-wing," she said, "I'll take you up on that," twisting up the straggling ends of her braid and looking askance at him with a sly smile, "I'll stay if you will perform a very special sort of African sacrifice for me."

"What do you mean?" Mateus asked, less confident now.

"I also grew strong among cattle," she said, "far away from here in a place you've never even heard of, a place I shall surely never see again. And when I was a very young girl I used to boast to my father that I'd never be taken by a man till I'd tasted of the tongue of the noblest steer. Now you understand?

"So," she said, after a long pause, "I guess you've decided your little *compadre* isn't worth so much after all. Can't we jump back over the bonfire and cancel out the spell?"

"It's not that. I love that animal as if he were my own, as if he were my very life," said Mateus, "but even so, O Boi is not mine, he's my master's steer, sired by the greatest bull in Ceareá. If he should be killed, there's no telling what would become of me. Do you want a dead man for a lover?"

"Better a dead man than a coward," Suuna said. "You are brazen, you are handsome, but I think for all your bravado that you're a lazy good-for-nothing Tapuía just like your ancestors—may they lie listless in the gourd! I don't want anything more to do with you."

Mateus turned away, his shoulders hunched into a sulk. Suuna ran back to Agõtíme at the gate.

Oia bamba, oia boumba bambia! The *pandeiros* began a frenzied call. The old women around the refreshment table whispered. Had that Mateus suddenly become possessed? Crazy *caboclo*. Look at him, wrenched the spear right out of her hand without even speaking to her. But what was that strange black woman doing with an Indian spear? Better not stand too near, better pretend not to notice her—sometimes that makes them go away. Make the sign of the *figa* with your left hand and the sign of the cross with your right. By all means don't let her catch your

eye. What makes you think the young one isn't just as dangerous? They're the same breed, that should be obvious to anyone.
And it was the young one who made Mateus run mad in the first
place. . . .

Oia bamba, oia boumba bambia. The poor beast grew hopelessly confused. What sort of a dance was this? Had that kindly
leather-skinned human being at last betrayed his friendship? His
nostrils flared. He lowered his head and began to rear. But it was
too late. One spear thrust and he dropped to the earth, his chest
rent with an excruciating pain.

Silence, then whispers. Now look what that crazy fellow's
done. Strike up the *pandeiros.* Keep dancing or they'll suspect
something's gone wrong. Such a beautiful animal. Such cruelty.
He must be possessed by The Warrior. No, it's that strange girl's
fault. She put him up to it. Why did Mateus want to jump over
the *fogueiro* with her? She's an ugly one. Where did she come
from? She's not so bad. It's the old one's spear. It's she put the
jinx on him. Both of them then. Don't just stand there. We'll all
suffer for this. Not just he alone. Call the *pagé.* Nonsense, what
good will a cure do? He's past that—look at all that blood. What
good, I say, what good? Call him anyway, you never know.
Maybe he's in league with those two. Start the music, Bastião, or
they'll think something's wrong, I tell you. To hell with them,
now's our chance. You fool, they've got guns. The Capitão's in
there. We couldn't possibly take the house. We'd all be killed, or
maimed for our pains, like Juca.

While little Roberto ran up the path to the thicket where the
Indian doctor lived, Gregorio and Bastião did begin to play again,
a few random rattles cut in, but nobody danced. They just stood
there, casting furtive glances at Agõtĩme and Suuna—everybody
but Mateus, that is.

Surely he's being ridden by someone, Agõtĩme thought, not
our Thunderer, not our Warrior, but by some barbarous feathered equivalent of one of them. I can feel his force; I can almost

see him. And she put up her hands to ward off whoever it was.
The old women shuddered, mistaking her gesture for a jinx.

Mateus meanwhile was riding the spear like a hobbyhorse,
zigzagging back and forth across the court, singing dolefully, as
if alone at night in the *campo grande:*

> Little cashew
> Filled with fire
> I too am burning
> With desire.
>
> My friend is dead.
> What's that to me?
> I'll find another
> In Piaui.
>
> Fall, little rain,
> I also weep
> My lovely ox
> Has fallen asleep.

Then, changing his tune, Mateus became inexplicably comical.
Jumping off his hobbyhorse, he rushed up the stairs, clapped his
hands three times and when he was sure of everyone's attention,
began to improvise a string of nonsense that purported to be
"The Last Will and Testament of a Slaughtered Beast."

> O Boi is dead
> Long live his beef,
> On his behalf
> I now bequeath
> His bloody tongue
> To the rising sun
> To keep my love
> Forever young,
> His cured hide
> To the timid bride

His gaping jaw
To the mother-in-law,
His cheerful tripe,
To the buxom wife;
His hindquarters
To thin daughters

Zabalinha—the spleen [faster, double time]
Legs to Gregorio
To Rosinha—the lean,
Lard to old Bastião;
Standing roast—to the Holy Ghost,
With tidbits left to the Jesuits
And bone marrow for every *vaqueiro*
And marrow for every *vaqueiro, Ai,*
And marrow for every *vaqueiro.*

Seeing the *pagé* at the gate, Mateus tied up his song with a refrain and rushed to the center of the yard with the others to watch the proceedings.

Fumigation first, of course, accompanied by imprecations in an unintelligible tongue. Then, handing his long pipe to the boy Roberto, the healer crouched close to the wounded part of the ox's body and gradually began to extract the various items imbedded there: thorns, fish scales, a housewife's need, a live lizard, and last of all a mysterious radiant stone. This, the *pagé* promptly reinserted into O Boi's end as a clyster. A hideous stench ensued. The crowd drew back in disgust. But look, the purge was doing its job!

O Boi opened his heavy eyes, lowed softly a couple of times, switched his tail and attempted, clumsily, to rise. Mateus pushed forward to help him. "He lives, he lives," everybody cried. "What a miraculous cure! Whoever would have thought that *pagé*, wise as he is, could raise a steer from the dead. Will wonders never cease!"

> My pale white ox has a valiant heart,
> Rise up and dance to the tambourine;
> Dance away darkness, dance out the light,
> *Bumba meu boi!*

sang Mateus.

"Come, wayfaring woman," said Tia Rosinha to Agõtĭme. "You are weary, anyone can see that, and ailing besides. Don't let those ill-mannered old women get you down. They think any stranger they meet is going to put the jinx on them. But tomorrow they'll have forgotten all about it. They'll outdo themselves to be nice, you can count on it. See, Mateus has returned your spear and taken your niece away to dance with him. There's no telling when or how it will end. You'd better come home with me. Please be my guest. Come, my poor house is not far from here." Agõtĭme nodded through the dense fatigue which had been gradually closing in on her like white fog from the riverbed, and allowed herself to be guided back along the wide path to the cluster of shanties on the bluff where Rosinha and the others lived.

At midnight on St. John's Eve all waters are sacred on account of the holy baptism of Our-Lord-of-the-Good-End. The muddy Itapecuru being no exception, the revelers in the courtyard of Fazenda Paraiso kept time by the Southern Cross and, at the enchanted hour, dispersed to fetch jars from their cabins.

Tired now beyond sleep, Agõtĭme, through the window in the back room of Rosinha's shanty, watched the shadowy procession disappear over the brim of the embankment and then return—earthenware jars silhouetted atop the moving heads.

In Dahomey, at the conclusion of the dry season, the Toxosu's priests (white chalk about their eyes, new palm leaves about their waists) returned in like manner from the sacred spring followed by stately *nesuxue* bearing the spirits of their ancestors. Thus, someday perhaps, downriver in Maranhão's seacoast city graceful white-gowned initiates would carry invisible Toxosu in their containers to the sanctuary. No, this was not a bad fate. She could, for the first time albeit in a shadowy way, imagine how it would really be. Were not Zomadonu and the rest already incipient in the silty waters of this slow-moving stream, ready to pop out at any minute? Caught up in some of these very jars, perhaps, without their carrier's knowing it? Tia Rosinha said the waters were sacred now, were they not always sacred? Who knows how many water spirits were clustered up there at the snags and roots of upturned trees along the Itapecuru? Those *Iaras* the wild Tapuías worshipped, and the ubiquitous Mãe d'aqua [the moon's daughter], the mysterious dolphins, the golden fish of the sun: how would the quarrelsome Toxosu manage to get along with all of these? She laughed at the thought, rolled over and fell asleep.

Up at the Big House, likewise, everyone was asleep at this hour, everyone, that is, except little Estrela who from her lonely window overlooking the balcony had witnessed everything. But they had swept away the blood in the courtyard. Her mother had gone to bed long before and she, Estrela, would never tell, no not she. The slaves were her friends and when she grew up she would inherit the estate and free them—Mateus first of all, whom she would marry and treat like a king. "I am a little butterfly," she sang softly, so that nobody, not even the beastie ghosts and night riders would hear her, "I am a little butterfly, who comes to you from the *sertão*." She wished that she hadn't failed so miserably before them all, that she could have sung it out there on the veranda as she sang it in her dreams. "I am a little butterfly, no, that's stupid. I'm not a little butterfly at all. I am Estrela, star of gold, yes, that's who I am, really,

> I am Estrela, star of gold
> Hovering over the *sertão*,
> Like the ancient secret told
> When the earth lay dark and cold.
> I bring the dawn. Awake, São João.

13 ◄► Rosinha's Shanty

Agõtĩme stayed many weeks at the Fazenda Paraiso, from São João's Eve until just before the onset of the heavy rains. It was a quiet time and she spent most of it inside Tia Rosinha's shanty or just outside on the stoop, surrounded by scarlet pepper plants that sprouted from pots hanging about the wooden frame of the door.

She never went into the fields with the other women, but she planned, when she grew stronger, to work Rosinha's plot in the communal garden across the flats from the *senzala*. (The slaves were allowed to grow their own vegetables, but Rosinha never seemed to have time to tend hers properly and her daughters-in-law were too spoiled to be of much help, much too spoiled in Agõtĩme's view.) Meanwhile she made herself as useful as she could and kept her own counsel. In the morning she set out the trays of rice and manioc (grains of the moon and sun, she told the children) to parch. In the afternoon when the thatched overhang began mercifully to shade the wrinkled mud façade, it was her pleasant chore to bring the wicker cages out. Hooking these over wooden pegs driven into the daub, she would sit down to grate, pound or grind food for the evening meal, all the while listening to the birds and keeping an eye on Tia Rosinha's grand-children as they toddled back and forth along the dusty road with their companions—other children, chickens, and a harum-scarum collection of dogs. Sometimes, in the evening, Mateus and Suuna came to call, not as often as she would have liked, but often enough, she supposed. This was Suuna's place, her story they had stumbled into; she had no claim on either of them. Mateus occasionally reminded her of Vivaldo; but he was not Vivaldo—not at all.

There hadn't been the slightest difficulty over the affair of the ox; on the contrary, O Boi now belonged legitimately to Mateus. From what neighboring ranch Mateus had abducted that spirited wife of his, Dom Verissmo had no wish to find out. Over-joyed that his prize *vaqueiro* was at last going to settle down (no more wild trips to Piaui or Para, thank God), Dom Verissmo sent a side of beef to his good friend the Capitão Mor (in case someone should lodge a complaint) and in an unprecedented fit of generosity, gave O Boi to Mateus.

No, that handsome gesture was not so extravagant as it might seem, the *fazendeiro* confided to his wife. To tell the truth he'd been rather concerned of late. O Boi had been behaving so strangely, he'd begun to suspect . . . that odd scar on his chest, for example. According to Mateus the animal had run mad in the stable one night and tried to gore himself with his own horns. Dom Verissmo didn't really believe this story. More likely some sort of sorcery was involved. Mateus must be covering up for the *pagé*, reputedly a distant cousin, or was it an uncle, of his. Ugh, what an evil-smelling old fellow that one was. He'd have kicked him off the place long ago, if he weren't afraid of leg cramps at night, or convulsions Yes, O Boi had grown too high-strung . . . better let Mateus have him, he knew how to handle him. After all, O Boi wasn't the only white ox in the world. In a few weeks he'd be going to Ceareá, just to look around, mind you, just to look around.

Even Agōtíme's presence at the *fazenda* was regarded with far less suspicion than anyone would have thought. The Capitão do mato came by on his rounds a week or so after her arrival and Dom Verissmo, who thought Mateus was just wild and generous-hearted enough to have abducted a mother-in-law for himself as well as a wife, said nothing about the old woman reputed to be living in Tia Rosinha's cabin. But the Capitão do mato could not be put off so easily. He'd got wind of someone, and if Dom Verissmo wouldn't talk of anything but the drought, well he'd just prowl around down at the *senzala*.

Rosinha had told the Capitão do mato that it was true, she did have a guest but the poor woman was very ill. "Nonsense," the Capitão do mato had said, "that surely means you've got a fugitive in there. Do you know how many lashes you'll get for concealing her?" And with that he pushed his way into the house.

Agōtíme had heard about *capitães do mato*, and had dreamed of being pursued by one as a child dreams of being devoured by Quibungo the monster with the hole in his back; but she and Suuna had been lucky. She had never met such a creature face to face before now. Well, there he stood, splayfooted and bulge-eyed, the rolled brim of his felt frontiersman's hat touching the roofbeam, the bandoleers crisscrossing his chest like strings of teeth ripped from the jaws of a monstrous iron-plated crocodile. And worst of all, he was a black man turned against black men. Semidelirious with fever as she was, Agōtíme would not be intimidated. She sat up in the *hamac*, swung her legs down, and narrowed her bright eyes. Nor did she flinch as he moved closer to study her forehead. "What? No 'F,' no fugitive?" he drawled, as if unwilling to concede that he had been wrong.

"Of course not, I told you she was not, *meu capitão*," Rosinha said. "She's an *akpalo* [wandering storyteller], surely you've seen the likes of her before, coming and going as you do. And as you can see, she has been very ill. She still is."

"When she's well, I'll pass by here again to listen to one of her tales," he laughed, "then I'll be able to judge."

"Wait a mo-ment," pointing his finger at Agōtīme's right eye, "here's something interesting. You, Senhora Akpalo, will you have the goodness to tell me how you got those scars? If I didn't know better I'd think, or would I?"

"That's true, what you think, Capitāo," said Agōtīme. "You've made a good guess; or, rather you've made two guesses, one good, one bad. These are indeed marks made by a jaguar's claws. But I am just as human as you are. Wandering from place to place, there's no telling what you may or may not run into. You must have second thoughts about your own profession, sometimes, camping at night by a dwindling fire, too close to a watering hole and miles and miles from the nearest *fazenda*. You travel armed, of course. Well now, in my own fashion, so do I. Look, over there in the corner; that *zagaia* spear actually killed such a one not too long ago."

"Very well, Senhora Akpalo," he said, backing into the curtained door, "very well."

To Tia Rosinha, once they were out of earshot, he said, "If you know what's good for you, old woman, get rid of her as soon as you can. You'll never be safe with someone like that around."

"I realize that, my captain."

When Tia Rosinha returned from showing the Capitāo do mato out, she found Agōtīme lying back in the *hamac*. She was drenched in sweat. Her eyes stared fixedly at the frayed palm ceiling through which the noonday sun grated golden specks. But her voice was natural, even intimate, as she said, "Tia Rosinha, I am better now, but in case of another bout, let me thank you while I can for all that you have already done for me. How clever you were to invent me such a character. Akpalo, how ingenious; I never would have thought of it and yet it suits me better than you can possibly know. Sometimes I've feared to be just that, storyteller and nothing more. I shan't object to making myself useful in that trade while I'm here. I've not forgotten how. My flock of noisy birds have flown away but they'll come back to build themselves yet another colony of nests before I send them off again, one by one. You won't regret having taken me in, and when the time comes, I'll unravel my *hamac* and be off in pursuit of them, beyond paradise." She laughed.

"Come to think of it," she went on, "I ought to practice. Why not begin with the true tale of how these scars appeared on my right temple. To you, my friend, an audience of one, to you and no other. You must have been curious about them yourself, but were too polite to ask."

"I never gave them a thought," lied Tia Rosinha, "and you must never, if you'll forgive my advice, bring up the subject again. You were most incautious just now. Your words had the intended effect on the Capitão, but you could have spoken indirectly to the same end. I don't know where you come from, but we never speak of The Destroyer here, never mention him by name, especially if he has had an unfortunate encounter with a spear, for his defeated spirit always seeks to revenge and one never knows, a chance reference might be enough to summon him."

"Forgive me," Agôtíme said, "I was feverish, and inexcusably afraid of the Capitão. Let us hope that his spirit was sleeping."

"This house is well protected," Tia Rosinha assured her. "Now you too must try to sleep."

Of The Destroyer one must never speak. Amid all the obscurity, this much leaked through the thatch. The Old World prohibition held good here; had stalked after her, in fact, all the way through the new forest. It had lain hidden in the thicket as, in the rocky recesses of her mind, she'd always known it would. And it had verified her. And beyond that, what was proved? The validity of a past life? Of all supernatural experience? Or was it, rather, the prophetic truth of the imagination? The storyteller's birds come home to roost? Who knew? Surely she did not, never would. This was as far as she could go along such an obscure path. The brand on the boat: that was unreal. There it was, still on her breast, but she had never accepted it. No, she was growing old, and she might be recaptured and sold many times, but she had never and would never be a slave, not in that sense anyway. To have been clawed by the unseen, however, and to have survived to tell the tale, even if it could never be told, this made an honest woman of her!

And so in the evenings before Tia Rosinha and the others returned from the fields, Agōtīme would take the wicker bird cages in and set the pots on their stone tripods over the banked charcoal fires in the cooking shed. She could never quite get used to rice, but there were always beans—she had become quite expert in preparing them with okra and little *maxixi* squashes from the garden. There were tomatoes and the leafy green they called João Gomez to make *caruru* with if one of Tia Rosinha's grandsons happened to be lucky with slingshot or net. They never lacked oil. And over all there were crushed peppers for stamina and dried manioc for grit. When Juca, Tia Rosinha's husband, came back from São Luis on the big plantation barge, he would bring a bag of coffee with him. Saturated with raw sugar, there was nothing like it for strength. Suuna said she thought Agōtīme was getting fat. "Nonsense," Juca said, "she's still as scrawny-legged as a water bird." She'd better stay on a while longer. She was good company for his wife.

Juca the bargeman was a bitterly lined, grey-haired man with a wooden leg. He had been maimed twenty years ago by Dom Verissmo's father for instigating a revolt. He had to ply the river. It was the only kind of work he could do.

At night Agōtīme played her part as Akpalo, the wandering storyteller of those bygone times. Tia Rosinha's cabin was always crowded with company, old and young; and it was little mouse-haired Estrela's secret delight to wrap herself in her mother's cast-off shawl and sneak down to the *senzala* after dark to listen to that tall, strange African woman tell of Orphan imprisoned in the drum, of Quibungo with the gaping hole in his back, of the three brothers—Foresight, Swiftness, and Healing. Which was best? Who knew? Agõtĩme even improvised on Tapuía tales. They were incomparable mimics, the Tapuía. Her own favorite was the one about the sun who became a golden fish in order to have feathered arrows shot at him. He envied the trees their crowns, the birds their crests, the Tapuías their headdresses. And she always ended her stories like this:

> *"Assim me contaram, assim vos contei;*
> I've told you this tale as it came to me;
> The next one to catch it will sing in a tree."

When the time came for Agõtĩme to leave Fazenda Paraiso, the children could not understand why she didn't want to stay on and on, forever.

"Because I have to get down to São Luis before the heavy rains."

"But that's no answer, Tia Agõtĩme; it rains just as hard there as here."

So Agõtĩme told them one more story. "This is a very special one," she said, "and while I tell it I will be glad I'm wearing the little *figa* Roberto carved for me. I heard it long ago in Dahomey. It's a secret. You must never repeat it. But if you listen closely, you'll understand fate. It's my son's story, really, not mine. It's the story he was born with and in our language we call it *Gbe Gouda* [It is patience that becomes king].

"A certain king had three sons who all lived in the same village across the lagoon from his palace. When the king died, messengers were sent across with the news. Each son, in his own way, prepared himself to go to the funeral. Ahouakaka, eldest and most diligent, reached the beach before the others and so was the first to step into the waiting canoe. In the middle of the passage, the ferryman ceased paddling and said, 'We've not discussed the fare. If you are to reach the other shore you must promise to give me food and drink, all your worldly goods, and your wife besides.'

" 'You must be crazy,' Ahouakaka said, 'I'm the king's eldest son and I refuse to pay you that or anything. Now get on with your paddling.' So the ferryman knocked him on the head, threw him overboard, and got on with his paddling. Ahouakaka drowned. The ferryman went on across with all the baggage, including Ahouakaka's wife, which he concealed on the other side.

"Returning to the landing whence he had set out, the ferryman found Ahoualele, the second son, ready to embark. Ahoualele, with all his goods, got in, and in the middle of the lagoon, the same thing happened to him.

"Gledo, the third son, was slightly delayed—not out of lack of respect for his father's memory, but because he took time to consult the nuts of divination. 'Gbe Gouda, am I,' his horoscope said. 'Give everything that's asked of you.' And Gledo vowed to be generous. When the ferryman stopped the canoe midway across and asked the third son for his payment, Gledo promised that once they had indeed reached the other side, he would give the ferryman everything he asked. Thus cheered, the ferryman began to beat the waters with a vigorous stroke, and as he paddled he sang:

> Ahouakaka refused. What happened to him? Drowned!
> Ahoualele wouldn't give. Where is he now? Drowned!
> Gledo will pay everything. A sensible fellow. Gledo will be
>   king!

To which the third son replied in a trembling voice:

> *Kumi lenle, tonu būkuto!*
> Paddle carefully, boatman of the lagoon,

> Paddle gently that my foot may reach firm ground,
> Foot in the canoe—protest impossible,
> Paddle cautiously, boatman of the lagoon.

Then the ferryman, growing expansive, confided in Gledo, telling him where he had hidden his dead brothers' things.

"When they reached the shore, Gledo handed over everything as promised—food, drinks, cloths, ornaments, and his wife. But no sooner had he been enthroned as king, than he called the rogue to the palace. Holding the ferryman prisoner until all the loot had been found and brought to the king's audience chamber, Gledo then and only then performed the execution. The ferryman's corpse was buried beneath the threshold of the royal gateway. Then Gledo once more consulted the nuts. This time Gbe Gouda said, 'You have done well. It is patience that becomes a king.'"

It was Sunday. The bushes by the riverbank were festooned with laundry—white shirts, petticoats, and head ties bleached in the sun. Against the stark blue of the sky, young girls could be seen walking across the flats carrying cumulus clouds on their heads. A group of boys were busy diving off the embankment and fighting their way back against the current. Everybody else was gathered about Agôtĭme on the mud steps watching Juca and his crew load the barge with baskets of rice and dried beef for market in São Luis. When it was time to go, Agôtĭme turned to say a last goodbye to each of her very special friends—Tia Rosinha, Suuna, Mateus, Roberto and little Estrela. Then, grasping the yellow-wood spear she had found that day by the carcass of Ianouare-the-Destroyer, she eased her way down to the landing. Someone gave her a hand onto the barge. She waved to everyone on the palisade. Pegleg Juca pushed off with his steering oar while all the boys in the water shoved at the bow. Within minutes she floated free. The current was strong. And within seconds they had rounded the bend.

14 ◣▶ Casa Xelegbata

She sat alone under the arcade. Leaning back against the cool whitewashed wall, she stared through half-closed eyelids at the cajàzeiro tree in the garden. On the other side of the wall, where she could neither see nor hear them, her dancers, like herself immaculately attired, sat ranged about the perimeter of the sanctuary. They were already in deep trance, but while they waited for the *tambor* to begin, the women, sitting primly as if not to muss their dresses, continued to hum the brief phrases with which they had just now drawn the impatient forces down. Rid of all particularity of expression, their impassive faces, sealed by heavy eyelids and up-thrust, overlapping lips, had become forms for casting the molten motives of existence. Thus in her mind's calm, Agõtĭme envisioned them. It was a lull over which she, like the goddess of storms, could remotely preside while waiting, waiting for the ambassadors.

Even if they were punctual, she would not have time for more than a brief exchange of courtesies before the ceremony. It was three o'clock. In a few minutes the *huntos* would arrive to tune the drums. The arcade would soon overflow with lay members of the cult and the usual stray visitors. The ambassadors would, therefore, be obliged to sit through the *tambor*—which Agõtĩme was not loath to have them do.

On the contrary! Bade was in excellent form this afternoon, and Leocadia could always be counted on to carry him well. Zomadonu was quarrelsome, naturally, but expertly controlled by Maria Fosi-Yome. This girl (a newly arrived Maxi) was the perfect medium for his quirkiness. She kept as tight a rein on him as he on her, so that he usually departed in a good humor. Or perhaps it was not entirely Maria's doing; perhaps the new world was imperceptibly mellowing the Toxosu, making him more amenable, as it slurred and morrowed everything. The *terreiro* was well-appointed, her dancers dignified, truly regal in their bearing. The achievement, after all, was real. Did anything else matter? Today there would be official witnesses. They would tell the king's birds, and the news would be passed onto future generations so that all Dahomey would know that their gods danced here. Would this satisfy Zomadonu? Would she then be free?

The ambassadors had arrived on the English admiral's ship and were staying with Doctor Quintus Almeida on Quebracosta Street. It was Benedito, her master drummer, who brought her this news. He worked as a stevedore at the docks and knew everything. She and her novices had heard the cannons as the flagship entered the harbor, and Benedito explained their significance, recounting everything that happened afterwards. But the "historic surrender" of the loyalist troops on Palace Square, the establishment of Brazilian "independence" on the Captaincy of Maranhão —what did that all mean to them? What did they care? Next to nothing, if it came right down to it. She wished the young emperor good fortune, but was there really any reason to believe that high-sounding phrases and a change of councilors would rid the people of their poverty, give their elders a voice in the young emperor's council, and open the eyes of those whites whose disdain for black people was all the more vicious for being disavowed? Supposing, just supposing young men like Luiz Braga succeeded in reaching the conscience of the young emperor, supposing all slaves were freed (which seemed most unlikely), what difference would that make now? A vicious collaboration of circumstances had brought over her people. Neither impassioned speeches nor ill-timed revolutions like the Imam's would right the balance. They would have to bide their time. Some day they would dominate. Some day they would be justified. Meanwhile the forces would sustain them. The forces were everywhere-in-the-world, as strong here as in Africa.

Who were these ambassadors? Would she recognize them? Not likely. Old men would not choose or be chosen to make such a trip. The women were curious. Supposing they were from Dahomey? But Agŏtíme had forbidden Benedito's going, as everybody wished, to tell them of her whereabouts. If indeed they were from Dahomey, let them smell her out, she said. It should not be difficult. Everyone in the black community knew her—if not by sight, for she seldom went out these days, then at least by reputation. Everyone knew this much about her—that in the old days she had been a queen there, and that now although she had a different kingdom, she still reigned supreme. Agŏtíme had not seen fit to tell even her initiates about the pact with Zomadonu, nor about her son.

Secretly, of course, and from the very first, she had known exactly where they were from and why they had come. When Doctor Almeida's servant had appeared at the door of Casa Xelegbata this morning with a wrought-iron staff discreetly wrapped in a white cloth, she had the presence to tell him to have the ambassadors call at three, adding, "Tell the esteemed gentlemen from Africa that I have been expecting them." They would probably begin by telling her that her son, now king, sent greetings. And this would be no news to her. Already for some time, for two or three years at least, her son's captives had been inun-

dating the rice fields of Maranhão with their Maxi sweat, their
Maxi lamentations. She had heard snatches of these last from
Maria-Fosi-Yome. They called him Gezo, the buffalo king:

When Gezo's armies broke through our well-guarded passes,
Surrounded Sokologbo, Kpaloko, Dassa-Zume,
We hastened to sow corn in our courtyards,
But the reservoirs, concealed deep in the cliffs,
Being outside the walls, were no use to us.
Who can wring water from grinding stones, or snare
The stampeding buffalo?
But can hawks harm the turtle till he's overturned?
There is a king overthrown, someone said,
His head turned spindle. Who holds the thread?
It is she, Gezo's favorite wife, Alotekã.
Night has fallen on the king of Savi, and the shadows
Slink down over Kpaloko, Minifin, Hũdjroto.
So one by one we came down from our mountains,
Those of us able to walk, or be carried, or led by the hand,
Forded the Zu and crossed blood-red ground to Gezo's king-
dom.
There he divided us, the men from the women,
And the old were put to work in the fields of Gobe.
But not all of us were to be sold.
From one hundred and sixty he chose
A group of musicians, saying, the rest would be slaves to
his wives.
But who can envy the bushfowl her feathers, besmirched as
they are.
Let us mourn for the pinioned eagles
Of Sokologbo, Kpaloko, Hũdjroto,
Let us weep and throw dust on our heads.

That the King Gezo of whom the slaves sang so bitterly
was Gãkpe by another name, Agõtĩme never doubted. Why

should she? She had performed her half of the bargain and had counted on Zomadonu to do his. Zomadonu was paramount—to all appearances, anyway. So far as the members of her cult were concerned, it was the water spirit who ruled her head and therefore ruled her house. And if it was wild, wily Legba who lent his name to the place as official guardian, no one commented on this anomaly, if anomaly it was—for nobody thought it such, not even Zomadonu. Why should he? At the beginning of each *tambor*, Legba was sent away while Zomadonu stayed on to dance at the head of the Royal Family—which was, apparently, all that counted with him. In Dahomey he had been merely chief Toxosu; here in São Luis there was no greater Dahomean force than Zomadonu; he dominated all the rest, even Thunder. Had he also, as a result of this increase of strength, grown proportionately important over there? She gathered as much from the increasingly pompous way he carried himself when he came down.

This she surmised without actually knowing for certain because their relation had gradually changed. For one thing, as mother of the house, she never danced him. After all, it was he who had forbidden this beforehand. But now that she had things well organized, he never appeared to her even in an informal way, never popped up out of fountains or waterjars or the nearest stream to needle or berate her, certainly not to indulge in confidences or to court her with incongruous dreams. It was as if, that afternoon on the Itapecuru, he had, without relinquishing his hold, given her up. If ever *vodū* were jealous, he was then; but now that far more dangerous rivals strove to possess her, he did not even seem to notice.

Well, their common enterprise was done. The cult was established. The Mãe de Santo would be amazed and, most likely, just the least bit envious—though São Luis was nowhere near so grand a place as Bahia. And over there? From this distance it seemed as if Zomadonu had but heaved an old enormity out of the muck and wrapped new cloth of gold about it. Yet who could argue that for Dahomey, Gǎkpe—now Gezo—was not a suitable, even an exemplary king? Surely he was successful, as Adǎdozǎ had never been, in expanding the kingdom's reach; and his cruelties seemed to be directed against his enemies.

Why blame Zomadonu? Who could have foreseen the way things would turn out? The slaves brought tales of the preeminence of de Souza. That man was in control of everything in Whydah town, on Whydah Beach. He had a hundred wives, they said, and he dressed like a king. So even the Ketu hunter had played, without knowing it, a destructive part. Gǎkpe and Chacha had, by means of the pact, both grown powerful enough to pervert it and had discovered how to make blood brotherhood pay. Never, people said, had there been such an influx of slaves from "the coast." But had not she herself been the first to mention the mulatto's name? Her own part had been by far the most reprehensible. Had she not given birth to everything?

So the youngest son had managed to get across the lake—thanks to Agǒtǐme, Zomadonu, the Hunter, and the Trader. In addition one would have to admit the Bokonǒ to this fabled company. If Gbe Gouda had not been the future Gezo's fate, would the wise diviner have made the palm kernels turn out that way? What was the primary significance, the urgency of the Dahomean Earth that its fate must at all costs be embodied in an energetic young king and be allowed unimpeded to act out its porous dream in iron fact and deed? She had not the Bokonǒ's superior vision of things. Nor could she intuitively understand. Her vision had always been that of the alien, the independent Maxi.

Nor did her countrywomen understand, yet still they came to swell the ranks of her congregation at Casa Xelegbata, came from the slaves' quarters of the townhouses, from the dilapidated shacks of the free, from as far as they could walk on a Sunday, to welcome the ancestral spirits of their first oppressor—first cause of all their griefs. True, the Royal Line was but one of three in the world of forces as she had envisaged and established it, the other lines were pure Maxi; but it was precisely the Royal Line, Zomadonu himself, that was most popular among her exiled people. And it was the Maxi women whom the royal *vodũ* deemed their best daughters, their best dancers.

The wives, the eternal wives of the panther.

She was now a mere caretaker of the garden, custodian of these restless vitalities that prowled the earth in search of a Dahomey. But once she had given birth to everything.

What was Gãkpe like now beneath that new name of his, those awful praises, those renowned feats of thick-necked bravery, that famous cloth of gold? Did she really want to see him in the flesh? Would there be anything to say? Should she not let him be? Had not their paths diverged, irrevocably?

Her heart had gone out to meet many children along the way—Fina, Oro, Suuna, Estrela and, by force of circumstance, most steadily to Luiz during these last years. Luiz, was he not closer to her than her own son?

He had been a pale-skinned boy of ten when his mother brought him along with her to Casa Xelegbata many years ago. The mother hoped that the Africanos, "who knew so much about simples," would be able to cure her of shooting pains along the scalp which troubled her and kept her awake night after night. Agõtĩme consulted the cowries on her behalf and said, "Senhora, one of the powerful spirits who lodges here among our sacred stones has already spoken for your child, and you in your ignorance have angered Him. Those pains of yours are but mild signs of what is to come. If you care for the life of your child, leave him here with us. Go your way, we here at the convent will take good care of him until the time comes for his initiation."

Thus Luiz Braga, forbidden by the oracle ever to see his uneasy mother again, began to play the role of the fortunate orphan beneath the flowering cajàzeiro tree in the walled garden they called "*Gôme*." It was the only bit of Africa he would ever see, but it was enough to make a dreamer out of him, a romantic poet with liberation his theme.

His white mother moved across the bay to Alcantra, married a policeman, some said, and in any event was never heard from again. Luiz, now a law student, at the *terreiro*'s expense, had recently moved to a room in the Faculdade; but he had formed the habit of coming most evenings to take a *cafezinho* with his "aunties."

To Agõtĭme, of course, he was especially devoted. Her stories had kindled the evening fires of Africa in him, fires from which torches were lit to herald the dawning of a new day. She told him many things—intermingling her own extraordinary experiences with those of fabled creatures from both sides of the Atlantic. Nor did she neglect the story of the Middle Passage or of Aligbonõ, although, in her confusion on the banks of the Itapecuru, she had sworn never to tell it to anyone again. Luiz in his turn remembered everything; and when, leafing through old copies of the *Diário Maranhense,* he happened upon an account of the Hausa Uprising of '07, he came running back to Casa Xelegbata to ask if by any chance the famous "Princess Aligbonon" was she. Then she had laughed and told him, for the first time, about Vivaldo: told him how destiny had seen to it that she keep exclusive company with spirits, diviner-priests, and kings, and how Legba, finding this path much too narrow and undeviating, had prevailed upon Fa to make an exception. "Let there be one ordinary man for Agõtĭme," Legba had said; and Vivaldo was he; but you could hardly call him ordinary.

And Luiz had said, "I never knew and I never shall know who fathered me; but I do know he was a black man, and I wish he could have been Vivaldo."

It had been a proud moment for both of them when Luiz brought his first hand-printed volume of *Versos Incendarios* to her. Standing in the shadow of the arcade, standing straight and slim in his clean white shirt that reflected light from the garden upon his sallow, sleepless face, Luiz standing thus had read the dedication:

To My African Queen

The ebb and flow of life knows no suspension;
In the eyes of my black mother are reflected
Ancestral lands my brothers have neglected
For shallow patrimonies of their own invention.
Pale as I am, I'm Negro—or Dog, or Fowl
I might have said. Stop looking at my face!
The world allows each creature enough space
To shout or sing in the darkness, whine or howl
Until the coming dawn when we shall rise
To follow the forces fathomed in her eyes.

Worthy sentiments but the words were stiff and glutinous. It was not poetry. Nothing breathed through the words; but she resolved at once not to betray her disappointment. What had she expected? Praise-songs in Portuguese? It was too vague a language for that. The sad elegance, the magic eloquence of the little *modinha* of the dark cliffs? Nonsense. Such sounds appealed only to degenerate aristocrats—like herself, she smiled. She would not hurt Luiz's feelings, and besides, such talk was useful; she could see that. So, drawing Luiz closer to her, she had said, "Vivaldo would have understood every word of what you say. Yours is a man's work, a continuation of what he began long before you were even thought of. Thank you, my son; I am unworthy of the dedication"—which was true, but in an obscurer sense than he would ever understand, honest Luiz.

The ebb and flow of life—these words, come to think of it, did say something to her, after all—but not exactly what Luiz had intended. Over the years the river had changed its course, stranding her dry and wrinkled. She was alone and unprotected. She glared at the clay mound in the garden. Its cowrie eyes

caught the glint of the afternoon sun—highlights. Heavy, heavy.
O no you don't, Elegba, not yet. Not today. I know you not,
Elegba.

The *huntos* had begun to tune. Striking the pegs with a
wooden mallet, Benedito tautened the ram skin so that Hũ would
speak properly to Gũpli and Hũpli. Esperança, the housekeeper,
tapped her gently on the shoulder, "Mãe Agõtĩme, Mãe Agõtĩme,
the ambassadors are here."

Dosuyovo was bald as a gourd. Age had streaked Atindebaku's face like the cross-section of a nutmeg; but she would have
known them both anywhere. They, clearly, were not so sure.
"Greetings after some time," she said, "after more than three
days, after long, long silence."

"Greetings to you, elderly woman, we hope your health is
good."

"How is everybody back at home?"

"They exist, thank you."

Still they were not sure, still they refrained from committing
themselves. Unrecognizable? Had she changed so much? The situation amused her. She could not resist exploiting it. "My heart
grieves," she said ambiguously, "for all the little details of your
very busy lives of which distance and the passing years have
spared me knowledge."

Again they hesitated. There was no hint of a smile on the
old priestess' face, but despite the commanding look in her eyes,
they would not prostrate themselves. They were wearing European frock coats. They would kiss her hand.

"When three lizards from Abomey turn up on the same rock
in another part of the world," she said, "is it not strange that they
should begin by demonstrating the advantages of travel? How is
it, countrymen, that not having seen or even inquired after me
for years, you should at our reunion further insult me by taking
me for a foreigner?"

"Forgive me, forgive us both, honored lady, so great was our delight in finding you at last that we could not believe our eyes," said Dosuyovo.

"Still cannot," Agõtĩme laughed. "Is it that you expected to find me perched in a tree instead of seated upon a shaded veranda?"

Atindebaku's smile was like a clear stream after a thundershower. "Na Agõtĩme . . ."

"We had to be certain," said Dosuyovo solemnly, "we could not discuss the king's business with just anyone. Gezo, formerly Gãkpe, now Buffalo, Toucan of the Incombustible Thicket, sends greetings to Agõtĩme of the Palm Groves. We have come to São Luis on the red-bearded admiral's ship, a privilege accorded us by His Imperial Majesty Dom Pedro—a very special friend of ours," he added.

"You have no need to impress me with your connections," she said, suddenly angered, "I remember you well. You have always been at the service of wealthy merchants and kings."

"Am I to be blamed for my destiny?" Dosuyovo asked. "I have but followed where fate has led me. Not many months after your deportation, my employer fell into disgrace and I with him; we were thrown into Cãboji Prison where as chance would have it I shared a cell with Xaxa de Souza, an even more eminent man of trade. We became very special friends, he, the then prince and I; and having suffered together, we naturally continued friends in times of prosperity. In a modest way I helped your son become king, and since that time I have served him indirectly as de Souza's linguist."

"All of us are our own best interpreters," Agõtĩme said. "Tell me," turning to Atindebaku, "how do you serve Gãkpe?"

"This is a difficult question to answer, Kpojito [Queen Mother]. Whether I have indeed come to America to find you with Gezo's blessing on an old trusted friend of the family, or whether I shall continue to serve him best by serving in exile, remains to be seen," he said, with a side look at Dosuyovo.

"Certainly for a Migã to leave the capital even for a short trip to some troubled place within the kingdom is unusual; but for a Migã to absent himself across the sea is without precedent," said Agõtĩme.

"Exactly," said Atindebaku, "you understand me perfectly."

"Tell me then how you have served him in the past? I always believed you partial to Gãkpe, despite Adãdozã's claims to the contrary. But in the old days you walked with discretion. When the opposing faction threatened revolt, you challenged to fire upon the thrones of the ancient kings. Then you hurried to Agõglo and told him to give in to Nahoue and name Adãdozã immediately. When I was imprisoned, you did nothing to help me; you stood by and watched me disgraced and sold, thinking only how fortunate it was that you did not have to kill me. Later, however, as the princes grew dissatisfied with Adãdozã, you must have come to risk more and more with increasing certainty of success. Am I correct?"

"It is a harsh view, but true in its outlines, Kpojito. You were always incautious, as a girl, if I may be forgiven for saying so; and I imagine you have found scant need for such wrappings over here in this vast territory. That Adãdozã had special powers at his command was common knowledge, sorcerer's powers in addition to those transmitted by his ancestors. It was also common knowledge that he had a particular talisman against enemies hid beneath the threshold of his audience chamber. Now when those who attended conspiratorial meetings were able to cross that threshold with impunity, I deemed those powers attenuated and took the pact with Gãkpe's nearest of kin. And when I, by other signs and prodigies became convinced that the royal ancestors had completely withdrawn their support from him, I set a secret date for the dethroning."

Agõtĩme smiled at the mention of prodigies. This was Zomadonu's work—a surfeit of hydrocephalic children, she supposed, unseasonable floods, the unexplained presence of mildew on brocade finery. "Go on," she said, "or shall I tell you? On the appointed day, Adãdozã and all his ministers, seated in council, were surprised to hear the distant voice of the great war drum heralding the king's arrival. Was not the king already where he was supposed to be? Dogba, the drum, however, was not. It was missing from its accustomed place by his side. Futilely, his fingers groped in the air. Hopelessly as a wounded animal he watched a hostile procession enter the throne room: first Dogba, then the royal musicians, then the royal birds, then the princes and princesses of the royal blood, and finally Gãkpe himself in a short-skirted hunter's tunic. At a sign from you, Atindebaku, the Minister of the Left Hand pulled the embroidered slippers from Adãdozã's feet. Then to the sound of drum you said, 'Two suns may not rule in the heavens at the same time. Step down. You are king no more. Long live the third son. The prophecy is fulfilled. We commit ourselves to the coolness of water.'"

"How did you know, Na Agõtíme? You have described the scene as if you had been there yourself, seated among the wives."

"A little bird told me," she laughed, "but it did not tell me everything. I have no idea, for example, how matters stand behind the high walls of the wives' court, walls I used vainly to wish that I might scale like a lizard or soar over in wild flight."

It was the prime minister's turn to laugh. "Things stand worse there than any place else in the kingdom, Na Agõtíme. Adãdozã is not dead, Gezo still dares not get rid of him—and who with the possible exception of yourself can blame him for that? However, your son has taken every precaution to make sure his memory will not survive—confiscated everything he ever used, all his regalia. His throne—you will be amused at this—was shrouded in black and white like a corpse, borne down to Whydah and shipped across the sea to be a coronation gift for the young emperor. We ourselves, on Gezo's behalf, presented it. Dom Pedro has no idea whose it is. I rather imagine he thinks our craftsmen carved it specially for him; but because I grew fond of Pedro the first time we lingered there in Rio City, I took the precaution of telling him he must never sit on it. Let us hope he never does.

"Well, as I was saying," Atindebaku continued, "Adãdozã still exists, albeit in Hedjanamonu Prison where not even the pigeons can see in, and as long as he does there are those of his former harem who will persist in remaining loyal. They quarrel with Gezo's chosen women, will take orders from no authority, certainly not from Alotekã—Gezo's favorite. Everybody in the wives' court hates her—the Maxi captives in particular. But the Maxi girls hate everything about Dahomey. They erode their good looks, their dispositions and everyone's peace of mind with their continuous wailing. They are seditious streams of discontent. I wish all of them, with apologies to you and your fate, sold away to make trouble for their masters and mistresses here in the new world. But Gezo will have them stay, keeps bringing new ones in with every additional conquest. He says he likes their spirit. Alotekã, being of their generation, cannot command their respect; nor can she ever aspire to. For she is evil, Na Agõtĭme, evil-tongued and evil-hearted. I wonder that Gezo ever married her. She has him bewitched. How you've been needed, Na Agõtĭme! Only the *kpojito* can rule over the *kposi*. Only Gezo's mother can restore order to the wives' court. And that is why we have gone to such lengths to find you. Until you are in your rightful place . . ."

"You go softly," she interrupted him, "and you are a very long time arriving, longer than the chameleon. The sea is wide, but if I remember correctly, it took us not much more than a month to complete our journey. And we had many inconveniences, many delays, changes. Tell me, old friend, did you travel by slave ship?"

The prime minister pretended not to hear the last question: "No sooner had Gezo become king than he said, 'Now at last I may send for my mother.' But his hands were tied. He had a kingdom to consolidate against enemies without and within. He had to show his strength immediately. When Gezo for the first time sent the Nago ambassadors back empty-handed, the people cheered; but the Nagos answered his defiance with invasion. He had to drive them back and one by one subdue the arrogant Maxi villages who collaborated with the Nago cavalry—lit flares, sent food to them—and while he was gone no one of any importance could be spared from the court. These battles won, he dispatched me in search of you, along with Dosuyovo as linguist plenipotentiary. I admit he should have considered that without domestic tranquility a man's external conquests can give no lasting satisfaction. But he, being young and eager for victories, may be forgiven his lack of wisdom."

"And I, who was growing old, my impatience," she said. "The post of *kpojito* being vacant, what have you done with the one who formerly reigned over the wives' court? Queen-mother's blood, can that be shed with impunity? Or have you exiled Nahoue, perhaps."

"Agōglo's first wife broke the stone long ago. No one closed her mouth for her. She was an old and very bitter woman. But now that she is gone, night has fallen doubly upon her. No one mentions her name. And to make doubly sure of this, Gezo has gone so far as to refuse to permit the installation of a living substitute."

"How kind of him to remember how I hated her," Agōtime smiled. "But is she not represented structurally by her gate?"

"That too is gone without a trace," Atindebaku said. "Gezo had the convicts wall it up and with the advent of the heavy rains the fresh clay became indistinguishable from the main. But a new gate has been cut through in your absence, Na Agōtime, making a path for the sun's last rays. You will find it where the wall now juts out to the northwest to accommodate more houses for common wives and their slaves. Not ten bamboos south of Senume's gate is Agōtime's."

"Yes," said Agõtĭme, "I know the place." With this she rose. "And now, honored visitors, I beg your indulgence. The *tambor* can no longer be delayed. You should be more comfortable over here by the low wall. There's a nice breeze from the garden. Our people call this garden *Gôme*. If you will be kind enough to take these seats I have reserved for you. Excuse me, excuse me, please. Here we are. Please sit down. We can continue our conversation afterwards. But you must be thirsty! What you had to say was so enthralling, I completely forgot. Forgive my discourtesy. Esperança, please bring these gentlemen some cool water." And with a slight nod to each of them, Agõtĭme turned away.

The congregation, of whose arrival she had been oblivious during the greater part of her talk with the ambassadors, greeted her warmly, but did not detain her as, smiling, she brushed past them on her way to the sanctuary.

> There was a saint,
> Sent by the lord,
> To wash away
> The sins of the world
> *Alleluia*, São João, *Alleluia*.

Globs of white wax in their shallow bowls set here and there upon the altarcloth of spume-white lace glowed like phosphorescent eyes of the sea, and the little tongues of flame rose now and then from their tallow beds to lap at the obscurity, briefly illuminate the ebony faces of the saints, and then subside again to await a fresh draught through the jalousies.

When they had finished singing the litany, Agõtĭme led the dancers out of the sanctuary on to the veranda: all three families in their proper order—Earth first, then Kings, and finally the combined hosts of Thunder and Sea. Bade rumbled forth with a blue sash about his dancer's waist. São João's day was his to dominate and Leocadia walked accordingly, with enjoyment. A royal welcome from the three drums broke upon their heads, spurging trance into ecstasy. The congregation clapped out in fours against the syncopated sevens of the gong. Hū, Hūpli and Gūpli spoke out their distinct patterns; and locked in that stampede of drum beats, the sisters sang the *Adajibe* [calling all gods], sang it for form's sake, joyously, after the fact, for in Agōtīme's house she saw to it that the forces came early, stayed firm and departed leisurely.

> *Adajike vodū daame*
> *Ahole vodū daame*
> *Emimaho pa pa be* . .

Having thus invoked the *vodū* and having once again, without incident, sent Elegba away, Agōtīme sat down on the bench beside the *asogwe* players to bless each daughter as her turn came to dance before the drums. There was no need for her to hold a silver bell. Her dancers never got too hot. Nor was there room on her veranda for a white wicker throne.

What a night that was! She didn't blame the Mãe-de-Santo for turning her out. Zomadonu had behaved atrociously. In the early days of Casa Xelegbata, she herself had been at pains to keep certain wild *caboclo* spirits from gate-crashing. In the suburbs of São Luis there were *terreiros* enough to take care of those bow and arrow brandishers. No Indian influences at all, no astral or even Angolan lines for her, no Nagos either. No weeds in the garden. Casa Xelegbata must be kept pure. That was their only chance for survival. But to play the queen—once yes, now no. Her style, although modeled upon that of the Mãe-de-Santo, was decidedly not Nago. More austere, more internal, it was her own.

During the week she maintained a quiet discipline, taught, listened, consulted Fa, told what she could, took proper care of the herbs in the garden, of the stones in the sanctuary. But come *tambor*, she, unknown to the others, in her own way, let herself go. At such times she considered herself to be a kind of counterweight, or restraining force. As each dancer's nerves, fragile as the veins of a leaf, became for a few splendid moments part of those unseen wefts of existence that make all fixed forms vibrate with strength, energy, the blood, the sap, the very breath of life, it was up to her to hold tight. And when, to the fierce energies released by the play of hand and stick upon master drum, the *vodū* responded, rode their mortal horses across earth, sea and sky, it was she who kept them, to the confines of the dancing floor; and at the same time it was she, the hidden fourth drum who absorbed the force, vibrating soundlessly until the song was done.

And Agōtǐme smiled that benign, placid smile all *mães-de-santo* unconsciously don, and glanced across the narrow veranda at the ambassadors.

Dosuyovo sat perfectly still—a look of tolerant boredom smoothed his face. Atindebaku scowled, intent—whether upon his own thoughts or upon the proceedings it was impossible to tell.

The *vodunsi*, on the other hand, were clearly doing their best to impress the ambassadors. Even in their entrancement, they were at some level of consciousness aware of the presence of the foreigners, of the importance of the occasion; and this restless excitement in turn communicated itself to the *vodū* and subtly conditioned their behavior. Zomadonu and Sakpata, for example, had taken this occasion to revive their ancient feud. As old gods, both were entitled to carry canes which they used to punctuate their stylized thrusts and parries:

Sakpata: Well, look at the savage animal we've got here!
             If Buffalo sees Goat, he gets agitated;
             If Eagle sees anything moving, down he swoops;
             Hyena's on the loose—better look to your kids!
             Guess what, Dog has chased Hyena out of the forest!

Zomadonu: No one dares make war on Zomadonu,
             Nor on Wemu who said he was a shark,

Nor on Adomu who ravished an anthill,
Water spirits all! Drought shrivels your yield?
Perhaps you have been insulting us.

Sakpata: Who ventures abroad at midday will behold
Nothing but scorched grass. If you chase me out,
I'll say
The land will be ruined. If you don't chase me out,
Chances are it'll be ruined anyway.
On the heads of kings falls a terrible malady.

Zomadonu: You go and you come, you come and you go;
Whatever you do, you can't get at my gills.

Sakpata: Zomadonu, you're a wily one.
Close relative of the panther kings,
I was just joking. I too believe
That nobody can make war on you.

And so it was with amicability resolved. Agŏtĭme nodded her approval and the gong set the pattern for the final praise of the Royal Family:

O Dako-donu, seller of slaves,
When you raise your sword,
It's to peel heads.
And you, Akaba, male yolk of twins,
And you, Agŏglo, who stood unscathed
Beneath the thunder-struck Dende palm,
And you Zomadonu . . . Dahomey,
Your force dominates the world. O kings,
My hands long to perform
All my elders have done,
Be all they have been.
We the strong survive;
We knock at the door;
Nobody answers.
The house is empty.
We remain outside.

Now the Kings sat down on the bench beside Agŏtĭme while the Thunder pantheon rose to perform. They were the youngest and most vigorous of the three lines, quick currents of energy connecting clouds to sea, justice to crime, fire to hearth.

There were no sky gods in Agŏtĭme's house. If Mawu and Lisa had deigned to descend, she would not have excluded them; but they never did, neither here nor there in Africa; and for reasons of her own she was determined not to establish shrines for them. These were the gods Na Huãjele had brought from her Nago community to reinforce her son Tegbesu's claim to the throne. But there had been a heavy price to pay for such an excess of maternal ambition in that case and so, she feared, there would be in her own. It was not merely that the sky gods' establishment legitimatized a political subservience to the Nago kingdom of Oyo. More importantly, those gods embodied an order beyond human conception and to steal an earthly throne in their name was to invite disaster. No wonder Dahomey was plagued by deformations and droughts at the beginning of Tegbesu's reign. Na Huãjele forced Zomadonu and his Toxosu out of the inchoate stream to play their parts in Dahomean family history. The murder of Agŏglo again upset the equilibrium, forcing the Toxosu into renewed aggressivity. Fa chose Gãkpe king. Zomadonu—his power magnified, intensified—installed him. That other elements would retaliate was sure; it was merely a question of time.

Thus rival factions seeking to authenticate their power generation after generation invoked opposing forces in the greater cosmos, little dreaming that it was they, the kings of this world, who were being manipulated to give expression to those primordial conflicts that infused life into everything. It was possible to see all human activity as possessed, and, strangely, only those who danced the forces themselves, who became their purest expression, contained—even if they could not sustain—the secret of equanimity.

No sky gods then, in Casa Xelegbata—although Nana-Buku,

the ancient crone in remembrance of whom Zomadonu had given Agōtǐme the cowries, had her special home in the sanctuary. But why did neither Hunter nor God of Iron ever descend to dance there? Could she, now that she was aware of so much more, continue to blame their absence on Zomadonu's jealousy? Each of these *vodū* had, at different times, showed her the way. Did these fraternal forces belong in another cult that she, Agōtǐme, under a different name, was destined to found in some as yet unimaginable place?

It had taken weeks, even months to find this one. Juca had helped her find a temporary place to live—a refuge in the midst of the tidal swamp where the freed people built their stilt-shacks on land nobody else wanted. From there she'd gone out every clement day to the compact little city of São Luis: down the narrow cobblestone streets between the tall shuttered townhouses, across Cathedral Square to the promenade overlooking the bay, descending this or that breakneck hill to the quays and then pushing by crowds of bare-torsoed stevedores, skirting crates, barrels and enormous baskets full of fish, avoiding slippery patches of pavement, to the market place where she would stop awhile for a cup of cane juice before trudging up and over the hill again, varying her route from one day to the next until every house on every street came to seem vaguely familiar.

And then one afternoon on her way out of town she had suddenly come upon the ruins of what must once have been a handsome retreat for Catholic friars or priests. She wondered why she had never noticed it before. Stepping across the rubble of the outer wall, she hurried expectantly across slabs of cracked tile flooring to stand in the shadow of what was left of the arcade and look out, through a rounded frame of mildewed stucco and exposed brick, onto the inner courtyard of her waking dream.

The herb garden was dead; the tiled pool dry and littered with refuse; but there was a tree, a cajàzeiro, with stubby deformed boughs. Shielding her eyes, she could see protruding from the fistlike nodules at the bough-ends of the blighted tree, the spikey promise of new twigs.

And as she stood, the declining sun reddened the bark until the tree seemed all aflame. Then the flames subsided and it seemed all leaf, the way it must have been once, and would be again. Now she observed the earth from which it sprang to be pitted, like laterite in the dry season, all flat save for a single mound, anthill-shaped, right at the base of it. And round about this stretch of porous ground a sleeping serpent coiled. Overhead a ring of thick black clouds was forming. A chill wind came up, skimmed the loose dust off the clay, swirled it up and whipped the heavy boughs into motion. There was a long roll of thunder. Lightning struck the tree. Rain fell, flooding the earth; and the sluggish contractions of the great snake begat the flux and reflux of a new-formed sea. But the invisible roots held. The rain eventually ceased; the waters retreated, and from the mound at the base of the tree a young antelope emerged, picking her way across the muddy surface of things. And touching earth at two points, from forked tongue to tail-tip the snake defined the arc of the sky, then disappeared, leaving his multicolored skin-cloth behind. And into the trench his sleeping body had made along the edge of the world, moisture began to seep, and seep, until there was a continuous stream from which fish lept, into which waterbirds dived deep; and the shallows teemed with multiple births and unrealizable conceptions. Then a panther appeared and began to pace up and down in the thicket grown up about the base of the tree. The antelope ran every which way, begging shelter from the sun-speckled leaves. Crouched on a low bough, Sky's eldest offspring, The Hunter, bow in hand, kept a cold eye on both of them. Night fell, and the vision vanished—all but the tree.

This ruined place, as it turned out, could be had for a pittance. The courtyard and crumbling arcade were the sole vestiges of a Jesuit seminary that had reverted to the Captaincy of Maranhão. The other buildings had gradually been torn down to make way for rooming houses and freed slaves' tenements on footage available upon payment of a small bribe to the prefect of police. But some neighborhood urchins having declared that odd-looking tree haunted, no one, until Agõtïme came along, had been willing to set foot in the garden.

(What's that strange woman doing living there in that place? Juca the one-legged bargeman from upriver helped her build a shack—hidden behind the old wall. You can't see it from the street. She was staying down in the flats before then. It was Juca brought her down from the interior in the first place. She says she's a queen from Africa come to establish the royal ancestors in São Luis. She's got Benedito and a couple of his friends to drum for her. How she managed to attract them away from the Nago house down the way I don't know. Sunday afternoons. No, there've been only a few possessions as yet, but she's begun to give beads; consultations at all hours of the day or night. Who wants to spend the night among the wailing ghosts of the Jesuits? Why not! That woman has force, more force than any Mãe-de-Santo I've ever seen. Just to look at her gives me the gooseflesh. Those eyes of hers. And what a grip she has. Do you know what they say . . . ?)

The lines of the original arcade pleased Agõtïme and when she had attracted enough followers to warrant the construction of a proper *terreiro*, she asked the men of her cult to restore the old cloister as best they could—with dirt floors rather than tile, of course, with adobe walls rather than imported masonry. That was why, unlike most new world *terreiros*, hers had no central pole about which the dancers turned, why the dancing area, being oblong, was so cramped. But in her mind's eye the *vodunsi* always danced counterclockwise about the cajàzeiro.

Beneath the tree Legba's cowrie features smirked upon an image of the anthill she had seen there that first day. Patron saint of the crossroads, he, guardian, extortionist . . .

> O Averekete,
>   I found you in the movement of the waves;

O Averekete,
   I found you in the ebb and flow of tides;
O Averekete,
   I took a walk all over the world, and
   I found you on the surface of the sea.

Averekete and Bade, having completed their solos, turned now to greet, as if after a long, long time, to demonstrate their indissoluble kinship. Hands up they approached (Averekete young and slim, Bade middle-aged and bulky), then palm to palm they pushed off in opposite directions, swirling round and round until they came up sharp against the knees of the congregation, then, moving away, they revolved again until they collided, back to back, unmovable as boulders. At last, after a long pause, they turned to embrace. The drums rolled and everybody clapped.

Now the gong took up the dismissal rhythm. The congregation rose while all the *vodunsi* danced in place. As usual, Agõtĩme led the Earth and Royal families out, then back again, to prevail upon the Thunder pantheon to quit the floor. Being young gods, they could have gone on all night, had not Agõtĩme implored them to cut their pleasure short. At this point a strange thing happened. Maria Fosi-Yome [Zomadonu] stepped out of line, strutted up to the ambassadors and without saying anything indicated that they prostrate themselves and kiss the ground in front of her. And Agõtĩme was amused to see that not only did they understand her, but, sheepishly, complied.

"Now gentlemen," said Agõtĩme, having greeted all the invited guests·and led them to the refreshment table in the dining room at the south end of the arcade, "we may continue our conversation. I commend you for sitting so long and, from the look on your faces, with so little enjoyment. We should be more comfortable in here," she said, ushering the weary ambassadors into the little room at the north end where the drums were stored. "You see, I have taken the horse by the tail and brought you each a glass of aguardente. Surely you, with your experienced tastes, will prefer this to the unfermented cane juice our ordinary guests are drinking. I have brought a third glass for myself. You can have supper later on, should you choose to stay. You'll be pleased to learn that we have *calulu, egô*, everything just the way it is prepared in Abomey. But perhaps you have grown accustomed to European food, to supping at the whiteman's table with a long-handled spoon. On the other hand, it's always nice to be able to relax."

"Na Agõtĩme," Dosuyovo broke in, "I do not understand. Why are you telling us all this? We did not come here to be put up, as at a traveler's inn. We have spent months, even years looking for you and now we must be getting back to Bahia and thence home. As soon as the Admiral returns from Belem, which should be any day now, he has promised us return passage on his flagship. How long will it take you to settle your affairs?"

"Yes," Agõtĩme said, "I can understand the need for haste. I imagine that my son, despite the soothing sounds of his captive orchestra, despite the charms of Alotekã or whoever, must rest uneasily when he thinks of his mother wrapped in a few rags on some filthy cockroach-ridden mat or sharing some straw with a colony of lice. Well, someone ought to have disabused him."

"Na Agõtĩme," Dosuyovo said, "you are tired. All this must put a terrible strain on you. You ought to get more rest, even at your age. Yes, we do admire your work. We had no idea . . . and if we have failed to respond the way you intended, it's just that . . . well, you can imagine . . . it was rather difficult to follow . . . familiar, yes . . . but in those white dresses, the women . . . However, our confusion, the product of our ignorance, should not in the least detract . . . Gezo will be humbled to learn that his ancestors are so honored here. No one is more pious than Gezo. You'll be glad to know that no sooner had he been made king than he called the Sakpatasi back. Your father's spirit must have rejoiced that day when they came dancing in to Sïboji Square, their straw skirts swirling, their straw veils shaking in the dry wind. No king has ever respected the cults with Gezo's enthusiasm, not just his own favorites—all of them. And the chief priests, when they learn of what you have performed here, they'll make you an honorary initiate of every cult there is, daub you with blood and feathers, streak you with kaolin, wind chains of cowries about your neck . . ."

"You don't understand."

"I think I do," Dosuyovo continued, "you're reluctant to let go. You're no longer young. Surely you must have your eye on a successor, trained to take your place."

"Tell me, Atindebaku," she interrupted quietly, "what the consequences would be if I didn't go? And I don't mean such matters as continued brawling in the wives' court. Do you understand me?"

"I think so. Things would run smoothly there, as here; in fact they already do. No, there'd be, I suppose, no consequences at all from the ceremonial point of view. They've got a substitute *kpojito*, an ample middle-aged woman (who looks nothing at all like you) to take your place in all processions until you return, with her long-handled cane and her broad-brimmed hat to strut about Sïboji Square at annual custom time, to dance the *botro* before distinguished visitors. Everything that happens has happened in the sky before, the old Bokonō used to say. Back in Abomey we make sure that everything continues to happen on earth as it happened before, and that everything which happens now happens in duplicate. At this very moment the female Prime Minister of the Right Hand is sitting in the palace somewhere—my counterpart; and fifty years hence an ample-buttocked woman will represent me in all the important processions, will walk beside priestesses personifying the spirits of the three kings I served during my lifetime—no, only two, I had forgot the curse on Adãdozã."

"You understand me perfectly," said Agõtĭme, "indeed the

depth of your understanding in these matters pleasantly surprises me. But there is a missing shard from the broken pot we have been reassembling: Gezo. The real Gezo who wears the embroidered sandals now, what is he like as a man? Would I recognize him? As a small boy he was so close-mouthed, so proud, so independent, so defiant of authority. What is he like now? Would we find anything further to say after the prescribed greetings had run out? Would we understand each other like the two insects in the fable?"

"I will praise him with pleasure: He's six feet tall, strong as the buffalo who lends him his name; thick-necked, heavy, although you could hardly call him fat; dignified, careful never to offend the forces, but full of self-confidence—not in the least like Agŏglo. The king? He is a clement friend, ambitious yes, an expansionist, eager for increase of wealth, of trade, yet he holds to the pact and will not plunder a blood brother's village for slaves. With all Europeans, especially those who speak with a double tongue, Gezo is defiant, but well-spoken, persuasive. With his wives, he's more playful than stern, rather afraid of them, if the truth be told, too inclined to let their intrigues trammel him —a weakness common to Dahomean kings, from my experience, and if one believes the old stories. This is the king.

"Yet to describe the medicine inside the gourd is to leave the most important words unsaid," the prime minister continued. "Know then, Na Agŏtĭme, that we are constantly at war and yet our fields burgeon with maize, red millet and other seeds; palm nuts pend from our trees like testicles; our children's bodies are sleek and fat and their mothers sing 'heel down hoe down' in the fields as they plant, sing *pocla-pocla* [pestle to mortar] as they prepare food in our well-swept courtyards. The Nagos all have gone. Gezo and the royal princes, all their wives, wear silk damask with impunity in Kana now. The slave trade is more lucrative than Agaja ever dreamed. All are satisfied. Under Gezo our kingdom has at length achieved health and renown."

"If such be the fate of Dahomean soil," said Agŏtĭme, "it is difficult to imagine why the king needs me. What was his real motive, Atindebaku? Does he wish to be known in song and story as the successful king who did not forget his mother, as the king who was powerful enough to seek her out no matter how far away, no matter how great the expense, to ransom, to redeem, to provide for her in her old age? Or was it a lingering hatred of Adādozā that moved him to dispatch you in search of me, a desire to undo everything, without exception, that his elder brother ever did? Or could it be, as we suggested earlier, that he sent you off with no thought that you would ever find me, sent you on an impossible mission for the failure of which you could, conveniently, be blamed and sent off again, and again, to spend the remainder of your life in pursuit of a phantom?"

Now Dosuyovo, who had been sitting in a sullen stupor as they talked, could no longer suppress his irritation. Turning first to Atindebaku he said, "It would seem that with all your talk of substitutes and representatives, you have, in the course of this conversation, decided that you don't really care whether she goes back or not. She's clever. I'll have to admit the thought had not occurred to me. Perhaps our mission was but a plot to get you out of the way—although why, I can't suppose. But I refuse to be used as an instrument in your banishment. I shall continue to interpret literally. We were sent for the queen mother. If we succeed in bringing her back, and there is every reason now we've found her that we should, Gezo can always invent some other excuse for getting you out of the country. He cannot, as you well know, under pain of his own death deliver night to the prime minister. So you are safe. But I am not.

"O we were stupid to have returned with empty hands the first time," Dosuyovo continued, "that was when we both should have stayed away, stayed on in Rio until Dom Pedro found a way to help us. We took a terrible chance, at least I did. Had it not been for the pact, de Souza would have had me murdered. I don't think even the pact would stay his hand a second unsuccess-

ful time. Nor can I stay on here in Brazil if she won't go home.
Not only are you immune, but you've already got an honored
place in official tradition. You are the man who dared depose
Adădoză. Not so I. The success of this undertaking will make
all the difference as far as my part in history is concerned. It's
my only chance to be remembered as more than the mere subordinate I've spent most of my lifetime being. We must discuss
this further.

"No matter what you and he decide to do," he said, turning
to Agõtĩme, "I shall not fail a second time. No matter what was
intended by those in authority, I shall go down in history as the
resourceful ambassador who brought back Queen Agõtĩme. And
if the king's birds cannot be relied upon to sing of it, my children
will repeat the story to their children and it shall be told again
and again by my kinfolk in prose until one day they cannot help
but weave that loose strand into their official poetry.

"Stay on in this backwater for all I care," he went on
rashly, "your true decision will have not the slightest bearing on
the facts. You know how legends are—mere nests into which invention lays credulity. As far as our friend Atindebaku's concerned, I know him well. He'll allow himself to be persuaded by
you, not the other way around. But then again, he, unlike me, has
a place to go in Brazil. Why should he spend his declining years
banished to some place he doesn't want to be? The young emperor likes him, liked him from the start, thought him an excellent horseman and a polished diplomat. Me Dom Pedro ignored. I might have been a servant of Atindebaku's. When the
English admiral Cochrane sailed north to pacify the Portuguese
loyalists, Dom Pedro sent us along in the flagship because he
thought you just might be found up here in Maranhão. But before we sailed, the young emperor knighted Atindebaku gave
him a title—so that he'd have to sit at the admiral's table. I, although I speak five European languages, sat with the crew. Let
him stay for all I care! He can get a job as hangman down there

in Rio, or if that job is filled, a stableboy or groom's job will suit.

"If you don't go back I shall tell Gezo the truth, and then I'll just as blandly suggest that he need not accept it. Let's pretend, I'll say, that I did bring her back. Let's say, however, that she's so old and ill that she's confined to her room, to her little house between the palace proper and the wives' court. Let's say that the *kpojito* will make her first public appearance at grand customs.

"Then I shall go back to Whydah. And in the evenings, when I recount our adventures to the listening ears of my young kinsmen, I shall amuse myself by whispering that some say you, Agõtĩme, are not really Gezo's mother at all, only his nurse, a last-minute substitute for a true Agõtĩme who, once upon a time, a generation ago, lay dying in childbirth. Thus planted, this seed of doubt shall grow until like the perfidious Clusia it shall in time surmount the true fig tree."

"That sounds like one of Nahoue's old threats," murmured Agõtĩme.

What else was there to say? She thought of pulling Atindebaku aside and telling him of the talisman she had buried long ago beneath the future site of her queen's-gate. But what good would that do? It would only give him cause for further anxiety. So she simply said, "Goodbye old friend, until tomorrow. We all have much to reflect upon. Matters such as these we have discussed cannot be decided hastily. I shall spend the night in seclusion among my stones, and I shall consult my cowries. Come back tomorrow afternoon when the sun is halfway down, when our shadows are the same length as we are, and I shall have a conclusive answer prepared for you.

"I must warn you," she said, unbolting the outer door, "to be careful on your way back to Doctor Almeida's house. It is St. John's Eve, a popular festival here. All sorts of revelers prowl the streets—wild Indians from the interior, fugitive slaves in disguise, renegade soldiers with their *caboclo* sweethearts, *vaqueiros* on the town and full of drink, simple hearts and desperate criminals, those whose wits have wandered and mere pranksters. You'll hear the same tune on many *pandeiros—bumba meu boi;* it sounds harmless enough, but the hidden motives are difficult to distinguish. Keep a sharp lookout. The masqueraders, if they can, will strip you of everything you have."

"We shall be circumspect," said Atindebaku. "We too shall go back over everything said tonight. May no shadow fall upon your path, or mine, until we meet again."

Dosuyovo bowed without saying anything.

She bolted the heavy door behind them. Well, that was that.

There was still work to be done about the *terreiro.* She and Esperança helped the *vodunsi* undress, carried their limp organdies to the laundry room, gave them whatever they wanted to eat, indulged their tired petulance and at last put them to bed like fretful children who have been kept up too late. Then she bade the other members of the household goodnight and asked to remain undisturbed until morning. It occurred to her that Luiz Braga had not put in an appearance at the *tambor.* Well, she supposed he had his reasons. He was young, and it was St. John's Eve. She decided against sending him a note. It was time to concentrate on other things: the jars first. She would try to get in touch with Zomadonu.

When the cocks in their pens behind the kitchen crowed for the first time, Agõtíme traced the tenth major sign on the ground just outside the sacred triangle containing the jars and the little pool of stones where the forces slumbered.

Flight, fanning the air, fire, and the flow of blood; swallow flying at dusk, wagtail, falcon hovering against the wind, oriole, linnet, nightjar, screech owl modulating its cry on a single note—all the sorcerous birds, ominous creatures of the winged night. (The tracks stopped at that watering place on the banks of the upper Itapecuru. It was time to take another path.) Palm groves delight me not. Let the name return to roost. I have had enough. Let me become Eagle's wife, mother of divination. I shall cling to the Earth, as the Bokonō long ago advised, but to an earth saturated with moonlight; I shall preside at the opening of eyes, at the inscription of signs. The legend of Agōtíme is complete; let others elaborate and alter as they will, discover, disregard, surmise. I shall become simply Na, an old crone of a queen, until I discover another name, another hearth, another doorway, a place to sit as once I sat in front of Tia Rosinha's shanty, another widow's hovel on another beach like Barra, another clearing.

She wiped out Sa Meji with her hand, then stood up, stiffly, and looked towards the door of the sanctuary. One can't go around the world burying amulets under thresholds, she laughed out loud, and yet—all strong souls are reborn to cross sixteen thresholds sixteen times. Her eye fell upon the row of sacramental implements on the altarcloth. "Gu be praised," she said, "O durable father of iron, even if I never installed you here, you've given me an idea. You are a youngest son, after all, and had I not been such an ambitious, god-ridden old woman never would I have said goodbye to that most faithful of your Servitors."

Taking up the knife with which Benedito slit the throats of fowls for her, Agōtíme pushed a chair over to the door. A step up brought her within easy reach of the lintel, for she was still tall, and upon this she began to carve the following exhortation: *Entra como entrei, beba come bebi, sai como sai* [Enter as I have entered, drink as I have drunk, depart as I have departed]. It was painful work. She was no longer used to holding her arms over her head to stabilize basket or water jar, or simply to adjust an elaborate coiffure. What an old crow I've become, she laughed as, finished at last, she hopped off the chair and pushed it back against the wall. One more thing. She went over to the little pool, picked out several stones, wrapped them up in her handkerchief and put them, together with the Toxosu's necklace, into the leather pouch she always wore tucked under her sash. Zomadonu had said he didn't mind, had wished her an easy journey, as a matter of fact; but she could no longer wear them as she once had, when she was young, and beautiful, like a palm. Now she left the room, went out to stand under the arcade for one last look at the cajàzeiro. The cocks crowed a second time. She ran down the main passage, threw the bolt and stepped out into the street.

It was near dawn. Dark forms were just beginning to emerge from the grey mist that inundated the island city at this hour. She could smell the dank, sweet smell of the estuary. All the bonfires had gone out, but there remained the muffled sound of the *pandeiros.*

Along the avenue leading out of town, she met a crowd of masqueraders returning to their homes. Some were dressed in feather headdresses and skirts, others in leather suits like the one Mateus wore. *Bumba meu boi, bumba,* throbbed the immense *pandeiros.* On they came, forcing their husky voices through the fog. There was a hoard of them and they were very drunk. Their lurching bodies formed a wall across the street. They began to yell obscenities at her. That terrible heaviness again. Her head pounded like the tambourine drums, *bumba, bumba.* Clutching her leather pouch, she fled off down a side street.

When the ambassadors arrived promptly at three that afternoon, Leocadia, rather mysteriously, informed them that Mãe Agõtĭme had disappeared.

In Pursuit of the Legend

I visited the house of an old man who claimed . . . Yes, the man of whom you speak was my grandfather. Dom Antonio Dosu-yovo, his full name. Stranded in Bahia. "Dosu" because of being the first son after twins, "Yovo" meaning whiteman, given him because, having served Europeans from an early age, he dressed, spoke and even walked like them. Please don't mind the flies. I don't see nearly so well as I used to. I keep trying to get my frames filled in Bahia, but I can't see well enough to write letters to that scoundrel any more. Perhaps you'd be good enough when you get back, I've mislaid his address. It used to be in that tin box over there, but I can't put my hands on it any more. Stranded, stranded in Bahia. Where were we?

Oh yes, my grandfather, the very image of a whiteman. He knew English perfectly, spoke all the European languages—Portuguese, naturally, French, German. It was for this reason Agōglo used to send him off on commissions to the other coasts. Various commissions, but mostly guns, I suppose. He was the perfect confidential agent, impeccably dressed.

No, it was in Abomey that he first met Gezo. No, not for a crime he committed himself. A wealthy trader whom he once served as secretary. You must remember he himself was the son of a commercial traveler's man from the Gold Coast who settled here in Sobadji Quarter when his service was up. Where were we? My grandfather's employer had been convicted of something against the state. That happened all the time in those days, and continued to happen under the French. My grandfather went with his unfortunate employer and when that man was beheaded, my grandfather was thrown into prison. There he had the good fortune to share a cell with the great Chacha. You've heard of him, I suppose? No, I don't know the meaning. It might have had something to do with the way he walked, like this: *chachacha-chacha*. But nobody really knows. Well, Chacha was a powerful man in his way even then and rather than behead him, Adãdozã hoped to shrink him down to size and then make use of him. But Gezo got there first. How he managed to get into the prison to speak to them is anyone's guess; but he did; and once there he made both of them, Chacha and my grandfather, pledge loyalty —"drink the Earth" they called it then. Once they had sworn to help Gezo take the throne away from Adãdozã, he promised to help them escape.

You'll find matches in that tin box over there. Excuse me for not getting up. My legs, you understand, in the rainy season. Once out of prison my grandfather became de Souza's man, helped him smuggle guns, rum and tobacco to Gezo's partisans. It was just about this time that the princes and princesses of the royal blood had begun to meet in secret after sundown. When the chief of the secret police got wind of these meetings, he dared not report them to Adãdozã because the Prime Minister of the Right Hand himself attended them. Yes, that's the man. Stranded. Would you care for a beer? I could send my great-nephew out for a cold one. Now where were we? When guns were discovered in their possession, the royal princes claimed to have formed their own hunting fraternity under the leadership of a certain famous Dega from Ketu town.

No, if Adãdozã was suspicious (and of course he was), he didn't show it, or so the story goes. For when the future king himself arrived at the court in a hunter's smock, Adãdozã spoke no threats but treated him rather with contempt, with condescension, praise—naming him Amadogũgũ [farina wrapped in a fraternal leaf]. Made bold by Adãdozã's harmless conduct the princes multiplied their alliances and soon many about the court were envied for their fine clothes, for the smell of their tobacco. "No man will make firewood out of the tree that shades him," Gezo often said, and my grandfather, upon whose back that strong tree grew, knew the truth of the adage better than anyone. When Gezo succeeded in his enterprise, Chacha was made Yevogã [liaison with the whites] and my grandfather, interpreter to Chacha. You see Adãdozã didn't care to revive the slave trade, he wanted to make guns himself. He misjudged the times, he'd be the man to have about now.

Now we come to the part you have been wondering about. You'll find clean glasses on the shelf over there. If you care for ice I can send for it. Gezo wanted his mother back, and he naturally turned to Chacha. He knew all the captains, all the traders, the big landowners too; anybody of any importance in those days—de Souza knew him, or knew someone who did. Now Chacha hardly could have gone himself, so he told Gezo that no more loyal and experienced, no readier person could be found for the undertaking than my grandfather.

The other one? The prime minister did go along. Why, I don't know. Before they left, Gezo, Chacha and my grandfather renewed their pact—this time including Atindebaku. They happened to arrive in Brazil at a very bad time. There were all sorts of delays. First they had to go see the king in his capital. They had trouble getting passage. When they finally did arrive he was too busy to see them, so they went back to Bahia, stranded in Bahia you might say.

Not one of the various traders and *fazendeiros* to whom they bore letters from Chacha had ever heard of anyone by the name of Agõtĩme, had ever seen anyone answering her description. She had gone over so many years before, she must have grown quite old by then, perhaps she had been sold many times. No one alive remembered buying her and no one could tell where she'd gone. They were advised to go north, all the way to Santo Domingo; but they had run out of money by then and you must have plenty of money for that kind of traveling. So they lingered on in Bahia, hoping for reimbursements to come over on one of the ships, and at length they gave up and went home on an outward-bound slaver.

No, no hard feelings, none at all, but Gezo was a king, after all, and a determined man. He would have his mother back. He refused to believe she was dead. So off they went again with three gold bars and a handsome gift for the young emperor, Dom Pedro. Stranded in Bahia? No. Not this time. They found her, of course.

Yes, I might as well tell you. You'll never get the truth out of them up there. They said, the official story went, that Gezo died of the smallpox. They always said that. Perhaps, before Gezo, the others all did die of the smallpox, but not that one. My grandfather heard from a priest who happened at that time to be visiting Ekpo. It was in the very year my father was born, the date's in the Bible, that's how I happen to remember exactly. It was at the beginning of the dry season, the time when our kings used to go out slave-hunting. The army, returning from a successful raid, passed by the outskirts of Ekpo town whose king was a blood-brother of Gezo. At this point the king told the guard to relax. Arriving at the crossroads of the main road and the path that led directly down to the town, Gezo saw a Legba shrine, and ordered his bearers to stop. He wished to pay his respects, you know. Just then a shot rang out. Gezo sank back. The assassin disappeared into the bush. The curtains were drawn about the king's litter and they rushed Gezo back to the capital. But he never recovered from the wound.

Imagine, to this day, a distant cousin of Gezo, a high and mighty old man with a mouth like a parched corn cob, claims that even if it were a bullet, it could not have been an ordinary one. Only a pellet made of dried buffalo hide could make the night fall upon Gezo. Against all else, he says, King Gezo was invulnerable, including, I imagine, the smallpox.

When you go up to Abomey they will tell you that Gezo was buried in Sīboji Square; and, for a fee, they will show you the tomb; but that's a lie, of course, for nobody knows where the kings were actually buried. Next to him, they will say, are buried the remains of his mother, Na Agōtīme, whom my grandfather brought back from Brazil. She may well be buried there, but not Gezo. Her gate? Yes, it's there. They call that gate *Gôme*. I don't know why, it's not a Fōgbe word, *Gôme*. And I'll tell you something else. There are some whose words are not lightly to be listened to who claim that she wasn't Gezo's real mother at all, only his nurse. There are others who whisper Gezo wasn't Adādozā's brother at all, only a usurping cousin. And there are still others who say that Agōtīme must have been an evil sorcerer and that's why Adādozā sold her. Perhaps Gezo would have been wiser never to have sent for her, but then, my grandfather would never have had the opportunity of visiting Brazil. Adādozā? No one knows where his remains are buried either. But when you visit the museum you'll see no throne of his; no altar in a royal tomb. Not one trace of his reign survives, not even a pipe or a piece of jewelry. First Gezo sent his sons to be taught sorcery by him and then the royal family blotted everything out. It is in Abomey as if Adādozā never existed. Down here we know that's all nonsense. And even up there, linger those who, if you talk to them long enough, will tell you that he outlived Gezo.

So much is obscure, I thought, as I walked out of the old man's house into the stinging light of late afternoon. Layer upon layer of lies concealing the heartwood. Hollow that out and you have a canoe. But I know that she did not return. Nothing that any old man could say would ever convince me to the contrary. You may ask what happened to her afterwards, where she thought she was going, where indeed she ended her life. That life. There are several possibilities, but she did not, not in any recognizable form, go home to Dahomey. No, when she left Casa Xelegbata, she was headed towards the interior—

Glossary

For the spelling of Dahomean names I have relied upon Father R.P.B. Segurola's dictionary, but I have occasionally kept the Anglicized form of place names.

Acarajé—An Afro-Brazilian dish made of beans, pepper and palm oil and rolled in banana leaves.

Agaja—King of Dahomey, 1708–1728.

Agasuvi—People of Agasu, the founder of the Royal Family.

Agõglo—King of Dahomey, 1789–1797.

Akãsã (Acaçá)—A cornflour dumpling. In Brazil also a fermented beverage made of diluted mush.

Akla-Meji—One of the major signs of the Fa system of divination.

Alabe—Chief of the *candomblé* orchestra.

Alotekã—King Gezo's favorite wife.

Asogwe—A percussion instrument consisting of a hollow gourd covered with a net into which beads, cowries, seeds or little bones are sewn; in Brazilian cult ceremonies this is usually shaken by women.

Averekete—Member of the Dahomean Thunder pantheon, responsible for the movement of the waves upon the surface of the sea; in São Luis Averekete, as a "young" god and therefore somewhat of a trickster, has gradually usurped functions once belonging only to Elegba.

Babalorixa—Male heads of cults.

Bumba!—An interjection expressing a wallop; as a percussive re-frain "Bumba meu boi" means something like "sock it to 'em old boy (my ox)."

Caatinga—A dry region characterized by thorny, stunted vegeta-tion; also (Bot.) a tropical trumpet creeper.

Caboceers—Headmen, local slave-dealers.

Caboclo—Used here to designate an inhabitant of the north-eastern hinterland of Brazil who may be part Indian/part European in origin or part African/part Indian; in any event, a man of the earth.

Cafezinho—A little cup of strong coffee, customarily sweetened.

Candomblé—The name in Bahia for African religious ceremonies —the institution of the cults as well as the particular occa-sions.

Captaincy (Capitania)—The name given to provinces in colonial Brazil.

Capitão-do-mato—A man whose occupation was the pursuit of runaway slaves.

Capoeira—An Afro-Brazilian form of self-defense which in its ceremonial form is danced to the accompaniment of music. Its origin is, undoubtedly, Angola.

Caruru—A stew made of fish, or shrimp, or chicken and palm oil with pepper.

Chacha (also Caca, XaXa)—The Dahomean king's representative in Whydah. The first to bear this title was Francisco de Souza, a Brazilian mulatto. Under his management, during the reign of Gezo, whom he helped secure the throne, the slave trade flourished. It is said that once he hustled 1,170 slaves aboard a ship in three hours in order to escape the surveillance of a British patrol. When he died in 1849 he had something very like a minor royal funeral.

Corveias—Gangs of forced labor.

Dã—The serpent, source of prosperity, motion, perpetuity; a *vodũ* from Mahiland who manifests himself as Dã-Aidohuedo [rainbow].

Dãgbe—The royal python of the Xueda people.

Dahomey (Daxome)—In the beginning this word designated the palace built "on the stomach of Dã." (Sacrificial corner-stones are common in antiquity.) Later Dahomey meant the city of Abomey itself and still later all the land administered from that city. The Dahomean kings astonished early European visitors with their wealth, with the complexity of their political organization, with their female military contingents, their system of male and female "doubles" for all state offices, and with the vast numbers of prisoners slaughtered on the occasion of "Customs" for the kingly dead. Sold to European slavers, those who survived the ordeal brought the religious culture of Dahomey, Mahiland and the Nago [Yoruba] to the new world, most especially to Haiti, Cuba and Brazil.

Dako-donu—An early Dahomean king.

Diqué—A large pond between the hills of the city of Salvador, Bahia.

Divination—The genius of divination is materialized in the sixteen palm nuts thrown by Fa's interpreter, the Bokonõ (or Babalão). There are 256 combinations or "signs" and to each of these is attached numerous meanings, usually presented in the form of parables, depending upon the client's question and his circumstances. Only men, with very rare exceptions, may be taken into the sacred forest of Fa to receive their ruling horoscope, one of the 256 signs. Divinations may be performed with a special necklace rather than with the nuts.

Egbado—The people living in the lagoon region east of Whydah.

Egun—The dead, worshipped in a cult by that name.

Fa-du—The oracular utterances of Fa, usually containing a story or fable.

Fazenda—A ranch; the owner is called a Fazendeiro.

Filha-de-santo—An initiated member of an Afro-Brazilian cult.

Fõ, Fõgbe—The people and the language they speak. The Dahomeans of this story belong, linguistically, to the Ewe cluster of the Twi branch of the Kwa subfamily of the Nigritic stock. They are related culturally to the Yoruba, but their political-social theory is quite different.

Fulani—A cattle-herding people ubiquitous in the West African savannah.

Ganhadores—Wage earners; certain slaves in colonial Brazil were allowed to earn wages for themselves in off-hours. These were also known as *negros de ganho.*

Ganzá—A rattle which, unlike the African *asogwe,* has seeds within.

Gbe-Gouda—One of the signs of the Fa system of divination.

Gôme (or Gumê)—Name given to the inner court of the Dahomean cult house in São Luis.

Gouda-Meji—Another major sign.

Gũdeme—The female counterpart of the Migã.

Hãye—A praise song sung by the king's wives to awaken him.

Huãjele—The mother of King Tegbesu, a priestess of the sky god cult; also name of succeeding priestesses of that cult.

Harmattan—A dry desert wind, also a season when this wind blows.

Huegbaja—The first "historical" Dahomean king (1650–1680).

Huntos—Drummers of the Dahomean cult in São Luis. The three drums are called Hũ, Hũpli and Gũpli.

Iara—Water spirit.

Ialorixa—Priestess in charge of a cult, a *mãe-de-santo.*

Jihad—A Moslem holy war to convert or exterminate the infidel.

Kpẽgla—Agõglo's father, King of Dahomey 1744–1789.

Kposi—"Wives of the Panther." About forty of them enjoyed a

privileged situation in the palace as distinguished from the hundreds of Axosi, ordinary wives.

Loko—A sacred tree: in Africa the ironwood, in Brazil the white gamilleira.

Mãe d'agua—Mother of the waters, a ubiquitous Brazilian spirit.

Malê—Thus were the Muslims called both in Abomey and in Bahia. Most of the Malês in Bahia in Agōtĭme's time were Hausas and Yoruba converts to Islam, victims of disruptions in the Oyo kingdom and the Fulani Jihad.

Malungos—Shipmates who, after leaving their slave ships, banded together in small groups to cooperate in freeing themselves. In this story Agōtĭme, Saliabsō and Suuna had sworn to be *malungos*.

Migã—The Dahomean Prime Minister of the Right Hand, also executioner.

Minas (or Minas-Geges)—The name given in Brazil to slaves from Dahomey or, roughly, from the Slave Coast on up into Mahiland.

Montaría—A small canoe used on the rivers of northern Brazil.

Muezzin—He who calls the faithful to prayer.

Nagos—The Dahomean and Brazilian name for people originating in the Kingdom of Oyo or any of the other Yoruba city-states or enclaves.

Nesuxue—The ancestors of the royal Dahomean family, represented by living substitutes.

Orisha (Orixa)—Generic name for divinities from Yorubaland.

Oro—A Yoruba secret society dedicated to the cult of the earth, the evocation and placation of the spirits of the dead and the punishment of political offenders.

Oya—One of Shango's three wives, goddess of the winds, lightning, the River Niger—she who can hold the spirits of the dead at bay. She was the source of the great quarrel between

Shango and Ogun (or some say between King Shango and the god of the hunt, Oshosi).

Pagé—Brazilian-Indian curer, or witch doctor.

Pandeiros—Huge Brazilian tambourines.

Pedro I (Dom Pedro)—In 1807 Pedro, barely ten years old, fled Napoleon's invasion of Portugal along with most of the members of his family, the Braganças. In 1821 Pedro's father made him regent of Brazil and sailed away to Portugal. In 1822 he became the first emperor of Brazil. Later, republican sentiment forced him to abdicate in favor of his son.

Quitandeira—A street vendor. This occupation was one way a slave woman with the status "de ganho" could earn money to buy her freedom.

Sa-Meji—A sign of divination.

São João—St. John the Baptist, whose festival, in Brazil, is celebrated in mid-winter with fires (*foquieros*).

Senume—King Kpẽgla's wife, mother of King Agõglo and therefore entitled to a gate.

Sertão—The dry northeast region of Brazil.

Tambor—The name for *candomblé* dances in São Luis.

Tapuía (Tapuya)—A large family of Amerindian tribes scattered throughout northern Brazil. Here used to refer to Indians untouched by the colonizing process. (Now often used in an obverse sense.)

Tegbesu—Dahomean king, 1728–1775, who among other things established the Toxosu.

Terreiro—Where *candomblé* takes place; the cult premises.

Vaqueiros—The cowboys of the northeast.

Vodū—The generic Dahomean name for god, equivalent to Orisha. These gods embody certain natural forces, human propensities, and often have a legendary past as well—that is, they may be deified culture heroes. To which *vodū* one belongs is determined by divination, although possession is a sure sign, and personality a fairly safe indication.

Weli Meji—A major sign of the system of Fa divination.

Whydah—The eighteenth-century port of trade on the so-called "slave coast" whose name derives from the English deformation of the word "Xueda" (see below). The Portuguese, who first landed on this coast in 1580, and whose language became the *lingua-franca* of the slaving game, called the place Ajuda. The French, whose economic interest in the area vacillated and then finally culminated in the military occupation and subsequent annexation of 1892, called the port Juda. But the local name is Glexue—meaning "the house in the field" or more broadly "Xueda farmlands." During the eighteenth century there were three well-established European forts (Portuguese, French, British) in Whydah. Slave trading had its ups and downs but in the 1730's an estimated 6,000 slaves were reaching Bahia (about one-tenth of the number of slaves annually extracted from Africa—all ports, all destinations). After a series of severe depressions the Whydah slave trade revived again under Gezo. In the 1850's it is estimated that Agōtīme's son exported 300,000 a year, for which he received about five dollars per head.

A final note on Whydah: When Dahomey became an independent state in 1960, the Portuguese burned their old fort—São João Baptista de Ajuda—to the ground rather than convert it into a consulate or museum.

Xu—The Xueda god of the sea. Xunō, his priest and chief priest of Whydah.

Xueda—The people whose sea-coast kingdom (with its capital inland at Savi) whom Agaja conquered in the 1720's.

Zagaia—Here specifically a Brazilian-Indian hunting spear.

Some artists, scholars and travelers who have opened the way to Abomey, colonial Bahia and Candomblé.

Mario de Andrade
I. A. Akinjogbin
William Bascom
Roger Bastide
Eduardo Campos
Carybé
Luis da Camara Cascudo
Octavio da Costa Eduardo
Abbé Étienne
Jean Baptiste Debret
Edouard Dunglas
Gilberto Freyre
Paul Hazoumé
Melville and Frances Herskovits
Henry Koster
Ruth Landes
A. Le Herrissé
Bernard Maupoil
Nunes Pereira
Donald Pierson
Maurice Rugendas
R. P. B. Segurola
Pierre Verger

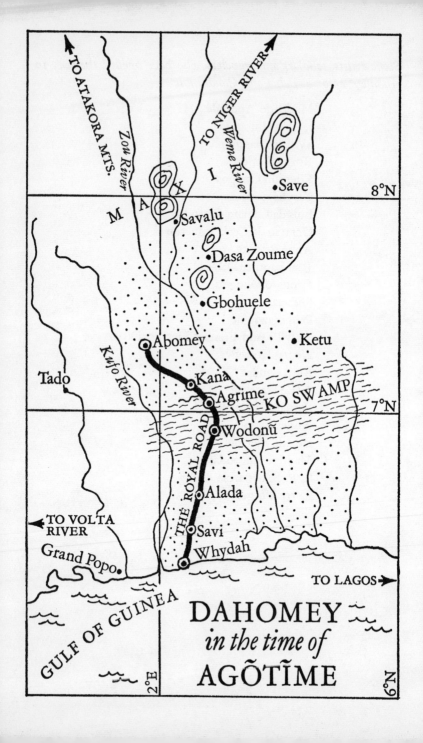

DAHOMEY in the time of AGŌTĪME

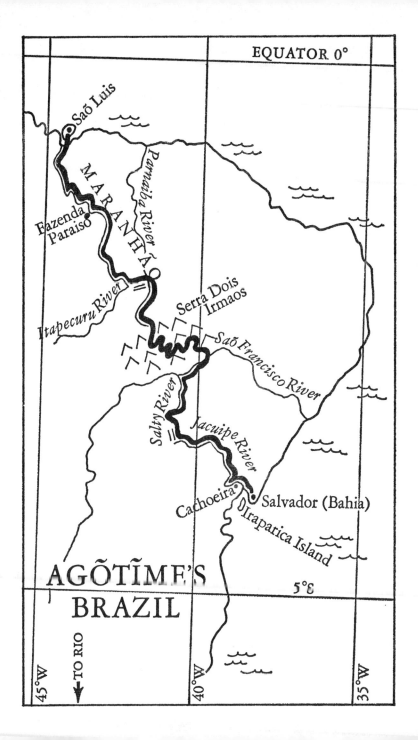

EQUATOR 0°

Saõ Luis

MARANHÃ

Parnaiba River

Fazenda
Paraiso

Itapecuru River

Serra Dois
Irmaos

Saõ Francisco River

Salty River

Jacuipe River

Cachoeira

Salvador (Bahia)

Iraparica Island

AGÕTĨME'S
BRAZIL

5°S

TO RIO

45°W

40°W

35°W